Richard Laymon was born in Chicago in 1947. He grew up in California and has a BA in English Literature from Williamette University, Oregon, and an MA from Loyola University, Los Angeles. He has worked as a school-teacher, a librarian and as a report writer for a law firm. He now works full time as a writer. Apart from his novels, he has published more than sixty short stories in magazines such as *Ellery Queen*, *Alfred Hitchcock* and *Cavalier* and in anthologies, including *Modern Masters of Horror*, *The Second Black Lizard Anthology of Crime* and *Night Visions 7*. His novel *Flesh* was named Best Horror novel of 1988 by *Science Fiction Chronicle* and also listed for the prestigious Bram Stoker Award, as was *Funland*. Richard Laymon is the author of more than twenty acclaimed novels, including *The Cellar*, *The Stake*, *Savage*, *Quake*, *Island*, *Bite*, *Body Rides*, *Fiends*, and *After Midnight*. He lives in California with his wife and daughter.

For up-to-date cyberspace news of Richard Laymon and his books, contact Richard Laymon Kills! at: http://www.crafti.com.au/~gerlach/rlaymon.htm

Also by Richard Laymon

The Cellar
The Woods Are Dark
Night Show
Beware!
Allhallow's Eve
The Beast House
Flesh
Funland
The Stake
One Rainy Night
Darkness, Tell Us
Blood Games
Dark Mountain*
Midnight's Lair*
Savage
Out Are The Lights
Alarums
Endless Night
In the Dark
Quake
Island
Body Rides
Bite
Fiends

* previously published under the pseudonym of Richard Kelly
Dark Mountain was first published as Tread Softly

Resurrection Dreams

Richard Laymon

The right of Richard Laymon to be identified as the author of the Work has been asserted by him in accordance with the Copyright, Designs and Patents Act 1988.

First published in paperback in 1986
by New English Library, the paperback division of W. H. Allen & Co Plc

Reprinted in this edition in 1990
by HEADLINE BOOK PUBLISHING

ISBN 0 7472 3534 7

Printed and bound in Great Britain by Clays Ltd, St Ives plc

HEADLINE BOOK PUBLISHING
A division of The Hodder Headline Plc

headline

I say, Jerry! You'd be in a blazing way,
if recalling to life was to come into fashion,
Jerry!
A Tale of Two Cities – Charles Dickens

First published in Great Britain in 1988
by W H Allen & Co Plc
First published in paperback in 1986
by Star Books, the paperback division of W H Allen & Co Plc

Reprinted in this edition in 1990
by HEADLINE BOOK PUBLISHING

A HEADLINE FEATURE Paperback

10

ISBN 978-0-7472-3534-7

Printed and bound in Great Britain by
Clays Ltd, St Ives plc

HEADLINE BOOK PUBLISHING
A division of Hodder Headline PLC
338 Euston Road
London NW1 3BH

Senior Year

CHAPTER ONE

That had to be Steve Kraft. It was Kraft's blue Trans Am, the one his dad gave him when he threw six touchdown passes against the Bay last fall. So that had to be Steve, all right.

The way his head looked reminded Wes of when you've got a marshmallow on a stick and you're trying to toast it to a nice golden tan and the bastard goes up in flames.

You blow out the fire. Then you go to pull the marshmallow off the stick. The stiff crust slips right off like a shell, and the white gooey centre stays on the stick.

Maybe Steve's face would slip off like that if you. . . .

Wes twisted away from the car's blazing wreckage and doubled over. 'Watch it!' Manny danced backward to save his shoes as Wes started heaving.

'Whatcha tryin' to do,' Manny asked, '*gross me out?*'

Wes heard him laughing and wondered how anyone – even Manny – could find something funny about Steve Kraft piling into the bridge's wall and burning like a marshmallow.

Then Manny patted his back. 'Should've lost it on Kraft, old buddy. Maybe you could've put him out.'

Wes straightened up. 'That's really sick,' he muttered.

'Hey, the guy was an asshole.' Manny took a swig of the Old Milwaukee he'd been drinking when they stopped to check out the fire. He passed the bottle to Wes.

Wes drank some, washing the sour taste of vomit out of his mouth. 'Maybe we better get outa here,' he said. 'Cops show up, they'll know we been drinking. 'Specially Pollock. He'll give us real shit.'

'Fuck Dexter Pollock,' Manny said. Standing in the middle

7

of the road, he swung his head from side to side as if searching for the police chief. 'Any car shows up, we'll just. . . .' His head jerked hard to the right. His mouth dropped open.

Wes looked.

The girl was halfway across the bridge, sprawled over the top of its low concrete parapet.

Wes *thought* it was a girl. He couldn't be sure, since her head was out of sight. But she looked as if she might be naked, and Steve Kraft wouldn't have had a naked *guy* in his car.

'I think she's bareass,' Manny said. His voice sounded hushed, secretive. 'Come on.'

They walked slowly toward her. Wes felt his heart drumming. His mouth was dry. He took another drink of beer.

'Bet it's Darlene,' Manny said.

'Yeah.'

Manny rubbed his mouth. 'Not a stitch on. No wonder Kraft piled up.'

The firelight fluttered and rolled over the bare skin of her back and rump and legs. Her left leg hung toward the walkway. The other was up on top of the wall as if she intended to climb over and leap into the creek.

'What's she doing?' Wes whispered.

'Lost a contact lense?' Manny suggested, and let out a short, nervous laugh. 'Not a stitch,' he said again.

That wasn't quite true, Wes realised. Now that he was closer to the girl, he could see that she wore white socks and white tennis shoes. Around her left ankle hung a pair of panties that looked glossy in the russet firelight.

'Think she'll be glad to see us?' Manny asked.

Wes didn't bother to answer. He suspected that Darlene would rather see just about anyone except Manny. She, like all those snob cheerleaders and most of the other kids in the senior class at Ellsworth High, thought Manny was the scum of the earth.

8

Manny called out, 'Hey, Darlene, don't jump! It's not that bad. Stevie's a goner, but *we're* here.'

She didn't move.

'Maybe she's hurt,' Wes said.

'Can't be hurt too bad, she came this far. Darle-e-e-ne.'

As they hurried closer, Wes looked back at the blazing car. Flames flapped through the space where the windshield belonged. He faced forward. Manny was already beside the sprawled girl. 'Hey, you don't suppose she got thrown all the way . . .'

'Not a chance.' He slapped the girl's rump. It jiggled slightly, but she didn't flinch or yelp. He leaned over her. 'Hey Wes,' he said. 'I think I know what she lost off the bridge.'

Wes didn't like the high, strange sound of Manny's voice. 'What?'

'Her head.'

'Quit joking around.'

'Look for yourself.'

West sidestepped past Manny, and looked.

Her left shoulder rested on top of the wall. The right was beyond the edge, drooping over the ravine, her arm hanging straight down.

Wes *knew* her head had to be there, just this side of the drooping shoulder, but he sure couldn't see it.

'No,' he said. 'It's there.' On that side of the wall, there was no light from the fire. That's why he couldn't see Darlene's head.

'Bitch got herself decapacitated.' To prove his point, he gave the body a tug.

Wes yelped and lurched backward as it came toward him. It rolled off the parapet, dropped, and hit the sidewalk at his feet.

'See?' Manny said, stepping out of the way so his shadow left her.

Wes saw, all right. He saw a stump of neck between her shoulders.

9

'That's Darlene, all right,' Manny said. 'Nobody's got a set like that.'

'I don't think we oughta be looking at her,' Wes said. 'You know? She's dead.'

'Yeah, I imagine she is.' Manny squatted down for a better view.

Wes felt angry at Manny, disgusted with himself. He knew it was wrong to look, but he kept staring at her.

'Ever see one before?' Manny asked.

'Just Steve.'

'Not a stiff, a naked babe.'

'Sure,' he lied.

Manny moved a hand up her thigh.

'Hey, don't.'

'Check her out, man. This is as close as a loser like you's ever gonna get to a babe like this.'

'For Godsake, get your hand off her.'

'Wish we had more light.' Manny started to pull her leg sideways.

Wes booted him in the shoulder and he tumbled over.

'Hey!'

'Don't mess with her. Just leave her alone!'

'Fuck you!' Manny leaped to his feet and whirled toward Wes. His fists were clenched at his sides.

Wes realised he still held the beer bottle. 'Stay back!' he warned. 'I'll bash you! I swear, I'll bust your head open!'

He raised the bottle like a club, and chilly liquid spilled down his arm.

'You think you can take me, man? I'll take that bottle and shove it up your tight ass.'

'I don't want to fight you,' Wes said.

'Damn straight, you don't.'

Wes tossed the bottle. It flew over the low wall where Darlene had been sprawled. A few seconds later, it hit the stream with a soft splash.

'Okay?' he asked. 'Okay?'

'Okay.' Smiling, Manny patted his shoulder. Then he

10

smashed his knee up into Wes's stomach. Wes dropped to his knees. 'Now we're even,' he said, and took Wes by the arm and helped him up. 'Don't know why you wanta act like such a dumb fuck. Come on, let's check her out. Isn't every day you get a chance like this.'

Wes, bent over and holding his stomach, fought to suck air into his lungs and shook his head.

'Just don't mess with me, then.'

Manny turned away and crouched over the body. And shot up straight as headlights glowed in the distance.

They ran. They ran away from Darlene's body and through the heat near the blazing Trans Am, into the cooler air beyond it. They flung themselves into Manny's car.

Manny started the engine. He looked at Wes and grinned. 'Tough luck,' he said. 'Coulda been a kick.' Then he swung his car into a tight U-turn, and they sped toward town.

CHAPTER TWO

When her clock blared Monday morning, Vicki set the snooze alarm to give herself another ten minutes. She stretched, rolled over, and pushed her face into the warm pocket of her pillow.

This was usually one of her favourite times of the day, a time to snuggle in the cozy warmth of her bed and let her mind roam.

Today, however, she felt uneasy, even a little frightened.

She knew it was because of what happened to Steve and Darlene.

It gave her a cold feeling inside.

She didn't feel sorry for them. Not exactly. After all, they had done it to themselves if it was true what Cynthia'd said. *No one* does seventy on River Road. And if they were really

11

nude when they hit the bridge, that was even worse. They'd been speeding and screwing around. It was no better than suicide.

Besides which, neither of them was any great shakes as a human being. Steve may have been a hunk and he *was* a pretty good quarterback if you happened to care, but he was also so conceited it made you want to throw up. Darlene was not only conceited, but she used her looks like a weapon to torment half the guys in school.

Vicki knew she wouldn't miss either one of them.

But they were dead.

Dead.

It made her feel *really* cold inside.

Lying here thinking about it wasn't making it any better.

She got up and shut off the snooze alarm. She stretched, hitched up her drooping pyjama pants, and stepped to her bedroom window.

Looked beautiful out there. The sky was clear and pale blue. Off in the distance, Mr Blain was on his dock, squatting down to untie his outboard.

The warm morning breeze stirred Vicki's pyjamas. The light fabric caressed her skin.

She heard the hum of insects, birdsongs and the cackle of a loon. A butterfly dipped past her window.

She thought how wonderful it was, and then thought about how Darlene and Steve would never see another morning.

She pictured Darlene in a dark narrow coffin, trapped under six feet of dirt. That seemed worse, somehow, than getting cremated like Steve.

She started to wonder whether she'd rather be cremated than buried. If you could feel the fire. . . .

Shivering, she turned away from the window. She went to the closet and put on her robe and told herself as she hurried from her room that they're both in Heaven. She wasn't real sure about Heaven, but it beat thinking about them being just dead forever.

12

In the hallway, she smelled coffee. She wondered how anything that smelled so good could taste so bitter.

Dad was at the breakfast table with his coffee. Mom, at the stove, looked over her shoulder as Vicki walked in. 'You want your egg fried or scrambled?' she asked.

'Fried, I guess.'

It all seemed so normal.

'Morning, Pops.'

'I'll *Pops* you!'

She bent over, put an arm around his shoulders, and kissed his cheek. He hadn't shaved yet.

She'd heard somewhere that whiskers kept growing for a while after a man's dead.

He patted Vicki's rump.

He's going to die someday, she thought. Mom, too.

Knock if off, she told herself. They're only thirty-eight, for godsake.

She gave him an extra squeeze, then straightened up and looked at her mother. Mom was breaking an egg into the skillet. She wore the blue robe Dad gave her two Christmases ago.

If I go around hugging everyone, Vicki thought, they'll figure I'm going weird.

So she sat in her usual chair and took a drink of orange juice. Dad watched her.

'Did you sleep all right?' he asked.

'Sure.'

'Bad dreams?'

She shrugged.

'We heard you talking in your sleep last night,' Mom said from the stove.

'Really? Did I say anything spectacular?'

'Just jibberish,' Dad told her.

Mom said, 'You sounded pretty upset.'

'I don't know. I don't remember.'

'If you're upset about something . . .'

'I'm fine, Mom. Really.'

13

'Like missing your period,' Dad said.

Vicki felt her face go hot. 'Very funny.'

'So that isn't the problem, I take it?'

'Not hardly.'

Mom brought the plate over. The fried egg rested on a slab of toast, the way Vicki liked it. There were two strips of bacon. While she cut up her breakfast and mixed it all together, Mom poured more coffee into Dad's cup. She gave herself a refill and sat down.

'It was a lovely service yesterday. You really should've gone with us.'

'Would've helped get it out of your system,' Dad said.

'My system's just fine, thank you.'

'Your science project could've waited,' Mom told her. 'You still have all week before the Fair.'

'I didn't like it hanging over my head. Besides, Darlene's parents were your friends, not mine.'

'They asked about you,' Mom said.

'Great,' she muttered. She got a piece of bacon onto her fork, stabbed the tines through a chunk of eggwhite and yolk-sodden toast, and stuffed them into her mouth. They didn't taste as good as usual.

Thanks for ruining my breakfast, folks.

'Well,' Dad said, 'it was your decision.'

'Mine, but wrong.'

'It would've been nice if you'd gone,' Mom said.

'Fine. Next time any kids get themselves wiped out doing seventy while they're screwing, I'll be sure to attend their funerals.'

Mom's face turned scarlet.

Dad raised his eyebrows and looked somewhat amused.

'That's a terrible thing to say.'

'I'm sorry, Mom.'

'If you could've seen her poor parents. . . .' Mom pressed her lower lip between her teeth. There were tears in her eyes. 'Their only daughter. . . .'

'I know. I'm sorry.'

14

'All I could think about was how I'd feel if that had been you.'

Now Dad's eyes were red.

'It wasn't me.'

'It could've been.'

'Sure, it could've been. Yeah. If I looked like Darlene and was head cheerleader and had all the guys drooling all over my body and had a red-hot boyfriend who thought it was cool to see how fast he can drive on a narrow road while I'm doing God-knows-what to him. Could've been me. Right! But I'm not a knockout and guys like Steve Kraft don't know or care that I exist and the only guy who does care is too timid and smart to drive like a maniac and if he ever did I'd pull out the damned ignition key and make him eat it.'

She stopped. She nodded her head once, hard, and jammed another bite of food into her mouth.

'So there,' Dad said. He still had wet eyes, but his mouth wore a tilted smile.

Mom's mouth hung open. She looked a trifle stunned and bewildered, but at least the weeping had stopped.

Dad got up from the table. 'Unfortunately, I have a living to earn. Now, don't you ladies launch into any tirades without me, okay?'

He stepped behind Vicki's chair and put his hands on her shoulders. 'You are too a knockout,' he said.

'Right. Sure.'

Mom nodded in agreement. 'You shouldn't belittle yourself, honey. You're a very attractive young woman – and very bright. Your father and I are both very proud of you. There's no reason in the world why you should ever feel the least bit jealous or envious of someone like Darlene.'

'I don't envy her, that's for sure.'

'Good,' Mom said. She didn't get it.

Dad did. He kissed the top of Vicki's head, muttered, 'Beast,' and left.

The rest of breakfast tasted just fine.

Getting things off your chest, she thought, must improve the appetite.

'Alice is here,' Mom called a few moments after Vicki heard the doorbell.

'I'll be out in a minute.' She finished tying her white Nikes, bounced up from the bed, and slung her book bag onto her back as she hurried from her room.

It was good to see Ace. It was always good to see her, but especially this morning.

'I know,' Ace was saying to Mom. 'It's a terrible tragedy.' She nodded a greeting to Vicki. Her face looked solemn. 'It's especially terrible for her loved ones.'

'Awful,' Mom said. Though she was Vicki's size and Vicki hardly considered herself a shrimp, she seemed small and fragile beside Ace.

Nearly everyone did.

Alice 'Ace' Mason was the tallest girl in the senior class, but plenty of boys had more height than she did – and most of them seemed smaller in her presence.

Imposing, Vicki thought. That's what she is.

And, at the moment, posing.

She turned sorrowful eyes to Vicki and said, 'I suppose we'd better get going. Have a nice day, Mrs Chandler.'

Vicki gave her mother a quick kiss on the cheek, then followed Ace outside. They reached the sidewalk. They were halfway down the block when Ace looked at Vicki with bright mischievous eyes.

'Where's your black threads, Vicks?' she asked in her usual brash voice.

'Where're yours?'

She snorted. 'Black panties, hon.' She took a long stride and swung her rump in Vicki's direction.

She wore white shorts that hugged her buttocks. A dark triangle and narrow waistband showed through the material.

'They really are black.'

16

'You can see them?' She twisted around and looked for herself. 'Well shitski.'

'Sexy, too.'

'Ordered them special. Want me to get you some?'

'Right. What happens when Mom does the wash?'

'We'll get her some, too. Drive your dad crazy with lust.'

'Please.'

'We order now, you'll get them in time for the dance.'

'Thanks anyway.'

'Give Henry a treat.'

'As close as Henry'll get to my underpants, I could be wearing polka-dot boxer shorts.'

'Poor guy. I can see he'll be having a memorable night.'

'How was your weekend?' Vicki asked, hoping to get away from the subject of Henry.

'Caught some rays. Aunt Lucy was her usual kick in the head. Wish I'd been here, though. Missed out on all the excitement. Your mom says you blew your chance to see Darlene get planted.'

'Couldn't go. No black panties.'

'We'll fix that. How about she was giving him head when they wiped out?'

'You're kidding. Where'd you hear that?'

'Thought it was common knowledge.'

'Nobody told me.'

Ace halted on the deserted sidewalk, looked all around as if to make sure nobody was within earshot, then bowed her head toward Vicki. 'Did you hear she was butt-naked?'

'Yeah. Cynthia called me Saturday morning. She overheard her mother on the phone with Thelma Clemens. She said Steve got burnt to a crisp and Darlene got thrown through the windshield – and how she was naked and how her head got . . . cut off.'

'That's all?' Ace asked.

From the gleeful look in her eyes, Vicki knew a major detail was missing from Cynthia's version. 'What?' she asked.

'Well, I talked to Roger last night and his brother's best

17

pals with Joey Milbourne. Joey's supposed to be the guy that found her head. It was way on the other side of the bridge under some bushes? Well, he's the biggest jerk-off ever to wear a badge, next to Pollock, and maybe he just made this up so he'd have a good story to tell, but he told Roger's brother that when he found Darlene's head . . .' Ace stopped talking and looked around again.

'Come *on*.'

'You sure you haven't heard this?'

'Quit goofing around and tell me.'

'She had Steve's dick in her mouth.'

'*What?*'

Ace bared her teeth and chomped them together.

'Holy shit,' Vicki muttered.

'When she bit it, she really *bit* it.'

Vicki cracked up and shoved Ace away from her.

'What a way to go!' Ace blurted through her own laughter.

'Makes me hurt,' Vicki gasped.

'You ain't even *got* one.'

'Well, if I did . . .'

'He came and went.'

'Ace, Ace!' She wiped her eyes. 'Stop it!'

'At least Darlene got a last meal.'

'Knockwurst!' Vicki squealed. 'Hold the sauerkraut!'

'More of a hot dog from what I heard. More of a *cocktail weenie*.'

'Oh, God. Stop it, Ace.'

'*Me?*'

Later, Vicki felt miserable with guilt. It was bad enough to feel no particular sorrow about the demise of her classmates. It seemed unforgivably gross·to have joked and laughed hysterically about it.

During fourth period study hall, she passed a note to Ace. The note said, 'He went to St Peter without his.'

Ace read it and snorted.

Mr Silverstein, who had been busy grading papers, jerked

18

his head up. 'Miss Mason, would you like to share with the rest of us?'

'Nah, I don't think so.'

'Is that a note I see clutched in your hand?'

'Nothing in my hand,' Ace told him. 'See?' She blatantly stuffed the note into her mouth, and held up both hands as she began to chew.

The performance drew applause from about half the kids in the room. Mr Silverstein shook his head. He frowned at Ace as if debating whether to pursue the matter, apparently decided not to risk it, offered a lame, 'Well, let's all try to keep it down; this is a study hall, not a sideshow,' and went back to grading papers.

Ace removed the sodden ball of paper from her mouth. She tossed it at Melvin Dobbs, who was sitting in the next row over, two desks up. It stuck to the back of his neck. Vicki tried to hold back her laugh. The air blew out her nose.

Normally, she felt a certain amount of sympathy for Melvin. He was a weird kid, odd enough to make himself the target of choice for everyone in the mood to cause trouble. Vicki wished Ace had thrown the spitball at someone else, but she couldn't help laughing.

Melvin flinched when the wet glob struck his neck. He sat up straight, picked it off his skin, then carefully plucked the wad open and studied it.

Oh great, Vicki thought.

Melvin turned around. He stared at Ace with his bulgy, half-shut eyes. Then he balled up the paper. He sniffed it, licked his thick lips, and stuffed the paper into his mouth. He chewed it slowly, smiling a bit and rolling his eyes as if really savouring the taste. Finally, he swallowed.

Vicki managed not to gag.

When the bell rang, she joined up with Ace.

Ace rolled her eyes, imitating Melvin. 'You see him chew it down?'

19

'I almost lost my breakfast.'

'That guy is *strange.*'

In the hallway on their way to the cafeteria, they saw Melvin ahead of them. He was walking stooped over, pumping vigorously with one arm while his other arm hung straight down with the weight of his briefcase. His pink shirt was untucked in the rear. It draped the seat of his gaudy plaid shorts.

'Got another piece of paper?' Ace asked.

'What for?'

'Maybe he'd like a second helping.'

Just then, Randy Montclair took a long sideways stride, cutting in front of Ace, and swatted the back of Melvin's head. 'Fucked up my appetite, you pig,' he said, and gave the kid another whack. Melvin cowered, but kept walking.

Randy had been in study hall. Obviously, he'd watched Melvin devour the spitball.

Doug, his buddy, skipped along beside him, laughing. 'Give him another!'

'Scum.' Randy slapped Melvin again.

'Knock it off!' Vicki snapped.

Still pursuing Melvin, he glanced over his shoulder. His lip curled out. 'Butt out.'

'Just leave him alone.'

Ignoring her, he backhanded Melvin's low head.

Vicki shrugged out of her book bag. Holding it by the straps, she swung it at Randy. The loaded satchel slammed into his shoulder. He staggered sideways, knocking into Doug. They almost went down, but not quite.

Then they were facing Vicki.

They didn't look happy.

'Just leave him alone,' she said. 'All right?'

Scowling, Randy waved a fist in front of her nose.

'Oh, I'm so scared.'

But not much. Not with Ace beside her.

'If you weren't a girl, I'd knock your face in.'

20

Doug looked as if he might echo his friend's remark, but he glanced at Ace and kept his mouth shut.

'Take a leap, guys,' Ace said.

Randy's scowl dissolved. He looked up at Ace. 'Just tell Vicki to keep her nose outa my business.'

Ace raised her eyebrows. 'I didn't hear the magic word.'

Randy muttered something inaudible and stepped out of the way, shoving Doug as if all this were somehow Doug's fault.

Vicki and Ace left them behind.

'Thanks,' Vicki said.

'You owe me a Ding-dong.'

'Only Twinkies today.'

'A Twinkie will do just fine. You all of a sudden Melvin's bodyguard or something?'

'It was my note he ate.'

'It was my spit.'

'It makes him your blood-brother,' Vicki explained.

'Gawd! Get a lobotomy, girl!'

CHAPTER THREE

On Saturday morning, Vicki's father helped load her science project into the trunk, and drove her to the Community Center.

The Spring Science Fair was one of the town's frequent events like the Antique Show, the Gun Show, and the Handicrafts Show that seemed to exist mostly for the sake of giving the residents of Ellsworth something unique to do on their weekends.

Most of the other shows brought in merchants and visitors from out of town, which was good for the motels and restaurants. But not the Science Fair. It was a showcase for the efforts of the local kids, who had to attend and demonstrate their creations if they wanted a passing mark in their school science classes. The kids and teachers got in free. It was $2.00 a head for everyone else, and it seemed that nobody in the entire town could bear to miss it.

Not only because most of the kids participating had a whole slew of relations, but because things never failed to go wrong and provide the folks with gossip – which seemed to be their chief recreation.

'Just think,' Dad said, 'this is your last Science Fair.'

'And not a moment too soon.'

It would be her twelfth – one a year since first grade. In the early years, she'd enjoyed the fair and looked forward to it almost gleefully. Her first project had been a chicken egg and a 100 watt lightbulb to warm it up. Later on, she'd made an electro-magnet with a nail and a dry-cell battery.

'Remember your volcano?' Dad asked. He, too, was apparently remembering the good old days.

'God, that was a disaster.'

When Vicki was in sixth grade, she'd made a terrific-looking volcano out of plaster of Paris and stood it on a platform concealing a dry chemical fire extinguisher. Every now and then, she gave the extinguisher a honk, shooting a white cloud out of the volcano's crater. The volcano actually *trembled* each time she triggered an eruption. But when the judges showed up, she wanted to give them an eruption to remember so she kept the lever down. The horn blared. All around, people cringed and covered their ears – then vanished behind the wall of white cast out by the extinguisher. The volcano shuddered. It all looked just great – what Vicki could see of it through the fog – until her hand slipped and the horn lost its perfect positioning beneath the crater and the powerful discharge blasted out the front of her volcano throwing plaster at the judges like shrapnel.

'You were the hit of the show,' Dad said.

'At least I didn't kill anyone.'

22

'I'd like to have seen a reprise of that. You could've resurrected the volcano for your final project.'

'Now that I'm a big girl,' Vicki told him, 'I don't get quite the same joy out of humiliating myself.'

Joy. She remembered the way she had cried afterwards. Everyone for godsake *clapping* hadn't made it any better.

'Displaying the parts of a dismantled rat,' Dad said, 'doesn't have half the flair of blowing up a volcano. Though it does have a certain gross-out potential.'

'I figured I might as well do something useful this year.'

'Just give you a few more years, you'll be cutting up cadavers.'

'Don't remind me.'

'Maybe you should go into law.'

'I'd rather heal people than screw them.'

Laughing, Dad swung the car into the parking lot of the Community Center. Though it was still early, most of the parking spaces near the open doors of the arena were already taken. Parents and kids were busy unloading tables and projects from cars, vans and pickup trucks. Dad drove as close to the door as he could get, which was a good distance away, and parked.

They went around to the trunk. When Dad opened it, the pungent aroma of formaldehyde swelled out. Vicki reached in. She picked up the dissection tray. The surgical gloves and implements she planned to use for her procedure were inside the tray. She handed it to her father, and lifted out the bottle containing the rat she would be dissecting during the course of the Fair. With that securely clamped under one arm, she took out the wooden display case in which the parts of a previously 'dismantled' rat were carefully mounted and labelled.

'Hiya, Vicki.'

The voice sounded familiar, but she couldn't quite place it. She turned around.

'Melvin.'

His wide head was tilted to one side, and he blinked and

23

smiled as he rubbed his hands together. 'Use some help?' he asked.

'Good man,' Dad said. 'So, they gave you a day off, huh?'

'Yep.'

'Think they can get along without you?'

He rolled his head around.

'Guess your father'll have to pump the gas himself, huh?'

'And wipe the windshields, too,' Melvin added.

Dad slipped the card-table out of the trunk and handed it to him.

'Don't you have your own project to set up?' Vicki asked.

'Done it already,' he said.

Dad shut the trunk, and the three of them started across the parking lot toward the arena. Melvin walked in the lead, balancing the table on top of his head.

He hadn't spoken a word to Vicki after the incident with Randy Montclair in the hallway on Monday. Though she hadn't relished the prospect of a conversation with him, she'd expected at least a word of thanks. Finally, she had decided that he was probably unaware of what she'd done. That didn't seem so likely, now. Offering to help carry her project was apparently his way of showing appreciation.

When he reached the door, he slid the table off his head, held it against his chest with both hands, and sidestepped through the entrance.

Vicki and her father followed him. The area set aside for the high school seniors was at the far end. She spotted Ace, who looked busy unloading a carton onto a table. Melvin knew enough to head for the big girl. He lowered the card-table in the open space beside Ace's display. When she said something to him, he darted a thumb over his shoulder. Ace saw Vicki approaching, and nodded.

Melvin folded out the legs and set the table upright.

'Thanks a lot for the help,' Vicki told him.

A corner of his mouth slid up. He nodded and blushed and turned away. A few shambling steps took him to the other side of the space that had been left open for a walkway

24

between the two rows of projects. He slipped a tattered paperback book out of a rear pocket of his baggy shorts, then sat on a stool facing the girls, and began to read. The book was *Frankenstein*.

'Want me to help you set up?' Dad asked.

'No, that's all right. Thanks.'

'Okay. We'll be back later. Have fun.'

He said good-bye to Ace, then walked away.

Vicki set her bottled rat on the table.

'I see you brought your lunch,' Ace said.

'You've got the bread, cheese and beverages. We'll have a feast.'

Ace's bread and cheese, neatly arranged atop her table, were coated with mould. She also had jars of coffee, red wine and apple juice. Each jar looked as if someone had dumped in a handful of fuzz from a vacuum cleaner bag. A pair of hand-lettered posters, joined together with tape, listed mould's beneficial uses.

'You'll get a blue ribbon for sure,' Vicki said.

'Eat my shorts.'

Vicki went ahead with her preparations. She opened her wooden display case and propped it up near the back of her table. Then she emptied her dissection tray and put on surgical gloves. She started to open the jar containing the formaldehyde and rat.

'Spare me, would you?' Ace said. 'The thing doesn't start for half an hour. Wait'll you've got an audience, for godsake.'

Vicki shrugged. 'Why not?' She put the bottle down and pulled the gloves off.

Ace was busy unfolding the two chairs she had brought from home. She set them up side by side with the backs to their tables. Both girls sat down.

Melvin, across from them, glanced up then resumed reading.

'What do you suppose *he's* got?' Ace asked in a quiet voice.

'Maybe he made that megaphone.'

25

The megaphone rested on the floor beside his stool. It didn't look homemade.

Behind him was an enclosure the size of an outhouse: a framework draped with blue bedsheets.

'What've you got in there?' Ace called over to him.

He raised his head and grinned. 'It's a surprise.'

'You got another car engine this year?'

'Maybe.'

'Come on, be a sport and give us a peek.'

'You'll see. I gotta wait for the right time.'

'When's that?'

'Not till the judges show up.'

'You're kidding.'

He shrugged his round shoulders. 'It's kind of a one-shot deal,' he said, and went back to reading.

'Turkey,' Ace muttered.

Vicki and Ace talked about other things for a while. When Ace's boyfriend, Rob, showed up, Vicki left her seat and wandered over to Henry's display. Not because she especially wanted to visit with him. But he was the closest thing Vicki had to a boyfriend, and he *was* taking her to the senior dance next week so she felt it would be weird of her to ignore him.

She found him seated at his computer, hunched over the keyboard, avidly pecking out commands that made Humphrey dance and wink though nobody seemed to be watching the performance.

Humphrey was a marionette, about three feet tall, decked out in a top hat and tails. He did his numbers beside Henry's computer, and looked somewhat as if he'd been impaled on the plastic pipe that ran from the control box to his rump.

'Howdy, Humphrey,' Vicki said.

The marionette waved to her and gave his legs a couple of spastic kicks.

Henry, seated on a swivel chair, swung around and looked up at Vicki. Behind his glasses, his eyes were wide with eagerness. They always seemed that way, as if Henry were

26

perpetually on the verge of making a startling announcement.

'How're things?' Vicki asked.

'Oh, fine.'

'Nifty outfit,' she said. Henry wore a bow tie and black dinner jacket. His outfit was identical to Humphrey's, though Henry wore no top hat. His hat rested on the table beside his keyboard, ready to be donned when the spectators started wandering by.

'You look very lovely this morning,' he said.

'Thanks.' Vicki wasn't especially pleased by the compliment. A day rarely went by that Henry didn't make a similar comment. But she'd never seen him really look her over. The words just came out like a programmed response to her arrival – as if he realised he ought to feign some interest in her physical appearance.

We've really got a red-hot romance cooking here, she thought.

But she supposed it was her fault as much as Henry's. Their relationship had started on an intellectual level when they'd been teamed up as lab partners in physiology last year, and neither of them had made any effort to get physical. They had gone out together at least a dozen times, and never even kissed. It was as if neither of them had bodies.

Vicki sometimes wondered what might happen if she should embrace him and kiss him hard and squirm against him, really let him know she was a woman, not just a discussion partner. Henry might suddenly turn into a lusting animal.

The idea didn't have much appeal.

So she'd done nothing to change the nature of the relationship – such as it was. She liked Henry, and he did fine in the role of boyfriend until something better might come along.

Which didn't seem too likely in the immediate future.

Of all the guys she could think of, there was not a single one who really interested her.

27

Thanks to Paul. When he moved away, it all fell apart.

She realised that Henry was talking to her. 'What?' she asked. 'My mind was wandering.'

'Did it wander someplace interesting?'

Someplace empty, she thought.

'No,' she said. 'What were you saying?'

'I thought that perhaps we might meet during the lunch break. We should discuss our plans for next Friday.'

'Sure. That'd be fine.' She glanced at her wristwatch. 'Well, it's about time for the fun to start. I'd better get back to my rats.'

'*Ciao*,' Henry said, and swivelled around to face his computer. His fingers fluttered over the keyboard, and Humphrey waved and winked.

Vicki walked back toward her table. Ace and Rob were standing in front of the chairs, facing each other, holding hands. Ace was nodding as she listened to him. Though three inches taller than Rob, she somehow always seemed less imposing when they were together, as if his presence transformed her into someone more feminine and vulnerable.

Vicki didn't want to intrude on the intimacy she sensed. She turned to her table and picked up her surgical gloves.

She wished she hadn't thought about Paul.

Sometimes she went for days at a time without thinking about him.

Her parents had called it 'puppy love,' which seemed like a way to make her feelings for Paul sound less important. Vicki had thought of it as love, and still did. When she'd been with Paul, she'd felt special and beautiful and full. Whether they were just sitting together in class, or holding hands in a movie, or spending a whole day exploring the woods or swimming or boating on the river, each moment seemed golden.

But his father was a Master Sergeant in the Marines. Paul showed up at Ellsworth High in the fall of Vicki's sophomore year. They met at once and fell in love and had just that school year and the following summer. Then new orders came down, and Paul left with his family for a base in South Carolina.

They'd had almost exactly one year together. It had been over so fast.

It was as if the best part of her life ended when Paul went away. 'You'll get over it,' her parents had said. She supposed she did get over it. In a way. More like getting used to it. The loss seemed always there, deep inside, a shadow that made every day a little less bright – a loss that would rise to the surface every time she was reminded of Paul.

A time like now.

Pulling on her gloves, she felt a hollow ache in her chest.

No point in getting yourself all upset, she thought. Hell, I'll probably meet some terrific guy at college in the fall.

Sure.

She unscrewed the lid of the jar, lifted out the rat with tongs and placed it on the dissection tray.

'That's *really* disgusting,' Ace said. 'Barforama.'

'Your mould is appetising?'

Ace watched over her shoulder as she pinned the rat's paws to the waxy bottom of the tray.

'What's Rob up to?' Vicki asked.

'He's taking me to the drive-in tonight.'

'What's playing?'

'Who cares?' Ace said, and let out a couple of cheery snorts.

Vicki alternated between exposing the vitals of her rat and sitting on the chair to chat with Ace, whose project was a display with no performance. They spent a lot of time watching Melvin ward off curious spectators wanting to see what was hidden inside his enclosure of bedsheets.

He explained that it was a 'one-shot deal' and that they should be sure to hurry back when he made the announcement with his megaphone.

'He's sure getting *me* curious,' Vicki said.

29

'Maybe he's got a guillotine in there and he'll do us all a favour and lop off his ugly head.'

'You think he's got the brains to make a guillotine?'

'If he had any brains, he'd be dangerous.'

Vicki was beginning to look forward to lunch by the time the four judges reached the project next to Melvin's. She checked her wristwatch. A quarter till twelve. At noon, there would be an hour-long break. Some of the parents, she knew from past Science Fairs, would have tables set up just outside the doors with beer and wine for the adults, soft drinks, hot dogs and pizza and tacos – all kinds of good stuff. Though she wasn't especially eager to spend the lunch hour with Henry, she was definitely hungry. Her mouth had been watering all morning because of the formaldehyde, which simply did that to you even if you were bent over cutting up a dead rat.

Ace patted her knee. 'The moment, ladies and gentlemen, is upon us.'

The judges stopped in front of Melvin. He climbed off his stool, picked up the megaphone, and flipped a switch. A high piercing whine stabbed Vicki's ears, then faded.

'Attention, everyone,' Melvin announced, his voice sounding tinny and loud. 'Come one, come all. Come and see Melvin's Amazing Miracle Machine.' As he spoke, he swayed from side to side and rolled his head. 'You don't want to miss it. Nosirree.'

'What a moron,' Ace whispered.

He *did* have a rather moronic look on his face, which wasn't all that unusual for Melvin.

Spectators were beginning to come over.

'Come and see it,' Melvin went on. 'The Amazing Miracle Machine. Hurry, hurry. Step right up. You've never seen anything like it. You don't want to miss it. Come one, come all.'

Mr Peters, the principal and head judge, stepped up to Melvin and said something – probably telling him to get on with it.

30

Melvin nodded, put the megaphone to his mouth, and said, 'The show is about to begin!'

By now, a substantial crowd was gathered in front of Melvin's display. Vicki followed Ace's example, and stood on the seat of her chair. From there, she had a fine view.

Melvin set his megaphone on the floor beside his stool. He stepped to a corner of his enclosure, hooked back one of the sheets enough to let him slip through, and vanished.

Nothing happened.

Everyone waited. More people showed up. There were murmured questions, heads shaking.

Mr Peters checked his wristwatch. 'We haven't got all day, Melvin,' he said.

'Is everybody ready?' Melvin finally called out. His voice sounded flat without the amplifier.

'*Do* it, doufuss,' Ace yelled.

A few people turned and looked up at her, some laughing, others frowning.

'And now – Melvin's Amazing Miracle Machine!'

The sheet across the front of the framework fell to the floor.

People gasped and went silent.

Vicki stared. For a moment, she didn't understand what she was seeing. Then, she couldn't believe it.

Surrounding Melvin and his 'project' were coils of razor-edged concertina wire. A poster at the rear proclaimed. 'I AM THE RESURRECTION AND THE LIFE.' In the centre, on a platform at least a foot high, rested a wheelchair.

In the wheelchair sat the corpse of Darlene Morgan. She wore the cheerleader outfit in which she had been buried: a pleated green skirt, a golden pullover sweater with a raised green E on its chest for Ellsworth High.

Her neck was wrapped in bandages to hold her head on. Her head was tipped back, her mouth hanging open. Her eyes were shut. Her face looked grey.

Between her feet was a car battery, jumper cables clamped to its posts. Melvin raised the other ends of the cables over-

31

head and bumped the clamps together. Current flashed and crackled.

Vicki, stunned, felt herself swaying. She grabbed Ace's arm to steady herself.

Somebody started to scream. Then everyone seemed to be yelling or shrieking.

'My God!'

'Stop him!'

'What's he *doing*?'

'Melvin, for godsake!'

'Do something!'

Instead of trying to stop Melvin, the people at the front of the group were backing away.

Melvin went on with business as if he were alone.

He clamped a jumper cable to each of Darlene's thumbs, then leaped aside, shouting, 'RISE! RISE! COME ON, BITCH, RISE!'

Darlene didn't rise. She just sat there. The battery charge seemed to have no effect at all.

'I COMMAND YOU TO RISE!' Melvin yelled. He rushed behind the wheelchair, grabbed its handles and shook it as if trying to stir her into action. 'COME ON! GET UP!'

Darlene shimmied and swayed. Her head wobbled. She didn't get up.

'UP! UP! I COMMAND YOU!'

Mr Peters leaped over the tangle of concertina wire.

Melvin jerked the handles ups. The wheelchair tipped forward, hurling Darlene from her seat. Mr Peters yelped as the body tumbled at him. He ducked under it.

Darlene flopped onto him. Her head came off, rolled down his back, and dropped face-first into the razor wire.

Melvin gave the screaming crowd a big, idiotic grin.

Homecoming

You'll be living here, Vicki told herself. You can't avoid him forever, so you might as well go ahead and get it over with.

There was enough gas left to reach Ace's, so she didn't absolutely have to stop. But that would leave the U-Haul with an empty tank and she needed to drive forty miles to Blayton tomorrow once she finished unloading at the new apartment Ace had found for her.

Maybe the Arco station at the other end of town would still be open. It used to close down early, but its hours might've changed.

Just go ahead and stop at Melvin's, she thought.

Though she was still at least a mile from the Ellsworth city limits, the decision made her heart thud faster. The steering wheel felt slick in her hands. Cool trickles slid down her sides all the way to the waistband of her shorts. She wiped a hand on the front of her blouse, then fastened the two top buttons she had opened earlier to let the air in.

Maybe he won't even be on duty, she thought. He could've hired a kid, or someone, to run the place. God knows, he could afford to.

He shouldn't have come back to Ellsworth. What was he, a glutton for punishment? He'd been an outcast even before he flipped out at the Science Far, and nobody was ever likely to let him forget the Darlene Morgan business.

When Ace told her on the phone last year that Melvin had returned, she'd been so appalled that she had given a lot of thought to changing her own plans. As much as she looked forward to returning to Ellsworth once she finished her residency, the idea of living in the same town as Melvin made her queasy. Maybe he was 'stable', maybe he would never do anything crazy again, but she knew that every time she saw him she would remember his Amazing Miracle Machine.

Still, Ellsworth was home. Even though her parents had moved to Blayton during her first year at medical school, it was Ellsworth that she longed for: the quiet, familiar streets of her childhood, the shops she used to visit, the woods and river, her friends. It was where she had been carefree and happy and where she had fallen in love.

Knowing that Melvin Dobbs had returned there after his release from the institution took away some of the town's nostalgic glow.

It might have been enough to make Vicki change her plans about returning. Except for one thing.

A $25,000.00 loan from Dr Gaines, offered to Vicki, and accepted, on the condition that she return to Ellsworth and help him in his family practice until the loan was paid back. A great deal, especially since she had always hoped to practice in Ellsworth. And she'd looked forward to working with Charlie Gaines, a charming old guy she liked a lot.

Her obligation to the doctor removed any real possibility of avoiding Ellsworth, where she wanted to live anyway, so she had resigned herself to an eventual encounter with Melvin.

The encounter had been eventual a year ago.

Now, it was imminent.

Vicki felt sick.

Calm down, she told herself. It's no big deal. He's not going to *do* anything to me.

Rounding the bend in River Road, she saw the lighted service station ahead. There was Melvin standing slouched in front of a car, apparently writing its licence plate number on a credit card receipt.

The way he was dressed, he might have looked ridiculous. He wore a baggy, bright Hawaiian shirt, plaid Bermuda shorts and dark socks that sagged around his ankles. But he didn't look ridiculous; there was nothing funny about it.

36

Vicki doubted that anything about Melvin, however odd, could ever strike her as amusing.

Her courage faltered.

Go to the Arco tomorrow, she thought.

But that would only postpone the inevitable. Better to face a nasty situation than to put it off and keep dwelling on it.

She slowed down, let out a shaky breath and swung off the road. The car was pulling away from the full-service island. She started for the self-service pumps, then changed her mind. This would be bad enough without having to get out of the truck. Especially the way she was dressed. So she drove to the full service area and shut off the engine.

Melvin hobbled over to her window, peered in, and tipped his head to one side. His lower eye narrowed. Up close, his face looked heavier than she remembered. Uglier, too. His eyes seemed bigger and farther apart, his black eyebrows bushier, his lips thicker. His long hair was combed straight back over the top of his head, and slicked down.

'I know you,' he said.

'Vicki Chandler. How are you doing, Melvin?'

He leaned closer. He'd been eating garlic. 'Vicki. Gosh.' His head bobbed and he smiled. 'Last time I saw you, you was standing on a chair looking green.' He chuckled, puffing his garlic breath into her face.

She wondered if it was a good sign that he could talk about that day, laugh about it.

'Well,' she said, 'I was a little shocked.'

'I guess you wasn't the only one.' He winked. 'That was the whole point, you know.'

'The whole point?'

'Giving Darlene a jump-start like that. Shoot, you don't think I thought it'd work, do you? No way. Only a crazy person'd think it'd work. Dead's dead, know what I mean?'

'Sure looked like you were trying,' Vicki said, astonished that he was discussing this with her, explaining himself.

'Put on a good show, didn't I?'

37

'Why'd you do it?'

'Got tired of being pestered. You remember how the kids used to pester me. You was always nice. You was about the *only* one didn't used to talk mean or knock me around. I figured it this way. I figured they was always after me on account of me being kind of different, so what I'd do, I'd shock their pants off and they'd be so scared of me they'd leave off.' He sniffed, and rubbed his nose. 'Course, I learned my lesson. I shouldn't of done it. Made me look like a crazy person.'

You *are* a crazy person, Vicki thought. Or at least you *were*.

'I'm sorry about your parents,' Vicki said.

'Thank you. They was pig vomit.'

'I could use a fill-up, Melvin. Unleaded.'

'They left me sitting pretty, that's about all the good I can say for them. Want me to check under the hood?'

'No, that's all right.'

He left the window, and Vicki took a deep breath.

Whatever they did to him in the institution, she thought, it sure hadn't changed him much.

In the side mirror, she saw him remove the gas cap and insert the nozzle of the pump. Then he came back to her window.

'You here for a visit, or what?' he asked.

She was surprised he didn't know. On the other hand, people probably didn't spend a lot of time chatting with him. 'I'll be working at Dr Gaines's office.'

'What'll you do there?'

'I'm a physician now.'

'A doctor?'

'Yeah.'

'No fooling. I got no use for doctors. Messing with people, you know?'

'I guess you've seen your share of them.'

'None as pretty as you, that's a fact.'

'Thanks,' she muttered.

38

'You married?'

'Not yet.'

'Saving yourself for me?' He laughed and rubbed his nose. 'Just a joke. I like to make jokes, sometimes. I used to have the orderlies and nurses cracking up. The patients didn't laugh much, they was too doped up. They didn't do much but drool.' He laughed at that one.

Vicki heard the gas pump click off.

'That be cash or charge?' he asked.

'Cash.'

He went away. While he was gone, Vicki lifted her handbag off the passenger seat and took out two twenties. Her hand was shaking badly, and the bills fluttered when she held them out the window to Melvin. He wandered off to get change.

Almost over, she thought. It wasn't so bad.

Wasn't so good, either.

When he returned, Vicki rested her wrist on the window sill to keep her hand from trembling. He counted the coins and bills into her palm.

'I'm real glad you're back,' he said.

'Thanks.' She tucked the money into the pocket of her blouse, and saw Melvin watch her do it.

'Hope you'll come around again anytime you need a fill-up.'

She nodded.

'Don't *you* be scared of me. Okay?'

'I'm not scared of you, Melvin.'

'Sure you are. They *all* are. Shoot, I'd go out of business if it wasn't for strangers passing through. Way folks around here act, you'd think *I'm* the one that killed Darlene. I never hurt her. All I just did was dig her up and play a little prank. But I don't want you scared of me. Okay?'

'Fine,' she said, forcing a smile. 'So long, now. I'll see you around.'

He stepped away from the side of the truck. Vicki started

39

the engine and pulled forward. She swung the truck onto River Road.

You could almost feel sorry for the guy, she thought.

The same way you could almost laugh at his peculiar appearance and mannerisms.

Except she didn't find him amusing or sympathetic.

Pig vomit. That's what he called his dead parents. You can't feel sorry for a guy who'd say·such a thing. Or for a guy who'd pull such a sick stunt with Darlene.

Sure, kids gave him a hard time. But that was no excuse. A lot of people get teased and don't go out and dig up a dead girl and put on a show with her body.

And he asked if I was *saving myself* for him.

Ace came to the door in a bright ·yellow nightshirt with Minnie Mouse on the front, and threw her arms around Vicki. Stepping back, she said, 'God, it's been a while.'

'Three years next month since my last visit,' Vicki told her.

'It's a shame the way you've aged.'

'You and the horse you rode in on.'

She grabbed up Vicki's suitcase and led the way through the house. 'How was the trip?'

'Endless.'

'We'll have a few snorts.'

'Sounds good.'

Ace swung the suitcase onto the bed in the guestroom. Then they went into the kitchen. 'Vodka and tonic?'

'Great.' Vicki sat at the table. 'Where's Jerry? Or shouldn't I ask?'

'Gave him the boot.'

'You're kidding. Everything was fine when we talked.'

'Well, a lot can happen in a week. He popped the big one Wednesday night. Can you imagine? The alimony and child support he's forking out, and he wants to marry me? That's a laugh. I'd be supporting him, the damn free-loader.'

She brought the drinks to the table, and sat down across from Vicki.

They raised their glasses.

'To living hard,' Ace said, 'dying young, and having a great-looking corpse.'

'Charming,' Vicki said. But she drank to it. Then she said, 'So you turned Jerry down?'

'I tossed him out on his bald ass.'

'Seems rather harsh.'

'He was no prize, anyway.'

'You're awfully picky for a gal in the springtime of her spinsterhood.'

Ace gave her the finger.

'Can't be many left.'

'Hon, there's plenty of fish in the sea. I've got no trouble hooking them. The problem is, I can't seem to land a keeper.'

'Jerry sounded pretty good to me.'

'This from the gal who dated Henry Peterson.'

Vicki rolled her eyes. 'Don't remind me. So what else has been going on?'

They talked and drank. It was after three a.m. when they quit.

Vicki staggered into the guest room. She sat down beside her suitcase on the bed, and flopped backward. Coins spilled out of her blouse pocket. They rested on her chest, and fell off her shoulder when she swung her legs up to remove her shoes and socks. She tugged down her shorts and panties, and kicked them away. Opening the buttons of her blouse, she noticed that her fingers were a little tingly. She would have to sit up to take the blouse off. She supposed she *could* sit up, but she didn't look forward to the attempt. To postpone it, she plucked the folded bills out of her pocket and let them fall onto the bed behind her shoulder. Then, moaning, she pushed herself up. She stood, slipped her blouse off and let it fall to the floor.

She dragged her suitcase off the bed. As it fell, she swung

41

it around, stumbling as it pulled at her. She steered the case down to the carpet and knelt in front of it. There was a knotted rope around its middle because one of the clasps was broken. She picked at the knot. It felt hard and tight. Working at it made her fingernails hurt.

Her nightgown was inside. Along with her toothbrush and toothpaste. She wanted them.

But not that much.

She crawled to the bed, pushed herself up and saw the scattered coins and bills.

The gas change.

Can't just leave it there, she thought. It'd end up on the floor.

So she bent over the mattress, bracing herself up with one arm, and swept the money into a pile. She closed her hand around it. Stepping back, she saw that she hadn't missed any. But one bill, caught only by a corner, fluttered loose on her way to the dresser. It brushed her thigh and swooped between her legs like a flying carpet. Her left hand made a snatch for it. And caught it.

Pretty darn good, Vicki thought. What speed! What agility!

She dumped the handful of money onto the bureau, then placed the captured bill neatly over the top of the pile.

Something was scribbled across it with a red pen.

Vicki lowered her head and squinted at the writing.

'MELVIN DROP DEAD AND DIE YOU SICK FUCK.'

In her dream, Vicki was sitting in darkness. She didn't know where, only that it was someplace bad to be. She wanted to get out fast. But she was bound to the chair. She felt ropes around her ankles, wrapping her wrists, criss-crossing her torso like bandoliers.

Gotta get out of here, she thought, close to panic. Haven't got much time. He'll be here any second.

She struggled to free herself. The ropes rubbed against her bare skin, but didn't come loose. Then she realised that

42

her bound hands, resting on her lap, weren't fastened down.
She raised them to her mouth. Her teeth found the bundle
of knots. She bit at the first knot and tugged it open, but
there was another knot beneath it. She tore that one loose
with her teeth, only to find still another knot waiting.

She started to whimper.

He's getting closer.

When the lights came on, she knew it was too late for
escape.

She was seated in the middle of the Community Centre
arena.

The clamour of a banging door reverberated through the
empty auditorium.

He's coming!

She saw him.

Melvin. He walked toward Vicki from a distant corner,
pushing a wheelchair. In the wheelchair sat Darlene. She
should've been wearing the letter sweater and pleated skirt
of her cheerleader outfit. Instead, she wore Vicki's white
nightgown.

So that's where it went.

I'll have to throw it away, Vicki thought. *I sure can't wear
it after it's had a dead person in it.*

Darlene looked very dead. Grey and withered. Even worse
than she did for real.

This is a dream, she suddenly realised. *This isn't
happening.*

But it sure seemed to be happening, and Vicki wondered
if she only *thought* she was dreaming.

She started biting the knots again, got another one open
as Melvin rolled the wheelchair closer, but there was still
another knot below it.

Melvin kept coming. Did he plan to ram her?

Eight or ten strides away, he stopped it.

The white bandage around Darlene's neck appeared to be
the same fabric as the nightgown. Through its diaphanous

43

layers, Vicki could see a bloodless, horizontal gash across the girl's throat.

Let's wake up now. Come on.

'You're looking lovely tonight,' Melvin said, tilting his head and nodding.

'Cut it out. Go away.'

'Have you saved yourself for me?'

'No.' She realised she was whimpering again. 'Leave me alone. Please. Just go away.'

'Be mine, darling, and I'll give you everlasting life.'

'No.'

'You'd like that, wouldn't you? To live forever?'

'I don't know.'

'Look at Darlene. Look at the face of death.'

Oh Jesus, Darlene's left eyelid bulged, slid up a bit, and a white *worm* squirmed out.

It's time to wake up, damn it!

'Don't you believe that I can give you life everlasting?'

'No.'

Melvin, leering, raised high the black rubber handles of jumper cables. 'Get this!' He bowed and swung the cables down over Darlene's shoulders. The clamps opened like jaws. They snapped shut on Darlene's nipples. Vicki heard a crackling buzz. The girl twitched and shimmied. White smoke began to roll out of her mouth. Blood welled out of her nipples around the teeth of the clamps and soaked the nightgown. Blood seeped into the fabric wrapping her neck. Her eyelids lifted. She had eyes, not empty sockets, and the worm was gone from her cheek. She blew out a puff of smoke. Smiling, she opened the clamps and tossed the cables back over her shoulders, where Melvin caught them.

Darlene rose from the chair. She took a few steps toward Vicki. Then, she snapped her body straight and planted her fists on her hips.

'Still think I can't?' Melvin asked.

Darlene, standing rigid, clapped her hands.

Clap – clap – clap – clap.

44

She shot a fist into the air.

'WE GOT PEP!'

Her other fist darted up.

'WE GOT STEAM!'

She danced and twirled.

'WE ARE THE GIRLS ON MELVIN'S TEAM!'

Shouting 'TEAM,' she leaped high, threw back her head, kicked her legs up behind her and flung her arms high. Vicki heard a ripping sound. Darlene's head went back farther and farther, the bandage splitting, her throat opening like a mouth. Her head dropped out of sight. It appeared behind her kicking legs. It thumped against the floor. She came down, her right foot landing on her face. Balance lost, she stumbled backward. As she fell into the wheelchair, her head rolled toward Vicki.

'NO!'

Melvin laughed.

The head rolled closer and closer.

Its mouth closed around Vicki's big toe and began to suck.

Yelping, she lurched up.

The bedroom was full of sunlight.

CHAPTER FIVE

Melvin looked up as headlights swept across the office windows. They belonged to a Duster that pulled up to the self-service island.

There was someone in the passenger seat.

Melvin peered through the window. Looked like it might be a gal, but he couldn't tell for sure.

He'd been waiting for a gal. He needed one.

His heart started thumping hard.

He folded his *Penthouse* shut and slipped it into the desk drawer.

The driver climbed out and walked around the rear of his car to the unleaded pump. He was a tall, skinny guy, probably in his early twenties. That meant the gal – if it was a gal – might be a young one.

Too bad she had to be with him. He looked like a hard case, the way he wore that T-shirt with the sleeve cut off, and those blue jeans hanging low and those cowboy boots.

You can't be too picky, though, Melvin told himself. It wasn't often a gal would drive into the station by herself, especially not this late at night. The last one to do it had been Vicki, three nights ago.

He'd planned to use her till he saw who she was. She would've been just right, coming along at that hour, and all alone. But she was a local, and people were probably expecting her, so it wouldn't have been smart even if she hadn't been someone he liked so much.

I'll just go out and take a look at this one, he thought.

He started to stand up, but the passenger door opened. He settled down in his chair again.

The passenger was a gal, all right. She swung her long, slim legs out of the car, stood up, and said something to the guy. Her hair was short, so it didn't hang down her neck at all. She wore cut-off blue jeans, and a white tube top that only stayed up because its elastic was hugging her around the middle. It left her midriff bare. Its upper edge was straight across her chest, high enough to cover her breasts completely. Her breasts looked like tennis balls and had been cut in half and stuffed under the stretchy fabric.

Pretty small, but right there. One good tug on that tube top. . . .

He rubbed the back of his hand across his mouth.

The gal shrugged at something her friend said, then started walking straight for the office. She didn't look where she was going because she had her head down and was searching inside her shoulder bag.

46

Her cut-offs hung very low. When she entered the office, Melvin saw that she had a small red rose tattooed midway between her navel and right hipbone. Its stem disappeared down the front of her shorts.

He raised his eyes before she looked at him.

She didn't have much of a face. Too long and narrow, with crooked slabs of teeth and an upper lip that wasn't long enough to keep her gums out of sight.

Though she looked at Melvin, she didn't appear to see him. Her face didn't change at all. It just turned away, and she started inspecting the munchies inside the vending machine.

Typical bitch. Plenty of them did that. Acted like he wasn't here.

You're no prize, yourself, you horse-face slut.

She reached out and dropped coins into the machine, then pressed a couple of buttons. Melvin saw a package of barbeque flavoured potato chips drop from a clamp. It thumped into the trough and the girl bent down to take it out. The seat of her jeans was frayed just below the right pocket, and pale skin showed through the loose threads. She straightened up, turned around and left the office.

Instead of heading back to the car, she walked past the window and rounded the corner. Looking for the restroom.

Making it easy for me, Melvin thought.

The guy, done filling his tank, came to the office. He stood in front of Melvin and dug some bills out of his jeans.

'Be needing anything else?' Melvin asked. 'Got a sale on wiper blades.'

'I don't see any rain,' the guy muttered, plucking bills out of his hand and tossing them on the counter.

Melvin stood up. First, he checked the windows. Then, he glanced at the computer, saw that he was owed $12.48, and picked up the money. A five and eight ones. 'That makes fifty-two cents back to you,' he said.

'You can count.'

'Sure can.'

47

He stuffed the bills into the left-hand pocket of his Bermuda shorts, reached into his other pocket, brought out a canister of tear gas and sprayed the guy in the face.

Got him right in the eyes. He squeezed them shut and grabbed his red face and staggered backward, bending over and going 'Uhhh uhhh uhhh.' He was on his knees by the time Melvin cleared the counter. The kick caught him in the ear and knocked him onto his side.

Melvin heard the faint sound of the toilet flushing, so he stomped the guy's head against the floor a few times. That seemed to do the trick. Maybe didn't finish him off, but at least he was out cold. Melvin grabbed him by the boots, dragged him around behind the counter, and sat down.

The gal probably could've seen him as she walked past the window, but she was busy using her teeth to rip open her package of potato chips. She didn't give the window even a glance. She just walked back to the car, got into the passenger seat, and shut the door.

Probably figuring her friend had gone to take a leak.

Her friend, Melvin noticed, *had* taken a leak. The front of his jeans was soaked pretty good. He was also taking a leak out of his left ear, but that was blood. It dripped into a little puddle on the linoleum under his head.

The gal sat in the car, eating.

After a while, her head turned. She must be starting to wonder what was taking the guy so long. He wasn't coming, so she went back to her chips.

Melvin opened the bottom drawer of his desk. He pulled out a box of plastic wrap, stripped off about a yard of the cellophane, and tore it free. He checked the gal. She wasn't looking. He lifted his shirt, held it up under his chin, and spread the filmy plastic sheet against his belly. It clung to him. It went most of the way around his back. He let his shirt fall, covering it.

Then he put the box away and watched the girl.

Finally, she climbed out of the car. She stood beside the

48

open door, frowned toward the corner of the building, and brushed her hands on her shorts.

Melvin guessed her patience had lasted about as long as the potato chips.

She headed for the corner of the building. Just to make sure she wouldn't look into the window and spot the guy on the floor, Melvin stood up and stared out at her. She caught a glimpse of him, and did as he expected – she looked the other way. He kept gazing at her, turning around when she reached the corner, and she kept looking elsewhere until there was no more window between them.

This was working out just fine.

Melvin figured she would come back into the office when she couldn't find the guy in the restroom, but he preferred to take care of her out back where he wouldn't have to worry about anyone driving past the station or stopping in for a fill-up.

He hurried out of the office and around the corner. Walking alongside the building, he heard her knocking. Then her voice. 'Rod? What're you doing in there?'

He reached the rear corner and stepped past it.

She was facing the men's room door. She knocked on it again. 'Rod, you either answer me or I'm coming in.'

Melvin stood motionless. She hadn't noticed him.

'All right for you, I'm coming in.' She turned the knob and pulled the door open. The light had been left on inside. She stood in the glow of it for a moment, then stepped through the doorway.

As the door swung shut, Melvin started moving. When it was completely closed, he ran.

He jerked it open and rushed in.

The gal whirled around, letting go of the toilet stall's door. This time, she didn't try to avoid his eyes.

Pretty hard to ignore me now, Melvin thought.

'Get out of here,' she said. Her voice was high-pitched. She didn't seem angry, yet, just surprised and confused as if she couldn't believe he'd blundered into the restroom with her. '*I'm* in here. Get out.'

'You're in the men's,' he said, and smiled.

'I know that. I was looking for someone.'

'Rod's in the office.'

'Okay.' She flapped a hand sideways, gesturing for him to step out of the way.

Melvin didn't move.

Her head turned a bit as if she figured that glaring at Melvin from the corners of her eyes, instead of straight on, was somehow more intimidating. 'You'd better just let me by.'

'Gonna tell Rod on me?'

She tipped her head back and kept staring at him. 'I'm warning you.'

With a shrug, Melvin stepped aside. He swept an arm toward the door.

'That's better,' she said. She walked toward the door, watching him with narrow eyes, looking sure of herself and eager to tell Rod about this creep who'd given her a hard time in the john. As she passed Melvin, she turned her face toward the door. She reached out and grabbed the knob. She pushed and the door opened.

Melvin snatched her hair and jerked. She yelped. Her hand, still on the knob, slammed the door as she flew backward. He swept a foot out from under her, gave her hair another yank and let go and watched her go down. Her back slapped the tile floor and she skidded.

Before she could start to get up, Melvin dropped onto her chest. Her breath whooshed out. Her eyes bugged. Her face went bright red. She squirmed, but her arms were pinned under Melvin's knees.

He lifted his shirt, peeled the cellophane away from his skin, folded the plastic film to double its thickness, and stretched it taut across her face.

With his hands clamped to the sides of her head, he had a good view through the clear plastic. Her face was distorted,

50

eyelids stretched sideways so she looked oriental like a robber in a stocking mask. Her nose, mashed down, had a white tip. The flattened lips of her wide mouth were pale. The disk of cellophane over her mouth crackled as she sucked and puffed. It fogged up.

She bucked and twisted and writhed under Melvin, but he rode her like a bronco.

Her tongue thrust into the plastic, making it bulge. Though the film didn't break, it stretched and formed a bubble. When she drew in her tongue, the bubble snapped into her mouth. It puffed out with a soft whupping sound, then was sucked in again. And she bit it. She caught it between her big crooked front teeth and worked her jaw back and forth – grinding it, chewing it. Her tongue pushed a hole through the plastic, darted back into her mouth, and she loudly sucked air into her lungs.

The air came out screaming.

Melvin slapped a hand across her mouth. That muffled the noise, but he doubted his ability to suffocate her with the hand. Especially the way she was flinging herself and shaking her head. The screaming soon stopped, but she kept breaking the seal and breathing.

Shit! He hadn't wanted to damage her. The cellophane usually worked.

She lurched violently, almost throwing Melvin, and suddenly her teeth found the edge of his hand. Before he could jerk it free, she bit. He felt her teeth sink into his palm, saw them break the skin on the back of his hand and go in. He heard himself cry, 'YEEEOOOW!' as pain bolted up his arm.

It took four punches with his left fist to her temple, each punch jarring her head and tearing his right hand, before he got it out of her mouth.

She was still conscious, her head rolling from side to side.

Melvin peeled the plastic wrap off her face.

Her eyes were half shut. She was moaning.

51

The side of her face was red from the punches, and starting to swell up.

Damn it.

Now she was marred.

She wouldn't have been pretty, anyway, Melvin consoled himself, but he hated the idea of leaving her bruised. After all, the bruise would probably be permanent.

Maybe some make-up.

She was stirring a little more.

With his left hand, Melvin grabbed the hair on top of her head. He lifted her head and gave it a bounce off the floor.

That settled her down.

He wrapped some plastic around his hand, partly to hold in the blood and partly to give himself a firm hold. Then he picked up the other end and stretched an unbroken section of the cellophane across her nose and mouth.

If at first you don't succeed. . . .

This time, she didn't fight it.

CHAPTER SIX

Vicki pressed the ten-minute snooze button on her alarm clock and snuggled down with her face in the pillow.

It's Wednesday, she thought. Charlie'd be heading out to the golf course, so this would be her first full day alone at the clinic. She felt a little nervous about that, and told herself to relax. Nothing was likely to come up that she couldn't handle – certainly nothing to compare with some of the emergencies she'd had to face during her residency at Good Samaritan.

Like Rhonda Jones. That was about the worst. Rhonda was brought to the ER by a truck driver who found her wandering along the highway, eyes slashed and both hands cut off by some maniac who'd raped her. One of the nurses actually fainted at the sight. Vicki, applying tourniquets and setting up the IV, kept a clear head and thought to herself at the time that she should be grateful to Melvin Dobbs and his Amazing Miracle Machine. Because, after seeing him try to jump-start Darlene and watching her head fall off, even the horrible mutilation of Rhonda Jones couldn't shock her senseless.

I don't believe I'll thank him, she thought.

Saving yourself for me?

She remembered that she'd dreamed about him again last night, and woke up gasping at around 2:30 with her night-gown soaked. She hadn't been able to remember the night-mare, but supposed it was pretty much the same as the one she'd had at Ace's house. She sure remembered that one.

She'd had dreams about Melvin every night since coming back. Three times, they'd caused her to wake up. She supposed the brief encounter with him at the gas station had done a number on her subconscious. The nightmares, bad as they were, didn't trouble her much except while she was in the midst of them.

After all, she was used to nightmares.

Following the Science Fair, she'd had them constantly for about two months. Then they'd become less frequent. Eventually, they'd dwindled down to one every two or three months, except when something disturbing came up to trigger a new series.

These would undoubtedly peter out, just like the old ones. Until that happened, she would just have to live with them.

She preferred the old nightmares. Those had pretty much been replays of the real event, lacking the weird variations present in the recent dreams. And in those, she'd been an observer, not a participant. Now, it seemed that Melvin's perverse stunt was *directed* at her.

All my fault, she thought. I shouldn't have stopped at his place for gas.

Vicki sighed. So much for enjoying a few extra minutes

snuggling in bed. She reached out, shut off the snooze alarm in time to prevent it from blaring, and got up.

She made her way through the darkness to the bathroom. After using the toilet, she returned to her bedroom and put on the running clothes that she had arranged on the chair the night before. She slipped a thin chain over her head. It held the apartment key and a police whistle. She dropped them down the front of her T-shirt.

The corridor outside her rooms was dimly lighted. She walked silently, and pressed a hand against her chest to stop the jangling of the key and whistle.

She didn't like this corridor. Not late at night, and not .at 5:00 in the morning.

It gave her the creeps.

All corridors gave her the creeps when she was by herself in a quiet building. You name it, she thought: school, dormitory, hospital, office building, apartment house. Just something about a deserted hallway when everybody else is either gone or asleep – or supposed to be.

A feeling that, if you make any noise, someone might just throw open a door and jump out at you.

This particular corridor was L-shaped so Vicki had to step around a corner before reaching the lobby and front entrance. She didn't much care for that corner.

But she stepped around it without hesitating.

The landlord's door was open.

Oh, great.

She cast a glance as she walked by, and sucked in a quick breath. Dexter Pollock was standing motionless just inside the doorway, wearing a bathrobe, bare-legged, staring out at her. She twisted her mouth into a smile of greeting, muttered 'Hi,' and kept walking.

'Word with you,' Dexter said.

Dandy.

He didn't come out of the doorway, so she had to go back to him. He stood there with his hands tucked into the pockets of his robe. His legs looked very pale in the faint light. He was a big man, well over sixty now and gone to fat, but when Vicki had been a girl he was chief of the Ellsworth Police Department, and she suspected that he still had the soul of a tyrant. She could kill Ace for choosing an apartment building that was *owned* by this man.

She leaned against the far wall of the corridor to keep the maximum distance from him, and crossed her ankles. He was known to be a lech. She was very aware of her bare legs – and his. She supposed he was probably naked under the robe.

'Early in the day to be going out,' he said.

'I suppose it is.'

'Still dark out there.'

'It's almost dawn.'

'You're a good-looking young woman.'

She didn't say anything. His words made her feel squirmy inside.

'Didn't your folks ever caution you about going out alone in the dark?'

'Sure they did.'

'I know they did. Your folks are fine people.'

'Thanks.'

'You think they'd approve, you going out at this hour and dressed in your skimpies?'

'I do it when I visit them. They don't seem to mind.' Then she added, 'I'm dressed fine,' though she wished at the moment that she was wearing her warmups instead of the T-shirt and flimsy shorts.

Dexter's eyes were pale blurs, but Vicki saw his head lower and rise as he inspected her. 'You're a rape,' he said, 'looking for a place to happen.'

'I have to get going,' she told him, hating the weak sound of her voice. You oughta tell him to shove it, she thought. She pushed herself off the wall and turned away from him.

'I'm still talking to you, Miss Chandler.'

'*Doctor* Chandler,' she said.

55

'Be that as it may. You have some respect and listen to me.'

She turned to him, frowning.

'You been away, so you're likely not on top of the local situation, and besides which, it's been kept pretty quiet. Nobody wants to get folks stirred up. Thing is, there's been half a dozen young women in this county vanish without so much as a trace being found of them. That's just in the past eight or ten months. And that's just the ones that got reported missing. Might be plenty more we don't even know about. So you'd best keep that in mind and think twice before you go off gallivanting at all hours in your underwear.'

'Thanks,' she said. 'I'll be extra careful. May I go now?'

'Do what you want.'

She pushed herself away from the wall and walked away, forcing herself not to hurry. As she reached the lobby, she glanced back. Dexter had stepped into the corridor. He was facing her.

She pulled open the glass door and stepped outside. The summer morning was warm, but she was trembling.

Thanks a real lot, pal, she thought.

His news about the disappearances was a little disturbing, but not much. She'd never kidded herself into thinking that Ellsworth was completely safe. No place was safe, especially for women.

What she found upsetting was Dexter ambushing her that way.

Had he been waiting for her? How did he know she'd come by?

Creep.

She liked to do her warm-up exercises on the broad stoop of the apartment building. But Dexter might just wander into the lobby and watch her through the glass, so she trotted down the stairs and started along the sidewalk.

She wondered if he would make a habit of waiting for her.

There was no way to leave the apartment without passing his door. The only other exit, conveniently located at her end of the corridor, would trigger an alarm if she tried to use it.

She came to the corner, and looked back. At least Dexter hadn't followed her. The sidewalk, grey in the glow of the streetlights, was deserted except for a cat sitting near the end of the block, rubbing a paw across its face.

Before starting to warm up, Vicki turned completely around and scanned every direction.

I always check, she told herself. Nothing to do with Dexter's warning.

Satisfied that no one was lurking nearby, she began bending at the waist and touching her toes.

I'm not going to put up with him, she thought. I'll just have to find a new place. Such a pain, though, moving.

Even with Ace's help, it had taken hours to unload the U-Haul and carry all her stuff into the apartment. And both of them with hangovers. Torture. She wasn't eager to repeat the process.

She sat down. The concrete felt cool through her shorts. She straightened out her legs, bent forward and grabbed the toes of her running shoes.

Give it some time, she told herself. Maybe Dexter won't make a habit of bugging me. He had his say. And I went out in spite of it.

But Vicki suspected that his 'say' was nothing more than an excuse to stop her, ogle her, and test his powers of intimidation.

Acts as if he's still the police chief.

He'd always been a jerk. Most of the kids in town used to despise him. He didn't just make them toe the line, he seemed to enjoy giving them grief. He probably picked on kids because he was such a coward when it came to adults.

The stories had it that he'd let his partner, Joey Milbourne, get beaten half to death by a couple of lumberjacks from the Bay who got drunk in the Riverfront Bar. He ran off and locked himself in his patrol car instead of giving Joey a hand.

But he sure was the tough guy, a regular Dirty Harry,

57

when it came to a teenager snowballing a car or knocking a baseball through somebody's window or parking by the river to neck.

He even gave Ace a bad time the night of the senior dance, which made Vicki especially glad they hadn't double-dated. According to Ace, she was butt-naked in the back seat of Rob's Firebird, going at it hot and heavy, when Dexter shined his flashlight through the window. He opened the door and ordered them both out of the car. He didn't even allow them time to put their clothes on. Ace snatched her gown off the floor as she crawled out, and held it against herself while Dexter brow-beat them about fornication and the possibility of getting themselves killed by a wandering lunatic. About the time he was threatening to run them in for indecent exposure and phone their parents, headlights appeared up the road. Ace dropped her gown and put her hands on top of her head. 'Guess you wanta frisk me,' she said. Dexter grabbed up her gown and shoved it at her and yelled, 'Get outa here, you crazy bitch!' And she and Rob scampered into his car and peeled away while the other car was still approaching.

Vicki got to her feet, brushed off the rear of her shorts, and started running.

Anyone other than Ace, she thought, would've been too humiliated from an experience like that to ever look Dexter in the eye again. So what does she do? She rents me an apartment from him.

When Vicki had found out, over vodka and tonic that first night at Ace's house, that Dexter Pollock was the owner, she'd said, 'Are you out of your mind?'

'I told him it was for you,' Ace said, 'and he dropped the rent ten per cent.'

'I hope you're kidding.'

'He said he figured it'd be handy having a doctor in the building.'

'I'm not a plumber, for Pete's sake.'

'Probably wants you to look after *his* plumbing.'

58

'Ha ha. Jesus.'

'He's not such a bad guy. He mellowed out some, after his Minnie kicked over.'

'You've sure got a short memory, Ace. You forget all about Senior Dance night?'

'Nope.' She grinned. 'Neither's he. Poor old fart goes red as a pimple every time he looks at me. The truth is, I scare him shitless. He thinks I'm nuts.'

'Because you dropped your dress in front of him?'

'Partly that.' Ace stirred her ice cubes with a finger, smiling down into her drink. 'You wouldn't remember those skimpy black panties I bought mail-order?'

'You wanted me to order some.'

'Those are the ones. Well, day after my run-in with Dexter, I mailed 'em to his house with a note. Said, "Dear Dex, Keep these as a souvenir of our ecstasy. Love and kisses, Honey Pot." '

'You didn't.'

'Wanta bet? And I personally saw Minnie take the envelope out of the mailbox the next morning.'

'Mean.'

'He's lucky that's all I did,' Ace said, her amused exterior cracking for just an instant and letting out the bitterness. Then she was grinning again. 'Poor jerk hasn't pestered me since.'

I oughta do something like that, Vicki thought as she rounded a corner and headed for Center Street. Make him think I'm crazy, so he'll leave me alone.

Or threaten to sic Ace on him if he gives me any more grief.

Better just to move out and find a new apartment.

Give it a couple of weeks, though, see how it goes.

She leaped off the curb at Center Street and looked to the right. The downtown business area of Ellsworth was grey in the pre-dawn light. A few cars were parked in front of the shops, but no one was about.

Light spilled onto the sidewalk from the windows of the

bakery a block away. On other mornings, she had run in that direction. She knew the bakery was the only place open. Though she couldn't smell the doughnuts from here, she remembered the delicious aromas and how they made her mouth water when she passed by.

It was sheer torture to run through those sweet smells and not stop in.

She decided to avoid that particular agony this morning, turned her back to the shops of the town, and headed north. She passed the dark windows of Riverfront Bait and Tackle, then left the walkway and ran through the grass of the long municipal park that bordered the river. A soft mist hung over the water. She saw a few boats far out, the silhouettes of fishermen sitting motionless with their poles. Somewhere, a loon cackled. She heard the distant putter of an outboard, but couldn't spot the moving boat. It was probably out behind Skeeter Island.

The ground sloped down toward the public beach and playground. She shortened her strides, wary of the dewy grass, and almost reached the bottom before her right foot slipped. Gasping, she saw both her feet fly up. She landed on her rump, tumbled backward, and dug her heels into the grass to stop her skid.

Brilliant, she thought.

She had that strange tightness in the throat familiar from other times (not very many and mostly long ago) when she'd fallen on her butt – a sensation that was like an urge to laugh and cry at the same time. It faded after a few seconds. Vicki told herself to get up, but she continued to lie there, panting for air. She felt the cool dew through her shorts and panties. The slide had pulled her T-shirt halfway up her back. The grass against her bare skin made her feel itchy, and it was the itch that soon convinced her to sit up.

She reached behind her with both hands and scratched. She was mildly allergic to grass. The itch would probably keep bothering her until she got back to the apartment and took a shower.

60

The back of her shirt was sodden. She had to peel it away from her skin before she could lower it. Then the wet fabric clung to her. She stood up, bent her arms behind her, and kept on scratching as she walked toward the beach.

She left the grass. Her shoes sank into the sand. At the water's edge, she was about to continue her run but spied a stick floating just offshore. It was about two feet long, and would make a wonderful back-scratcher. Since her shoes and socks were already wet from the dew, she went ahead and waded into the river. The chilly water rose around her ankles. She crouched, snatched up the stick, reached behind her back with it, and sighed as she scratched herself through the damp T-shirt.

The sky in the east was lighter now. Soon, the first rays of sunlight would break through the trees across the river.

She remembered the time she watched the sunrise with Paul. That was only a week before he went away. Late in the night, they had both crept out of their houses. They met and spent hours roaming the woods north of town, holding hands and talking quietly. It was a sad, sweet time. Long before dawn arrived, they found themselves here at the beach. They sat on the swings for a while. They silently climbed to the top of the slide and sat up there, his arms around her. Then they slid down together and wandered to the shore.

Vicki let the stick fall from her hand. She stared at the diving platform floating on oil drums a distance offshore.

They left their shoes and socks on the beach, that morning, and swam out to it. They sat on its weathered planks, shivering in their wet clothes. Then they lay down and hugged each other and the chill went away. It was as if she and Paul were the only people in the world. They kissed so long and hard that their faces were red around the mouth when the sun finally came up.

Remembering it, Vicki felt a hollow ache.

So many people, later in life, claim they have no regrets, say they'd do nothing differently if they had a chance to go back. But Vicki had a major regret. It filled her with sadness whenever she thought about that morning with Paul on the diving raft. If she had it to do over again, she would've made love with him there before dawn on the gently rocking platform. She had opened her wet blouse for him, and he had fumbled open her bra and lifted it up around her neck and caressed her breasts. That was far more than they had ever done before. It seemed daring and wonderful. Paul had never seen or touched a girl's breasts before, and he was the first to look at Vicki's and touch them. His hands never strayed below the waistband of her jeans, and she never touched him down there though she could feel him while they embraced and squirmed against each other. She thought about it, but the idea of actually taking off their pants and *doing* it seemed huge and grownup and terrifying. So it didn't happen. When the sun started to rise, they untangled and sat up. Even as she fastened her bra and buttoned her blouse, she felt a peculiar emptiness. Something – she wasn't quite sure what – had been missed or lost. She wept as she watched the sun come up over the river, and Paul put an arm around her back and said, 'This was the best night of my life, Vicki. I love you so much. I'll always love you, no matter what.'

'I'll always love you, too,' she said.

Standing in the river's shallow water, Vicki sniffed and wiped her eyes. Should've done it, she thought. Would've been so beautiful.

Those are the breaks, she told herself.

She turned away from the raft. Head down, she waded ashore. She was in no mood to continue her run. She scratched her back. She decided to return to the apartment and take her shower and get rid of the itch.

It'll be an interesting day, she told herself, trying to shake loose the mood of gloom. Charlie's golf day. I'll be in charge.

So who cares?

Her feet made sloshing sounds inside her soaked shoes.

She wiped her eyes again.

'You okay?' a man called.

The voice stunned her.

She looked up.

Near the far corner of the beach, where the playground equipment stood, a man was perched at the very top of the slide. Paul? Had some strange twist of fate lured him back to the beach at dawn, all these years later? It seemed impossible, but she hurried toward him, staring, her heart pounding wildly.

It can't be Paul, she told herself. If he'd moved back to town, Ace would've told me.

Maybe Ace doesn't know.

Maybe he just arrived.

He seemed about the right age. His hair was the same sandy blond colour as Paul's. He looked bigger, though. Paul had been slim, whereas this man had broad shoulders, a muscular chest and arms. Maybe Paul filled out, she thought.

Then she was close enough to see the features of his face, and her hopes collapsed.

Paul might've grown big and strong, but his face couldn't have changed this way. The man's eyes were farther apart than Paul's. His nose was larger, his mouth wider, his chin more prominent. Even his ears were different: they were bigger than Paul's, and lay close to the sides of his head.

Silly to think he *could* be Paul, she told herself.

'Are you all right?' he asked when she stopped near the foot of the slide.

'I guess so.' She felt cheated. And violated; she'd thought she was alone, but this man had been spying on her. 'What're you doing up there?' she asked.

'Seemed like a nice place to watch the sunrise.'

'Been up there long?'

'A while.'

She wondered if he'd seen her fall.

'I have to get going,' she muttered.

'See you around,' he said.

Vicki turned away and ran toward the road.

63

The little red light at the back of the HotTopper went off, letting him know that the stick of butter had melted. Melvin's right hand was bandaged and still painful from the bite, so he used his left hand to unplug the device, aim it down at the popcorn and squirt. The butter sprayed out as if from the shower nozzle, turning his popcorn golden. He sprinkled salt, shook the bowl, then sprayed more butter and sprinkled more salt.

He carried the bowl of popcorn into the living room, placed it on the table in front of his sofa, and returned to the kitchen. He filled a glass with ice, took it out to the living room, then went into the kitchen again and removed a two-litre plastic bottle of Pepsi from the refrigerator. He carried that into the living room.

He sat on the sofa. He filled his glass. On the television, David Letterman was introducing a Stupid Human Trick. Melvin pressed the Play button on his remote. Letterman vanished.

Melvin grabbed a handful of popcorn and started to munch.

His video camera, mounted near the ceiling of the basement laboratory and aimed downward at a forty-five degree angle, gave him a great view of the work table and the area around it.

Elizabeth's naked corpse lay stretched on the work table, strapped down with leather belts. The belts secured her wrists and ankles to the table top. Another belt crossed her throat. Another crossed her chest, just below her small breasts.

Melvin watched himself step in front of the camera and smile up at it.

'Handsome devil,' he muttered, and ate some more popcorn.

The Melvin on the screen wore a glossy robe of red satin

purchased by mail order from a sporting goods company that made such robes for boxers. He rubbed the back of his bandaged hand across his mouth, then said, 'Tonight, we'll be trying a method from page 214 of *Hizgoth's Book of the Dead*. My subject will be Elizabeth Crogan of Black River Falls.' He stepped back and swept an arm toward the corpse on the table behind him.

Turning away, he stepped to a cluttered cart next to the table. The back of his robe read, 'The Amazing Melvin' in swirling golden letters.

Melvin's hand trembled as he lifted his glass off the table. He took a drink of Pepsi, set it down, and watched himself bend over an open book on the cart.

Checking the recipe.

He picked up a mayonnaise jar and raised it towards the camera. 'The blood of three bats killed under the full moon,' he explained. He unscrewed the lid and stepped over to Elizabeth. Holding the jar in his right hand, grimacing at the pain, he poured some blood into his cupped left hand, and spread it over her face. When her face was red-brown with the syrupy fluid, he waved the jar over the rest of her body, spilling trails of blood onto her neck and arms and chest, her breasts and belly, her groin, and down the tops of her legs to her strapped ankles. He set the bottle aside. With his left hand, he rubbed the blood, smoothing it over her skin.

Melvin let his handful of popcorn fall back into the bowl. He gazed at the television. His heart was pounding, his mouth dry.

He spent a long time spreading the blood on Elizabeth. Then he stepped away and disappeared from the screen. Melvin heard splashing water while he cleaned his hand in the wash basin.

Every visible inch of the girl's body was painted. His fingers had left streaks and swirls.

Maybe should've turned her over and done the back, he thought.

He took a drink of Pepsi. The glass was slick in his buttery, shaking hand.

Melvin came back, stared at the body, then stepped over to the cart and checked the book again. He raised another jar towards the camera. Pieces of this and that hung suspended in a cloudy white liquid. 'Milk of goat,' he said. 'Eye of cat, tail of newt, henbane and mandragore, spider legs, ashes of a dead sinner. Brought to a boil at midnight.'

He opened the jar, set it down beside Elizabeth's head, then slipped an aluminum funnel into her mouth. Standing behind her head so his body wouldn't block the camera's view, he poured the substance into the funnel. It made soft, slurpy sounds. After a while, it began trickling from the corners of her mouth. Little bits of things rolled with the liquid down her cheeks.

The jar was only half empty.

He frowned at it, glanced into the funnel, then stepped sideways. With his good left hand, he shoved down hard on her belly. Stuff gushed out of her mouth. The funnel overflowed, spilling onto her face and neck. He let up, and the funnel began to drain into her. He pushed again, let up, pushed, let up. Soon, the funnel was empty. He picked up the jar and dumped more in. It went down for a while, then started backing up again. He glanced at Elizabeth's stomach, which was beginning to look bloated.

Shrugging, Melvin set the jar aside. It was nearly empty. He took the funnel out of her mouth. Goop poured from its spout as he cast it away. Her open mouth was full. A dark lump floated in the middle on the milky pond.

Melvin took another handful of popcorn and filled his mouth. He watched himself wink at the camera as he returned to the cart.

He studied the book again, then addressed the camera. 'Three candles, midnight black.' One at a time, he lighted the wicks, dripped pools of black wax onto the body, and placed the burning candles upright in the wax. When he was done, a candle stood in the tangled hair of her pubis and the other two rose from her breasts.

Melvin bent over the book, slipped handwritten papers out from under the top page, and read aloud.

'Master of Darkness, I, your servant, do humbly beseech you. I have prepared the earthly remains of Elizabeth Crogan in the manner prescribed. She has been annointed with the blood of the bat; she has consumed the Nectar of Hizgoth; the candles of the Black Triumvirate are burning at the three corners of the luminex. Her remains are in readiness. I beseech you, send me the soul of Elizabeth Crogan that she might join me in the service of your realm.'

Melvin, listening to his voice, refilled his glass with Pepsi, took a drink, and ate more popcorn.

On the screen, he kept on reading.

Finally, he came to the end. 'This I ask in the name of the Black Triumvirate.'

He stepped around the cart. Standing beside the body, he plucked the lower candle from its bed of stiff wax, and plunged it, flame first, into her mouth. The Nectar of Hizgoth spilled down her cheeks. He tossed the extinguished candle aside, then dunked each of the remaining candles into the Nectar.

Stepping behind Elizabeth's head, he raised both arms high. Blood had soaked through the bandage on his right hand, and trickled down his wrist and forearm. He shut his eyes. He mumbled, 'Come on, babe.'

He looked down at her.

Nothing.

Melvin stopped chewing his mouthful of popcorn. He leaned forward, staring at the body, half expecting its eyes to open, its head to turn. He'd been there; he knew she wouldn't move. But he could almost *see* it happening.

'Come on, come on,' he said on the television.

That Melvin lowered his arms, dug a Kleenex out of his robe pocket, and mopped the dribbles of blood off his right arm and wrist. Looking up, he glared into the camera.

He bent over the corpse, thumbed up an eyelid, and gazed at the eye.

The lid stayed open when he released it.

He stepped around to the side of the table. He shook her shoulder. Her head, with its single open eye, wobbled from side to side, slopping out the white Nectar.

He bent over and pressed an ear to her chest.

His face came up. He scowled at the camera. The left side of his face was smeared with bat blood.

'Didn't work,' he said to the camera in a calm voice. Then he yelled, 'SHIT!' and hammered his fist down between her breasts. Nectar erupted from her mouth. He pounded her again and again, using both hands, crying out in pain as he punched her with his wounded hand.

Melvin scowled as he watched. He didn't much enjoy seeing himself in the throes of his disappointment and rage and agony. He especially didn't like the way he'd lost control. He picked up the remote and pressed the Fast-Forward button.

In fast-forward, he *really* looked like a lunatic punching her, shaking her, prancing around the table waving his arms as he silently shouted, cuffing her some more, rushing off-screen and reappearing with a mirror that he held under her nose, scowling at the mirror, hurling it away in disgust. As he scurried up onto the table, Melvin pushed the Stop button.

The basement laboratory vanished. On the screen, a cute gymnast in leotards did the splits on a balance beam while she talked about the 'safe, sure feeling of confidence' she got from using Lite-Days Mini-Pads.

Melvin shut the television off. He finished the Pepsi in his glass.

He turned sideways on the sofa and looked at Elizabeth Crogan sitting there next to him, leaning back against the cushions, hands folded on her lap, legs stretched out, feet propped up on the table and crossed at the ankles. She didn't look too bad. He'd cleaned her up after last night's

68

experiment, had even bandaged her broken skin, applied makeup and brushed her hair.

'Still dead?' he asked.

She didn't move. She just stared at the blank television.

'Last call for a come-back,' he said.

Nothing.

'Speak now, or forever hold your peace. I'm gonna bury you. Want me to bury you?'

Nothing.

'Okay. You had your chance.'

He took a last mouthful of popcorn. Chewing it, he slung the body onto his shoulder and headed for the garage.

CHAPTER EIGHT

Dexter was waiting for her, that morning, when Vicki passed his door. It came as no big surprise. She had dressed in a warm-up suit.

'Good morning,' she said and kept on walking.

'Hold on, there.'

She turned around, but didn't approach his door. Dexter stepped out into the corridor.

'Come here. I won't bite.'

Maybe you won't bite, she thought, but you're still a creep. She took a couple of steps towards him, anyway.

He wore his faded blue robe. His hands were stuffed in its pockets. 'You gonna keep going out in the dark, no matter what I say.'

'I need to get my exercise.'

'You kids always think it can't happen to you.'

'I don't think that at all,' Vicki told him. 'But I'm not about to spend my life hiding. Besides, who's to say I'd be safe in my room? An airplane could crash on the building.'

'That's about as dumb a remark . . .'

'It's nice that you're concerned about my safety,' she said. She doubted that he *was* concerned about that. More than likely, it was just a convenient subject. All he really cared about was stopping her for a talk and a look. 'I appreciate it,' she said. 'But I wish you'd quit bothering me about this business. I've gone running in places a lot more dangerous than Ellsworth, and I'm still around to talk about it. Nothing you can say is going to change things. So how about just letting it drop? Okay? I'm in no mood for lectures at this hour in the morning.'

Dexter raised his thick eyebrows. A corner of his mouth turned up, but he didn't look amused. 'Aren't you the feisty one.'

'I don't appreciate getting hassled by you every time I try to go out.'

'Hassled? I'm just giving you some friendly advice. You want hassle, just wait till some lunatic throws you down in the dark while you're out there running your little butt off, and sticks his peter in you.'

Heat rushed to Vicki's face. She felt her heart slamming. 'That's what you'd like to do, isn't it?'

Dexter's face darkened. 'You don't talk to me that way.'

'I'll talk to you any way I please.'

He grinned, baring his upper teeth. 'You béen taking smart-mouth lessons from your pal, Ass?'

She went rigid and glared at him. 'I'm outa here. You can rent your damned apartment to somebody else.'

'Hey, now, you can't . . .'

'Just watch.' She whirled away from him and headed for the lobby.

'Bitch!'

She pushed through the door and rushed for the sidewalk.

After her stretching exercise near the end of the block, she ran. The running quieted her outrage. She decided that the blow up with Dexter had been a good thing. She might have stayed on at the apartment, otherwise, and tried to put up with him. Moving would be a drag, but not nearly as bad as suffering more encounters with that son of a bitch. She would make some calls from the office, later on. With any luck, she'd be able to find a new place today. Move out in a few days. The last of Dexter Pollock.

When she reached Central Street, she headed north and ran through the park. But starting down the slope towards the beach, she looked towards the playground equipment. Someone was sitting on one of the swings.

The guy from yesterday?

Just a vague shape in the darkness, but he seemed to be about the same size as the man who had watched her from the slide.

What's he doing, *waiting* for me?

First Pollock, now this guy.

Sorry to disappoint you, mister.

Wary of slipping again on the dewy grass, Vicki waited until she reached the bottom of the slope. There, she turned to the left and ran towards the sidewalk.

You ought to be flattered, she thought, that he came back this morning. Yeah? Who says that's why he did it? He was in the park yesterday without knowing I'd show up. Maybe he just likes to sit over there and watch the sunrise.

But he would've said something if I'd tried to run by.

What's so bad about that?

He didn't seem like such a bad guy. He might even be very nice.

You'll never know if you don't give him a chance.

Not today, folks. Not after Dexter.

Though she felt a little guilty about it, she didn't turn around and go back to the stranger. She reached the sidewalk bordering Central, and kept running north.

She wondered if he'd noticed her on the slope, seen her turn away and known the change of course was for no other reason than to avoid an encounter with him. She hoped not. He might think she was afraid of him, or simply stuck up.

It's not that, she thought as if apologising to him,

71

explaining herself. It has nothing to do with you. You seem like a nice guy. I'm just in a foul mood, that's all.

If he's there tomorrow . . . ?

Cross that bridge when we come to it.

The sky was growing pale as Vicki ran past the junction where Central ended just north of town and became River Road. The sidewalk ended with Central. Usually, she turned around here and headed back for the apartment. Not today. She was in no hurry to return and possibly face Dexter again.

She stayed close to the edge of the road and listened for traffic, ready to bolt onto the dirt shoulder if she should hear a car coming up behind her.

There were only a few homes out this way, mostly cottages close to the shore with private docks in the rear. When the road curved away from the river, the homes vanished. Vicki felt as if she were alone on a woodland trail. A paved trail, but shadowed by trees and silent except for the forest sounds of birds and insects and leaves rustling in the breeze. The sweet, warm aromas seemed even more wonderful than those from the bakery on Central Street.

Vicki felt great. But hot. Thanks to Dexter. She should've been wearing her lightweight shorts and T-shirt, not this warm-up suit. She hadn't even thought to put the jacket and pants on *over* her regular outfit. Once she was clear of Dexter, she could've dumped the warm-ups behind some bushes near the stoop. She wished she'd thought of that. But she came out wearing only a bra and panties under the heavy clothes.

The road was deserted, so she slid her zipper down almost to her waist. Air poured in, cooling the sweat on her chest and belly. Much better.

She considered leaving the road. The forest had plenty of footpaths, and she used to know all of them like friends. She could find a place to leave her warm-ups.

Right, and run in your undies.

The idea was tempting, but she turned it down. After all,

72

what if she met somebody on the trails? Slim chance of that, but she didn't want to risk it.

Even dressed, it might not be such a hot idea to go into the woods alone.

She rounded a bend in the road. Her stomach went tight. Ahead was the bridge over Laurel Creek. In her jarring vision, she saw the low stone wall that Steve Kraft had hit. Her mind filled with images of Darlene in the wheelchair, Melvin clamping the jumper cables to her thumbs, Darlene tumbling onto the back of the principal and her head dropping onto the razor wire. Then her nightmare version swarmed in: *Have you saved yourself for me?* and *I'll give you life everlasting;* the worm in Darlene's eye; the teeth of the cable clamps biting into the girl's nipples and how she bloomed smoke and rose from the chair and went into the cheerleader routine that ended in a leap with her head falling off; the head rolling towards Vicki, rolling.

God, I shouldn't have come out this way.

She turned her back to the bridge and ran from it.

After Elsie Johnson left the office, Vicki had a free hour before the next scheduled appointment. She opened the *Ellsworth Outlook* to the classified section and began searching for an apartment. She found three ads that looked promising, and made two calls before Thelma knocked and poked her head in. 'Melvin Dobbs just walked in,' she said. 'He doesn't have an appointment, but he'd like to see you. Apparently, he's injured his hand.'

Melvin.

'Is Charlie back from his house call?'

'Afraid not. Would you like me to tell him you're busy?'

'No, that wouldn't be right. I'll see him.'

Thelma shut the door.

Vicki stood up. Her legs felt a little shaky. Maybe because of the longer run this morning, maybe because she dreaded facing Melvin. She couldn't blame her goosebumps on the run. Rubbing her arms, she stepped to the office door. She removed her white jacket from its hanger, put it on over her sundress, and buttoned its front.

I should've stayed in bed today, she thought.

Entering the corridor, she saw that the door of Examination Room B was shut. That's where Thelma would've put Melvin. She hesitated in front of the door.

The more I see of him, she told herself, the less he'll spook me.

She wasn't sure she believed that. After all, it was seeing him at the gas station that apparently triggered her fresh round of nightmares.

She opened the door and stepped into the room. Melvin was seated, shoulders hunched and legs dangling, on the end of the paper-covered examination table. He looked as if he'd dressed up for the occasion. Instead of his gaudy shirt and shorts, he wore a blue dress shirt and slacks. His right hand, resting on his thigh, was wrapped with gauze and adhesive tape.

'Good morning, Melvin.' Her voice sounded steady. 'You have a problem with your hand?'

He squeezed an eye half-shut and bobbed his head. He raised the hand towards her. 'It got bit.'

'Oh? You have a run-in with a dog?'

'A scum-sucking kid. I went to give a credit card back to his old man, and the little shit took a bite out of me. I think it's infected.'

Nodding, Vicki took scissors off the instrument tray. She held his hand and began to snip the bandage. 'When did this happen?'

'I guess about three days ago. I figured it'd get better, but it just keeps hurting.'

'Well, let's see what the damage is.' She finished cutting through the bandage. The bottom layers of gauze were glued to his wound with pus and blood. She soaked a cotton ball with alcohol and used that to loosen the grip of the sticky fluids. At last, she was able to peel the last of the gauze

74

away. She swung the lamp closer, held his hand beneath its powerful light, and inspected both sides.

'That's a pretty nasty bite he gave you,' she said.

The teeth had left shallow, crescent-shaped wounds on the back of Melvin's hand. There were similar wounds, but deeper, on his palm. The kid must've snapped at Melvin, caught the edge of his hand, and bit down very hard. The area surrounding the injuries looked slightly red and swollen.

'It might not be a bad idea to get some x-rays of this. Just to rule out the possibility of a fracture. We don't do that here, but I could refer you to a radiologist over at Blayton Memorial.'

'No x-rays. You kidding?'

'Oh, they're harmless, Melvin.'

'Sure. They're so harmless, how come they can cause a spontaneous abortion if a fetus gets zapped?'

His question surprised Vicki. How could he know such a thing?

Give him some credit. He's not as stupid as he seems.

'That's fairly rare,' she said. 'And you're not a fetus.'

'Just the same, nobody's gonna zap me with no radiation.'

'Does your hand seem to work all right? Any loss of motion in the fingers?'

'They move okay. They're just sore. Whole hand feels sore.'

'Well, you're right about it being infected.'

'Gonna have to amputate?' Melvin asked.

'Oh, not today. I don't think there's much to worry about. I'll just clean and dress the wound for you, and give you a prescription for some antibiotics. Human saliva's a regular cesspool of bacteria. You would've been better off if a dog *had* bit you.'

He grinned up at her. 'Been a dog,' he said, 'I'd of brought you its head so you'd give it the rabies test.'

The words made a cold place inside Vicki.

'The kid's old man almost knocked *his* head off.'

75

She started to clean the wounds. 'Did you get their names?'

'On the credit card.'

'His family really should have to pay for the medical care.'

'I got insurance. I'm not gonna mess with going after them.'

That was refreshing. Most people were ready to sue over the slightest injury. In this case, a lawsuit seemed more than justified. She could understand, though, how someone with Melvin's history might prefer to avoid stirring up trouble.

'You should try to avoid using this hand,' she said. 'Do you have somebody to help you out at the station?'

'I got Manny Stubbins helping me out.'

'That's good. You definitely don't want to be pumping gas or changing tyres or anything like that. Has the pain been bothering you much? Have you had trouble sleeping?'

'Some.'

'Have you taken anything for it?'

'Just aspirin.'

'And that's helped?'

'I guess.'

'Well, I could prescribe you something for the pain if it's really bad. Some Darvon or Valium. But I'd prefer not to. You'd be better off sticking with aspirin or Tylenol, as long as that's helping.'

'Yeah, I don't want no dope. Turn me into a zombie. Had enough of that in the looney-bin.'

Vicki started to apply a fresh bandage.

She could feel Melvin staring at her. Almost done, she told herself. A few more minutes, and he'll be gone.

'Much as I generally hate doctors,' he said, 'it's sure nice coming to one as pretty as you.'

'Thanks.'

Saving yourself for me?

'You got a piece of this?' he asked.

'A piece of what?'

'The clinic here. You a partner, or something?'

76

'No, I just work here.'

'You oughta have a practice of your own.'

She managed a smile. 'Yeah, I could go for that. But it costs a lot of money to start up a practice. Besides, I wouldn't want to go into competition against Dr Gaines.'

'How come?'

'He's a nice man, and he's done a lot for me. If it weren't for him, I probably couldn't have made it through medical school.'

'What'd he do, pay for it or something?'

This is getting awfully personal, Vicki thought.

Though the subject made her uncomfortable, she realised she was the one who had brought up Charlie's helping her. And what did it really matter if Melvin knew?

'He gave me a pretty good loan,' she said. 'My parents helped out, and I had scholarships and I worked part of the time, but without . . .'

'So you're here because you owe him?'

'Well, I'm here because I want to be here. It's not just the loan. I'm sure I'll stick around, even after it's paid back.'

'How much do you owe him?'

'That's between me and Dr Gaines.'

'Just asking,' he muttered. 'Didn't mean to make you mad.'

'I'm not mad.'

''Cause I could help you out, you know. I'm pretty rich.'

'Well, thanks. I'm fine.' She finished bandaging him, turned away, and scribbled out a prescription. Her hand trembled as she wrote. Just great, she thought. He wants to give me money. What next?

'I want you to get this filled,' she said, giving the slip to him. 'Take the tablets three times a day. And change your bandage every night. If your hand doesn't get better, come back and we'll have another look at it.'

'So, we're done?'

'Yep.'

77

Nodding, he hopped off the examination table. Vicki stepped into the corridor ahead of him.

'Thanks for fixing me up,' he said.

'Any time.'

Tilting his head sideways, he narrowed an eye and peered at her. 'You're awful nice to me,' he said. 'I'm gonna be nice to you.'

She forced herself to smile. 'Have a good day, Melvin.'

He lurched up the corridor, stopped at the door to the waiting room, looked back over his shoulder and winked at her. Then he was gone.

CHAPTER NINE

A few minutes before five that afternoon, Melvin slid into a booth at Webby's Diner and ordered a cup of coffee. As he sipped it, he kept watch through the window.

From there, he had a fine view of the Gaines Family Medical Clinic across the street. He could see not only the front entrance, but also the small parking lot along the side of the building.

After a while, Dr Gaines came out. He went to a white Mercedes in the lot, and drove away. That left a green Plymouth station wagon, a yellow VW bug, and a white Dodge Dart. The bug, he knew, belonged to Thelma the receptionist. Vicki had driven into town in a U-Haul. She might've bought a car, but neither the wagon nor the Dart looked new.

She hasn't got much money, he reminded himself. Not if she had to borrow from Gaines. So she probably couldn't afford a new car. Maybe she doesn't have any car at all. Or maybe she bought a used one, or she borrowed one.

While Melvin was thinking about this, a pregnant woman

78

left the building. She drove away in the Dart. That left the wagon. It didn't seem like the kind of car Vicki would drive.

Beggars can't be choosers, he thought.

While the waitress was refilling his coffee mug, a man came from the wrong direction, carrying cans of paint, and opened the tail gate of the station wagon. He must've been in Handiboy, next door to the clinic. When the paint was loaded, he drove away.

That left only Thelma's VW.

Melvin frowned.

Maybe he'd missed Vicki.

Or she's still in there, but doesn't have a car. Or has a car, but walked. She might only live a few blocks away.

At twenty after five, the front door of the clinic swung open and Vicki stepped out. Melvin stared. He rubbed the back of his hand across his mouth. She looked beautiful. He liked her more in the white doctor jacket she had worn that morning; it was a stiff, formal costume that somehow made Vicki seems all the more soft and vulnerable, as if she needed to wear it for protection. But she looked just fine without it, too. Without her shell. She wore a yellow sundress that had no sleeves at all. Her legs looked very bare below the swaying skirt.

As she walked away, Melvin snapped a quarter tip onto the table. He headed for the door, forcing himself to move slowly so he wouldn't arouse the suspicion of the waitress or Webby behind the counter. He knew they were watching him. *Everyone* always watched him, except for strangers in town who didn't know what he'd done.

Outside, the heat of the afternoon closed around him. He squinted across the street. Vicki was halfway up the block, walking fast. His car was parked at the curb. It'd be stupid, he thought, trying to follow her with the car. Unless he got in and went after her and asked if she'd like a lift. Would she accept a ride from him? Maybe. But she might wonder how come he happened to show up just then.

He decided to follow her on foot.

He stayed on his side of the street, and didn't hurry.

On the next block, Vicki entered Ace Sportswear.

'Getcha something spiffy in the way of a bikini? Give you our sawbones discount.'

'Not today.'

'Well, then, fuck you. Get outa here.'

A young woman was standing nearby. She whirled around and gaped at Ace.

'Jennifer,' Ace told her, 'do me a favour and throw this gal out.'

Jennifer's mouth fell open. Her face went bright red. She looked no older than seventeen or eighteen.

'Oh, don't get your shorts in a knot, hon. This is my old bud Vicki Chandler.'

The girl rolled her eyes upwards. 'I thought you'd flipped out. I mean, Jesus hunchin' Christ. I mean, shitski, I never heard you take off after a *customer* like that.'

Vicki grinned at Ace. 'You been giving speech lessons around here?'

'What do you mean? Hey, how do you like Jen's outfit? Spiffy, huh?'

The girl wore a black and white striped dress that looked like an umpire's shirt. It wasn't much longer than a shirt, either. The belt was a loose silver chain with a silver whistle that hung against her left thigh. She wore white knee socks and black running shoes.

'Unusual,' Vicki commented.

'Guys love it. Has the sports motif, the little girl motif . . .'

'The nightshirt motif,' Vicki added.

'Hottest item in the store,' Ace said. 'When I get my new shipment in, I'll give you one. It drives the guys wild.'

'You ready to go?'

'Been waiting for you.' To Jennifer, she said, 'Things stay slow, you can close up early. So long.'

'Nice meeting you, Jennifer.'

'You, too,' the girl said.

They left the shop and walked around the corner to Ace's car. Hot air poured out against Vicki when she opened the passenger door. She rolled the window down before climbing in. The sun had been burning down on the seat. She winced, feeling scorched, and shoved herself up and hooked her elbows over the seatback to keep her rump off the searing upholstery.

'You okay?' Ace asked.

'Medium well,' Vicki said.

Ace sat down on a beach towel folded neatly on the driver's seat. 'Sorry about that, hon. I've got another towel in the trunk.'

'Any burn ointment?'

'Want to stop in at the clinic?'

'I'll live. I guess.' Vicki lowered herself slowly. It didn't hurt so much, this time. She sighed.

'Where to?' Ace asked, starting the car.

'The first place is on George Street. Near the church.'

Ace made a right onto Central. 'Oh, looky there.' She swung her thumb to the left.

Vicki leaned forward, peered past her, and saw Melvin. His back was turned. He was facing the display window of Johnson's Pharmacy, scratching his cheek with his left hand.

It was odd to see him. Vicki felt as if time had gone haywire. He'd left her office about seven hours ago, hadn't he?

'He was in this morning,' she muttered.

'I know. You told me on the phone. Going senile?'

'Weird.'

'What's weird? After seeing you, he probably got inspired to buy some condoms.'

'Oh, charming. Thanks.' Vicki looked over her shoulder and tried to spot Melvin through the rear window. The angle wasn't right. She couldn't see him.

'It's not uncommon, you know, for patients to fall in love with their doctors.'

81

'It's not uncommon for doctors to perform frontal lobotomies on wiseass friends.'

Ace glanced down at her breasts. 'Think I need one?'

'What?'

'That operation. On my frontal lobes. They look fine to me.'

Vicki ignored that one. She dug into her handbag and took ut the folded paper on which she'd written the address of the two apartment buildings they planned to visit.

'I really am sorry about Pollock,' Ace said. 'That piss-bag. I'm gonna have a few words with him.'

'Please don't. I just want to get out of that apartment and be done with him.'

'Dirty old fart.'

'I just hope I can get into one of these places fast.'

'I wouldn't count on moving in tonight. I tell you what, we'll stop by your room after we've checked these places out. You can pack up whatever you'll need, and stay with me till they let you move in.'

'It's a deal.'

'Great. We'll have us a blast.'

Melvin supposed they might've seen him as they drove by, but he guessed it didn't matter much. After all, he was right in front of the drugstore, and Vicki *had* given him a prescription. He'd gotten it filled that morning, but Vicki wouldn't know that.

When the sound of Ace's Mustang faded, he turned around and spotted it heading north on Central. He kept an eye on it as he rushed back for his car.

It turned left on George Street.

He reached his car, made a U-turn, and went left on George. The red Mustang wasn't in sight. 'Shit!' He punched the steering wheel. With his right hand. And cried out in pain.

When the agony subsided, he muttered, 'Okay, it don't matter.' He really wanted to find out where she lived, but

82

he'd just have to try again tomorrow. And the next day, if tomorrow didn't work out. It shouldn't be hard. He knew he would find out, sooner or later.

Coming to an intersection, he glanced both ways. No sign of Ace's car.

He kept heading west on George Street, figuring he might as well stick with it for a few more minutes.

On the next block, he found the red Mustang parked at the curb in front of a two-storey brick apartment house. No sign of the girls.

He stared at the building.

That's gotta be it.

He drove on.

That night, a little before ten, Melvin parked around the corner from the apartment house. His heart pounded fast as he walked towards the entrance. The pounding made his right hand throb.

He needed a new gal. He wouldn't use Vicki for that, though. Someday. Once he got it right. But it'd be awful to mess up with her and have to bury her like the others. She'd just have to wait.

In the meantime, he'd settle for looking at her.

He stopped at the door. Peering through its glass, he saw a small, dimly lighted foyer with a panel of mail boxes on the wall. On the left was a narrow stairway to the second floor. To the right of the stairs, a corridor stretched the length of the building. He saw no one.

He tried the door. It opened, which was hardly surprising. In Ellsworth, nobody gave much thought to security.

He stepped up to the mailboxes. There were a dozen, each labelled with the apartment number and name of the renter. The first box had an extra label that read Manager. Melvin moved his finger down the row, touching each name label.

No Chandler.

But the name on the card taped over the mail slot for 4 had been scratched out with a blue pen.

83

That's gotta be Vicki's, Melvin decided.

She'd only been here a few days, probably hadn't bothered to put her name up yet.

The hardwood floor of the corridor creaked under his shoes. He winced at the noise. But he didn't have to go far. Apartment #4 was the second door on the right. As soon as he spotted it, he turned around and hurried outside.

He crossed the lawn. At the corner of the building, he found a narrow lane of grass. Light spilled out from the windows of apartment #2, slanting down and casting a glow on the hedge that bordered the property. Melvin ducked below those windows, and made his way through the darkness to the windows of #4.

He peered through the glass. The curtains seemed to be open, but the room beyond was so dark that he could see nothing.

Either Vicki had already gone to bed, or she was away somewhere.

If she'd gone to bed, he wouldn't get to see her unless maybe she woke up to use the john, or something. Not much chance of that.

He wondered if he should stick around, just in case she was out.

He didn't want to waste the night, though. It'd be worth waiting for, if he knew for sure that she'd come in pretty soon. Just spying on her would be great, and even if she shut the curtains there might be a gap so he could see her undress.

But she might already be asleep.

And maybe this wasn't her apartment. After all, her name wasn't on the mailbox.

Waste tonight, he thought, and it'll just be that much longer before you can *do* things with her.

I'll try again tomorrow, he decided. I'll come earlier.

He crept away, ducked under the lighted windows of the neighbouring apartment, then thought he might as well take a peek. Slowly, he rose from his crouch. The curtains were open. The woman on the reclining chair looked familiar. He couldn't place her at first, then realised she worked as a

84

check-out girl at the Riverside Market. Melba, that was her name.

A fat pig.

She was sitting there, leaning back in the chair with her feet propped up. Her hair was in rollers. She wore a beige bra and panties. She held a paperback book in front of her face, so she couldn't see Melvin. An open bag of taco chips rested between her legs, and a can of Diet Pepsi rested on the lamp table within easy reach.

She looked like a bloated, bulging wad of raw dough.

Melvin considered killing her. She was repulsive. At the store, she acted like a snot.

It'd be nice to kick her swollen belly till she puked up blood.

Don't be dumb, he told himself. You don't want to mess around with someone you won't use.

He wouldn't be able to get her body out to the car, even if he wanted to.

Besides, he'd have to touch her to kill her. He could just *feel* his fingers sinking into that puffy white skin.

Melvin ducked down below the window, and headed for the street wishing he hadn't looked at Melba. He wished it had been Vicki sitting in that chair. Vicki, for sure, wouldn't wear cruddy beige undies. Maybe red. Maybe black.

He imagined her sitting there in nothing but her white doctor jacket. It was unbuttoned, hanging open.

He climbed into his car, and began the forty mile drive to Blayton Memorial Hospital.

CHAPTER TEN

A little after midnight, they started coming into the hospital parking lot. The area was brightly lighted. Melvin, sitting low in the driver's seat, watched them through the windshield.

85

There were both men and women. Some wore street clothes, but others were dressed in white. He supposed they were doctors, nurses, lab technicians, orderlies, janitors, all ready to head home now that their shift had ended.

Melvin settled on a tall, slim gal in a white dress. Probably a nurse. At this distance, he couldn't see her face too well. But she had short blonde hair like Vicki, and her figure looked good. She looked better than any of the others.

She walked with a stocky woman who was likely another nurse, and a man in overalls. The three of them stopped beside a van. They chatted for a while. Melvin heard the quiet sounds of their voices, but he couldn't make out what they were saying. The man soon climbed into the van. The two nurses stayed together as they passed several cars in the area of the lot reserved for staff. Then, the slim one climbed into a VW Rabbit and the stocky one kept walking.

Melvin backed his car out of its space, joined the small line of other vehicles waiting to exit the lot, then rolled onto the street and swung to the curb. Peering over his shoulder, he watched the Rabbit VW turn onto the road.

It turned right, just as he had.

A good omen, he thought.

The Rabbit passed him. He quickly moved out behind it, then eased off his accelerator and let himself drop back a ways. No point in hugging the gal's tail, even though she probably assumed he was just another hospital employee heading home.

She might not be easy to get.

The ones who stopped at his gas station were always easy. A couple of those, he just did them while they sat in the driver's seat, all set to pay him for the gas. Some, he followed them into the john and took care of them there. Others, they'd stop at the full-service island and he'd make a slice on the fan belt while he was under there checking the oil. After they drove off, he would shut the station and head up River Road in his tow truck. He'd find them stranded on the roadside a couple miles out of town, and they'd think it was a miracle that he'd happened to show up. Easy.

But this was a lot different. He wasn't sure how to handle it.

He'd given the matter considerable thought while he was waiting in the hospital lot. He knew how he *wanted* to get her. He wanted to just follow her home, wait till she was inside, then sneak in and take her by surprise. That way, he would have all the privacy and time he might want. For all he knew, though, the gal might be married or staying with her parents or have a roommate. In fact, he had to admit that it was most likely she *didn't* live alone.

He could go in and get her, anyway, but he wasn't sure he wanted to bother with that.

The other choice was to nail her before she got home. Either figure a way to stop her on the road, or try to get her after she parked, while she was on her way to the door. Those methods would only work if nobody else was nearby.

Just play it by ear, Melvin told himself.

The Rabbit turned left. Melvin followed. He checked his rearview mirror. None of the cars behind him made the turn. The road ahead was empty, with only a few houses in sight up ahead. He knew this road. It led to Cedar Junction, eight miles west of Blayton. Soon, there would be a long stretch through farm land before the outskirts of Cedar Junction. If she just doesn't pull into one of these driveways . . .

She didn't.

Headlights appeared in the distance, so he held off. The lights drew nearer. He squinted against their glare. A pickup whooshed by, and the glare was gone. Melvin watched the tail lights in his rearview. When they were tiny red specks, he swung across the centre line and stepped on the accelerator. He gained on the Rabbit, sped past it, then eased back onto his side of the road.

Nothing ahead except the moonlit road and fields.

He studied the Rabbit in his rearview mirror. It seemed to be about three car lengths behind him.

Melvin grinned at his craftiness. He knew he could've swerved into the car's path while he was passing it, but a weird manoeuver like that would've put the woman on guard. This way, she might not be suspicious at all until it was too late.

He braced, left hand tight on the steering wheel, arm locked straight, pressing himself against the seat back and the headrest.

And jammed down on the brake pedal.

His tyres grabbed the pavement, skidded and shrieked.

The Rabbit bore down on him.

He heard its squeal.

His car lurched with the impact. Not much of a jolt, really, but enough. He heard no breaking glass, so he doubted that either car had been damaged.

He swung onto the hard dirt shoulder of the road, and stopped. The Rabbit moved slowly past him, both its headlights still working. For a bad moment, he feared the nurse might keep on going. But she turned her car onto the shoulder and stopped a few yards in front of him.

Her door opened. As she climbed out, Melvin slumped against the steering wheel. He heard the quick scrape of her shoes on the road. The sounds stopped beside him. He slowly sat up straight, shaking his head.

'Are you all right?' the woman asked. Her voice was trembling.

'I guess,' he muttered. He rubbed the back of his neck.

She was standing close to his door, bending down to look in at him. He wished he could see her better, but the light was too faint. What he could see looked good. He guessed she was in her early twenties. Her white dress had a name tag over the left breast, but he couldn't read it.

'What happened?' she asked. 'Why did you stop?'

'Something . . . ran out in front of me. Maybe a cat. I don't know. It all happened so fast. Guess I should've gone ahead and hit it.'

88

'I'm so sorry. I shouldn't have been following so close. Did you hit your head?'

'I don't know.' He rubbed his forehead. 'I'm all right, I guess.' He turned off the engine, and took out the keys with his bandaged right hand. He slowly opened his door and stepped out onto the road. Pretending to ignore the woman, he wandered to the rear of his car.

'I don't think there's any damage,' she said as she followed him.

The tail and brake lights glowed red.

'Don't look like it,' Melvin mumbled. 'I got a flash in the trunk. I'd better get it.'

'I'll give you my name and number,' the woman said. 'If there are any problems, I'd be more than happy to pay.'

He unlocked the trunk. Its lid swung up.

'We don't have to get the insurance companies involved, do we?' she asked. 'I'd rather take care of this just between us, if it's okay.'

'Sure,' he said.

'Great.' She sounded very relieved.

Melvin took the flashlight out of his trunk. He turned it on, and shined it on the woman's hands as she searched her purse. She found a pen and notepad. He watched her hands shake as she tried to hold the pad steady and write on it.

'You may develop some stiffness in the neck,' she said as she wrote. She sounded a lot like Vicki talking about his bite. 'That wouldn't be at all uncommon in a situation like this. But if you'll come to the hospital and ask for me . . .'

'Fine,' Melvin said.

'I'll see that you're taken care of. We have a fine physical therapy department.'

'Okay.'

She tore a page off the pad. It fluttered as she gave it to him. He held it under the flashlight beam. Her name, Patricia Gordon, was scribbled in shivery ink. Beneath the name was a telephone number. Melvin tucked the paper into his shirt pocket.

89

As she slipped the pad into her purse, he aimed the light at her face.

She squinted and turned her head.

Not bad looking at all. A cute little nose. Freckles. Sandy-coloured hair sweeping across her forehead.

The name tag read, Patricia Gordon, RN. The dress had a zipper down the front. It was low enough to show a small wedge of bare skin below her throat.

'Could you . . . ?' she started to say, but her breath exploded out as Melvin rammed the flashlight into her belly. Pain bolted up his own right arm. He cried out and dropped the flashlight at the same moment Patricia doubled. He drove his knee up into her so hard she was lifted off her feet. before she could fall, he wrapped his arms around her waist. He hoisted her and flung her into the trunk. She landed on her back, legs in the air. The slamming trunk lid knocked her legs down. The trunk latched.

Melvin picked up the flashlight with his left hand. He thumbed the switch back and forth a couple of times, but the light was dead.

The red rear lights gave enough brightness for him to check the area behind his car. While he looked around, he heard bumps and muffled shouts from the trunk.

The purse, he decided, must've gone into the trunk with Patricia. It had been on a shoulder strap. He didn't see anything on the pavement or ground.

He walked over to her car. The engine was still running. He opened the driver's door, leaned in, pulled out the ignition key and punched off the headlights with a knuckle. When he shut the door, the car rested in darkness.

He wiped the door handle with the hanging front of his shirt.

Back at his own car, he removed the key from the trunk lock. Patricia shouted, 'Let me out of here! You can't do this!'

'Wanta bet?' he muttered.

He climbed into his car, made a U-turn, and drove away.

He knew he might be leaving his tyre tracks on the dirt shoulder of the road. He thought about going back and rubbing them out. Someone might come along, though. He'd been lucky to take care of Patricia without another car showing up. Tomorrow, he'd send Manny away and put different tyres on his car, get rid of these. Easy.

At home, Melvin parked inside his two-car garage. He used the remote control on his dash to lower the door. As it rumbled down, he climbed out of the car.

This was the first gal he'd brought home alive.

Exciting, a live one in his trunk. But a little scary, too.

He stood at the rear of his car and stared at the trunk.

What'm I gonna do with her now?

During the long drive, he'd had plenty of time to consider the problem. But he hadn't come up with any great ideas. It was a toss-up between killing her immediately and keeping her alive for a while. It might be fun if he didn't kill her right away. He could tie her up and fool around with her. On the other hand, he was eager to try a new method on her. That, after all, was the reason he took her.

I'm not a goddamn rapist, he told himself.

Besides, how would he tie her up without hurting his bad hand? She was bound to put up a fight. He'd either have to gas her or pound the daylight out of her. Then, if she wasn't out cold, he'd have to hide her face with something. He sure didn't want her *looking* at him while he screwed her. All that contempt in her eyes. Gals nearly always had contempt in their eyes when they looked at him. She would, for sure.

But if he held off till after he killed her and brought her back, she'd be so grateful she'd do anything to please him. Hell, she'd love him.

He went into the house. He came out with his Colt .44 revolver and a green, double-ply plastic trash bag. He shoved the folded bag into a front pocket of his pants. Holding the revolver in his left hand, he unlocked the trunk. The lid rose.

91

Patricia lay curled on her side, hands covering her face. She was sobbing quietly.

'Climb out,' Melvin said. 'I'm not gonna hurt you.'

'Don't hurt me,' she said through her hands.

'Told you I won't. Come on.'

She got to her hands and knees inside the trunk, never once looking at him. Her back shook as she wept. A string of snot dangled from her nose, swaying. Slowly, keeping her head down, she climbed out of the trunk. She stood with her back to Melvin, and hunched over and held onto the car.

'What are you going to do to me?'

'Just don't try nothing, you'll be okay.'

He pushed the revolver under his belt, took the trash bag out of his pocket, and shook it open.

'What's that?'

'Nothing. Just a bag. You're gonna wear it so you don't see where we're going. Stand up straight, arms at your sides.'

She followed his orders. Melvin spread the bag apart, slipped it over her head, and pulled it down her body. It covered her almost to the knees. He took off his belt and made a loop by slipping one end through the buckle. He dropped the loop over her head. The plastic bag crackled as he pulled, closing it around her neck. He left enough slack in the belt so she could still get air.

'Can you breathe okay?' he asked.

Her covered head nodded. Melvin heard her sniffle.

'It's not too tight?'

'No.'

'Okay, face me.'

She turned around. Melvin shook the belt sideways and watched the buckle slide around to her front. He walked backward, leading her across the garage to the side door of the house. He led her into the house, through the kitchen to another closed door. Opening the door, he said, 'Stairs. Be careful.'

'Where're you taking me?' she asked in a high, whiny voice.

92

'The basement.' Melvin grinned. 'That's where you're gonna stay till they come up with the ransom.'

'Ransom?'

'Sure. What did you think, I was gonna murder you or something?'

'All you want's money?'

'Course.'

Melvin switched on the basement light. Turning his back to the stairway, he took a careful step down. His left hand held the belt. His right hovered over the banister. Patricia hesitated on the top stair. 'Go ahead and hold the railing,' he said. 'I don't want you to fall and hurt yourself.'

She hitched the plastic bag up around her waist, reached out and clutched the wooden rail.

Melvin stayed two stairs below Patricia, and watched her as they descended. She took slow, careful steps. Her shoes and stockings were white. He hated those white stockings.

They'll be the first to go, he decided.

'Who's supposed to pay for me?' she asked. She didn't sound so upset anymore.

'You tell me.'

'I have some savings.'

'How much?'

Melvin reached the floor of the basement. Patricia stepped down the final two stairs. When the banister ended, she pulled the bag down as far as it would go, apparently preferring to be covered and out of sight.

'I've got about eight hundred,' she said. 'Will that be enough? You can have it all.'

'Eight hundred?' Melvin stepped behind her. 'Sure. That sounds fine.' He wrapped the belt around his left hand.

'Well, good. Then that . . .'

He jerked the belt. Patricia stumbled towards him as the loop shut, cinching the trash bag tight around her neck. He lurched out of the way. Her rump hit the concrete floor. He scrambled backward up the first three stairs, keeping the belt taut, dragging her until she lay against the steps. She kicked and squirmed. She worked the bag up her body, freeing her arms, and clutched the choking belt.

Melvin frowned. He wanted to suffocate her, not strangle her. He didn't want marks on her throat. So he gave the belt some slack. She yanked on it. Melvin released his grip. The belt uncoiled from his hand and flew past her feet.

She took a noisy breath and sat up. Her hands plucked at the top of the bag, trying to pull it off her head as if it were a stubborn jersey.

Melvin dropped down behind her. Sitting on the next stair up, he forced Patricia's arms down and wrapped his legs around her, pinning the arms to her sides. Then, he bent over her head and hugged the bag against her face.

When she was dead, he took off her white stockings first.

CHAPTER ELEVEN

Vicki flinched awake, gasping. She rolled onto her side, hushed the clamour of the alarm clock, and flopped onto her back. She stared at the dark ceiling. She was breathless, her heart slamming, her head throbbing with pain.

She couldn't recall the nightmare, but it must've been a doozy. No doubt featuring Melvin.

She lifted an arm out from under the sheet, and rubbed her forehead. It felt hot and damp. When she rubbed her scalp, she found her hair drenched.

Coming down with something? she wondered. Felt like a hangover. Though she'd stayed up late last night in the kitchen with Ace, she'd had nothing to drink except Coke. Probably just a bad case of nightmare.

Though Vicki's breathing and heart rate seemed to be normal again, she still had the headache. And she felt leaden.

Forget about running this morning, she thought. Just take

some aspirin, try to go back to sleep, and hope you can shake the headache.

She brushed the sheet aside. Moaning with the effort, she sat up. From the feel of the warm breeze on her skin, she knew that something was wrong. She looked down. Her left breast was bare. The bodice of the nightgown hung below it. Thinking that the spaghetti strap must've slipped off her shoulder, she ran a hand up her arm. The strap wasn't there.

Must've pulled loose.

She swung her legs off the bed and turned on the lamp. Squinting against the brightness, she lifted the pocket of lacy fabric over her breast. At its edge was a ragged notch.

Vicki scowled at it.

She stood and peeled the damp nightgown off her body. She caught the dangling cord. At its tip was the small patch of fabric torn from the front.

'Good God,' she muttered.

Normal tossing and turning couldn't have done this, no matter how feverish her sleep had been.

She stepped over to the closet door and looked at herself in the full-length mirror. The strap had left a thin red mark on the top of her left shoulder.

Someone had grabbed the nightgown and ripped it from her breast.

Someone, she thought. Guess who.

Unless her room had been invaded during the night by a roaming molester, or Ace was a closet lesbian, Vivki had torn the nightgown herself. The other two possibilities seemed remote. Ace had never shown any inclination towards sexual contact with Vicki. Even if she *was* interested, she was hardly the type to sneak around copping feels. As for a stranger visiting the room, who was likely to come in and do no more than expose one of her breasts?

Vicki felt certain that nobody could've given the nightgown a yank like that without waking her up. It must've hurt, the cord abrading her shoulder that way.

95

She'd done it herself, probably in the throes of the nightmare.

And that frightened her.

She'd been assuming that the nightmares would taper off. Instead, they seemed to be getting worse.

What's next, sleep-walking?

She tossed the nightgown across a chair, opened the closet door and put on her light, satin robe. Then she made her way through the hall, past Ace's open door, and entered the bathroom. After using the toilet, she took a bottle of aspirin out of her overnight bag and washed down three tablets with a glass of water.

Back in the bedroom, she shed the robe, re-set her alarm clock for eight and turned off the lamp. She stretched out on the bed. The damp, cool sheet felt good against her bare skin. The breeze from the open window roamed over her. She rubbed the back of her stiff neck, folded her hands beneath her wet hair and gazed at the ceiling, wondering if she would be able to fall asleep – wondering if she dared.

She dreamed she was on the diving raft with Paul. The sun hadn't come up yet, and a heavy mist hung over the river. She could see nothing beyond the edges of the platform. 'I love you so much,' she said.

'I'll always love you,' he told her.

She felt a terrible ache of emptiness and longing. 'I want this morning to be special, something we can always have and always remember, even if we never see each other again.'

He took her into his arms and kissed her. Vicki began to weep.

'What's wrong?' he asked.

'You'll be going away.'

'I'll come back. Someday, I'll come back to you.'

'Do you promise?'

'Cross my heart and hope to die.' He crossed his heart. Then Vicki began to unbutton his shirt. 'What're you doing?'

'We're going to make love.'

'Here?'

96

'Nobody can see us.'

Soon, they both were naked. Vicki lay on her back. Paul, stretched out beside her, braced up on an elbow, slid his hand softly over her skin. 'You're so beautiful,' he said.

She curled her fingers around his penis.

Moaning, he climbed onto her. He knelt between her spread legs. He kissed her breasts. 'You're awful nice to me,' he said. But it wasn't Paul's voice. 'I'm gonna be nice to you.' He licked her nipple and Vicki grabbed him by the hair and jerked his head up. Melvin grinned at her.

She started to scream. Melvin slapped a bandaged hand across her mouth. 'I'm gonna be *real* nice to you.'

'No, please!' Somehow, she was able to speak in spite of his hand.

'It's okay. See?' He held a foil-wrapped condom above her face.

'No!' she cried out. 'Please!'

'Get on with it, would you? We haven't got all day.' Someone else was with them on the raft.

Vicki turned her head.

Dexter Pollock was kneeling beside them. He took off his robe. He was naked except for a gun belt, and a police badge pinned to his chest. Trickles of blood ran down his breast from the pin holes made by the badge.

'Hey!' someone yelled from a distance. 'What's going on out there?'

The mist lifted. Across the water, far up the beach, was a man sitting atop the playground slide.

Dexter drew his revolver and fired. The man toppled backward and fell to the ground behind the slide's ladder.

Melvin, kneeling above her, now had jumper cables in his hands. He touched the clamps together and sparks exploded from the sharp copper teeth.

Vicki, yelping, clutched her breasts and lurched upright in bed. The room was bright with sunlight. The clock showed 7:50. In ten more minutes, the alarm would've gone off. She

97

wished it had. If the alarm had blared, the sudden waking might've shocked the dream from her memory.

Every detail remained vivid.

Her headache seemed to be gone, but her neck muscles felt like iron.

Ace opened the door and peered in. 'You okay?'

Vicki nodded. She pulled the sheet up to cover herself.

'You yelled.'

'Had a nightmare.'

'You look like death warmed over and pissed on.'

'Thanks. Feel like it, too.'

Ace came in. She was holding a mug of coffee. Her hair was in curlers. She wore her Minnie Mouse nightshirt. Its front bobbed and swayed and she walked. 'Here,' she said, 'take this.' She handed the mug to Vicki. 'You need it more than me.'

Vicki sipped the hot coffee. She sighed.

Ace sat on the edge of the bed. 'Must've been a sweetie of a nightmare.'

'Started off just great. Then Melvin and Pollock showed up.'

'I would've yelled, too.'

'Jesus.'

'You're dripping.'

'I know. That's twice in one night.'

'Same dream?'

Vicki shrugged. 'I don't remember the first one. I've been having these damn things ever since I got into town.'

'Every night?'

'I think so.'

'Your psyche must be a wreck.'

'It's being around Melvin again. He's in all of them, coming after me. At least the ones I remember.'

'Subconsciously, you desire him.'

'Oh, right. Take a leap.'

'Hope they aren't premonitions.'

Vicki sneered at her.

Ace patted her leg through the sheet. 'I know just what'll fix you up, hon. A boyfriend, that's what you need. Fall in love, that'll take your mind off the Amazing Melvin.'

'Right.'

'Barring that, maybe a shrink.'

'It may come to that.'

For just a moment, Ace's concern showed in her eyes. Then she smiled. 'You'll be fine,' she said. 'I'll throw some breakfast together.' She stood up.

'While you're throwing, I guess I'll take a shower.'

'Better take two,' Ace told her, and left the room.

After a long, cool shower, Vicki put on a clean T-shirt and shorts. She found Ace in the kitchen, making a stack of pancakes to go with the sausage links sizzling on the skillet. She leaned over the sausages and sniffed them.

'Maybe I'll just stay with you. The hell with a new apartment.'

'If you think I'd mind, you're crazy.'

'We've already established I'm crazy.'

'I've got no use for that guest room.' She grinned over her shoulder at Vicki. 'When I have guests, that ain't where they sleep.'

Vicki poured more coffee for herself, and filled Ace's mug on the table. 'I don't know,' she said. 'It might be fine for a few days, but . . .'

Ace hoisted an arm and sniffed her armpit. 'Like roses,' she announced. 'So what's the problem? My breath offensive?'

'I'd just be in your way.'

'It'd help me out. Not that I'm hurting or nothing, but you could make a small contribution toward your food and lodging. I'd charge a hell of a bunch less than Agnes Monksby. You'd have the run of the house instead of just some little apartment, no landlady or creepy tenants to deal with, not to mention you'd have a nice yard for sunbathing . . .'

'Not to mention a cook,' Vicki added.

99

'Yeah, well that's not necessarily part of the bargain, hotshot. We'd take turns on that kind of shitski.'

'I don't know, Ace. I already told Agnes I'd take the place.'

'I didn't see any money change hands.'

'Well . . .'

'Call her up and tell her you changed your mind.'

'I wish you'd mentioned this yesterday, before we talked to her.'

'Yesterday, I didn't think you'd go for it.'

'What makes you think I'll go it today?'

Ace looked at her and raised an eyebrow. 'You're having all those nightmares, for one thing. You don't want to be waking up in an empty apartment. You need to have a friend around. I'm it. Least till you find some guy who'll fuck you silly and make you forget about Melvin. And I'll help you find the guy, too. I'm not without contacts. In the meantime, tell Monksby you changed your mind. We'll go over to Pollock's after work and get the rest of your stuff.'

The idea of staying here appealed to Vicki. It would almost be the same as having a home or her own. Ace was such a close friend she was like family, and it appeared now that she might be upset if Vicki refused her generosity.

Also, there were the nightmares. They seemed to be getting worse, and Ace was right about the comfort of having a friend under the same roof.

If it doesn't work out, she thought, I can always find a new place later.

'Are you sure you don't mind having me around for a while?'

'Would I ask you if I minded?'

'I mean, I don't want you doing it out of pity or . . .'

'Don't be a pain in the crack.'

After breakfast, she got ready for work. Ace offered to give her a lift.

'You don't open for another hour,' Vicki said.

100

'It'll only take me five minutes to run you over to the clinic.'

'Thanks. I think I'll walk, though. I missed my workout this morning.'

'Yeah. You'd better walk. Turn into a fat slob, we won't be able to foist you off on some charmer, I'll be stuck with you forever.'

'Right.'

'Stop by the shop after you're done, we'll go over and get your stuff.'

'Great. See you then.'

Vicki left the house. Though the morning was hot, the trees shaded the sidewalk and there was a hint of mild breeze. She felt good. Her headache was gone. Her neck still seemed a little stiff, but that was a minor irritation.

It was a major relief to know that she would be living with Ace. And tomorrow was Saturday. The clinic remained open on Saturdays, but Charlie had given her the weekends off. She could spend the day relaxing, settling in. She looked forward to it.

Her good mood lasted until the clinic came into view and she spotted Melvin Dobbs sitting on the stoop. His hair looked slicked back and oily. His eyes were hidden behind mirror sunglasses. He wore a shiny red Hawaiian shirt decorated with blue flowers, plaid Bermudas, and black socks. His Oxfords gleamed in the sunlight.

As Vicki approached, he raised his bandaged hand in greeting, and stood up.

'Good morning, Melvin.' Though she felt shaky inside, her voice sounded calm. 'How's the hand?'

'About the same.'

She could see that he hadn't changed the bandage. If she mentioned it, however, he might ask her to apply a fresh one.

'You look real pretty,' he said.

'Thanks.' She felt a little sick. The reflecting sunglasses prevented her from seeing the direction of his gaze. The

101

neckline of her sundress wasn't so low that it revealed even the tops of her breasts, but she suddenly wished she'd worn something that covered her better.

Armour would do nicely.

'Did you want to see me about something?' she asked.

He nodded. He rubbed the back of his left hand across his thick lips. 'You got a car?'

'No, not yet.'

'Didn't think so. You came in with that U-Haul, and you rode off with Ace yesterday. I was over at the drug store when you left. You oughta have a car.'

'Well, I'm saving up for one.'

'Come on.' He stepped past Vicki, waved a hand for her to follow, and shambled to the corner of the building.

As she walked toward him, his left hand slipped into a pocket of his shorts and came out with a key ring.

Oh, no.

Parked in the clinic lot beside Thelma's VW bug was a bright red Plymouth Duster.

'Melvin.'

'Like it?'

'It's very nice, but . . .'

'Yours.' He held the keys toward her.

She didn't reach for the keys. She shook her head and rubbed her moist hands on her dress. 'What do you mean?'

'You can have it.'

'I can't accept a car from you.'

His head bobbed. 'Sure you can. I got no use for it.'

'I still can't.'

'I painted it up special for you.'

'That's very sweet of you, but . . .'

'You're my friend. You been real nice to me. You oughta have a car.'

'Melvin.' She sighed. 'That's very thoughtful of you, and I appreciate it, but a gift like that . . . I can't. Really.'

'Okay. Okay.' He was grinning. Vicki wished he would stop grinning. 'Figure it's a loan, then. You can just borrow

102

it off me till you save up and get a new car of your own. How's that?'

'I really don't need a car, anyway, Melvin. I live close enough to walk.'

'Sure you need one. You got this one.' He took a lurching step forward, thrusting the keys at her.

She clasped her hands behind her back, shook her head.

'No. Please, Melvin, I don't . . .'

His bandaged hand darted out. A fingertip hooked out the top of her dress. He dropped the keys down her front. She felt them tumble between her breasts and skitter down her belly. The belt at her waist stopped their fall.

Shocked, she stared at Melvin.

He sidestepped around her, grinning. As he hurried away, he looked over his shoulder. 'When you don't need it no more, just let me know.'

'Melvin!'

'Any trouble with it, come by the station.'

'You can't leave it!'

He vanished beyond the corner of the Handiboy building.

Vicki plucked the front of the belt away from her body. The keys dropped, brushing against her panties, hitting the pavement between her feet with a jangle.

She crouched and picked them up.

Two keys, one for the ignition and one for the trunk, on a small steel loop connected to a plastic disk that read, 'Dobbs Service Station, 126 South River Road, Ellsworth, Wisconsin.'

She considered chasing Melvin and hurling the keys at him.

She looked at the car.

A nice little car, fire-engine red.

How could he do this to me!

103

CHAPTER TWELVE

Melvin got melted cheese on his bandage as he reached into the bowl beside him on the couch. He poked the coated nacho chip into his mouth, licked the cheese off the tape, and started to chew. Then he pressed the Play button on his remote control. The McDonalds commercial vanished from the television screen and he saw himself in the basement laboratory, wearing his red satin robe, gazing up at the camera.

'Tonight,' he said, 'we'll try a method from page 621 of *Curses, Spells and Incantations* by Amed Magdal, translated from Coptic by Guy de Villier. My subject will be Patricia Gordon of Cedar Junction.' He stepped away from the camera and swept an arm toward the work table. Stretched out on the table, wrists and ankles belted down, was the naked cadaver of the nurse.

Melvin took a drink of Pepsi as he watched himself approach the cart and check the open book. The Melvin on the television looked up, frowning. 'I don't like this one much,' he said. 'I don't want to mark 'em up. But I'm gonna do it anyhow. If it works, it works.'

He lifted an Exacto knife off the cart, stepped over to the body, and pierced its skin just above the pubic mound. Slowly, he began to carve a curving line. In the trail of the blade, blood seeped out. Not much. She had been dead for more than an hour before he began the procedure. When he withdrew the blade, the strip of blood formed a circle nearly twelve inches in diameter on Patricia's abdomen. He stepped back, inspected it, rubbed his mouth, winked at the camera.

Bending over the corpse again, he carved an inverted pyramid inside the circle, large enough so that each of its points met the edge. This was to become the 'Face of Ram-Chotep.' So far, it looked pretty much like the diagram in the book. He nodded, and cut eyes into Patricia's skin just within the upper points of the triangle.

Then he cut the mouth – a deep slash just above her navel four inches in length.

Melvin watched himself return to the cart, pick up a chunk of root from the 'Tree of Life', stick it into his mouth and start to chew. Recalling its bitter taste, he took a drink of Pepsi. He remembered thinking as he chewed the root to paste that this better be the real thing. The Shop of Charms in San Francisco had charged him $150.00 per ounce, and that included the 20% 'favoured customer' discount. It was the most costly item in the store's catalogue. He'd ordered ten ounces, just to have it in case it worked.

While he chewed the root, he picked up a threaded needle.

He returned to Patricia. He poked the needle into her thigh, just to have it handy. What's one more wound? he'd thought at the time.

Bending over the corpse, he spread the edges of the 'Mouth of Ram-Chotep', pressed his own mouth against the gash, and used his tongue to thrust the masticated root inside.

When he took his mouth away, the green glop began to ooze out. He stuffed it back in with his fingers, and kept stuffing while he used the needle and thread to sew the wound shut.

Finished, he stepped back. The slash, now cross-hatched with stitches, really did resemble a mouth.

As he returned to the cart, Melvin lifted the bowl of chips onto his lap. He ate, watching his image on the screen but paying little attention to the gibberish he was reading from the book.

He'd had little hope for this method. It seemed too simple, requiring almost no preparation at all – just the cutting and the masticated root. No bat's blood or eye of newt. No ashes of a dead sinner, which was good since his father's urn had been depleted from other tries and the Shop of Charms didn't carry that particular ingredient.

But the incantation was in the original language. That seemed like a plus. In so many of the other books he'd used, the chants had been translated, which seemed like a good way to ruin the whole process.

Melvin had a cheese-covered chip almost to his mouth when the reading ended. He let it fall into the bowl, and watched himself return to the table.

He stood on the far side of the corpse so he wouldn't block the camera's view.

'Okay, babe,' he muttered, 'do your stuff.'

Slowly, the lines of blood forming the Face of Ram-Chotep began to widen. Trickles started to roll down the slopes of her body. They streamed across the Face, slid down her sides.

Melvin whirled toward the camera, leaped and shot his fists into the air. 'ALL RIGHT!' he yelled. 'ALL RIGHT!!!' He pranced around, whooping and waving his arms, and froze with one foot high as a loud inhaling noise came from Patricia. She sounded like a drowning woman coming up for a breath. He bent over the table. Her eyes were open. They jittered this way and that, spotted Melvin and stared at him as she wheezed.

He patted her shoulder. 'I saved you,' he said. 'I brought you back. Me. You were dead and I brought you back.'

She frowned. She looked as if she didn't understand.

'You died,' Melvin told her. 'Do you remember dying?'

Her head shook slightly from side to side. She was no longer huffing for air. She lay there, motionless except for the slow rise and fall of her chest, and stared at him. If she was in pain, it didn't show. She simply seemed confused.

'Don't worry, huh? You're all right, now. I worked my magic on you, and made you live again.'

She raised her head and looked down at herself. Alarm began to replace the puzzlement on her face.

'The blood's nothing,' he assured her. 'Just part of the magic. The straps, they were just so you wouldn't hurt yourself. Do you want me to take them off?'

She nodded.

'Can you talk?'

Her lips twitched. She made no sounds.

'That's okay. Now, don't move.' He unbuckled the belt holding her left wrist to the table. He lifted the wrist. His fingertips sought her pulse.

Watching, Melvin remembered the strange beat of her pulse. Strong, but very slow. Twelve beats per minute, he'd found out later when he timed it. The slow heart rate, he figured, probably accounted for the cool feel of her.

He stepped down to the end of the table. As he unstrapped her feet, Patricia slowly lifted her hand. She touched the Mouth of Ram-Chotep. She raised the hand above her face. Her fingertips glistened with blood and the green ooze of the chewed root. She licked them clean while Melvin released her right hand.

He looked at the camera and rolled his eyes upward.

Melvin, watching, chuckled at his expression.

Being dead had made her a little weird. Licking the stuff off her fingers had been the first sign of that, but only the first of many.

She started to sit up.

'Lie still,' he told her. She obeyed. Melvin took a moist sponge off the cart. She lay motionless, watching him as he gently swabbed the blood off her body. The Mouth kept leaking. He taped a gauze pad across it, then went back to the shallower cuts. When he was done, the design remained distinct with shiny thread of blood. But the lines didn't thicken or drip. The bandage made the Face of Ram-Chotep look gagged.

Melvin set the sponge on the table beside Patricia's hip.

Her hand felt for it. She found it, lifted it above her face, and squeezed it into her mouth. Pink liquid spilled from the sponge at first, then slowed to a trickle. Stuffing half the sponge into her mouth, she began to suck and chew on it.

'Hits the spot?' Melvin asked.

She grunted.

She stuffed the rest of the sponge into her mouth.

'Hey, that's enough. You can't eat that.'

She didn't hesitate for an instant, just pulled the sponge out and gave it to him.

'Go ahead and sit up,' he told her.

She sat up, crossed her legs, rested her hands on her knees, and looked at Melvin as if waiting for the next order. A few little drops of blood broke away from the lines and crept down her skin.

'Try to say something,' Melvin said. 'What's your name?'

She frowned, shook her head, shrugged. 'What's yours?' she asked.

Melvin saw his back go straight.

'You *can* talk.'

'I guess so.'

She could not only talk, but her voice sounded *normal*.

'What's your name?' she asked again.

'Melvin.'

She smiled. 'That's a nice name.'

Melvin looked at the camera and shook his head.

'What's wrong?' she asked.

'Nothing. Huh-uh. Everything's fine. Jesus.'

He'd felt as if he must be dreaming. This *couldn't* be happening. It was more than he'd even hoped for. He had never really quite believed he would succeed in bringing one of these gals back to life. It was an ambition – hell, an obsession. But even though he'd told himself over and over that he would eventually stumble onto a formula that would work, he'd always doubted he could pull it off.

And if somehow one of them *did* come back, he'd imagined she would be pretty much along the lines of your standard zombie: bug-eyed, zoned out, a regular retard.

Patricia might not be entirely normal, but she was close. Very close.

'Boggles the mind,' he muttered.

'Do I have a name?' she asked.

'You don't know?'

She shook her head.

'What's the last thing you remember?'

'You said, "You don't know?" '

'No, I mean . . . what did you do this morning?'

She knitted her brow. She chewed her lower lip. She shrugged. The shrugging made her breasts rise and fall. 'Nothing, I guess.'

'Do you remember the hospital?'

'Is that where I died?'

'You worked there. You were a nurse.'

She smiled. 'Really?'

'Who's the President of the United States?'

'I don't know. How should I know?'

'Do you know *anything?*'

Her smiled widened. 'You're Melvin.' Her eyes lowered. She lifted his bandaged hand. 'What happened here?'

'Somebody bit me.'

'Can I?'

Melvin thought he heard something. He pressed the Mute button on the remote. The conversation on the television died.

'Melll-vin,' came Patricia's voice.

'Yeah?' he called.

'Melvin?'

He shut off the VCR, moved the bowl off his lap, and hurried upstairs to his bedroom. He switched on the light. Patricia, sitting up in bed, looked worried for a moment, then smiled and combed fingers through her mussed blonde hair. She had been wearing one of his mother's nightgowns, but now it lay on the floor. The rumpled sheet lay across her legs.

'Something wrong?' Melvin asked.

'I woke up and you weren't here.'

'I just went downstairs to look at some television.'

The hand in her hair moved down. It curled over her left breast. Staring into Melvin's eyes, she squeezed her breast. Then she circled the nipple with a fingertip. The centre grew and jutted. She pinched the nub between her thumb and forefinger and pulled, stretching it.

109

'Do you want to play?' she asked.

'Again?' Melvin asked, grinning.

'I like it.' She twisted her nipple and squirmed. 'You like it, too, don't you?'

'I don't like getting bit.'

'I won't.'

'That's what you said last time.'

'I promise.'

'Okay.' Melvin turned toward the door.

'Where are you going?'

He looked around at her. She had let go of her nipple, which was a relief to Melvin. He knew that she seemed oblivious to pain, but it had still made him nervous to watch her pulling and twisting so hard. 'I'll come right back.'

'Can I come, too?' She looked worried again. Clearly, she didn't want him out of her sight. Ever. That morning, she'd actually cried when Melvin explained that he needed to leave her alone. She'd begged to go with him. Finally, he'd locked her in the basement. By the time he returned from taking the car to Vicki, she was hysterical.

This could get to be a real nuisance.

'Just wait here,' he told her.

Frowning, she nodded bravely.

Melvin hurried down the hallway to the bathroom. He took a fresh roll of adhesive tape out of the medicine cabinet, then returned to the bedroom.

While he was away, Patricia had moved the top sheet to the end of the bed and stretched out. Her hands were folded beneath her head.

'Was that quick enough?' he asked.

'I guess.'

He draped his robe across the chair. Patricia, staring at him, licked her lips as he walked to the bed. He climbed onto her and sat across her hips. Her skin was cool under his rump. He felt the tickle of her pubic hair.

The pad of gauze just above her navel had come loose at one end. He tried to lift it for a peek at the wound, but it was

110

stuck to her. He remembered how Vicki had used alcohol to loosen the bandage on his hand. Maybe he would try that. Later.

He touched the pyramid he had carved into Patricia last night, and felt the stiff, thin ridge of a scab.

'I guess you're healing,' he said.

'Is that good?'

'Sure.'

She bounced gently a couple of times, thrusting herself up against him. 'Aren't we going to play?'

'In a minute.' He peeled a four-inch strip of adhesive tape off the spool and tore it loose. 'Close your mouth,' he said.

'I won't bite.'

'I know.'

She closed her mouth and smiled. She slipped a hand from beneath her head. It slid down her body and touched him. Her fingers curled around him and lightly slid up and down his shaft while he applied two strips of tape. When he was done, her lips were sealed by the big white X. 'Isn't gonna hold you,' he said. 'But if you make the tape come off, I'm leaving. Understand?'

Patricia nodded.

'Cause it really hurts when you bite.'

CHAPTER THIRTEEN

It seemed rather silly to be sunbathing since the lotion would prevent her from getting a tan, but Vicki felt good sprawling on the lounge, the sun hot on her back, the late afternoon breeze sometimes sliding over her.

She supposed she might get *some* tan, in spite of the screening lotion. She hoped so. She wanted to look good in her new bikini, just in case she should ever wear it to the beach.

Could've skipped the sun block, she thought. A little exposure this time of day wouldn't kill me.

But she knew that without the block she would've felt too guilty to enjoy the sunbathing.

Reaching behind her back, Vivki tied the strings of her bikini top. Then she rolled over, folded her hands beneath her head, and shut her eyes.

It had been a fine Saturday.

There may have been nightmares last night, but she'd awakened without any memory of them. Nor had she torn her nightgown in her sleep – because she'd left it off. Smart move, that.

The running couldn't have been much finer. No Dexter Pollock annoyed her on the way out. A mist hung over the town, muffling the streetlights so they looked like glowing balls of cotton. The mist also seemed to muffle sounds, making the morning seem unnaturally silent and peaceful. The heavy air, while not exactly cool, felt less warm than usual. She wore her shorts and T-shirt. No need for a warm-up suit with Dexter out of the way. She ran fast. The air washed over her. Instead of taking her usual route, she ran south so she wouldn't have to see Melvin's car sitting in the clinic lot, wouldn't have to worry about confronting or avoiding the stranger who'd been in the park those other two mornings.

On the way back, she stopped in the bakery and bought doughnuts with money she had tucked into her sock for that purpose. When Ace got up, they pigged out.

Then she went with Ace to the shop. Ace opened up, and Vicki browsed for a long time, and finally bought shorts and a knit shirt and a skimpy white string bikini – all at the 20% 'sawbones' discount.

After that, she returned to the house and spent hours just sitting around, catching up on the medical journals and taking breaks to read a mystery. Ace came home early, leaving Jennifer in charge of the store, and they got into their bikinis to 'catch some rays.'

112

All in all, a great way to spend a Saturday. Vicki couldn't remember the last time she'd spent such a peaceful, relaxing day.

As she lay there thinking about it, she heard the shower go on. Though she wasn't eager to move, she knew that she would shower after Ace got out. That would feel good. The plan, then, was to linger over a batch of margaritas and fire up the grill and make hamburgers for supper. Then, they would head into town, pick up two or three movies at the video store, and spend the evening in front of the television. Sounded good to Vicki. Sounded perfect.

The telephone rang.

Ace in the shower.

Sighing, Vicki flung herself off the lounge. She raced barefoot across the patio, jerked open the screen door, and rushed through the kitchen to the wall phone. She snatched up the handset. 'Hello?'

'Who's this?' A male voice. Familiar.

'Vicki. Alice can't come to the phone, right now. Would you like to leave a message?'

'Hi, Vicki.' Suddenly, too familiar.

'Melvin?'

'Thought you might be there. How you doing?'

I *was* doing just great. 'Okay. I wish you'd stop over at the clinic and pick up your car.'

'I got no use for it. You go ahead and keep it.'

'I don't want it, Melvin. Honest. I appreciate your gesture. It was very thoughtful, but please.'

'You don't like it? You want a different kind?'

'There's nothing wrong with the car. I just can't accept a gift like that – not even as a loan. Okay? So if you'd just take it away again, I'd . . .'

'I can't. You've got the keys.'

You dropped them down my dress.

'Do you have another set?' she asked.

'Nope.'

'Okay. Then I'll drop the car off at the station.'

113

'I'm home. You wanta bring it here?'

'I can't do it now, anyway. I'm pretty busy right now. I'll just take it to the station sometime, maybe tomorrow or Monday. Okay?'

'Okay.' He sounded disappointed. 'Vicki?'

'Yes?'

'I'm sorry. I only just wanted to help. I figured you could use a car, you know? I wasn't trying to cause you no trouble. Guess I messed up, huh?'

'No, you didn't mess up.'

'Are you mad at me?'

'No. You were just being nice. I understand that. I just can't go around accepting gifts like that.'

'From me.'

'From anyone. Don't put yourself down, Melvin.'

'Why not? Everybody else does.'

'I've really got to go, now. Have a nice evening.'

'You, too.'

'Bye.' She hung up, slumped against the wall, and muttered, 'Why me, Lord?'

Hearing the water shut off, Vicki went to her bedroom. She picked up her robe, sat on the edge of the bed, and wondered what to do about Melvin.

The car business wouldn't be the end of it.

What next? Would he send flowers, ask her for a date?

She wanted nothing to do with him, damn it. But she didn't want to hurt his feelings. God knows, he'd spent his life getting dumped on.

Through the doorway, she saw Ace leave the bathroom. A towel was wrapped around her head. Another, tucked together between her breasts, hung down just far enough to cover her groin.

'Save me any hot water?' Vicki called, rising from the bed and stepping into the hall.

'I took that shower so fast I hardly got my butt wet.'

'Why the hurry?'

'I got me a powerful thirst.'

114

'Did you hear the phone?'

'One of my myriad admirers?'

'Melvin.'

'No shit?' Grinning, she leaned sideways against the door frame. 'He's tracked you to your lair.'

'You may think it's funny.'

'I think it's love.'

'You'd be smirking out the other side of your face if it was *you* he had the hots for.'

'I wouldn't be smirking at all, hon, I'd be barfing.'

Vicki leaned against the wall, the robe draped over her forearm, and stared at Ace. Ace stared back. Her grin slipped away. 'So what're you gonna do?'

'I don't know.'

'You scared?'

'A little, I guess.'

'Never should've been nice to him. That was your first mistake. You take a loser like that and treat him nice, you're asking for it. You can afford to be nice to somebody normal, a normal guy isn't gonna blow it all out of proportion and fall in love with you and get crazy. A guy like Melvin, you've gotta either ignore him or treat him bad. That's the only way to play it safe.'

'Yeah, well the damage is already done.'

'Tell me about it.'

'What'll I do?' Vicki asked.

'Tell him to fuck off.'

'I can't do that.'

'Want me to do it for you?'

'No.'

'Don't want him mad at you.'

'It's not that, exactly.'

'I know. You feel sorry for him. That's what got you into this.'

'But how do I get out of it?'

'Short of moving out of town? Well, I know something that worked for me. There was this guy, Blake Bennington.

115

You wouldn't know him, he showed up while you were in med school. A real yuck. He came into the shop one day and I sold him a swimming suit and I thought I'd never see the end of him. Talk about a royal pain. He wouldn't leave me alone. The more I told him to fuck off, the more he wanted to fuck *me*. I just couldn't get rid of him.

'There's this *thing* about guys like that. They think they're in love with you, but they aren't. What they love is their *idea* of you. And that just grows if you keep your distance from the guy. So what you've got to do is get up-close and personal. Shatter the image.

'What I did, I finally let Blake take me out. We went to the Fireside Chalet. I tell you, he thought he'd died and gone to heaven. We're both sitting there in our fancy duds, drinking and having lobster tails, the way he looked at me, you'd think I was Venus or something. So then about half way through the meal, I laid this gorgeous fart.'

'Oh, no,' Vicki said.

'During dessert, I kind of casually started picking my nose. I actually got out a pretty good-sized booger and wiped it on the edge of my plate. He kept glancing at it. Couldn't keep his eyes off the thing.

'He was down, but not out. He went ahead and took me to his apartment after dinner. He tried to get me out of my dress, and I told him I didn't think he'd better because, after all, my skin rash might be contagious.'

'Gawd,' Vicki said.

'And I told him that even if it *wasn't* contagious, I was pretty embarrassed and didn't want anybody to see my runny sores. And besides which, it was my time of the month and did he really want blood all over everything?'

'Sounds like you laid it on a little thick.'

'He got pretty depressed. We both drank more and more. Finally, I threw up on his coffee table.'

Vicki shook her head.

Ace grinned. 'All this apparently had a subtle but profound effect on the fantasies he'd built up around me.'

'Subtle.'

'He never asked me out again. In fact, he seemed to go out of his way to avoid me.'

'And you think I should try something like that with Melvin.'

'Just a thought. It's a tried and true method. And it's a way to get rid of him without wounding his pride. You don't tell him to take a hike, he decides he *wants* to take a hike. Perfect solution to your little dilemma.'

Vicki pushed herself away from the wall. 'Know something, Ace?'

'Plenty.'

'You're crazier than shit.'

Ace laughed. 'I might be crazy, but I got rid of the guy. Think about it.' She headed for her room.

While Vicki took her shower, she did think about it. She knew she couldn't pull off such stunts as Ace had described. Even if she had the guts, her sense of dignity wouldn't permit it.

But Ace had a good point about idealising.

Melvin doesn't know me. If he thinks he's in love, or something, it's because of fantasies. The more I try to avoid him, the more he'll probably want me.

Spend some time with him?

Ugh!

When she finished her shower, she put on shorts and a T-shirt and joined Ace in the kitchen. Ace had already prepared a batch of margaritas in the blender. The glasses were rimmed with salt, waiting for her arrival. Ace gave the blender another buzz, then filled the glasses with the frothy cocktail.

They went out to the patio and sat at the table.

Vicki sipped her drink. 'Delicious.'

'*And* good for you.'

'I've been thinking about what you said.'

'Gonna barf on Melvin?'

'Hardly. God, I don't really want to do this, but it makes sense.'

'What? Spell it out, Einstein.'

'Meet with him. Not to gross him out, or anything. But I can see a couple of ways it could help. For one thing, it's bound to put a crimp in his fantasy life if he spends some time with the real me.'

'Except the real you is so adorable.'

'Right. I know I'm wonderful, but I bet I don't live up to his image, whatever that might be.'

'Especially if you cut the cheese.'

'The other thing is, even if he isn't turned off by a dose of my adorable self, it still ought to take some of the fuel out of the fire. Just because of access.'

'You gonna give him *access?*'

'People mostly desire what they can't have.'

'Right. Go to bed with him.'

'The more I try to avoid him, the more he'll need to be with me. It's like roots. If a plant isn't getting enough water, its roots keep growing longer and longer.'

'Christ. You go away to school, you come back deep. Roots, for godsake.'

'You know what I mean.'

'Right. You don't want Melvin's root growing longer and longer. So what's the plan?'

'Meet him someplace in public. Have a couple of drinks with him. Just socialise for maybe an hour or so. With you along for moral support.'

'Oh, good. I'd hate to miss it.'

'How about the Riverfront Bar? Tonight?'

'That's about as public as you can get.'

They drank up, and went into the kitchen. While Ace refilled their glasses, Vicki checked the telephone directory. Melvin was listed.

Ace stood there, watching as she dialled.

Through the earpiece, Vicki listened to the ringing. She felt a little breathless. Her heart was pounding, her stomach knotted. After the sixth ring, she began to hope he wasn't home.

Maybe this isn't such a hot idea, she thought.

Maybe try it for another night.

Like next month.

After the tenth ring, Melvin answered. 'Who's this?'

'Vicki.'

'Vicki?' He sounded amazed. 'Hi!'

'I was thinking about the car.'

'Yeah. You wanta keep it?'

'No, but I thought you might want to pick it up. Ace and I are going to be at the Riverfront Bar tonight at about ten o'clock. Why don't you stop in, we'll have a couple of drinks, and I'll give you the keys. Then you can stop by the clinic later on and take the car home with you.'

'Have drinks with you?'

'Sure. It'll give us a little chance to chat.'

'Gosh.'

'Okay?'

'Sure. Sure. Ten o'clock?'

'Right. See you then, Melvin.'

'Sure. See you then.'

Vicki hung up. She let out a deep, trembling breath. 'I must be crazy,' she muttered.

Ace handed a glass to her. 'Crazy, but smart. It may work. Or it may not. Either way, you'll have the joy of knowing you brought joy, however fleeting, into the otherwise drab existence of that young, adoring, demented, shit-for-brains dork.'

CHAPTER FOURTEEN

Melvin whistled as he prepared his hamburger.

Whistled, 'Everything's Coming Up Roses.'

He couldn't believe his good fortune. Only two nights ago, he had resurrected the dead. Now, this. Vicki had actually invited him out for drinks.

Giving her the car had been a bright idea, after all. Though she was apparently too shy to accept such a gift, she appreciated the offer of it. This was her way of thanking him.

Melvin didn't know how he could stand to wait for ten o'clock.

He turned his hamburger over. Grease sizzled and snapped on the skillet.

It's not *all* coming up roses, he told himself. He wasn't real happy about going into the Riverfront Bar. At that hour on a Saturday night, half the assholes in Ellsworth would be drinking in there.

Nor was he exactly delighted that Ace would be sitting in on the festivities. She wasn't an asshole. She was okay, he supposed. Still, three's a crowd.

If only he could be alone with Vicki, someplace private.

But this was a start. This was a *great* start.

Melvin draped a slab of sharp cheddar over the top of his burger, and put the lid on the skillet. While he waited for the cheese to melt, he spread mayonnaise over his bun. He picked up a knife and was about to saw off a thick slice of red onion when he thought, What am I, nuts?

Onion breath on his first date with Vicki?

No way.

Not that she's gonna kiss me, he told himself.

But maybe she will. Who knows?

He took the lid off the skillet. The cheese had melted and run down the sides of the burger. He slid a spatula under the patty, and lifted it over to his bun. He pressed the top of the bun down on it. Then he turned off the stove, picked up his plate, and sat down at the table.

Patricia, sitting there, smiled at him and stuffed a wad of raw ground beef into her mouth. There wasn't much left of the half pound he'd set in front of her before starting to cook the burger for himself.

Eats like an animal, he thought. Nothing but uncooked meat, and of course there was the jar of bat blood in his laboratory. She'd gulped that down the first night. He doubted that she'd had an appetite for such things before he killed her. It was like the biting, somehow connected with having been dead.

As Melvin ate his hamburger and watched her, a drop of pink juice fell from her chin, joining the other stains on the white front of her T-shirt. The spots were in the middle between her breasts.

Melvin could see the dark of her nipples through the thin shirt.

He never would've guessed he'd get tired of looking at a naked woman, especially one as attractive as Patricia. But there was just so much to see, and seeing it constantly – not to mention 'playing' with her to the point of exhaustion – had finally started to bore him. So he'd given her the shirt this morning and told her to wear it. She obeyed.

Melvin hadn't expected the shirt to turn him on. It was intended simply to spare him from always seeing her naked. But the way he could sort of see through it, the way it took on the shape of her breasts and moved with them, and how it almost wasn't long enough. . . . He found a whole new joy in watching her.

They had spent most of the day cleaning house. *Patricia* cleaned, Melvin supervised. House-cleaning was wonderful. It required a lot of motion: walking, reaching, bending, kneeling. The T-shirt bobbed and swayed, and rose and fell mere inches like a stage curtain controlled by a tease. He loved it. He watched, but didn't touch. Finally, unable to stand it any longer, he went ahead and took her. On the carpet of the upstairs hall. With the vacuum cleaner still running, humming beside their heads. He made her keep the T-shirt on. He'd been in such a frenzy that he didn't take time to tape her mouth, and she gave his shoulder a nasty bite. Worth it, though. Out of this world.

He watched Patricia stuff the last of the raw meat into her mouth. Juice dribbled down her chin, spilled onto the shirt.

She was mostly obedient except for the biting. It seemed that she simply couldn't control it.

121

Can't go on this way, he thought.

Two days, and he already had four bites on his shoulders, another on his upper left arm. Once, she'd come very close to opening his throat.

She always did it to him when he was about to go off, and too distracted to stop her. The sudden pain of the bites never failed to push him over the edge. He had incredible orgasms. They weren't half as good the few times she didn't bite.

In spite of that, he knew that he couldn't go on letting Patricia sink her teeth into him every time they screwed. The pain of the wounds lasted a long time after the ecstasy was over.

And the wound worried him. In those Romero movies, a single bite from the living dead was enough to turn *you* into one. He tried to convince himself that was a pile of shit, but he couldn't quite get the idea out of his head. Besides, even if that was shit, he knew for a fact that the bites weren't doing him any good. Like Vicki had said, human saliva's a regular cesspool of bacteria.

The antibiotics he'd been taking for the bite on his hand should help with the others, maybe keep him from getting infected, but still. . . .

Try screwing her right after she's eaten?

Could try it now, and see if she bites.

But he didn't feel like it. He would be seeing Vicki in just a few more hours.

If he used the method on Vicki, would she turn out the same as Patricia? He didn't especially want that to happen. Too soon to tell, though.

The smart thing was to try it with a few others, see how it goes, before taking a chance with Vicki.

Maybe they can bite each other, he thought, and smiled.

Patricia smiled back. She lifted her T-shirt, baring her breasts, and used the shirt to wipe her wet lips and chin. 'Do you want to play?' she asked.

'Let's watch television.'

She nodded. She seemed to like television almost as much as playing.

They went into the living room and sat together on the couch. He gave the remote to Patricia. She spent a while changing channels, then settled for a rerun of 'Gilligan's Island.'

Melvin gazed at the show. He didn't even try to pay attention. He imagined how it would be tonight with Vicki. Whenever his mind returned to the present, he glanced at the red numbers of the digital clock on the VCR. How could time possibly pass so slowly?

The shows changed. He fidgeted. He watched the clock.

Finally, it was eight-thirty.

He squeezed Patricia's leg. 'Stay here,' he said. 'I've gotta take a shower.'

'I'll come with you.'

'Stay here.'

She gave him a pouty look, then turned her eyes to the television.

Melvin went upstairs. In the bathroom, he hung his robe on the door. He stood before the mirror and watched himself remove the bandages. His hand was looking better. The swelling and inflammation had gone down. The newer bites on his arm and shoulders didn't appear infected.

But they burned like flaming oil when the hot spray of the shower splashed onto them.

Gritting his teeth against the pain, he shampooed his hair and lathered himself with soap. He was rinsing when he glimpsed a vague, moving shape through the plastic curtain. *Psycho*. Goosebumps crawled up his back. The curtain skidded open and of course it was Patricia standing there, not Norman's mother with a butcher knife.

'Damn it!' he snapped.

She lowered her head as if ashamed. 'I missed you, Melvin.'

'Go downstairs.'

'Don't you like me anymore?'

123

'I like you to obey me.'

She sobbed. She raised her face. Her eyes shimmered with tears.

Melvin sighed. This possessive business was almost as bad as the biting. In a way, it was nice, but . . .

'I'll go,' she said. She turned away. Melvin saw the way the T-shirt curved over her buttocks. He felt a stir.

'Okay,' he said. 'Come on back. Get in here, but leave your shirt on.'

She faced him, grinning, and stepped into the tub. Melvin slid the curtain shut. He stepped back and watched. Patricia seemed to know what he wanted. She stood beneath the spray, turning slowly. As the T-shirt became wet, it hugged her skin and became nearly transparent.

He rubbed her through the fabric. She reached up and held onto the shower arm and smiled at him through the spray. He peeled the shirt up above her breasts. The water made her skin shiny and slick. His fingertips traced the face of Ram-Chotep, the stitches cross-hatching the Mouth. She squirmed as he slid a hand between her legs. He kissed her nipples, licked them, sucked.

Before he took her, he stuffed his wash cloth into her mouth.

Shortly before ten, Vicki and Ace entered the Riverfront Bar. It was dimly lighted, hazy with cigarette smoke, noisy. People spoke loudly to be heard over the juke box blaring Waylon Jennings. Glasses and bottles clinked. Pool balls clacked together on the two tables at the far side. Beeps and jingles came from a row of electronic games.

Vicki spotted many familiar faces on her way across the floor: strange grown-up faces that resembled kids she hadn't seen for nearly a decade, others that looked just the same as she remembered them from all those years ago, several she'd seen during her more recent visits to town, and a few she'd come to recognise during the past week. She didn't spot Melvin. Nor could she find the man from the playground

124

by the river. Some of the people noticed her, nodded a greeting or simply looked perplexed as if they couldn't quite place her. Ace said 'hi,' to some friends, but didn't stop to chat.

They found a deserted booth along the wall. Vicki scooted across the seat and motioned for Ace to slide in beside her. That way, Melvin would have to sit across the table.

'Let's try and get rid of him fast,' Ace said. 'Then maybe we can scrounge up a couple of guys, get something going.'

Vicki shrugged. She was in no mood to scrounge up anyone. She didn't like the smoke or the noise. She would just as soon leave when the meeting with Melvin ended.

A barmaid came. No one Vicki recognised. She wore blue jeans shorts and a pale blue T-shirt printed with, 'I'm a Good Sport – I Scored at Ace's.' Her shirt was the same as the one Ace wore.

'What'll it be, gal?' she asked.

'Let's have a pitcher of Blatz and three mugs.'

'Comin' right up.' She rushed away.

'That's Lucy. She's from the Bay. Married Randy Montclair.'

The name seemed vaguely familiar to Vicki. Then she remembered. He used to pal around with Doug. Both of them, royal pains. They'd hoisted Henry into a trash bin after school, one day. And Randy was the one who gave Melvin those whacks, just a week before the Science Fair. Vicki, ticked off, had shoved him or hit him or something to make him stop. She wondered, now, if that little show of gallantry may have been what started Melvin liking her. Maybe she had Randy to thank for her present problems with the guy.

Lucy brought the pitcher and mugs to the table. Vicki paid her.

While Ace was filling the mugs, Melvin appeared.

'Greetings,' he said. He scooted over the seat until he was directly across from Vicki. He brought a sweet, cloying aroma with him as if he'd been drenched in after-shave.

'You're looking dapper,' Ace said, and poured him a drink.

He wore a shiny Hawaiian shirt and a pink sports jacket. His black hair was slicked straight back. Maybe the smell, Vicki thought, came from hair oil.

Ace slid the mug to him. He winked at her. Then he grinned at Vicki. 'You look real nice,' he said. His gaze wandered down. Vicki had worn a dark plaid blouse, long-sleeved and too heavy for the weather, chosen solely to prevent Melvin from getting even a hint of what was underneath. But the way he looked at her, it might've been transparent. She had an urge to finger the buttons just to make sure they all were fastened. His stare made her feel squirmy. He rubbed his lips with the back of his bandaged hand.

The bandage was fresh and white, as if he'd put on a new one for the occasion as part of dressing up.

'Well,' Vicki said, 'I might as well give you the keys.'

'If you're sure.'

She took them from her purse and pushed them across the table. He put them into a pocket of his jacket.

Vicki lifted her mug. 'Well, here's looking at you.'

They all drank.

'So whatcha been doing with yourself?' Ace asked him. 'Resurrected anyone lately?'

Vicki cringed.

Melvin grinned and bobbed his head. 'Oh, I gave that up. They taught me better in the funny farm.'

'You sure sparked up that Science Fair,' Ace said.

'That's what I had in mind.' He hunched over the table, leered at Ace, then at Vicki. 'Like I told Vicki, I only just did it to give the finger to all the assholes.'

'Guess you managed that, all right.'

Vicki wished they would change the subject. On the other hand, she was rather glad that Ace was sparing her from having to make conversation.

'So how'd you pull it off, anyway? You sneak into the bone orchard and dig her up?'

126

'Sure. Took a lot of digging, too.'

'You did it at night, I guess.'

'The Wednesday before the Fair.' He seemed to enjoy talking about it.. He kept grinning and nodding. 'The graveyard gate was chained. I had to get through that with a hacksaw. Then I just snuck in and started digging.'

'Weren't you scared?'

'I didn't wanta get caught, you know. But I weren't scared of no ghosts or stiffs, if that's what you mean.'

'How'd you get her out of the coffin?'

Vicki rolled her eyes.

'Had a pry bar along. It was easy. The hard thing was hefting her up.'

'Dead weight,' Ace said.

'Jesus,' Vicki muttered.

Melvin chuckled. 'She wasn't just skin and bones, you know. She had a build on her.'

'Shit, yes,' Ace said. 'Her tits alone must've weighed in at twenty pounds each.'

'I wouldn't know about that. All I know, she was tough to lug around.'

'If you'd waited a year or two, she might've been easier to carry.'

Melvin laughed with a mouthful of beer and sprayed it back into his mug.

'So, did you carry her all the way home?'

'No, no. Would've herniated myself. What I did, I put her in the trunk of my car, then went back and filled in the hole. Didn't want anyone catching on, you know.'

'Yeah, that would've ruined it.'

'Wanta hear a good one? I almost forgot her head. Yeah. See, I left it sitting on this tombstone while I worked on filling up the hole. Then my hands were full, what with the shovel and pry bar and everything. I got back in the car and drove halfway home before I remembered about her head.'

'Dumb you.'

He chuckled. 'Yeah, but it was still there when I went back for it. Hadn't walked off.'

'Or rolled,' Ace added, 'as the case may be.'

'This is really revolting,' Vicki muttered.

Melvin grinned at her.

'So then you took her home with you?' Ace asked.

'Kept her in the basement. My folks, they never went down there. Then Friday night, I drove over and broke into the Center. Had my stuff all set up before sunup, and had the door open and everything by the time people started coming along to set up for the Fair.'

'You sure put a lot of effort into your project,' Ace said. 'I tell you, me and Vicki didn't go to half the trouble you did. And I bet they didn't even give you a blue ribbon.'

'Gave me a straitjacket, that's what they did.'

'And well-deserved, too.'

Melvin laughed. He shook his head and wiped his mouth and took another drink of beer.

'Lucy didn't bring us any peanuts,' Ace said. With that, she got up and left.

Oh, great, Vicki thought. She leaves me alone with him. That wasn't part of the deal. Hell, there was no deal. But she knows how I feel about Melvin.

Maybe that's *why* she left. Figured the encounter'll do me more good if she's not here like a security blanket.

No, she just wants peanuts.

Vicki managed a smile. 'How's your hand doing?' she asked.

'Oh, it's getting better. I got a real good doctor.'

'I see you changed your bandage.'

'Took a shower tonight.'

There's a pretty picture.

'Do you ever think about that movie, *Psycho*, when you take a shower?'

'I try not to,' Vicki said.

'We had this gal at the funny farm, they couldn't get her to take a shower. That's 'cause she saw *Psycho* when she

128

was like ten years old. She'd get real ripe after about a week. Then they'd take her into the shower room, a couple of orderlies, and you'd hear her screaming.' With his left hand, Melvin picked up the pitcher. He filled his mug with beer, then poured more into Vicki's mug. 'My mother, she never took showers. She took baths. Do you like baths?'

'Yeah,' she said. 'I do both.'

Great. His mind's on bathing.

'My mother, she used to shave her legs in the tub.'

How does he know that?

He tipped his head to one side and grinned. 'Do you shave in the tub?'

'That's none of your business, Melvin.'

His grin slipped away. 'I'm sorry. Didn't mean to make you mad.'

'Why don't we talk about something else?'

Where the hell is Ace?

'What did you do today?' she asked.

'Oh, cleaned house.'

'That's a huge house. It must be a real chore, having to keep it up.'

'Oh, it's not so bad.'

'You haven't been working at the station?'

'Doctor's orders. I guess I'll go back next week, maybe. Or maybe not. I kinda like staying home.'

Out of the corner of her eye, Vicki noticed someone approaching the table. She turned her head, expecting to see Ace with a bowl of peanuts.

It was Dexter Pollock with a mug of beer.

'Mind if I sit?'

Before she could respond, Dexter slid in beside her. 'That's Ace's seat,' she said.

'Ass won't mind. She's over gabbing with some folks.' He glanced across the table at Melvin, then looked at Vicki. 'You must be hard-up, keeping company like this.'

'Why don't you get out of here,' Vicki said.

'I didn't get a chance to tell you goodbye. Guess I was

away when you took your stuff out. I would've lent you a hand.'

'I didn't need a hand. We had some local movers take care of it.'

'We? You and Melvin?' He squinted across the table. 'She move in with you, lover boy?'

Melvin's face flooded with scarlet.

'You're one lucky fella,' Dexter told him. 'She's a nice piece of ass.'

Vicki felt a rage growing inside her.

Melvin glared at Dexter. 'You don't say shit like that.'

'Aw, isn't that sweet.' He smiled at Vicki. 'You got yourself a regular knight in shining armour, that's what you got. Nutty as a nigger-toe, but he's sure full of chivalry. You ever notice, girl, you got a regular habit of attracting crazy folks? You got your bosom buddy, Ass, and now you got your lover boy, Melvin. Both of 'em mad as Hatters. How come you think that is? You got a *smell* or something, draws lunatics?'

She didn't trust herself to speak. She just stared at him.

'You better get outa here,' Melvin warned.

Dexter ignored him. 'Must be your aroma.' He leaned sideways. His shoulder pressed against her. He lowered his head, sniffing. 'Knew it. Seems to come from down farther.' He hunched down, still sniffing. The side of his face brushed against her breast.

Vicki grabbed his hair and jerked his head back and dumped her full mug of beer onto his lap. He gasped and flinched rigid. He stared at her, eyes bulging, mouth open. 'Why, you little cunt,' he muttered. Then he snatched up his own mug of beer and swung it at her. For a moment, Vicki thought he intended to smash the glass into her face. But it stopped short. The beer flew out, stinging her eyes, splashing over her face and ears.

As she wiped her eyes, Dexter snapped, 'Sit down, you fucking maniac. She had it coming.'

'You'll get it for this,' Melvin said.

'Oh, I'm trembling. I'm shaking in my boots.'

130

'What're you *doing*, you scum-fucking trash heap!'

Ace's voice.

Vicki stopped rubbing her eyes and looked. Dexter was on his feet, face to face with Ace. Almost face to face. She was three or four inches taller. 'I didn't do nothing,' he said. His voice sounded just a bit whiny, as if he were a schoolkid caught in a nasty act by his teacher.

'Looks to me like you pissed yourself.'

'Get out of my way.' He tried to step past her, but she blocked his way. 'I've got no business with you, Alice.'

'I saw what you did. Tell Vicki you're sorry. In fact, apologise to both of them.'

'You gonna make me?'

'I'm going to count to three, turd-face. One. Two.'

He whirled around. 'Okay, I'm sorry.'

'Buy us another pitcher.'

'I didn't *use* your beer, goddamn it!'

'That's not an issue. Just give me five bucks for another pitcher, and we'll forget this ever happened.'

'You're gonna push me too far, you overgrown . . .'

'Overgrown what?' Ace asked.

'Nothing,' he muttered.

Ace snapped her fingers. Dexter took out his wallet, removed a five dollar bill, and handed it to her. 'Thanks,' she said. 'Now, get out of here.'

Dexter turned away and walked into the noisy, milling crowd.

Ace set the bowl of peanuts on the table. She bent over and used a napkin to wipe a few drops of beer of the red vinyl cushion, then sat down. Smiling from Melvin to Vicki, she cracked open a shell. She tossed a pair of peanuts into her mouth, chewed a few times, and said, 'Can't leave you two alone for a minute.'

'That dirty, toe-sucking pig,' Melvin said.

'Such language,' said Ace.

'You sure took care of him. He acted like he was scared of you.'

131

'That's 'cause he knows what I'm capable of.'

'I oughta kill him. Stuff he said to Vicki.'

'Well, if you kill Pollock, don't try and jump-start him. Just let him rot.'

'Yeah.'

'I want to leave,' Vicki told them.

'Come on, we've got to get another pitcher.'

'You stay if you want, I'm going home.'

'Do you have to?' Melvin asked, looking disappointed.

'Yeah. I've had enough fun for one night.'

Ace filled the pockets of her shorts with peanuts.

Vicki, Ace and Melvin left the Riverfront Bar together. On the sidewalk outside, Melvin said, 'I'm sure sorry he came along and ruined our time. But it was real nice, anyway. Maybe we can do it again, only I'll pay.'

'We'll see,' Vicki said. 'Goodnight.'

CHAPTER FIFTEEN

Dexter stuffed his damp trousers and boxer shorts into the dirty clothes hamper.

That damn bitch, she had no business dumping the beer on me. She's as crazy as her lunatic friends.

I was still chief, I'd run her in for it. See how she likes a night in the lock-up.

Dexter *could* have still been chief of the Ellsworth Police Department. That's what made it so galling. It was his own stupid fault. Nobody forced him out. He'd put in his thirty years and retired at age fifty-two, figuring there was no point in hanging onto a job when he didn't have to. Retirement had looked good. No responsibilities. No Minnie around anymore to nag him. Plenty of income, what with the pension and the property. He'd have all the time in the world to do whatever he wanted: fish, play golf, drink, chase the women.

By the time he realised his mistake, it was too late.

He was used to folks turning nervous when he showed up. Watch out, here comes Pollock. Don't fuck with him. Step out of line, he'll bust your ass. They feared him. They respected him.

No two-bit slut would've dared dump a beer on his crotch. *Doctor* Chandler.

Reaching into the closet, he unhooked a hanger and took out one of his uniforms. It was still inside a filmy plastic bag from the cleaners in Blayton.

Dexter always took his uniforms to Blayton or Cedar Junction to have them cleaned. If he had them done here in town, people might start to wonder.

He removed the plastic bag and stuffed it into the wastebasket. Then he got dressed: dark blue trousers; light blue shirt with its chief's shield and name plate on the chest, department patch on the shoulder; black socks and spit-shined shoes. He strapped his gun belt around his waist. He slid his nightstick into its ring on the belt, his .38 caliber Chief's Special into the holster. Last, he put on his police hat.

He swung the closet door shut, and stared at himself in the full-length mirror.

Damn, he looked fine.

And felt fine, too.

He'd been in his blues at the Riverfront, no way Chandler would've pulled any shit. Or Asshole, either. Five bucks for a new pitcher of beer.

And I gave it to her.

Not *me*, that other Pollock. She'd asked *me* for five bucks, she'd be one sorry bitch.

Dexter drew his nightstick. He raised its blunt head toward the mirror.

'Five bucks, huh?' he asked. 'How'd you like this shoved up your ass, Ass?'

133

Oh yeah?

'Yeah!' Club in both hands, he lunged and imagined himself ramming it into Ace's belly, saw her double over, fall to her knees. 'Still feeling tough?' he asked. He saw himself step behind her. With the end of his club, he flicked her skirt up. Her ass was bare. Of course it was. That's 'cause she mailed her fucking panties to Minnie. 'See how you like *this*,' he said, and shoved the nightstick into her anus.

In the mirror, he watched himself crouching, thrusting with the club. He could almost see it going in and out, almost hear Ace squealing.

He stood up straight. 'That takes care of you, I guess,' he told the area in front of his feet. He twirled the stick a few times by its leather thong, then slid it into the belt ring.

He spread his feet and planted his fists on his hips. He glanced at the mirror image of his jutting trousers, and smirked. 'See that, *Doctor?* It gets that way when someone pours beer on it.' He unzipped his fly and freed himself. 'How about licking it clean for me? Huh? You'll like that, won't you?' He slid his fingers around the engorged shaft.

The doorbell rang.

Dexter saw his face go red, his hands quickly trying to force his penis back inside the trousers. Wouldn't go. Heart slamming, he gave up and threw open the closet door. He snatched his robe off the hook and put it on. He tossed his police hat onto the shelf.

He shut the door. In the mirror, he saw that the robe hardly concealed the fact that he was wearing his uniform.

So, there's no law I've gotta open the door.

He glanced at the clock. Almost eleven. Who'd be ringing the doorbell at this hour?

Maybe one of the tenants.

It rang again.

Heart thundering, he hurried from his room. The leather of his gunbelt creaked as he walked. He fumbled inside the

134

robe, got his shrunken penis back inside his pants and closed the fly.

At the door, he squinted through the peephole.

For just a moment, he thought that the young woman standing in the hallway was Vicki Chandler. Then, he realised she was a stranger. Blond hair like Vicki, but not quite as pretty. She wore a white dress. What was she, a nurse?

The main thing, I don't know her, she doesn't know me.

She rang the bell again.

Dexter slipped his robe off and tossed it over the back of a nearby chair. He opened the door. 'What can I do for you?' he asked.

'Oh, you're a police officer?' She looked glad about that.

'Chief Pollock, ma'am. Is there some kind of trouble?'

'Well, not exactly, no.' She smiled, shook her head, and fingered the hair over her ear. The name tag over her left breast read Patricia Gordon, R.N. Her white dress had a zipper down the front. It was open enough to reveal a long V of bare skin that ended between her breasts. 'My car broke down,' she explained. 'I was hoping to find someone with a phone, so I could call and have my girlfriend pick me up. Do you have a phone I could use?'

'Sure do. Come on in, Patricia.'

'Thank you. You're very kind.'

He backed away from the door. She entered, and he swung it shut.

'Would you like me to take a look at your car?' he offered. 'What seems to be the trouble with it?'

'Oh, it just died on me.'

'I'd be happy to take a look at it.'

'No, that's all right. I'll worry about it tomorrow. If I can just use your phone.'

Dexter pointed at the telephone on the end table. Thanking him, Patricia sat down on the couch. Her white skirt slid partway up her thighs. She wore no stockings. Her legs looked very bare. She lifted the telephone onto her lap,

135

picked up the handset, and dialled. Dexter took the night-stick out of his belt, placed it on the floor beside his easy chair, and sat down. He tried not to look at her legs.

Sighing, she shook her head slightly. 'Answering machine,' she said. She waited a few moments, then spoke into the phone. 'It's me, Patricia. The damn car broke down again. Call me as soon as you get back.' She checked the plate in the centre of the dial, and read off Dexter's number. Then she hung up. She placed the phone back onto the table. 'Do you mind if I wait?' she asked. 'I'm sure Sue will be back in just a couple of minutes. She probably just went out to buy some cigarettes. She does that all the time. Smokes like a fiend.'

'You're welcome to stay,' Dexter assured her. 'Could I get you something to drink?'

'No, thank you. But you go on ahead. Did you just now get off duty?'

Dexter felt heat rush to his face. He told himself there was no reason to be embarrassed – Patricia had no way of knowing anything. 'Just got back about five minutes before you showed up,' he explained.

'Neat uniform,' she said.

'Thanks. You look good in yours, too. So, you're a nurse. I haven't seen you around these parts.'

'I'm new in town.' Her gaze lowered. Dexter tried to remember if he'd zipped his pants. 'Have you ever shot anyone with that?'

He realised that her gaze was on the revolver.

. 'Sure. A few times.' He'd fired it many times while on duty over the years, but never *at* anyone. Mostly just in order to scare people shitless. Like drunks, teenagers making out.

'Have you *killed* anyone?'

'Just four times,' he said.

Patricia pursed her lips and blew softly, almost whistling. 'With that gun?' she asked.

Nodding, he patted the holster.

136

'Let me see it,' she said, patting the cushion beside her.

Holy Toledo, Dexter thought. Got us a live one, here.

He stood up, popped open the snap of the leather guard strap, and drew his revolver. He smiled at Patricia. 'Safety first,' he told her. He broke open the cylinder, dropped the cartridges into his palm, and snapped the cylinder back into place. Stepping toward her, he dumped the ammunition into a front pocket of his trousers.

He sat down on the couch and handed the revolver to Patricia. 'Ooh, it's so heavy.' Her fingertips caressed the six-inch barrel. She curled her fingers around it, slid them up and down the length of it.

Dexter felt himself getting hard as he watched her.

Moaning, she stroked her cheek with the side of the barrel. Her eyes were half-shut. She eased herself backward against the cushion, and kept rubbing the revolver on her face.

Dexter shook his head. This was one strange gal. Comes in to use the phone and starts getting cozy with his sidearm. Like some kind of hot dream.

She slid the muzzle into her mouth, way in, and started working her lips as if she were milking it.

'Jeee-zus,' Dexter murmured.

She slid the barrel out of her mouth. It came out wet. She turned her face toward him and made a lazy smile.

'Are you . . . all right?' he asked.

'Fine.' A mere whisper.

'Guess you sure like that revolver.'

'Yeah.'

'Maybe you ought to get one of your own.'

She smiled. She slid the barrel inside the top of her dress. Dexter saw its bulge moving under the fabric as she ran the barrel over her breast. 'It's so long and hard,' she whispered.

So am I, he thought. God, so am I.

Her other hand lowered the zipper a few inches. With the gun muzzle, she nudged the cloth aside, baring her breast. Her nipple was standing erect. She slid the barrel over it. The steel pressed it flat, then let it spring up again.

'I don't believe this,' Dexter muttered.

Slowly, she swung the revolver toward him. She touched the muzzle to his lips. 'Open up,' she said.

This is nuts.

He opened his mouth and felt the barrel glide in over his lips.

Her thumb drew back the hammer.

Jesus, he thought. Good thing I unloaded it.

I *did* unload it, didn't I?

Sure.

Still, having the thing in his mouth like that made the skin go tight on the back of his neck.

Patricia said nothing. Holding the gun in his mouth with one hand, she used her other to unbutton the shirt of his uniform. She tugged at it, and he felt the tails pull up out of his trousers.

She unbuckled his gunbelt.

She unbuckled the belt of his trousers, opened the waist button, and drew the zipper down. He felt himself spring out. Then he felt her fingers.

Man alive, what a gal!

Then the gun was no longer in his mouth. Patricia tossed it. It landed on the coffee table, skidded across a couple of magazines and dropped to the floor.

She went down on him.

Holy fucking Toledo! Dexter threw back his head and spread out his arms and held onto the back of the couch.

She comes in to use the phone.

She takes my gun in her mouth.

She takes *me* in her mouth.

God what did I do to deserve this?

He moaned and writhed as Patricia's mouth slid up and down, as she sucked.

He'd had head before.

Never like this.

'Oh babe,' he moaned. 'Oh babe!'

Then, he shrieked.

138

'At the top of the local news, retired Ellsworth Police Chief Dexter Pollock was brutally slain last night in his Fourth Street apartment.'

Vicki lurched rigid. Coffee sloshed from her mug and splashed the floor between her feet. She stared at the radio.

'A tenant residing in the building, Perry Watts, discovered the grisly scene when he returned from a party shortly after midnight, and noticed that the victim's door was ajar. Mr Watts immediately notified the authorities. Responding officers found the retired chief dead at the scene, the apparent victim of multiple wounds. The nature of the murder weapon has not been disclosed.

'Patricia Gordon, a registered nurse in the employ of Blayton Community Hospital, is being sought for questioning in connection with the murder. Miss Gordon, herself previously thought to have been a victim of foul play, had last been seen when she left the hospital at the end of her shift Thursday night. Her abandoned car was found Friday on Harker Road, three miles east of Cedar Junction. An extensive search failed to reveal any clue as to her whereabouts.

'According to Chief Ralph Raines, who assumed the position of Ellsworth Police Chief following Pollock's retirement, "We have substantial evidence that the missing nurse, Patricia Gordon, was present in the victim's apartment at the time of the murder. Anyone with knowledge of Miss Gordon's whereabouts should contact the authorities immediately. She may be armed, and should be considered extremely dangerous." '

'The WBBR news team will keep you informed on all further developments in this shocking and tragic situation. In Ellsworth, today, the Antique Fair continues . . .'

Vicki wiped the coffee off the floor, and left the kitchen. She walked down the hallway to Ace's room. Ace was

139

sprawled on the bed, her face sideways on the pillow, the top sheet down around her feet, her nightshirt halfway up her back. The skin of her legs and back was pink from yesterday's long exposure to the sun. The skimpy seat of her bikini had left a stark white triangle on her rump. Vicki lifted the sheet and covered her.

She sat on the edge of the bed. Blonde hair hung over Ace's face. A few strands were caught in the corner of her mouth. Vicki brushed the hair aside. Ace didn't wake up.

The clock on the nightstand showed 8:05.

Maybe I should let her sleep, Vicki thought. No. She can spend the rest of the day sleeping, if she wants, but I've got to talk to her now.

She gently shook Ace's shoulder, heard her moan, saw an eye open slightly. 'Wha . . . ?'

'Dexter's been killed.'

She raised her head.

'I just heard it on the radio. He was murdered last night.'

'Holy shit.' Ace rolled onto her back. A wrinkle on the pillow had pressed a red, scar-like crease down the right side of her face. 'Murdered? *Our* Dexter?'

'Yeah.'

'Melvin do it?'

'They seem to think it was some nurse. The one who disappeared a few days ago.'

'They get her?'

'They're looking for her.'

'Oh, weird.' She struggled against the mattress, sat up and leaned back against the headboard. 'Let me have some of that.'

Vicki handed the mug to her. Ace took a few swallows, and sighed. 'That nurse, they figured she'd been nailed by some roving nut-case.'

'I know. Dexter, he'd warned me . . .'

'His little morning lectures . . .'

'Yeah, about the disappearances. Then the latest missing

140

gal turns up in his apartment and kills him. At least, they *think* she killed him.'

'Melvin sure as hell threatened to kill him last night.'

'Is it just a coincidence?' Vicki asked.

'I wonder what makes them think it was the nurse.'

'They found something in the apartment. It sounded as if they're pretty certain she's the one who killed him.'

'Be nice if it *was* Melvin. They could put him away, he'd be outa your hair.'

'It doesn't sound too likely.'

'Maybe he's in on it with the nurse.'

'Oh, sure.'

'You sound like you don't want it to be Melvin.'

'We just shouldn't jump to conclusions,' Vicki said.

'A, he's nuts. B, he threatened to kill Dexter. C, Dexter got murdered. That doesn't sound like jumping to conclusions. Not to me, it doesn't.'

'So how'd he get the nurse to do it?'

Ace shrugged, and drank some more coffee.

'You know how Dexter warned me about all those missing gals?' Vicki asked. 'Suppose *he's* the one who was doing it?'

'Our own local Ted Bundy?'

'Maybe he's the one who abducted the nurse. Maybe kept her tied up in his apartment, or something. Last night, she got loose and killed him. You know, to save herself.'

'Big problem with that theory, Watson. She would've run straight to the cops.'

'Well . . .' Vicki realised that, if she thought about it, she could probably come up with several reasons why the nurse might *not* have run to the cops after killing Dexter. He'd been a cop himself, after all, and . . . . That would be stretching it, though. Ace was right. If the nurse had been his prisoner, she would've gone for help the moment she escaped.

'You honestly don't think Melvin had anything to do with it?' Ace asked.

'God, I hate to get him involved if he's innocent.'

141

'If he's innocent, I'll eat my shorts.'

'I guess we should tell the police what we know, huh?'

'Yer durn tootin'.'

'Oh, boy,' Vicki muttered. 'I've never done anything like that. What do we do, just walk into the station?'

'Hell no. Let them come over here.'

Vicki wrinkled her nose. 'Okay. I guess I'll . . . what, just call them up and . . . ?'

'You want me to do the calling?' Ace asked.

She felt enormous relief. 'Well, I could do it, but . . . Yeah, you want to?'

'Why not.'

'You're a pal. Thanks.'

'Don't thank me, buy me a Ding-dong.' She gave the mug to Vicki. 'I'll call right now, before we come to our senses.' She tossed the sheet aside. Vicki stood and turned toward the door. 'Think I'll try Joey Milbourne at home. Let him get the glory.'

In the kitchen, she checked her address book and dialled. Vicki refilled the mug with coffee. 'Hello, Iris? It's Ace. Joey there? . . . He was? That's great. That's what I want to talk to him about . . .' Ace rolled her eyes. 'No, I didn't call to get the gory details. I *know* something about it. Vicki and I were *with* Pollock last night. . . . Fine, you don't want to wake him up, I'll call the station and somebody else can be the one to break the case wide open. I'm sure Joey will thank you for it.' Covering the mouthpiece, Ace whispered, 'Twat.' Then, she nodded. 'Yes, why don't you.' Again, she covered the mouthpiece. 'Going to see if he's awake. He was at Dexter's last night. She's gonna check and see if the phone woke him up.'

Ace took her hand away. 'Morning, hot stuff. Sorry I woke you, but I thought you might want to trot over here and interrogate me and Vicki Chandler. We were with Dexter at the Riverfront last night at about ten-thirty and we *know* something. . . . Yes, about the murder. . . . Half an hour's

142

fine.. See you then, sport.' She hung up. 'You might want to check this guy out.'

'I remember him.'

'He's a hunk. You could do worse.'

'Who's Iris?'

'His mother.'

'He lives with his *mother?* He must be at least thirty-five.'

'Closer to forty.'

'He's that age and lives with his mother, he's got problems.'

'So, who doesn't?'

Vicki ignored that. She filled a mug for Ace, then headed for her bedroom. She had showered after her morning run, and was wearing her robe. She changed into white jeans and a yellow blouse, and went into the living room to wait for Joey's arrival.

A hunk. Pollock's murdered and we're planning to finger Melvin and Ace is playing matchmaker. The guy lives with his mother, no less. Last thing I need.

Ace came into the room. She was barefoot, wearing paint-spattered cut-off jeans and a baggy sleeveless grey sweatshirt.

'I see you dressed to impress the hunk,' Vicki said.

'Don't want to steal your thunder, hon.'

'Oh, thanks.'

'You could do worse.'

'How come *you're* not after him?'

'I've had my turn.'

'What's wrong with him?'

'Nothing.'

'I'll bet.'

'He's not my type.'

'Oh, but you think he's mine?'

'As we say in the sportswear biz, can't hurt to try it on for size.'

'As we say in the doctor biz, bend over and spread 'em.'

Ace snorted.

A few minutes later, Vicki heard the faint thud of a car

143

door shutting. Then came the quick sound of footsteps on the walkway, then the doorbell. Ace opened the door. The man who entered was as tall as Ace. His light brown hair was cut short, and he had a neatly trimmed moustache. Vicki could see why Ace considered him a hunk: his face was tanned and handsome; his white knit shirt hugged bulging muscles and a flat belly. He looked tightly packed into his faded jeans.

Vicki remembered him as a baby-faced beanpole. He'd grown the moustache and apparently taken up body building since she last saw him.

'Joey, you remember Vicki Chandler?'

'Of course. Vicki? I hear you're working with Charlie Gaines over at the clinic.'

'Just started last week,' she said. 'How are you doing?'

'I could've used a couple more hours of sleep.'

'You'll be glad I woke you,' Ace told him.

'I actually require eight hours to function at top form, so I'm two hours short.'

'Better take a load off before you collapse.'

He arched an eyebrow at Ace. Then, he sat at the other end of the couch and crossed a leg over his knee, which must've been painful in those tight jeans. He rested a clipboard against his upthrust leg. 'Now,' he said, 'I understand that you two were with Pollock last night.'

'At the Riverfront,' Ace said. 'We were there with Melvin Dobbs.'

'What on earth for?'

'He seems to have the hots for Vicki.'

Joey looked at Vicki. The eyebrow went up again.

'I'm not encouraging it,' she explained.

'I wouldn't. He's an odd bird. So, the four of you were drinking at the Riverfront.'

'The three of us,' Vicki said. 'Me, Ace, and Melvin. Then Ace left the table to get some peanuts . . .'

'Salted in the shell,' Ace added.

144

'You should be careful of salt,' Joey said. 'Bad for the cardio-vascular system.'

'While she was away, Pollock showed up and started bothering us.'

'Bothering you how?'

'I'd been a tenant in his apartment building, but he kept pestering me so I moved out. He wasn't very happy about that.'

'Pestering you how?'

'By being his normal lecherous self,' Ace said.

'He'd stop me in the hall, make crude remarks, that sort of thing. Supposedly trying to warn me about running early in the morning. He seemed to think I was asking to get myself assaulted.'

'Which is probably what *he* wanted to do,' Ace suggested.

Joey frowned at her. 'The man's dead.'

'That doesn't make him suddenly a saint.'

'His point may have been well taken. There have been several incidents, recently, of attractive young women disappearing without a trace.'

'Like the nurse who turned up at Pollock's last night?' Ace asked.

'I think we're straying from the point here,' Joey said. He looked at Vicki. 'So you were drinking with Dobbs, and Pollock showed up and began bothering you? What time was this?'

'About ten-fifteen, ten-thirty.'

'And his behaviour was abusive?'

'I'd say so, yes.'

'Was he alone?'

'He seemed to be.'

'Did you notice anyone in the establishment wearing a nurse's white dress?'

'No. Not that I saw.'

'Me neither,' Ace said.

'So how does this tie in with the subsequent murder?'

'Melvin threatened to kill him,' Ace said.

145

Both Joey's eyebrows shot up.

'I *thought* that might get your attention.'

'Exactly what did Dobbs say?'

' "I oughta kill him." '

Vicki nodded agreement. 'Those were his exact words.'

Joey wrote on his clipboard. 'And by "him," he was referring to Dexter Pollock?'

'No, Eddie Rabbit. Of *course* he was referring to Pollock. Why do you think we're telling you this?'

'So, both of you heard him threaten Pollock's life between ten-fifteen and ten-thirty last night?'

'That's right,' Vicki said. 'But we were all upset with Pollock. I poured some beer on him, myself.'

'Why was that?'

'He was getting cute. The thing is, he was being a jerk and Melvin's remark seemed pretty normal, under the circumstances. I could've said the same thing, myself.'

'But you're not a lunatic who'll go out and *do* it,' Ace pointed out.

'What transpired after the altercation?'

'Ace and I went home.'

'What about Dobbs?'

'He left the bar when we did. Right after we got rid of Pollock.'

'So the three of you left the Riverfront together.'

'At about ten-thirty or so.'

'And went directly home – here?'

'Here.'

'What about Dobbs?'

'He came with us and we had an orgy.'

Joey narrowed his eyes at Ace. 'We're talking about a murder investigation.'

'So sorry.'

'Melvin didn't come with us,' Vicki said. 'We don't know where he went afterwards.'

'Was Pollock still in the tavern when you left?'

146

Vicki looked at Ace. Ace shrugged. 'He might've still been there.'

'I didn't see him leave,' Ace said.

'You both came directly here after leaving the Riverfront? Did either of you leave the house again last night?'

'What, are *we* suddenly suspects?' Ace asked.

'I'm just asking.'

'We watched TV,' Vicki said, 'until about one o'clock. Then we went to bed.'

'Anything else to add?'

'That's about it,' Ace told him. 'So, you going over and question Melvin?'

He slipped his pen under the clamp of the clipboard. 'I'm not sure there's any reason to bother Dobbs about this.'

'What, it doesn't matter that he threatened to kill Pollock?'

'We already have a suspect in this.'

'The nurse,' Vicki said.

'What makes you think she's the one who killed him?'

'Physical evidence at the scene.'

'Such as?'

'I'm not at liberty to reveal the details of our investigation.'

'Bug-squat.'

'I will say that we found a dress in Pollock's apartment. The name tag identified it as belonging to the suspect.'

'So did she leave starkers?'

Joey shook his head.

'Couldn't her dress have been planted to mislead you?' Vicki asked.

'By Melvin, for instance,' Ace said.

'We have some indications that the perpetrator was a female. And we should be able to confirm, today, that it was actually Patricia Gordon who inflicted the wounds. Once we've checked her dental charts . . .' He stopped abruptly and looked annoyed.

'She bite him?'

'I didn't say that.'

'Of course you didn't.'

147

'Damn it.'

'We won't say anything,' Vicki told him.

'I would appreciate that.'

'If this nurse disappeared Thursday,' she asked, 'how did she end up in Pollock's apartment?'

'We have no idea.'

'He hadn't been . . . keeping her?'

'It occurred to us. But we found nothing to indicate that she'd been there for any period of time.'

'The earlier theory was that she'd been abducted?'

'That's what we'd assumed. It followed the pattern of the other disappearances, at least until she turned up last night and killed him.'

'Don't you think that's pretty strange?' Ace asked.

'Everything about this is strange.'

'But you're pretty sure,' Vicki said, 'that Pollock isn't the one who abducted her, and maybe kept her tied up or something, and she killed him to escape?'

'We didn't find any ropes in the apartment. His handcuffs were in their case on his utility belt. We didn't find anything that looked as if it might've been used as a gag. There weren't any drugs in his apartment that he might've used to render her unconscious. So it certainly doesn't appear that he was keeping the woman against her will. From the latent prints we found, it doesn't even look as if *anyone* had been in the apartment except Pollock.'

'So where was she since Thursday night?' Ace asked.

'When we find her, we'll ask.'

'Maybe you'll find her at Melvin's house,' Vicki said.

Joey looked at her and hoisted an eyebrow. 'You're thinking that Dobbs abducted her Thursday night, kept her, and sent her over to Pollock's last night to make good on his threat?'

'It's occurred to us,' Vicki said.

'Pretty farfetched. What do you think Dobbs did, hypnotise her?'

Vicki ignored his sarcasm.

148

'Possibly,' she said. 'I understand it's widely believed that a person can't be forced under hypnosis to do something she would otherwise consider abhorrent, but there are ways around that problem. If the subject is given an acceptable rationale for the behaviour . . .'

'Like he told her Pollock is a ham sandwich,' Ace elaborated.

'I might as well get going,' Joey said. 'This isn't getting us anywhere.'

He started to rise.

'No, wait. Keep out of it for a minute, would you, Ace? This is serious.'

'It's starting to sound pretty half-assed, even to me.'

'Melvin actually *might* have kidnapped that nurse and hypnotised her into killing Pollock for him. If he was able to convince her that Pollock was a threat, that maybe he intended to rape or murder her, then that could provide a sufficient motive to allow her to justify using violence against him. It's been done. I read a case study in a psychology journal that described *exactly* that . . .'

'It didn't go down that way,' Joey said. 'Gordon didn't behave like a gal defending herself. She went well beyond anything that could've possibly been justified by the kind of hypnotic suggestion you're talking about. The savagery . . . You have no idea. And I'm not about to enlighten you.'

'Okay. Suppose we forget the hypnosis angle. What if Melvin was with her in the apartment? Maybe he had a gun, or something, and forced her to attack Pollock.'

Joey shook his head. 'I already explained there was no indication that anyone else was present. Besides, if he was there, why didn't *he* simply shoot Pollock, or whatever, rather than force the woman to do the killing?'

'I don't know. He might've had some sort of weird reason.'

'What I think this boils down to,' Joey said, 'is that Dobbs made a casual remark last night in the heat of anger – a remark that you yourself said was fairly normal under the circumstances – and Pollock just happened to be killed a

149

couple of hours later. From what you've told me, I might just as easily suspect you as Dobbs. After all, you were upset enough to pour beer on Pollock.'

'You could at least go over to Melvin's house and ask him about it.'

'Did anyone other than you and Ace hear his threat against Pollock?'

'I doubt it.'

'I could go over there. I could probably even get a search warrant on the basis of what you told me. Not that I think I'd find anything. But I could do that. And Dobbs would know exactly who put me onto him. Do you want that?'

'Not especially,' Vicki admitted. She'd realised Melvin would probably find out that she and Ace had told on him, but she had pushed the knowledge aside, not wanting to confront it. Hearing her suspicions confirmed by Joey gave her a bad feeling in the stomach.

'I'd be out there in a minute if I thought you were onto something,' he explained. 'But I frankly just don't see how Dobbs could've possibly been involved in this. The nurse killed Pollock. It's as simple as that. The only thing I'd accomplish by confronting Dobbs would be to make him extremely put out with you and Ace. I really can't imagine you want to have someone like him mad at you.'

'We could live with it,' Vicki said.

'On the bright side,' Ace told her, 'it might put a damper on his affection for you.'

Joey's eyebrows went up again. 'I hope you ladies didn't bring me over here because of your own personal problems with Dobbs. Get the cop to roust him . . .'

Vicki felt her face go red. 'Just forget it. We told you what we had to tell you. If you don't want to follow up on it, that's your business.'

'Better go home and catch up on your beauty sleep,' Ace told him. 'Sorry we bothered you.'

Now, his face was red. 'Maybe I spoke out of line . . .'

'I'd say so,' Vicki said. 'We didn't ask you over here to

cause trouble for Melvin. He threatened to kill Pollock and we felt we had a duty to report it. That's all. And if you don't think it's relevant, fine. Don't do anything about it. No skin off our noses. In fact, it's a relief.'

'I just don't think . . .'

'We know,' Ace said.

Sighing, Joey rose to his feet. 'If anything else comes up,' he said, 'don't hesitate to contact me. I mean that. But I honestly need more than an idle threat before I can go barging in on someone. This is America, after all. Freedom of speech is guaranteed by the Constitution.'

'Thanks,' Ace said. She gave Vicki a look of concern. 'I guess we'd forgotten that. What fools we've been.' She got up and walked to the door and opened it. 'Thanks for coming by, officer. And thank you for reminding us that we live in a country where personal liberty is thus cherished.'

Shaking his head, he left the house.

Ace shut the door. 'Freedom of speech my lily white ass.'

'Some cop,' Vicki muttered.

'About as useful as a limp dick.'

'If I were a cop, I'd hot-foot it over to Melvin's with a search warrant.'

'You sound like you're convinced.'

'Oh, yeah,' Vicki said. 'In fact, I don't see how Melvin could've been involved. It *doesn't* make sense. But I'd go out there, regardless. I'd check him out. I'd search his house. I'd want to make sure the nurse *isn't* there. What kind of a cop is Milbourne, anyway?'

'The kind that has a yellow streak up his back. He knows damn well he oughta go out there. He's just too chicken-shit to do it. The question is, are we?'

'You're kidding. You couldn't drag me over to Melvin's. Besides, if the cops can't be bothered. . . . It's their job, after all. We did our part.'

'You just want to forget about it, then?'

'I'm not about to play Nancy Drew.'

'Might be fun.'

151

'Yeah. Like a sharp stick in the eye.'

'You could give Melvin a call, ask him out for a picnic or something. I'm sure he'd be delighted. While you keep him busy, I sneak into the house and have a look around.'

'Great idea. I only see two problems. One, I'm not about to take Melvin on a picnic. Two, what if the nurse *is* in there and kills your butt?'

'We both know she isn't, of course.'

'Right. So what's the point?'

'Good point. Never mind. Let's go over to Blayton, check out the shopping mall, and take your folks out to dinner.'

'Yeah!'

CHAPTER SEVENTEEN

Thelma's VW bug was in the clinic parking lot Monday morning. So was Charlie's white Mercedes. The red Duster was gone.

Thank God.

With the car gone, the gift taken back, Vicki felt as if Melvin might be receding from her life. It was too much to hope that she was rid of him entirely. But the car had been a link that was now broken.

And yesterday, he'd neither called nor put in an appearance. Of course, Vicki'd spent the afternoon and evening in Blayton, so he might've tried while she was away.

Going an entire day without any contact from Melvin, however, made her feel encouraged.

She was very glad that Joey Milbourne had refused to see him about the threat. She and Ace had done the right thing, telling him, if only because they both would've felt guilty keeping the knowledge to themselves, but the more she'd thought about the situation, the more certain she was that

Joey had been wise not to act on it. Obviously, Melvin hadn't been involved in Pollock's death. Confronting him about it would've made things messy, and for no good reason.

Very messy, she thought. Melvin would think we'd stabbed him in the back. And he'd be right.

Just have to hope he never finds out we told.

Don't worry, he won't.

Now, if I can get through today Melvin-free. That'll be two days in a row.

With a last look at the empty space in the parking lot, Vicki turned away and entered the clinic. The waiting room was deserted. Thelma, behind the reception window, raised her head and smiled. 'Morning,' Vicki said. 'Have a nice weekend?'

'Oh, it was too short, I'd say. Aside from that . . . we went to the Antique Fair yesterday. Jim paid good money for a beat-up old Roy Rogers lunch box, which didn't set too well with me, but he said he had one just like it when he was a kid so what the hell. Men are such children, more often than not. Isn't it something about Dexter Pollock?'

'Terrible,' Vicki said. She'd been feeling pretty good. Not anymore.

'Lord only knows why that gal did him in,' Thelma said, 'but I bet she had her reasons. Wouldn't surprise me at all, they find out Pollock was up to no good with her. I always figured, if he lived long enough and didn't mend his ways, one gal or another would up and do him in. In my younger days, I had a couple of occasions to slap him down, myself. Course, I never killed him. But I might've, I'd had a gun handy. I suspect, if they ever nab that nurse, there're plenty of folks hereabouts who'd like to pin a medal on her. They'd have to stand in line behind yours truly.'

'Well,' Vicki said, 'I wasn't especially fond of Pollock, myself. I doubt if he deserved to get murdered, though.'

'I suspect he deserved it, all right. But it's a shocking thing, anyhow, I guess, that kind of bloodbath happening

153

here in our own town. You want to go in and see Charlie? He said he wanted to see you first thing.'

Vicki felt a small flutter of concern. 'Do you know what it's about?'

Thelma shook her head. 'No idea. But he's got Jack Randolph with him.'

'Who's Jack Randolph?'

'A lawyer.'

Oh, God. What's going on?

He heart pounded as she stepped through the waiting room doorway. She walked slowly down the corridor toward Charlie's office.

A lawyer. *Malpractice?* That seemed unlikely. She hadn't seen anyone with a major problem last week. Complications were always possible, of course. But if somebody had a problem . . .

She knocked on the door of Charlie's office. 'Come in,' he called.

She opened the door. Charlie smiled at her from behind his desk. In spite of the smile, he looked confused for just a moment as if he didn't recognise her.

'You wanted to see me?'

The confusion seemed to clear. 'Vicki? Indeed I did. Have you met Jack Randolph?'

'No, I . . .' As she stepped into the room, the man rose from his chair beside Charlie's desk and smiled at her.

'Dr Chandler,' he said.

She knew she was staring at him. She knew she was blushing, that her mouth was hanging open.

The man from the playground. Who'd watched her from his perch atop the slide. Who'd been there the next day, on a swing, as if waiting for her. Who'd shown up, even in one of her nightmares, only to be shot off the slide by Dexter Pollock. Or was it Melvin? She couldn't remember.

'Hello,' she managed.

'Nice to see you again,' he said.

'Oh,' Charlie said, 'you've met?'

154

'Briefly,' Jack told him.

'Well good, that's fine. Jack's an attorney, Vicki.'

'Is there some kind of problem?'

'No, no,' Charlie said. 'Take a seat.'

She sat on the chair in front of his desk. No problem, he'd told her. That was a relief, but she still felt confused and tense. And strangely excited by the presence of the man from the playground. She watched him sit down on the other chair.

What's he doing here? she wondered. It must have something to do with me. How did he know where I work?

'Vicki,' Charlie began, 'I've given some thought to your position here. I find that you're an extremely valuable asset, and I'd like to think that you'll stay here in town and possibly even take over the clinic after I'm gone.'

After I'm gone.

He looked the same as usual: his white hair neatly combed, his face ruddy, his blue eyes bright. But Vicki remembered how he'd seemed a bit confused when she first opened the door. 'Are you okay, Charlie?' she asked. 'Is something wrong?'

'No, no.' He waved a hand as if dismissing the thought, then scratched his stomach. 'I suspect I've got a few good years left in me yet. But I am getting on, Vicki. I've spent my life looking after the folks of this town, and I'd like to see you stay here and take over the clinic after I'm gone.'

There, he'd said it again.

'I don't have any plans to leave,' Vicki told him.

'Well, that's good to hear. The thing is, I want to make it worth your while to stay on.' He scratched himself again. 'I'm asking you to be my full partner here at the clinic.'

'Geez.'

'Is that a yes?' Charlie asked.

'Well . . . yes. Of course. I'm just so shocked . . .'

'We'll be fifty-fifty partners.'

'God. I . . .'

'Jack will draw up the papers today.' He looked at Jack.

155

'And I want you to put in there that Vicki'will assume full ownership upon my death.'

Vicki frowned. 'I'm very grateful, Charlie, but. . . . Are you sure you're all right?'

'Fit as a fiddle.'

'This is too much. I don't deserve to have you just *give* me your practice.'

'I want it to be in your capable and caring hands. I wouldn't want to trust it to a stranger. I've spent my whole life caring for the folks of this town, and I wouldn't want to see it all fall apart after I'm gone.'

That's three.

He looked at Jack. 'You'll write all that up and have it ready for my signature this afternoon?'

Jack nodded.

Scratching his stomach, Charlie smiled at Vicki. 'There's also the matter of the loan. Let's just call that a gift.'

'Charlie, you can't . . .'

'Sure, I can. No arguments, now.' She saw a tiny speck of blood appear on the front of his white shirt over the place where he'd been scratching. 'You were a young lady with promise, and I always hoped you'd turn into a fine doctor and come back here to take up for me. Lending you that money was just my way of hooking you back. Now that you're here, we'll just forget about it.'

'That's *twenty-five thousand dollars*, Charlie.'

'I've got no use for it, anyway.' He looked again at Jack. 'Maybe you can put that down on paper, too. Make it official that I'm cancelling out the IOU.'

'Fine,' Jack said.

'Charlie. I . . .'

'Now, I won't hear any more arguments from you or I just might change my mind.' He scratched his stomach again. Now, the front of his shirt was marked by a thread of blood nearly an inch long.

'You're bleeding, Charlie.'

'Am I?' He looked down. 'So I am.' He sounded amused.

'Scratched the scab off, I suppose. Those pesky rose bushes. I was pruning them yesterday. Those thorns are treacherous.'

'Would you like me to have a look?' Vicki asked.

'Lord, no. It's nothing.' He slipped a finger inside his shirt, rubbed, took it out and glanced at the smear of blood on his fingertip. Then he licked it. 'I do suppose I'd better head home and fetch a clean shirt.' To Jack, he said, 'Can you have the papers ready for my signature by, say, five o'clock?'

'No problem,' Jack said.

'Fine. I'll be here waiting. You can go on about your business, now, Vicki. I'm delighted to have you as a partner.'

'Well, thank you. Thank you very much, Charlie.'

'My pleasure.'

As she rose from her chair, Jack smiled at her. 'I'll see you later, Dr Chandler.'

At a quarter past five that afternoon, Vicki was at her desk reviewing records from Blayton Memorial about the rotator cuff repair surgery on a patient she would be seeing tomorrow for a follow-up examination. She was having a hard time concentrating. All day, her mind had been drifting back to the incredible meeting in Charlie's office.

She still felt dazed.

A year or two down the road, it might've been different; she had hoped to be offered a partnership, eventually. But not this soon. Not after she'd been here a week. It seemed outlandish, unreal.

Wonderful, but troubling. What could've prompted Charlie to make such a momentous decision so suddenly?

And to cancel the debt?

Vicki had to believe that something was gravely wrong with him. All that talk about 'after I'm gone'. Almost as if he'd just found out he had a terminal illness. He'd claimed to be perfectly fine, but she just couldn't believe it.

He'd seemed cheerful, though.

Someone knocked on her office door. 'Yes?'

The door swung open and Jack Randolph stepped in. 'I

157

have the partnership papers for you to countersign.' He came to her desk and handed the stapled packet to her. 'After you've looked them over, if you'll initial the bottom of each page and sign the final page.'

Vicki stared at the top sheet and shook her head. 'What do you know about all this?'

'Well, the agreement indicates that you'll take a $4,000.00 draw each month. At the end of each fiscal year, you'll receive a fifty per cent share of any profits. You'll also assume that portion of any debts incurred by the partnership.'

'Debts?'

'It's nothing to be concerned about. I had an opportunity to look at the books, and the clinic is in fine shape financially.'

'Do you think I should sign?'

'I sure would, if I were you.'

'Why's he doing this? It's so sudden. I just don't understand.'

'You suspect some ulterior motive?'

'Did he say anything to you . . . about his health?'

'Nothing that you didn't hear.'

'It seems so weird. As if he thinks he might be dying, or something.'

'I don't think you should be too concerned about that. Certainly not on the basis of his decisions this morning.'

'Why would he do it, though?'

'I've seen similar behaviour quite a few times with people who come in to have their wills drawn up. They suddenly get an urge, feel they absolutely have to do it right away. Sometimes, it's because they just had a close call of some kind and they suddenly realise they aren't going to live forever. Maybe a friend has just died unexpectedly. Or they're going in for surgery and have a premonition they won't survive it. Sometimes, it's as simple as having a birthday. All of a sudden, they can't let another day go by without having a will. But it's nothing to worry about. Just

158

humam nature. I think Dr Gaines suddenly woke up this morning and realised he'd better make you a partner before a safe falls on his head.'

'I hope that's all it is.' She felt at least a little relieved by Jack's explanation. 'Did he seem all right to you?'

'Maybe a bit confused about a few things. Nothing that struck me as especially odd. But I don't know the man. You're probably a better judge of whether . . .'

'You don't know him?' Vicki asked.

Jack shook his head. 'He phoned me this morning. Said he picked my name out of the yellow pages. Which makes it very interesting that I'm here, since he might just as easily have chosen a different attorney. Enough to make a person wonder about such things as Fate. I've been wanting to see you again, Dr Chandler.'

All she could manage was, 'Oh?'

'We didn't have much chance to get acquainted, last time.'

'Yeah, I'm sorry about that. You kind of caught me at a bad moment.'

'I'm sure it must've been a shock, realising you weren't alone.'

'I didn't expect to find someone sitting on top of a slide at that hour. That's for sure. You do it often?'

'Once in a while. I'm an early riser.'

Vicki found herself smiling. 'So you like to leap out of bed and hot-foot it to the nearest playground?'

'Oh, I take my time. I just wander around and sniff the morning and listen to the silence. It's a nice time of the day. I guess you know that. It's one of the reasons I'd like to know you better.'

'Well . . .'

'If you have a fellow waiting at home for you, or . . .'

'No. At least I *hope* not.'

He gave her an odd look.

'It's nothing.'

'How would you feel about having dinner with me tonight? Your new business arrangement calls for a celebration, and

159

the Fireside Chalet seems like just the place for that kind of thing. What do you say?'

'Best offer I've had all day.' All month, she thought. All year. 'Sure,' she said. 'I'd like that.'

'Great. I'll hot-foot it home and make the reservations. Does eight o'clock sound good?'

'Fine.'

She scribbled Ace's address and telephone number onto a prescription pad, tore off the sheet and gave it to him. 'Can you read that?'

'Your handwriting's pretty good, for a doctor.'

'I'm still new at it.' She glanced down at the agreement papers.

'No hurry about that,' Jack told her. 'You should take your time and read it carefully before you sign. Just give it to Dr Gaines before you leave, and keep a copy for yourself.'

'All right.'

'See you at about a quarter till eight?'

Vicki nodded. Jack, backed away, smiling, a look on his face as if he couldn't quite believe his luck. 'Well, see you,' he said.

'See you.'

He went out the door.

CHAPTER EIGHTEEN

Melvin and Patricia were in the living room watching television when the doorbell rang. The clock on the VCR read 9:01. 'Now, that's prompt,' Melvin said. 'Wait here.'

Patricia stayed on the couch, but watched over her shoulder as he went to the door. He peered through the peephole. 'It's all right,' he told her. Then he opened the door.

And staggered back as Charlie Gaines threw himself forward and wrapped his arms around Melvin.

'Hey, hey, cut it out,' he said, patting the man's back.

Charlie squeezed him hard.

'Come on, let go, now.'

Charlie released him. Melvin shut the door and locked it. When he turned around, the doctor was wiping tears from his eyes.

'What's wrong?'

'It's nothing. I'm all right. You won't make me leave again, will you?'

'Depends.'

'I did everything like you told me.'

He took Charlie by the arm and led him to the couch. Charlie sat down in the middle. As Melvin sat beside him, Patricia scurried around both of the men and squeezed in between the end of the couch and Melvin. She put her arm across his shoulders. Melvin slid a hand up her bare thigh and under the draping tail of the big blue police uniform shirt she had worn away from Pollock's apartment. 'Charlie and me, we've got stuff to talk over. So just sit quiet.'

Though her eyes looked troubled, she nodded.

Melvin started to take his hand away as he turned toward Charlie. Patricia grabbed his hand and stopped it. 'Let go,' he said in a firm voice.

Pouting, she released his hand.

He faced Charlie, and found the man scowling at Patricia. 'Did you make sure nobody followed you here?'

'I checked very carefully.'

'Good. Were there any problems?'

'No problems at all.'

'Vicki didn't put up a fuss about you giving her the partnership?'

'She suspected I was ill.'

'Shit, you're not ill, you're dead.'

Charlie laughed. 'If this is dead, I don't know what I was worried about all those years.'

161

'She went and signed the papers, though?'

'Sure did.'

'Where did you leave them?'

'Exactly where you told me to.'

'In the top drawer of your desk?'

'That's right.'

'And you took care of the loan?'

'I did. She tried to talk me out of that, but I told her just what you said and she acquiesced.'

'How much was the debt?'

'Twenty-five thousand dollars.'

Wouldn't even take a car from me, Melvin thought, but didn't bat an eyelash over twenty-five grand and a partnership from the old doctor.

'How'd you find out how much it was?' he asked.

'Thelma gave me the books.'

'Did she suspect anything?'

'Thelma? No, I don't believe she did.'

'And you didn't say anything about me, did you?'

'To Thelma?'

'To anyone.'

'No. Nary a word.'

'What about the lawyer. Did he give you any trouble?'

'He was just fine. He took care of everything.'

Melvin leaned back. Sighing, he put a hand on Charlie's leg, a hand on Patricia's. 'Well,' he said, 'it sure looks good.' To Charlie, he said, 'Did Vicki seem real happy about the whole thing?'

'She appeared more confused and worried than happy.'

'Well, it must've been a pretty big surprise. I guess she'll be real happy once it all sinks in.'

'I don't know how come you wanted to bother,' Patricia muttered.

'None of your business.'

'You've got me. I don't see why . . .'

'Don't give me any of your shit, or I'll lock you up.'

'Are you planning to revivify Vicki?' Charlie asked.

162

'None of *your* business.'

'In my personal opinion, it would be a grand plan. After all, she's a lovely young lady.'

Melvin smashed an elbow into Charlie's side. 'Don't you even *think* about her that way.'

He hung his head. 'I'm sorry. I didn't mean to suggest anything untoward. However, it doesn't seem especially fair to me that you should have Patricia and yet I'm without a woman.'

'You're an old man.'

'There may be snow on the roof, but I assure you there's still plenty of fire in the . . .'

'You're not getting Vicki, so forget it you old fart.'

'Perhaps a different woman, then. I would certainly be appreciative.'

'This ain't a fucking *dating service!*'

'I'm sorry. It was only a suggestion.'

'Keep your suggestions to yourself.'

'Yes. I will. I'm sorry.'

'Stay here and watch the TV,' Melvin told him. He squeezed Patricia's leg. 'Come with me.'

She gave Charlie a look of triumph, then stood and followed Melvin upstairs. He led her into the bedroom. Her shirt was already unbuttoned. She plucked open his robe, pressed herself against him, and pushed her tongue into his mouth as her hands roamed his back and rump. Soon, he eased her away. 'Get in bed.'

She let the shirt fall to the floor. Its badge hit the carpet with a soft thump. She climbed onto the bed, crawled to the middle, and lay down. Gazing at him, she licked her lips. She caressed her breasts, pulled at the nipples.

'Stop that.'

She folded her hands beneath her head.

'Now, go to sleep.'

'You want to play, don't you?'

'Maybe later.'

'Oh, come on.'

'I have stuff to do.'

'With Charlie?'

'Yeah.'

She frowned and pushed her lips out.

'I'll be back in a while.'

'I bet you're gonna play with Charlie.'

'Fat chance.'

'Sure.'

'I'm gonna kill him.'

That brightened her up. 'Honest?'

'Yep.'

She nodded, smiling, then frowned again. This time, she looked confused rather than pouty. 'He's dead already. How can you kill him when he's dead already?'

'I'll figure a way;' Melvin said.

Though the problem had been lingering in the back of his mind since he first came up with the scheme to use Charlie Gaines, he'd been too busy to worry about the details of how he might go about rekilling the man.

The first order of business had been abducting Charlie. That turned out to be easy with the help of the revolver Patricia had taken from Pollock. He'd simply hiked over to Charlie's house last night, knocked on the door and stuck the gun in his face. The man offered no resistance, since he didn't want to be shot. He drove his car. Melvin sat in back with the muzzle pressed against his head.

Then came the killing of Charlie. He got him down into the basement and held the cocked revolver in his face while Patricia strapped him to the table. Then he suffocated the old man with cellophane. Simple. No problem at all until Patricia climbed onto the table, all set to bite his neck. A whack on the ear put a stop to that.

Then came the matter of bringing him back. That took Patricia's mind off biting him. She was probably so fascinated by the process because she realized that she'd gone through the same treatment, herself. She'd actually begged to help, so Melvin allowed her to chew the Root of Life and tongue

164

the messy glop into stomach gash. Then he let her do the stitching. Why not? She was a woman, after all, so she'd likely had more experience than Melvin when it came to needles and threads. She did a fine job of it, too. She acted happy and proud while she worked. Only after Charlie revived did she start getting moody.

Training him came next. Since he woke up with amnesia, the same as Patricia, it took all night to prepare him for Monday's tasks. He'd been a quick learner, but Patricia had made a constant pest of herself. Starting with snide remarks about Charlie. 'I don't think he's so special . . . He's awfully old and ugly. . . . He's not very smart, is he?' Melvin ignored her, so she tried being seductive. She stripped and tried a variety of poses. She caressed herself, pulled at herself. When Melvin failed to respond, she found a pair of scissors. That was the last straw. Though Melvin didn't want to be bothered, he didn't care to have Patricia mutilate herself. So he took the scissors away, led her up to the bedroom and wasted a precious hour appeasing her. Then he locked her in the room and returned to Charlie.

By eight o'clock in the morning, Charlie seemed ready. Melvin studied the telephone directory, chose a lawyer, and listened while Charlie made the call. An answering machine took the message to meet Charlie at the clinic at nine.

Finally, Charlie drove away. Melvin, exhausted and unwilling to endure another confrontation with Patricia, staggered up to his parents' bedroom and fell onto their king-sized bed. He slept until mid-afternoon, when he was roused by shouts and pounding from his own room.

He found Patricia breathless and blubbering, her face streaked with tears. In her tantrum, she had raked herself with her fingernails. Her thighs and belly and breasts were lined with weals and scratches, some bleeding. A thread of blood had leaded from a corner of the Mouth of Ram-Chotep as if the ancient deity had snaked and dribbled. Her right forearm was tooth-torn and bleeding.

He had left Patricia alone several times before. Some-

165

times, he returned to find her asleep. Other times, she was weeping. But she had never done anything like this.

'Are you nuts!' Melvin blurted. He drew back a fist, but she looked so pitiful that he couldn't bring himself to strike her. Instead, he eased the sobbing girl against him and held her. 'It's all right,' he murmured.

'You don't love me, anymore.'

'Yeah, sure I do.'

'You've got *him*, now.'

'I don't care about him.'

'You didn't . . . come back all night.'

'I'm here. You shouldn't go hurting yourself like that.'

'I couldn't . . . help it. You locked me in.'

'I can't be with you all the time. There's a lot of stuff I've gotta do.'

She kept on crying and clinging to him. Melvin stroked her hair. Then, he lifted her and carried her into the bathroom. They stood together beneath the shower. As Melvin gently soaped her wounds, she stopped crying. She peeled the sodden bandages off his shoulders and chest, kissed his bite marks, slid the soap over them, then ran the slippery bar down his body. Staring into his eyes with a look that seemed both solemn and a little shy, she lathered and fondled him.

'I love you so much,' she said.

'I love you, too,' he told her. Watching the spray bounce off her hair and shoulders, seeing the look in her eyes, feeling the slick glide of her hands, he almost believed it.

When they finally went downstairs, it was late afternoon and Melvin's stomach was growling. He knew he'd better start thinking about ways to rekill Charlie, but the old man wasn't due back until nine. So he threw a frozen pizza in the oven for himself. When it was ready, he took a T-bone steak from the refrigerator and gave it to Patricia. He began to eat his pizza. Patricia unwrapped her steak over a plate, then wrung it out like a washcloth. When the plate shimmered with a puddle of red juice, she poured it into a wine glass.

She sipped it while she dined. She used a napkin frequently to dry her chin. She was starting to become very tidy about her meals, as if making an effort to improve her manners. When she finished, her blue police shirt was still spotless.

It had crossed Melvin's mind, after dinner, that he should go down to the basement and search the Magdal book for a way to rekill Charlie. But he simply hadn't felt like it. The task of studying the book seemed like too great a burden. So he took Patricia into the living room and turned on the television and didn't stir from the couch until the doorbell rang.

Now, it was Charlie watching TV. Standing beside the bed, Melvin wondered just how he *would* go about rekilling the man. Just go ahead and do it, he told himself. It'll probably be as easy as it was to kill him in the first place.

'Why don't we just shoot him?' Patricia suggested.

'It has to look like an accident. I think I'll take him out in his car.'

'I can come with you, can't I?'

Here we go again.

'I'd like to let you,' he said. 'The thing is, you've gotta stay inside. The police are looking for you because of the Pollock murder.'

She seemed to shrink with gloom.

'Don't start carrying on, honey.'

'You're going to leave me again.'

'It won't take long.'

'Oh, sure.'

Melvin sat on the edge of the bed. He slid a hand up her leg, feeling the hard ridges of scabs from last night's tantrum. 'If you don't want me to go,' he said, 'I won't.'

'Really?'

'Honest.'

She beamed at him.

'Charlie will have to stay with us, though. That okay with you?'

Her smile faded. 'I don't want him here.'

167

'Me neither. But I'd have to take him somewhere to get rid of him, and I can't do that without leaving you alone for a little while.'

She seemed to ponder the problem for a few moments. 'How long would you be gone?'

'Half an hour, maybe.'

'That isn't so long.'

'I'd be back before you knew it.'

'Do you have to do it now?'

'I guess not.' He glanced at the clock beside the bed. Nine-thirty. It really was too early. He'd wanted to take care of it right away, get it finished, but there would be far less risk if he waited. The ideal time would be two or three o'clock in the morning.

He didn't know if he could wait that long.

But the longer he put it off, the better.

'I don't have to go for a while,' he said.

'Don't go till after I'm asleep, okay?'

'Okay.'

Patricia rolled over, reached to the nightstand, and snatched up the roll of masking tape. She tore off several strips. She pressed them across her mouth.

CHAPTER NINETEEN

Jack took her by the arm and led her toward his car. 'Thank you so much,' she said. 'Dinner was wonderful.'

'My pleasure. I haven't had such a great time in . . . oh, days.'

'Jerk.' She bumped him gently with her elbow.

'If I'd said "years", you might have thought I was smitten.'

'Smitten?'

'Smote?'

168

'But you're not?'

'Actually, I am. But I'm not about to admit it.'

He opened the passenger door for Vicki. She climbed in and leaned across the seat to unlock the driver's door for him. Starting to fasten her safety harness, she considered going without it and sitting in the centre, close to Jack. But if she did that, she might appear too eager.

Let him make the first moves, she thought.

Jack had made it clear during dinner that he found pushy women disagreeable. 'I'm all for equal rights,' he'd said. 'I'm all for women having careers if that's what they want. But so many of them these days have this obnoxious "take-charge" attitude that drives me up the wall. It's as if they see everyone else as a competitors and need to keep the upper hand.'

'You prefer your women meek and submissive?' Vicki had asked, in sympathy with his complaint but feeling obliged to put in a word on behalf of the home team.

'I prefer them like you.'

'And how is that?'

'Aside from all your more obvious attributes, you possess the wonderful, rare quality of being able to laugh at yourself.'

'So, you like clowns.'

'I like people who don't take themselves too seriously. My impression of you is that you see life as an adventure, not as a war.'

'Uh-oh, there's a fine distinction.'

'An adventure may be fairly similar to a war in its day-to-day events and hazards . . .'

'Like running, ducking, getting your butt shot off . . .'

'Right. But the difference is in a person's attitude. The warrior sees everything as a battle to be fought and won. The adventurer sees it all as experiences – exciting or scary or funny or sad. The adventurer is moving toward a goal, the warrior toward a conquest.'

'So you prefer the Amelia Earharts of the world as opposed to the Joan of Arcs?'

'Right.'

'They both went up in smoke.'

Jack managed to swallow his mouthful of wine in time to avoid spraying it across the table when the laughter burst out.

Vicki found out later that he'd been married to an attorney who'd decided that having children would put a crimp in her career, only to become pregnant due to a faulty IUD. She terminated the pregnancy against Jack's protests, and Jack had divorced her. Which explained a lot.

'You haven't told me much about yourself,' Jack said as he drove out of the restaurant's parking lot.

'What would you like to know?'

'Have you ever been in jail?'

'Would my ten years on a chain-gang count?'

'What were you in for?'

'*Man*slaughter.'

He looked at her through the darkness. 'Have you been married?'

'Not yet.'

'How many proposals have you turned down?'

'What makes you think there were any?'

'You're fishing for compliments.'

'Three proposals,' Vicki said.

'But you were determined to finish your schooling and embark on your career . . .'

She snapped her head toward him. 'Hey, now.'

'Perfectly understandable.'

'Don't jump to conclusions.'

'I *know* how it is. Marriage and children, if any, were relegated to the good old "back burner". Certainly in the future, you told yourself. Before the good old "biological clock" ran out of time. Thirty – there's a fine age to start thinking about a family. By thirty, you'd be settled in your career and might be able to find time for such secondary matters.'

He sounded a little malicious, mostly disappointed. He had her all figured out, and he didn't like what he'd found.

170

'Thanks,' Vicki muttered. She felt cold and hard inside.

What did you think, she asked herself, you'd found Mr Right?

This guy must be one hell of a lawyer. Doesn't know a single goddamn thing about it and decides I'm some kind of super-bitch career broad because I didn't marry the first guy that popped the question.

Well, screw him.

When hell freezes over.

Her eyes burned and the tail-lights of the car ahead went blurry. Her breath suddenly hitched. She turned her face to the side window. She gritted her teeth and willed herself not to sob.

The car slowed. It swung to the curb, and stopped. Vicki wiped her eyes. The houses on the block weren't familiar.

'What'd you stop here for?' she asked.

'You're crying.'

'No, I'm not.'

He put a hand on her shoulder.

'Don't touch me.'

He took the hand away.

'Vicki.'

'Go to hell.'

'Why are you acting this way? For God's sake, all I said . . .'

'Yeah, I sure want to hear it again.'

'I'm *delighted* that you turned down those guys.'

'Delighted, my ass.'

'If you hadn't, you'd be married now, and . . .'

'Would you please take me home?'

'Not until . . .'

She opened the door.

'Okay, okay.'

She closed it, and Jack started the car moving again.

'I didn't mean to upset you,' he muttered,

She turned and stared at him. 'Thought I'd laugh it off? Ha ha? The girl who doesn't take herself seriously? I'm

171

supposed to just write it off as another episode in the Adventures of Doc Chandler? Only I'm not an adventurer, am I? I don't fit into that flattering category anymore. Now I'm the warrior. The ball-chopping Amazon. Well, you and the horse you rode in on, buddy.'

Jack shook his head as if he couldn't believe she was throwing such a fit.

Vicki slugged him in the shoulder.

'Ow! Hey!'

'Amazons like to do that.'

Jack held his shoulder and kept glancing at her as he drove. He said nothing. Neither did Vicki. At last, he stopped the car in front of Ace's house.

Vicki opened her door.

'Wait.'

'What?' she asked.

'I'm sorry.'

'So am I. But that doesn't make it go away. You don't stick a knife in someone and say you're sorry and presto the wound's gone. It doesn't work that way.'

'It hurt, Vicki.'

'Good. It was supposed to. That's what a punch is all about.'

'Not that. I wanted to believe you were different. I didn't want you to be one of *them*. But . . .'

'You don't know what I am.' She climbed out and slammed the door and ran to the house. As she took out her keys, she heard the car speed away.

She turned around. Jack's car vanished around a corner. She leaned against the door, sank down feeling the cool painted wood slide on her back, came to rest on the stiff prickly brush of the doormat, raised her knees and hugged them.

'Bastard,' she muttered.

She'd *really* liked him.

How could he do that, just suddenly lump me in with his

ex-wife and all the bitches of the world because I'd turned down those three proposals?

Shouldn't have told him.

Screw that. I'm not going to lie. If he can't handle it, that's his problem.

I could've explained.

Who gave me a chance? The creep. He didn't wait for any explanation, didn't *need* any, because he knew. Right, he knew. Career comes first, guys, tough luck.

Who needs him, anyway?

Didn't even give me the benefit of the doubt. Didn't even *ask* why I turned them down.

The bristles of the doormat made her rump itch. With a sigh, she stood up. She rubbed her buttocks, then unlocked the door and entered the house.

Ace, on the couch, looked at her and turned off the television with the remote. 'What went wrong?'

The plan had been for Jack to be asked in for drinks – if they didn't go to his place instead – and Vicki would introduce him to Ace, and then Ace would make herself scarce.

The plan had made Vicki nervous and excited all through dinner. She'd imagined how it would go. The tentative first touches, the first kiss, the inevitable moment when Jack would press a hand to a breast. While they ate, while they talked and laughed, the living room scene played in a back corner of her mind. She saw him sliding the straps of her dress down her arms. She worried about Ace coming into the room. Ace wouldn't do that, but still she was reluctant to go on with this in the living room. Did she have the nerve to suggest they move to her bedroom? Maybe she should call a halt before it came to that.

Was she sure that she actually wanted to sleep with this man? Yes, she had decided about the time the chocolate mousse arrived at the table. Yes, but it'd be better to hold off. All the more exciting to build up toward it slowly – see him again and again, moving closer each time as if they were taking a long, romantic trip, stopping here and there to enjoy the sights, growing all the time more eager to reach the final destination but savouring each moment along the way.

That's how it should be. Not from first dinner to bed all in the space of a couple of hours, missing out on the small but wonderful joys of journey.

Jack might not look at it that way, though. Most men didn't. They felt cheated if you didn't go straight to bed with them. Vicki wondered how persistent Jack would be. She wondered if even she would have the willpower to hold off.

As he placed his Mastercard on the small plastic tray with the bill, she wondered if he had a condom. If not, that would settle the problem. She didn't have any (no need, since she hadn't been seeing anyone), and though Ace undoubtedly had a trunk-load somewhere, Vicki certainly had no intention of asking her for one.

She had a diaphragm. She could put it in. But she wouldn't.

It wasn't pregnancy that worried her.

Might get a little embarrassing, but he certainly couldn't accuse her of being a prig or a tease if she called a halt to things for lack of a rubber. Not with AIDS rolling through the country like a plague.

Maybe he carried one, just in case he got lucky.

Well, he didn't get lucky.

Neither did I, Vicki thought.

'We had a disagreement,' she told Ace.

'You're kidding.'

'You don't see him, do you?'

'Well, shit, how'd you manage that?'

'It was easy.'

'He turn out to be an asshole?'

'Not exactly.' Vicki sat down on the couch. She kicked her shoes off, stretched out her legs and rested her feet on the corner of the coffee table.

'Let me guess,' Ace said. 'He's married.'

'Divorced.'

'Ah-ha. And therefore bitter, resentful, suspicious, wary

174

of any involvement because he doesn't want to get hurt again. Who's to say you're not his ex, cleverly disguised?'

Vicki smiled. 'How'd you get so smart?'

'The school of soft knocks, hon.'

'Beneath my clown suit beats the heart of an Amazon career bitch baby-killer.'

'Baby-killer?'

'His ex had an abortion because she decided a kid would mess up her law practice.'

'And Jack wanted the kid?'

'Yeah. So now he assumes I must be the type to pull a stunt like that.'

'Naturally.'

'The bastard.'

'So how was he otherwise?'

'What does it matter?'

'You must've thought he was pretty nifty, or you wouldn't be so upset about this little development.'

'He was okay, I guess.'

'You were crazy about him.'

'Maybe. But . . .'

'Facts of life, hon. Fact one, you're pushing thirty. Fact two, I don't think you're into pimply, vapid teenagers. Fact three, there are no guys out there of a suitable age who aren't carrying some kind of garbage.'

'The good ones are all taken?' Vicki muttered.

'Or *were*. And we know damn well you wouldn't want to mess with the others. You find a guy over about twenty-five who hasn't been married, or at least had a long-term relationship with some gal, he's gotta be totally fucked. One way or another. Take our friend Melvin, for instance.'

'Thanks, I'd rather not.'

'He's available, hasn't been divorced.'

'And I thought I was depressed *before*.'

'I'm trying to cheer you up.'

'And doing a good job of it, too.'

'What I'm getting at, you just aren't going to find a guy

175

who doesn't have a certain load of garbage. If he's available – and isn't totally fucked that he never had a relationship – there has to be a woman in his past who either messed him up or died on him. Either way, you inherit the shit she dumped on him. It goes with the territory.'

'You're so full of understanding, you should go out with him. I'm sure he'd classify you as an adventurer. Just watch out if he asks how many proposals you've turned down.'

'That's the trick question, huh?'

'Was for me.'

'What'd you tell him?'

'Three.'

'Where's the problem? That just shows you're picky.'

'Not to him. The way he sees it, I laid waste to the guys because marriage would conflict with my career goals.'

'Was he right?'

'Good question. Excellent question. He didn't bother to ask it. That's the whole damn reason . . .' Her voice slipped upward. Her eyes flooded.

Here I go again, she thought.

Ace scooted across the couch and put an arm across Vicki's shoulders. Vicki turned to her, held her, wept against her neck. She felt Ace stroking her hair.

She should've been here on the couch in Jack's arms. That was the plan. It was supposed to be Jack, not Ace. They'd be here right now, and she'd be wondering about condoms, and . . . she cried all the harder.

'It's all right,' Ace murmured. 'It's all right.'

'I . . . *wanted* him,' she blurted.

'I know.'

'What's . . . wrong . . . with me?'

'Nothing. Nothing, honey. You're just lonely. It's been too long and you had too many hopes pinned on this guy.'

'The bastard.'

'Look on the bright side.'

'What . . . brights side?'

'You've got me.'

176

'I know. I know.'

'That was supposed to be a joke, hon.'

'Even so . . .'

Ace squeezed her, gently kissed the side of her head. 'We've got each other,' she whispered. 'No joke.'

'I know. God, Ace . . .'

'Just keep your hands off my tits.'

Vicki laughed and choked on a sob.

'Poor thing, you've struck out twice in one night.'

'Bitch.'

Ace eased her away. *Her* eyes were red and wet. Her fingertips stroked the tears off Vicki's cheeks. 'Better?'

Vicki sniffled. 'Yeah. Thanks.'

'So what are you going to do now?'

'Go out and buy a vibrator?'

'Other than that.'

'I don't know.'

'Guess what? Jack's probably not overjoyed by the way things turned out tonight, either.'

'I'm sure.'

'He's probably home alone right now, crying out his own little eyes.'

'I bet.'

'Being a guy, of course, he's more likely getting drunk and crushing beer cans on his face.'

Vicki laughed and wiped her nose.

'Why don't you give him a call?'

'Are you kidding?'

Ace shook her head.

'I don't know.'

'What've you got to lose?'

'What's the point?'

'He's a man. You're crazy about him, or were, till you had this misunderstanding. He's probably breaking a leg trying to kick his ass about all this.'

'Or just grateful he "found me out" and got while the getting was good.'

177

'So call him up, find out which it is.'

'No. Huh-uh. It's *his* problem. Let him do the phoning if he wants. I'm going to bed.'

Vicki stood up.

'Sure you don't want to wait up for his call?'

'There won't be one.'

'Right. He'll probably drop by, instead. Maybe I'll slip into my nightie, just in case.'

'My friend.'

Later, lying in bed, Vicki stared at the dark ceiling. She heard quiet voices and background music from the television. She heard no ring of the telephone, no doorbell. But she stayed awake for a long time, listening.

CHAPTER TWENTY

'Okay,' Melvin said, 'stop the car.'

Charlie stepped on the brake. The car jerked to a halt, throwing Melvin forward. He slapped a hand against the dashboard to brace himself. Then he opened the passenger door.

'Where y'goin'?' Charlie asked, his words slurred by the martinis he'd been gulping for the past hour.

'Nowhere,' Melvin said. 'Sit tight.' The gasoline inside the doctor's medical bag sloshed as he lifted it off the floor and placed it on the seat. He climbed from the car, shut the door, and stepped around to the driver's side. 'Take off your seat belt,' he said.

Charlie unlatched the safety harness and reached for the door handle.

'No, don't get out.'

'Huh?'

'When I say "go", I want you to push the accelerator all

the way to the floor. Drive around the bend as fast as you can, and run into the bridge over the creek.'

'Wha' y'mean, run into it?' He sounded confused.

'Crash against it. As hard as you can. That wall on the side of the bridge.'

'The parapuh?'

'The parapet, right. I want you to hit it full speed.'

The man frowned up at Melvin through the open window and scratched the side of his head. 'Y'wan' me t'crash?'

'That's right.'

'That'd ligely kill me.'

'Nah. Don't be an idiot. You're already dead.'

'Well, yes 'n no.'

'Do it!'

'Wha' for?'

'Because I told you to. I brought you back to life, I could make you dead again if I want. So do what I tell you.'

Charlie sniffed and rubbed a hand under his nose. 'I don' wanna make you mad.'

Melvin patted his shoulder. 'I'm not mad. I just want you to crash into the bridge. I promise you won't get hurt. I have a real good reason for wanting the car smashed, and I'll tell you all about it on the way home.'

'How'll we ge' home, I wreck my car?'

'We'll walk back to my station, and take the tow truck.'

'Oh. Ogay.' Charlie shrugged, then drew the safety harness across his body.

'You don't need that,' Melvin told him.

'Y'wan' me t'jump clear?'

Melvin sighed. Though he heard no cars approaching, he glanced up and down River Road. 'If you jump out, the car will slow down. I want it to hit full-speed.'

'How y'know I won' get hurt?'

'Trust me, Charlie. You're my pal. Besides, I've got big plans for you.'

'Yeah?'

179

'I'll need your help getting me some more gals. And I'll let you take your pick. You can have one all for yourself.'

'Yeah?'

'Right.' Melvin squeezed his shoulder.

Charlie nodded.

Melvin stepped back. 'Ready, set . . . go!'

The engine roared. The Mercedes shot forward. It was powered by gas, not diesel fuel, so it had great pick-up. It rushed around the bend, out of sight beyond the trees. 'Go go go!' Melvin yelled. He clapped his hands, winced at the pain from his bite, and waited for the night to shake with the noise of the collision.

The crash, when it came, didn't shake the night.

Melvin raced around the bend. The car wasn't a ball of flames, as he'd hoped. It just sat there.

He muttered, 'Shit.'

Charlie, holding his forehead, looked out the window. 'How'd I do?' he asked.

'Fine,' Melvin said. 'Just fine.' He stepped to the front of the car. The concrete wall had bent the bumper on the right side, smashed the grill slightly, dented the front of the hood, and broken the headlight. From the look of the damage, Charlie must've hit the parapet going all of ten miles per hour.

Damned old fart.

Charlie swung the door open.

'Stay in there!'

He shut the door.

Melvin went to him.

Charlie looked out the window. He was pressing a handkerchief to his forehead. 'Aren' we gonna go home, now?'

'In a minute.'

Charlie lowered the handkerchief. His forehead had a nice gash. He looked at the bloody cloth, then pressed it to his mouth and began sucking on it.

'Hand me your bag,' Melvin said.

180

Charlie searched, found his medical bag on the floor, and lifted it to the window. 'Wha's in here?' he asked, shaking it.

Melvin didn't answer. He opened it, dumped gasoline onto Charlie's lap, then bent down and hurled the remaining gas under the front of the car.

'Wha' y'doing?' Charlie asked. He sounded worried.

Melvin ignored him. He struck a match and touched it to the moist pavement near the tyre. A faint bluish flame rose and spread over the spill. Melvin stood up. He dropped the burning match into the doctor's bag. With a soft *whup*, the satchel filled with fire. He tossed it onto Charlie's lap.

'Hey now!' Charlie blurted as he went up. One of his flaming arms knocked the bag aside. The door started to open. Melvin kicked it shut.

'Stay,' he ordered.

'Wha's the big idea?' Charlie asked, frowning through the blaze. His shirt was on fire. So were his eyebrows and hair. 'Le' me out, 'fore I'm ruined.'

'Stay.'

Charlie rammed a burning shoulder against the door. The door flew open. He swung a leg out. It wasn't burning yet. Melvin hurled the door shut. There was a soft thud as it struck the man's leg. Melvin tried to hold the door shut, but Charlie reached out the window for him. He lurched away from the blazing arms.

The door flew open again. Charlie, afire from the knees up, climbed out of the car and looked down at himself. He started slapping at the front of his tattered, burning pants and shirt. Then he gave up. He planted his fists on his hips and turned his head toward Melvin. He swept a hand across his face a few times as if trying to bat the flames aside to allow himself to see better. 'You're tryin' t'kill me all over again,' he said.

Melvin glanced at the car. Flames were licking up through the cracks around the hood. Before long, a gas line would burn through.

'Get back in the car,' he said.

'Why, I don' imagine I will, y'damn back-stabbin' s.o.b.'

With that, Charlie raised his blazing arms as if reaching for Melvin, and started limping toward him.

Melvin lurched past the old man and ran to the middle of the bridge. Charlie staggered after him.

The front end of the car was now engulfed in flames.

If only Charlie was still inside!

How could it go this bad? Melvin wondered. He never guessed it would go *this* bad.

Melvin backed against the parapet.

The blazing man, arms out like a movie zombie, stumbled closer and closer. He littered the pavement with flaming bits of cloth. His hair had burned away, leaving his head black and charred. His pants and shirt still burned. Flames still fluttered in front of his face. One eye was a bubbling pool. It burst, and fluid streamed down his cheek.

He was on the walkway, only a few steps from Melvin, when the other eye went.

Melvin sprang away from the parapet. He ran out into the road, then rushed Charlie from the side.

His bandaged hand rammed the man's burning shoulder.

Charlie stumbled sideways. The edge of the wall caught his hip. One leg flew up, but Melvin saw that he wasn't going to tumble over the top without some help. So he grabbed Charlie's ankle and shoved it high. The old man, his weight on the broad top of the parapet, squirmed and kicked as Melvin forced his leg higher and higher.

The car exploded.

Melvin felt a hot blast of wind.

With both hands, he thrust Charlie's ankle toward the sky.

Charlie dropped from the wall.

Melvin leaned over. He watched the burning man twirl and somersault and finally belly-flop into Laurel Creek. With the sound of the splash, Charlie went dark.

Melvin sagged on the wall.

It's over, he told himself. It's probably okay, they'll just think Charlie made it out after the crash, but he was on fire so he jumped into the creek to put the fire out. It'll look like an accident, okay.

'Damn back-stabbing s.o.b.!'

A chill squirmed up Melvin's back.

He cupped hands around his eyes and peered down at the stream. He saw nothing but darkness.

But he heard a quiet splash.

He hurried to the far end of the bridge, stepped off the walkway, and began to make his way down the steep slope. The weeds under his feet were wet with dew. He skidded. He grabbed bushes and saplings to hold himself steady. Halfway down, his feet shot out. He landed hard and slid over rocks and twigs, wincing, gritting his teeth, eyes filling with tears as his back was scratched and gouged. A boulder finally stopped his slide. He lay there with his feet against the rock and took deep, hitching breaths. His back burned and itched. The wetness of his shirt felt good, though. He didn't want to move.

But he knew that he had to get up. He had to find Charlie and finish him off. Fast. People far away might've heard the explosion of the car. Or a motorist might come along.

There was a rock under his left hand when he pushed himself up. It was half buried in the ground. He tugged it loose. It was the size of a softball, but a lot heavier.

He stood, climbed onto the boulder that had stopped him, and crouched. The stream, a few yards below, looked black except for a few flecks of moonlight. He couldn't see Charlie.

Might be anywhere.

A chill of fear spread through Melvin at the thought of the burnt old man sneaking up on him. He told himself not to worry about that.

The old fart's blind. He can't get me.

The thing to worry about was letting him get away. Messed up as he was, he could still talk.

Tell on me.

Melvin climbed down the front of the boulder. He made

183

his way carefully to the bottom of the slope and stepped into the stream. The water was cold. It wrapped him to the knees. The rocks of the stream bed felt slippery beneath his shoes.

He looked under the bridge. Black in there, but light from the other side would've silhouetted Charlie, at least if he was standing. If he wasn't standing . . .

Melvin squatted down. The cold water seized his groin, stole the heat from between his buttocks. It climbed to his chest and made his nipples ache. But he was low enough for the dim glow beyond the bridge to backlight anything more than a few inches above the surface.

A dark lump near the middle made his heart jump. He squinted at it. Charlie's head? Maybe just a rock or the end of a thick branch. Whatever it was, it didn't move. Melvin thought about wading closer to it.

Awfully dark in there.

He felt cold prickles on the back of his neck.

That's not Charlie, he told himself.

Might be.

'Charlie?' he asked. His voice came out husky, not very loud.

No answer.

Melvin stood up and started to turn away from the bridge, but suddenly he didn't have the nerve to turn his back on all that darkness – and whatever was in there. Standing, he could no longer see the thing. He imagined it gliding toward him. He waded backward as fast as he could.

He looked up at the blazing car. It felt good, comforting, to see all that light. He wished he were up there, right now. In the brightness, feeling the warmth.

When he lowered his gaze, he knew it had been a mistake to look at the fire. His night vision was ruined. Before, he could *see*. Not much, but some. Now, except for the fire way up there, he could see nothing at all.

I'm blind, he thought.

As blind as Charlie.

He could sneak up on me easy.

Melvin whirled around and staggered through the water. He knew he should search for Charlie, finish him off somehow, but all he felt now was fear and a need to get away. It seemed best to follow the stream until he was a good distance from the road, then head through the woods and make his way home.

He flinched at the first blast of the fire alert.

It filled the night, loud and piercing, a siren noise that grew and faded and died, then came again.

Even as it roused the volunteers from their sleep, a police car would be speeding toward the bridge.

Whimpering, Melvin started to run downstream. He pumped his knees, but the water dragged at him, held him back. Then his left foot stepped on something that moved under his weight. His foot slipped off it. He stumbled, dropped his rock, gasped and fell. Water splashed up around him. Closed over him. *Arms wrapped his back.*

OH JESUS NO!

He ached to shriek, but held his breath as he was embraced by the thing beneath him on the stream bottom – the thing that had to be Charlie Gaines. It squeezed him hard. It wrapped its legs over the backs of Melvin's legs. Something slithered across his lips. *Charlie's tongue?* Then he felt the edges of teeth against his lower lip and chin. He jerked his head back, heard the clash of the teeth snapping shut.

Tried to bite me!

Just like Patricia.

In that instant, it all changed for Melvin. His stunned horror shattered like a shell that had been enclosing and smothering his mind. He felt the shell burst and fly apart, felt his mind breathe and flex and smile.

Suddenly, he was *Melvin* again, not some whimpering sissy, and the thing embracing him and hugging him and trying to bite him was nothing more than Charlie Gaines. Not a hideous zombie, just an old fart who'd been burnt to a crisp and didn't know when to die.

A charbroiled steak.

185

With teeth.

And now the teeth were scraping the side of Melvin's neck. Though Charlie clung to him like a frantic lover, the embrace was *below* Melvin's arms. That left his hands free. He clutched the side of Charlie's face. It felt slick and crumbly. His thumb found the empty eye socket. He hooked his thumb inside the hole. Like pudding in there, but the bone was a solid ring and when he jerked it with his thumb, Charlie's head turned with it. He forced the head sideways and down. He grabbed the near side of the face with his bandaged hand. Pressing the head against the bottom, he shoved himself upward. Charlie's embrace wasn't powerful enough to hold him. The arms opened just enough. Melvin's shoulders and head broke the surface. He gasped for air.

The fire alert blared again.

He wondered if anyone had arrived at the fire.

As the noise stopped, he heard a car door slam.

He looked over his shoulder. The bridge was out of sight beyond a bend in the stream. High to the right, the leaves of the trees shimmered with firelight.

He almost screamed as Charlie raked his back, splitting his shirt and ripping his skin. Hissing instead, he let go of Charlie's face, tried to keep it down with the thumb of his other hand, and felt along the stream bottom, searching for a rock. He grabbed one. Charlie released Melvin's legs and shoved at his chest. Melvin went backward, thumb pulling out of the socket with quick suck. Now he was on his knees. Charlie rose up in front of him. Blacker than the stream. Water sprayed Melvin's face. 'Gonna kill you,' Charlie said. His voice had a gurgle to it. 'Back-stabbin' s.o.b.'

Melvin slammed the side of Charlie's head with the rock. The blow snapped his head sideways. Melvin struck again. This time, he felt the skull crush and go soft. Charlie started to flop backward. With his left hand, Melvin caught the back of the old man's head. Holding it above the water, he pounded the rock again into the soft place. It made a wet sound as if slapping mud. He hit it again and again.

186

Charlie lay limp beneath him, not moving at all.

So that's how you rekill the fuckers, Melvin thought. Bash their brains in.

He heard voices in the distance behind him. There were sirens, but they sounded much farther away than the voices.

He lowered the rock into the water, and let it fall.

He crawled around Charlie. He found both the man's arms, grabbed his wrists, and began wading backward, towing him downstream.

He did it for a long time.

Sooner or later, he knew, they'd find the body. They'd think Charlie had jumped into the stream to put himself out, had cracked his head open on the rocky bed, and been carried downstream by the current.

They'd think that for a while, at least. A good autopsy would change their minds, for sure. He'd read up on such things. Just one whack in the head, and they might figure it happened when Charlie went off the bridge. But Melvin had clobbered him five or six times. They'd know that wasn't any accident.

They'd figure Charlie'd been murdered. Then they'd find samples of Melvin's skin under his fingernails. They'd know he'd been scratched. They might even learn his blood type.

It was sure getting complicated.

Melvin kept towing Charlie downstream.

The only good solution, he finally decided, was to dispose of the body. If they couldn't find it, they couldn't do an autopsy. They might just stick with the theory that Charlie had jumped off the bridge because he was on fire, and gotten himself swept out to the river and lost.

So how do I get rid of it? he wondered.

That one had him stumped.

Even if he was strong enough to carry Charlie around all night, and he doubted he had the strength to pick him up at all, where would he take him?

He kept pulling Charlie along, certain that he would come up with an answer to the problem. He began to ache from the strain of bending over and wading backward with the body.

Finally, he towed it ashore. He held onto one wrist to keep Charlie from drifting away, and sat on the trunk of a deadfall, feet dangling in the stream. After catching his breath, he listened. He heard the murmur of the stream, the breeze stirring the leaves, birds chirping, mosquitos humming. No human sounds. He guessed that he must be at least half a mile from the bridge. There wasn't much chance of anyone wandering this far downstream. Not for a long while yet.

'What'm I gonna do with you?' he muttered.

'Bah stah s.o.b.'

Melvin squealed.

He flung himself down, hugged Charlie's head to his chest, ripped out broken shards of skull, flung them, dug in, grabbed brains and jerked them out. He squeezed the sodden mass, felt it ooze between his fingers, heard bits of it splash into the stream. He dug in again, pulled out another mushy handful, hurled it away, and scooped out more and threw it.

'Dead yet?' he gasped. 'Huh? Fuckin' pig!'

Charlie sure *seemed* dead, but he'd seemed dead before.

Melvin yanked the man's jaw down. He tugged on the tongue, tried to tear it out by the roots, but his hand slipped off. So he wrenched Charlie around, slammed the back of his head against the tree trunk, held it there and pulled the tongue out as far as he could.

He bent down close to the face. It didn't look much like a face. It looked like charcoal, except for the white teeth and slightly pale shape of the tongue drooping out between them.

Melvin sucked the tongue into his mouth. Drew it in deep. Bit into it, gnashed, and jerked back his head. Moaning, he picked up Charlie's arm and pulled him to the middle of the stream. He let go. The body started to float away.

Melvin opened his mouth. He pulled out the slab of tongue and flipped it into the bushes.

Let them find the damn body.

'That's one dead fucker won't tell no tales,' he said.

Then he waded ashore, entered the woods, and headed for home.

CHAPTER TWENTY-ONE

'You've been a very bad girl,' Melvin said. 'You were supposed to save yourself for me.'

He was standing beside her bed, frowning down at her. He bent over. Vicki couldn't see what his hand was doing, but a motor hummed and the back of the bed began to rise. A hospital bed? As it lifted her, she saw that she wasn't in a hospital. The bed was in the middle of the Community Center auditorium. And as it lifted, the sheet on top of Vicki began to slide. She tried to grab the sheet. Couldn't. Her wrists were bound to the guardrails of the bed.

The sheet drifted down, falling away from her breasts and the huge mound of her belly.

'You see?' Melvin asked. 'You didn't save yourself for me. I'm deeply disappointed in you, Vicki. I love you. You *know* how I love you. How could you let another man have you? How could you let him *knock you up?*'

Impossible, Vicki thought. A false pregnancy, that's what it is.

'I didn't,' she said. 'It's a mistake.'

'Oh, really?' He thumped her belly with his knuckles. It sounded like a ripe watermelon. 'Who's inside there, huh? I know who it isn't. It isn't Melvin junior. Could it be Jack junior?'

'No. It's nobody.'

'We'll see about that.'

'I *can't* be pregnant. I haven't slept with anyone.'

189

'I'm sure you didn't *sleep*. You fucked, though. There's the proof.'

'But I didn't! Honest!'

'Liar, liar, pants on fire.'

It *was* a lie, she supposed. But the last time was so long ago. Bart. He was the last. That was almost three years ago. New Year's Eve. They'd both been smashed, she forgot her diaphragm and he didn't use a rubber ('Like wearing a glove') and then her period was late and she was sick with worry, but then it came. It *did* come. The blood poured out and she wept with relief.

She got her period and, besides, that was *three years ago*. Couldn't be Bart junior. No way. And she never *did* it with Jack.

Unless she forgot.

'We didn't,' she said. 'Jack and I . . . we had a fight.'

Maybe we made up, though.

She could see herself on the couch with him. Or was that Ace? No, it was Jack. He slid the straps of her dress down her arms, lowered the bodice, kissed her breasts. 'Not here,' she said. 'Let's go in the bedroom.'

Vicki realised, with some relief, that she was no longer Melvin's captive in the auditorium. Jack was carrying her down the hallway of Ace's house. He took her into the bedroom. He put her onto the bed. He removed all her clothed, then his own.

She writhed against the smooth bare length of his body, kissing him, moaning as he caressed her all over. Then she was on her back, Jack kneeling between her legs. And she thought, he can't. Not without a rubber. But if I speak up, he'll think I don't want his baby.

I want your baby. I don't want AIDS.

He won't believe that.

I can't tell him. It'll all be over if I tell him.

Then Jack had a foil pack in his hands. He was tearing it open.

Oh, thank God.

190

Oh, Jack, I was so wrong about you.

She raised her hands toward him. She took the condom. She slipped its rubber ring over the head of his penis and slowly unrolled it, feeling his heat and hard thickness through the moist sheath.

Trembling, she whispered, 'I love you. I love you so much.'

'You should've *saved yourself* for me!'

Melvin rammed his arm in all the way to the elbow, jerked it out, and flung the torn-off leg of an infant at her face. 'TELL HIM YOU DIDN'T WANT HIS LITTLE PIGGIE!'

'NO!' she cried out.

Lurched upright and found herself in the bedroom, whimpering, shaking, naked, the sheet bunched at the end of the bed, both her hands clamped tightly between her legs.

Her heart was pounding. Though she panted, she couldn't seem to get enough air. She crossed her legs Indian-style, arched her back, tilted her face up, pointed her elbows at the ceiling, and interlaced her fingers behind her head. Her hair was dripping wet. So was the rest of her body. She felt runnels of sweat trickle down her face, her back, her sides, her chest. Her eyes stung as if daubed with saltwater.

Trying not to think about the nightmare, she let her mind follow a single drop of sweat as it slid past the front of her ear, down her jaw and neck, over her collarbone, onto her breast. It stopped at the tip of her nipple. It hung there, a tiny trembling weight, turning a little chilly, until another bead of sweat came down and joined it. They fell together as a single dollop, made a cool splash on her thigh, and rolled down the side and under it to be blotted out against the bottom sheet.

Soon, Vicki's breathing and heartbeat were nearly normal again. She reached behind her back, found her pillow, and used it to mop her face. Then, she let it drop down through the circle of her arms. She pressed it against the wet chilled skin of her breasts and belly. It felt soft and warm. Cosy. She eased herself down onto the bed. Embracing the pillow gently, she sighed.

191

She could almost fall asleep again.

And dream?

She turned her head. The clock on the nightstand showed 2:08. Three more hours before time to get up. She'd better go ahead and sleep, or she would be wasted tomorrow.

Maybe she'd finished with Melvin for the night. One good dose of the creep, like that, ought to be enough to satisfy whatever damn corner of her mind was so obsessed with him. It had given her the mandatory nightly horror show.

Now, leave me alone, she thought.

The part of her dream about Jack had been a very nice fantasy. Let's have some more of that – just leave Melvin out of it.

Jack.

He hadn't phoned. He hadn't come by.

The hell with him.

The dream-Jack had it all over the real thing. Didn't give me any grief. Actually had a condom. And I put it on him. Lord. I've never done that. Obviously, I'd like to.

Stroking the pillow, she remembered the feel of him.

And flinched at the sudden wail of the fire alert. It climbed to a shriek, and died. A few seconds later, it came again.

All over Ellsworth, the volunteer fireman were being blasted awake.

Along with everyone else.

Including Jack.

Vicki slid her pillow aside, climbed from bed and went to the window. Bending over, she put her hands on the sill. The warm breeze drifted over her skin. The street beyond the yard was deserted except for a few parked cars.

The noise of the fire alert continued, blaring to a high pitch, sinking and dying out, leaving an empty stretch of silence, then rising again.

Jack has to be awake, Vicki thought. Nobody could sleep through this racket.

She wondered if he was thinking about her, wondered if

he regretted the way it had gone. Maybe he only felt relief that he had found her out so quickly.

He's so wrong about me, she thought.

She heard a car engine. Headlights brightened the street. Then a car raced by, a blue light flashing on its dashboard.

One of the volunteer firemen speeding toward the station.

Vicki felt a small pull of guilt.

Here I am, wrapped up in my own petty problem, and someone out there has *real* troubles. A house might be burning down. A car might've crashed. Someone could be injured or dead.

A doctor might be needed.

The ambulance attendants were trained to render first aid at the scene. By the time she could get there, they'd probably be rushing any victims toward the ER at Blayton Memorial.

She wouldn't know where to go, anyway.

Get directions at the fire station, same as the volunteers.

You *might* get there in time to help.

The alternative, she knew, was to return to bed and try to sleep and maybe have another nightmare.

Her heart pumped as if the decision were already made.

'I'm Dr Chandler,' she said through the open window of Ace's Mustang. 'I'd like to help, if I can.'

The man in the driveway of the fire station nodded. 'It's a car fire out on River Road at the Laurel Creek Bridge. You're welcome to head out there, see what you can do.'

She thanked him, backed onto the street, and sped toward River Road.

A car fire at the bridge. Where Steve Kraft piled up, all those years ago. Where he was burnt, where Darlene was decapitated.

Vicki pictured Darlene in the wheelchair, centre stage at the Science Fair, all decked out in her cheerleader suit, neck wrapped to keep her head on – Melvin clamping the jumper cables to her thumbs.

She shook her head as if to jar the image loose, and prayed it wasn't kids in the car.

It probably *would* be kids. Teenagers. Only kids would be up at such an hour, probably drinking beer and hot-rodding it up River Road. They loved to see how fast they could take those curves. Loved to prove they were Big Men.

Big Men risking Death.

Easy to risk it when you don't believe in it. And most teenagers don't. Vicki knew that for a fact. They just didn't believe in death. Not their own. Not even when they committed suicide. Somehow figured they'd go on living, dead or not. The blessing and curse of youth. *They'd be more goddamn careful*.

She swung onto River Road.

She hoped, if this was some kid trying to prove himself, he didn't have his girlfriend along. Or a carload of pals.

Though the road was still empty ahead, Vicki saw red and blue glows flashing through the air, sweeping the pavement, glancing off trees on the far side. She moved her foot to the brake and slowed down. She rounded the bed.

A line of flares crossed the road. Beyond them, both lanes were blocked by cars. In among the cars stood the pump truck. She saw no fire, just a few wisps of smoke, red then blue in the spinning lights of the firetruck and ambulance and police cruisers. Cars and men blocked her view of the wreck.

Striding toward the line of flares was Joey Milbourne. He raised a hand, signaling Vicki to stop. She set her brake. He walked up to her window and bent down. 'Bridge is . . . Vicki?'

'I thought I'd come out and see if I could be of any help.'

'Pull on ahead,' he told her.

She steered between two of the flares, stopped and climbed out with her medical bag.

'I don't think you'll be needing that,' Joey said, nodding at the bag. 'Not yet, anyhow. All we've got so far's the car.'

'No driver?'

194

'Nobody.'

She left her bag on the seat. Walking with Joey through the cluster of cars, she saw men with lights searching the roadside ditches near the bridge, one wandering into the trees. Another man, head down, was on the bridge and seemed to be studying its sidewalk and parapet. Two more were searching the area beyond the bridge.

'The driver's door was open when we arrived,' Joey said. 'Looks as if he just wandered off. Maybe in shock. Doesn't look like much of an impact, but you never know. He might've cracked his head on the steering wheel. Looks like he was on fire, too. We found some charred cloth on the . . .'

'My God,' Vicki muttered as she saw the burnt-out husk of the car. It was all black except for patches of white left by the chemical extinguishers. The tires were flat and smoking. The windows had been blasted out. The hood was up. The trunk lid, torn from its hinges, rested atop the car's roof.

In spite of the destruction, the car's size and squared corners were unmistakable to Vicki.

A Mercedes.

After I'm gone.

Tight and sick inside, she rushed toward the rear of the car thinking, it's not Charlie's, can't be, he's not the only guy in the world with a Mercedes . . . just maybe the only guy in Ellsworth.

She crouched at the bumper. Heat radiated off the wreck. The stench of burnt rubber seared her nostrils. Holding her breath, she squinted at the license plate. The beam of Joey's flashlight found it. In spite of the raised metal, she couldn't make out the numerals through the blackness. She reached out to rub the soot off, scorched her fingers, jerked them back, then slipped her hand inside her T-shirt and, leaning forward, used the fabric like a thin glove to wipe the plate.

It read DOC CG. 'It's Charlie's car,' Vicki said. 'Dr Gaines.'

'Christ,' Joey said.

195

'Got something here!' a voice called from the distance.

Dazed, Vicki stood and followed Joey. They headed for the man in the middle of the bridge. Was he the one who called?

Charlie killed himself, she thought. My God, he killed himself. That's why he turned everything over to me. He had it all planned. I was right, he was sick. Found out he had cancer? Something. Should I tell? Let them come to their own conclusions.

Dimly, she realised that the man on the bridge was another cop.

'What is it, chief?' Joey asked.

Chief Raines? Pollock's replacement?

'Look here,' the chief said, and aimed the beam of his flashlight at the top of the parapet. The concrete was smudged with black. 'He must've come out burning, took a header off the bridge.'

'Dr Gaines,' Joey said.

'Charlie Gaines?'

'His car.'

'Shit.'

Both men leaned against the parapet and shined their flashlights into the ravine. Vicki, stepping up beside Joey, gazed down and watched their pale beams slide over the surface of the stream, over the rocks and bushes along its shores.

'Figured he'd land in the water,' the chief said.

'Must've been crazy.'

'I guess, you're on fire, you'll do most anything.'

Hell, Vicki thought, the *fall* will probably kill you. What was that? A line from some movie. *Butch Cassidy and the Sundance Kid*, that was it. This wasn't a fall like those guys took. Maybe fifty or sixty feet. But she'd been down there many times when she was a kid, and the stream was normally about two feet deep.

'I don't see him,' the chief said.

'Me neither,' said Joey. 'Think he could've wandered off?'

196

'Possible. More likely, the current took him. We'll probably find him hung up a ways downstream.' The chief backed away from the parapet. Some of the searchers were already on their way over. He called in the rest of them. When everyone was gathered on the bridge, he explained that the driver was Charlie Gaines and must've jumped off hoping to douse the flames in the creek. 'He might've survived and made it ashore. So check around in the trees. My guess, though, we'll find him downstream.'

'Think he might be alive?' asked a white-shirted ambulance attendant.

'Won't know that till we find him, will we? Let's get moving.'

The group split up, men heading for the ends of the bridge.

Vicki stayed with the chief and Joey as they walked back toward the wreck. 'I'll go on down and direct the search,' the chief said. 'Milbourne, you stay up here and control the scene. We don't want a bunch of rubber-neckers showing up and mucking around.' He looked at Vicki. 'What's your business here, young lady?'

'This is Dr Chandler,' Joey said.

'I'm Dr Gaines's partner,' she explained. 'I'd like to help in the search.'

His eyes narrowed. 'You do get around.'

What does he mean by that? she wondered.

'I heard the fire alert and thought I might be able to help.'

'She's the one who identified the car as Charlie's,' Joey pointed out.

'I don't suppose you were *with* him tonight?'

'No,' Vicki said. 'I saw him at about five-thirty, just before I left the clinic.'

'You weren't *drinking* with him at the Riverfront?'

'No, I . . .'

'You didn't hear Melvin Dobbs threaten Charlie's life, did you?'

Vicki felt heat rush to her face. 'Oh,' she said, 'terrific.

197

I'm some kind of a nut because I reported a threat on Pollock's life.'

'And now you're here. What is it, some kind of a hobby with you to butt into police business?'

'I'm a *doctor*,' she said, pushing her voice out so it sounded firm, so it wouldn't reveal how timid and bitter she suddenly felt. 'I came out here to offer my assistance in case anyone needed medical attention.'

'Well, pack up your Bandaids and go on home, *doctor*.'

'I'd like to help in the search.'

'I'm sure you would. Thing is, we don't need you down there gumming up the works. So trot on home.'

'He's my *friend*.' This time, she couldn't stop her voice from trembling.

'Milbourne, get her out of here.'

'Yes, sir.'

With that, the chief stepped past Vicki and strode toward the end of the bridge.

'You'd better leave, now,' Joey said.

'He thinks I'm some kind of a *groupie!*'

'He's just upset, that's all. He's under a lot of pressure over the Pollock mess, and to have something like this happen right on top of it . . .'

'Can't I just wait up here till they find Charlie?'

'I'm afraid not.'

'Well, geez . . .'

'Go on home, now. There's nothing for you to do here. I'll notify you as soon as we find him.'

She stopped at the end of the parapet where the front of Charlie's car was tight against the concrete. Peering over the side, she saw Chief Raines on the wooded slope. He was nearly down to the bank of the creek. Other men were roaming the shore, others wading through the water. The beams of their lights swept and darted.

She turned to Joey. 'Why don't you just lend me your flashlight, and . . .'

'Want to get me in trouble with the chief?'

198

'Damn it, don't be such a wimp.'

Joey grabbed her arm. Not gently. 'Time to move on out, honey.'

He led her toward her car. Lifting on her arm so her feet barely touched the pavement.

'Let go of me!'

He didn't.

When they reached Ace's Mustang, he jerked the door, open, swung her around it and released her arm. It felt hot where his fingers had pressed into her flesh.

Vicki climbed into the car. As she moved her medical bag to the passenger seat, Joey threw the door shut.

'Go,' he said.

She started the car, made a tight U-turn, and sped away. Her heart was thudding. She panted for air. She was trembling with rage and humiliation.

They'd shooed her off like a stray dog.

What's *wrong* with those men?

Joey had been okay until the chief took off after her. Why didn't he stick up for her? That was easy. He's chicken. What didn't make sense was the chief's attitude. He had her all figured out as a nuisance, just on the basis of whatever Joey had told him about their reporting Melvin's threat against Pollock.

What were we supposed to do, keep it to ourselves?

Even if it didn't lead anywhere (and Vicki would bet they didn't bother to check Melvin out), the chief should've appreciated getting any kind of information about the killing. Instead, he seemed to look at it as an intrusion.

A couple of broads trying to tell him how to run his investigation.

So I show up and he dumps on me. I could've helped look for Charlie. I'm another body, damn it. I've got eyes. I'm not blind, even if I am a woman.

That's the crux of it right there, Vicki realised. I'm a woman.

That's why I couldn't help look for Charlie. That's why

199

they ignored the tip about Melvin's threat. I'm just a meddling broad who gets her kicks by butting into *their* business.

Some kind of flake.

What are all the men in this town, woman-haters?

Not Charlie, she thought.

Oh Charlie, *what happened to you?*

CHAPTER TWENTY-TWO

She parked the car in Ace's driveway, then went into the house. No lights were on. She left them off, and made her way through the darkness to her bedroom.

She knew there was no point trying to sleep. She would just toss and turn, wide awake, worrying about Charlie and reliving all the rotten things that had happened during the past few hours: the fight with Jack; the nightmare; the horrible scene at the bridge and knowing that Charlie, on fire, had leaped for the creek; and on top of all that, the humiliating encounter with the police chief. Enough to keep her awake for *days*.

She peeled off her sooty T-shirt, took a fresh one from the drawer, and put it on. Then, she looped the chain with the house key and whistle over her head.

Running would help. It always helped.

On her way back through the house, she wondered if she shouldn't stay and wait for Joey's call. He'd promised to let her know, when they found Charlie. But that might be an hour from now. Or never. No point hanging around.

Besides, the news, when it came, was almost sure to be bad.

Vicki stepped outside. On the sidewalk in front of the house, she did her stretching exercises. Then, she ran.

She ran fast, darting her legs far out, pumping her arms, feeling the warm air rush against the bare skin of her face and arms and legs. She had no destination in mind, but when she found herself on Center Street racing northward past the deserted shops, she remembered a few mornings ago when she followed Central to its junction with River Road and turned back at the Laurel Creek Bridge.

She thought, what if I stick to the shoreline? I'll come to the Laurel Creek inlet. I can follow the creek upstream and look for Charlie without anyone interfering.

It hurt to think about Charlie. She wanted to block him out of her mind, to block out everything, to run and, for a white at least, to be free.

But she wondered if she *could* reach the inlet. There was private property along the shore beyond the north end of town. There might be fences blocking her way.

I could swim around them, she thought.

Ahead was the park. She left the sidewalk and ran on the grass. It felt soft and springy under her shoes.

Go down to the beach and follow the shoreline. Might work.

What's the point, though? Charlie wouldn't have *walked* toward the river. If he survived the jump from the bridge, he would've climbed back up to the road. If he's down-stream, he got carried there by the current.

I wouldn't find him alive.

The searchers may have already found him.

I owe him a try.

Vicki shortened her stride as she started down the slope toward the public beach. Gazing beyond the sand, she saw the dim shape of a fence stretching down to the water's edge.

I can wade around it, she told herself. I can swim all the way to the inlet, if I have to. It's probably no more than half a mile.

At the bottom of the slope, she picked up her pace. She came to the beach. She raced across the moonwashed sand.

'Vicki?'

She recognised the voice.

Her head snapped to the left.

Jack was speeding down the silvery ramp of the slide. He flew off its end and ran toward her.

Vicki stopped and faced him. He was barefoot and wearing only shorts. He stopped a few steps away from her.

'Early for your morning jog,' he said.

'What are you doing here?'

He shrugged his broad shoulders. 'I don't know. I couldn't sleep. I was just lying in bed, thinking about you. When I heard the fire alarm, I decided to get up. I just wandered for a while, and ended up here. I guess I hoped you'd show up, sooner or later.'

'What for?' she asked. Her heart was thumping. She felt as if she couldn't get enough air.

'Oh, Vicki.' He started to raise his arms toward her, then let them fall to his sides. He shook his head. 'I'm sorry. I was wrong to jump on you. You're not Gloria. You're so different from her that . . . I guess I've still got a lot of anger in me, and for just a minute there I let it out at *you*. I shouldn't have done that.'

'I'm *not* Gloria.'

'I know.'

'I'm not an Amazon career bitch.'

'Partly Amazon, maybe.' As he said that, a corner of his mouth tipped up and he rubbed his right arm just below the shoulder. 'You pack a pretty mean wallop.'

He turned sideways and pointed. His skin, milky in the moonlight, had a faint smudge of darkness like a shadow where she had punched him.

'I did that?' Vicki asked.

Reaching out, she let her fingertips drift over the contusion. The dark area felt slightly warmer than the skin around it.

'I'm sorry,' she said.

'It's all right.'

'I shouldn't have hit you.'

202

'It was assault and battery, you know. But don't worry, I won't press charges.'

'The cops would love it if you did.' She slid her hand down his arm and took hold of his hand. 'The chief seems to hate my guts. He just gave me the bum's rush. All I wanted to do was help look for Charlie.'

'Charlie Gaines?'

'He's missing. That's what the fire alert was about. He crashed on River Road. They think he was on fire and jumped off the bridge into the creek, but they couldn't find him. I wanted to help and they kicked me out.'

Jack squeezed her hand. 'Why wouldn't they let you help?'

'I don't know. But I thought I might sneak in the back way and search upstream. The inlet's not far from here.' She nodded toward the fence at the boundary of the beach.

'Want some company?' Jack asked.

'I'd like that.'

'Lead on. I'll try to keep up.'

He released Vicki's hand. She whirled away and rushed across the beach. She heard him running behind her. Then, he caught up and ran at her side.

She angled toward the end of the chainlink fence. A sign near the final post read, 'Public Prohibited Beyond this Point.' The water splashed up her legs as she rounded the post. On the other side, she leaped onto the bank and hurried across the back yard of a cottage. The windows of the cottage were dark. Ahead, a pier stretched into the river. An outboard floated alongside it.

Jack caught up to her, then passed her.

She stared at his wide, pale back, at the dark seat of his shorts, at his strong legs pumping out.

And it felt so good to be with him.

Vicki could hardly believe they were suddenly together. It had happened so fast. One moment, she was alone and Jack little more than a bitter memory: the next, he was back and she felt closer to him than *before* their fight in the car.

He was waiting for me, she thought. Hoping I'd show up.

She followed him past the pier, past a small beach, and through a gap in a hedge at the far side of the yard. They came out behind a two-story house with a wooded lawn. A car tire was suspended from one of the limbs. This house had a larger beach area than the cottage they had left behind. A canoe rested, hull up, on the sand. Some distance ahead was a dock with a boathouse on the other side.

Jack turned toward the beach. He came to a stop beside the canoe, crouched down and flipped it over, uncovering a pair of paddles that had been left beneath it.

'What're you doing?' Vicki whispered.

'Let's borrow it. We'll get there in no time, if we take it.'

'Are you kidding? It isn't ours.'

'This is an emergency. They'll understand. Besides, they'll never find out we took it. Probably.'

Vicki glanced toward the house. She could only see bits of it through the trees.

Jack handed a paddle to her. He kept the other for himself, and lifted the prow. Vicki grabbed the stern. The aluminum canoe felt nearly weightless as she hurried behind Jack, rushing it down the beach.

She half expected someone to shout from the house and come running out to stop them. But no one did.

They waded into the river and eased the canoe down. Jack held it steady while Vicki climbed in. As she knelt and dipped her paddle into the water, Jack swung himself aboard.

She looked over her shoulder.

We're getting away with it!

She felt a strange thrill. She'd never stolen anything before.

We're not stealing it, she reminded herself. Just borrowing it. And this is an emergency.

Though she hadn't been in a canoe for years, she used to spend long hours in them exploring the river's shoreline and islands. It felt so familiar: the narrow wooden slats under her knees, the paddle in her hands, the weight of the water against the blade as she swept it back, the sound of the drops

204

spilling away when she lifted the paddle out, the soft rushing lap of the river under the hull as the canoe glided forward.

Jack acted as if he too, had spent much of his youth in such a craft. He knelt upright, drawing his paddle through the water with smooth, graceful strokes, leaving the steering to Vicki, seeming to know that the job was hers and realising immediately that she was good at it.

She matched his strokes. Soon, the canoe was speeding over the calm suface of the river. When they were out beyond the end of the pier, she turned them northward.

The air was warm. The river was calm, black except for silvery moonlight sprinkled across its ripples. Vicki saw no boat lights. She heard no motors. There seemed to be no one else on the river. A few specks of light glimmered along the far shore. The stillness and beauty gave her a hollow feeling of regret.

If only she were out here with Jack and no terrible errand. They could paddle out to the middle of the river and let the canoe drift. She would go to him. He would put his arms around her. They would kiss. They would lie down in the bottom of the canoe . . .

Some other night, she told herself. Maybe next week or next month. All of this will be a bad memory, and we'll come out here for no other reason than to be with each other.

She pictured Charlie floating dead in the creek, and felt a hot jolt of guilt.

We're out here for you, Charlie. It doesn't matter about me and Jack.

Not tonight.

She turned her face to the left. They were gliding past the dock of the last house before the woods. In the distance, she saw a point of land. She remembered from long ago that it reached into the river just this side of the Laurel Creek inlet.

Holding the paddle straight down beside the canoe, she twisted its blade against the flow. Water swooshed and bubbled up. The canoe turned. When it was aimed toward the point, she resumed stroking.

Soon, they slipped past the jut of land.

'It's just ahead,' Vicki said.

Jack, nodding, rested his paddle across the gunnels.

Vicki eased the canoe forward. She peered into the darkness of the bushes and trees along the bank, but didn't see the narrow opening until Jack pointed. Sweeping the canoe toward it, she heard the soft rush of the running water. She gave the paddle a final, strong pull.

As the canoe glided closer to the inlet, she scanned the woods. She saw no lights. She heard voices faint with distance.

Either the searchers hadn't yet come this far, or they'd already reached the river and turned back.

Jack slipped into the river. It covered him to the waist. Gripping the prow with one hand, he waded ashore and dragged the canoe partway up the embankment near the edge of the creek. He crouched and held it steady for Vicki. Staying low, she scurried to the front. Jack gave her a hand as she climbed out. It was wet. Together, they pulled the canoe farther up the low slope.

'Now what?' he whispered.

'I guess we walk upstream.'

His big hand closed around her forearm. They stepped around a cluster of bushes and entered Laurel Creek. Its rocky bed felt slick under her shoes. As they approached the middle, the water level rose above her knees.

'Too bad we don't have a flashlight,' Jack said.

'I hadn't really planned to do this.'

Side by side, they waded slowly forward. The creek and its shores were dark except for a few flecks of moonlight. Vicki heard the voices of the searchers, but they seemed no closer than before. She couldn't make out the words.

Though she often checked the black path of the creek in front of her, she concentrated on studying the shores. If Charlie's in the water, she thought, we won't have to see him. We'll feel him. This stretch of the creek was so narrow that they wouldn't be able to miss the body. It would strike their legs.

And she prayed that Charlie was not in the water. They were too far downstream from the bridge.

If he's still alive, she thought, he's either on the shore or the searchers already found him.

Her heart gave a sudden lurch as she spotted a pale shape floating toward her. Jack squeezed her hand, then let go. He hurried toward the thing. 'Just a branch,' he whispered.

'Thank God.'

He bent down and pushed it. The branch slid out of the way, scraping against rocks along the shore.

They continued walking up the creek.

While Vicki's eyes roamed the dim shapes of bushes and rocks alongside the stream, she listened for the searchers. Minutes went by when all she heard were birds and insects, an occasional frog, the slurp of their own legs moving through the water.

Then, a voice would come from the distance ahead. Another would usually answer. Then, more silence.

The voices seemed *farther* away then before.

That pleased Vicki, at first. She certainly didn't want to run into any of the men from the chief's party. But she began wondering what it meant.

It could mean, she decided, one of two things: either Charlie had already been found, or the searchers had finished hunting downstream.

She hoped that they had turned back because Charlie had been found. Found alive.

But what she believed, in spite of her hopes, was that the men had made their way to the river's edge without finding him. Some time before she and Jack arrived. Once he was in the river, there was no point in continuing the search. The body would be lost. Until it washed ashore somewhere, maybe miles downriver. Or until it decomposed and the gases sent the bloated corpse popping to the surface. So the men had given up and headed back for the bridge.

We might as well quit, she thought.

No. Too soon.

Jack made a quiet 'Hmm?' He waded to the right. Vicki stayed beside him, peering at the shore, wondering what he'd noticed. He stopped and looked down. Vicki saw the vague shape of a cigarette butt on top of a dark rock.

'My hands are wet,' he whispered. 'Do you mind?'

Vicki shrugged, unsure of what he meant.

He pressed his right hand against the front of her T-shirt. She felt it rub across her belly, and she realised he was using her shirt as a towel because he wore no shirt, himself, and shorts were damp. He turned his hand over, rubbed the back of it against her, then clenched the shirt in his fist. When his hand went away, she felt the moisture it had left on the fabric. And she still felt his touch like a warm, exciting after-image.

He bent down. He picked up the remains of the cigarette. He rolled it between his thumb and forefinger. 'Fresh,' he whispered. 'Filter's still wet.'

'So the searchers got this far,' Vicki said. It confirmed her suspicions.

'They might've missed him, I guess.'

'They've got lights.'

'Do you want to turn back?' Jack asked, and tossed the cigarette into the bushes.

'I don't know.'

'It's fine with me if you want to keep looking.'

'We'd just be going over ground they already searched.'

'It's up to you,' he said.

'I guess there's not much point.'

'Maybe they found him.'

'Maybe.'

Jack took a step closer to Vicki. He gave her upper arm a gentle squeeze, then kept his hand there. 'I wish there was something we could do for Charlie.'

208

'We did all we could.'

'He means a lot to you, doesn't he?'

Vicki nodded. 'He helped me so much. I was his patient, you know. He was my doctor when I was a kid. When he found out I was interested in medicine, he kind of took me under his wing. I'd go over to the clinic after school, sometimes, and he'd show me things and we'd talk.'

'I suppose he must be like a father to you.'

'I never needed a father figure . . . have a perfectly good real one, you know? Charlie and I were never even all that close. We were friends, but it was pretty much on a professional level. He was always encouraging me.'

'He must've cared a lot for you,' Jack said, lightly caressing her arm.

'More than I ever suspected. I wish . . .' Her throat tightened. 'I wish I'd paid more attention to him. I should've seen him outside the clinic, had dinners with him, or . . .'

'Does he have a family?'

'He's divorced. He never had children. He was all alone, and I just ignored him.'

'You joined him in his work,' Jack said. 'It sounds as if that's exactly what he wanted all along. I think you fulfilled whatever hopes he had for you. You shouldn't feel guilty for not doing more.'

That's a good way to look at it, she thought. 'He never acted as if he . . . I mean, I went my way and he went his. I don't know what he did when he left the clinic. He had *lots* of money, a beautiful home. He was fairly handsome for a man his age. So I just assumed he was getting along fine. I never worried about him. I hardly gave him any thought at all. I should've.'

Jack caressed the side of her face. 'Do you want to keep looking?'

'I don't think so.'

'We'll go back to town and find out what's happening. For all we know, Charlie's made it through all this. He might be in a hospital room, right now, giving orders to the nurses.'

'That'd be nice,' Vicki said. 'If only it's true.'

They turned away from the shore. Vicki held his hand. Side by side, they waded down the middle of the creek. Though she had no more hopes of finding Charlie, she scanned the darkness anway.

I should've cared more about him, she thought. I should've made sure he was happy. He wasn't a father figure to me, but was I like a daughter to him? Maybe. Probably. He did what a father does for a daughter: encouraged me, taught me, gave me advice and guidance . . . paid for my schooling.

God, Charlie, I'm sorry.

You fulfilled whatever hopes he had for you.

Did I?

If you're still alive, Charlie. I'll make it up to you. I will.

Soon, she saw the moonlit river through a break in the trees ahead.

'Almost there,' Jack said.

'I'll be glad when we're rid of the canoe.'

'We can go to my place, and I'll drive you over to the bridge.'

'Okay.'

That's the one good thing about all this, she thought. Being with Jack. If only the rest hadn't happened . . .

We'll be together a lot from now on, she told herself, and squeezed his hand.

He looked at her. She wished she could see his face.

They waded forward. As they neared the mouth of the creek, the view of the river widened.

And Vicki saw the canoe.

On the river.

Twenty or thirty feet out.

Drifting away.

CHAPTER TWENTY-THREE

'Oh no,' Vicki muttered.

'How the hell . . . ?'

She let go of Jack and lurched forward. He grabbed her arm. 'No. Wait here. I'll get it.' He backed away, held up a hand signalling her to stay put, then swung around and hit the creek in a low dive. Water exploded up. Vicki trudged after him, watching him swim through the last of the narrow channel and into the river.

Wait here?

I don't think so.

She glanced at the slope where they had left the canoe. Saw no one. But *somebody* had been there. The canoe hadn't just slipped into the river. Someone had pushed it. And might be nearby.

Goosebumps swarmed over her skin as she searched the darkness of the slope.

She looked at Jack. He was halfway to the canoe.

She threw herself forward, hit the water flat, knifed through it, glided up to the surface and began to swim. Lifting her head, she snatched a breath. She spotted Jack. 'Slow down', she called.

He stopped swimming. She saw only his head while he waited for her to catch up.

'I would've come back for you,' he said.

'I know,' she told him, treading water. 'I just didn't want to stay there alone. Somebody *did* this, you know.'

'The possibility occurred to me.'

She saw that the canoe was drifting farther away. 'We'd better get a move on,' she said.

They swam for it.

Jack reached the canoe first. He ducked beneath it. Vicki realised he intended to hold the other side of the vessel to keep it steady while she boarded. 'Okay,' he said. 'Climb on in.'

Stretching out an arm, she grabbed the gunnel. She pulled herself forward, lifted herself high enough to seek Jack's fingers curled over the aluminum gunnel, and glimpsed something large and dark lying in the bottom of the canoe.

A man?

'Jaaaaack?' Her voice came out tight and rising.

'What's . . . ?' His head came up. 'Holy Jesus,' he muttered. 'Is it Charlie?'

'I don't know. I can't . . .'

The thing in the bottom of the boat sat up fast and smashed a forearm across Jack's face. Jack flew backward. The canoe rocked toward Vicki as she heard a hard splash. She tried to thrust herself away. A hand grabbed her hair. Yanked her up. For a moment that seemed to last a long time, she hung there, the canoe skidding on its side about to capsize, her scalp burning with pain, her waist against the gunnel, water rushing around her legs as the canoe slid, her gaze on the black moonlit face that *couldn't* belong to Charlie.

Charred. Cracked. Holes where his eyes should be. No hair. One side of the head gaping open as if his skull had And in the lasting moment, she thought, It's Charlie. Has to be. Alive!

She felt no elation. Just pain and shock and terror.

What's he doing alive with that kind of head trauma?

Why'd he hit Jack? Why's he *doing* this?

Jack might drown!

She swung a fist up to strike at the outstretched arm, but he twisted away and she felt herself rise up and drop forward. The shift in weight made the canoe drop from its wild tilt. It rocked from side to side, the gunnel pressing into her thighs, raising and lowering them. She felt air on her kicking legs, then water, than air again. Her face rested on something that felt cool and wet and crusted. She knew it was Charlie's burnt leg.

With a gurgling sound that might have been a laugh, Charlie shoved her hip. Her legs scooted along the gunnel. She twisted and squirmed, trying to get away from him. He

212

pushed her, turned her as she struggled. At the moment Vicki's legs dropped into the canoe, he threw her onto her back.

She fell sprawling on top of him.

She bucked and writhed. He held her down.

'Charlie!' she gasped. 'Charlie, it's me! It's Vicki! Let go! What are you *doing?*'

He yanked her T-shirt up until it was stopped by her armpits.

Vicki grabbed the gunnels with both hands and tried to pull herself up.

Charlie tore at her bra. The clasp between the cups gave way. She felt his crisp hands close on the bare skin of her breasts.

'No!' she cried out. 'Charlie.'

He answered with a gurgle.

She grabbed one of the fondling hands and pulled it away. Just for an instant. Then, there was a damp crumbling sound, and a husk of burnt flesh slid off in her hands. With a squeal, she flung it away. Charlie's hand clasped her breast again. Now, it felt warm and slick and she knew it was blood and tendon and muscle caressing her.

His other hand went to her belly and moved down. It pushed beneath the waistband of her shorts.

'NO!' She grabbed it.

Teeth clamped down on her shoulder.

She shrieked.

The canoe lurched, tipped onto its port side, and Vicki threw herself that way. The canoe flopped, spilling her into the river with Charlie on her back. His hands stayed where they were. His teeth kept their painful grip on her shoulder.

His weight pressed her downward as if he had no buoyancy at all.

Vicki, with only an instant to react before the water shut over her, had only managed to snatch a little air. Her lungs ached to inflate.

She kicked and flapped her arms, struggling to stop her descent. But Charlie kept sinking her.

His teeth ground into her shoulder.

His one hand slid to her breast and crawled over it like a huge, scabby spider.

The other, inside her shorts, moved to her hip. Fingertips scraped her skin. She felt a quick tug. The thin elastic band of her panties broke.

She grabbed Charlie's wrist with both hands. She jerked it hard, forcing the hand upward. It didn't let go of her panties. The crotch dug into her, but she kept pulling. The fabric split. Charlie's hand came out from inside her shorts and up against her belly. She twisted his wrist, turned his arm away.

Something more than Charlie's weight thrust her down. Slimy weed licked her skin.

She suddenly felt his head jerk. His teeth ripped her shoulder and let go. His clenching hand was torn away from her breast. Shoving his other arm away, she rolled from under him, tumbled through the clinging fronds, started to rise and kicked madly for the surface.

A hand grabbed the back of her right thigh.

NO!

But instead of dragging her downward, it shoved her up and went away.

Her head broke the surface. She filled her burning lungs with air, saw that she was facing the shore, whirled around and spotted the overturned canoe and swam for it as fast as she could. Moments later, hearing a splash behind her, she slipped onto her side and looked back.

'Go!' Jack yelled. He began swimming after her.

She wanted to wait, but she pictured Charlie coming up out of the depths, reaching for her feet. So she raced for the canoe. She slowed down only long enough to grab a floating paddle. Pressing it against her body, she side-stroked using her free arm until she reached the canoe. She held the prow and looked back.

Jack was moving fast.

She swept her eyes over the rippling surface of the river all around him. No sign of Charlie.

Again, she imagined his black, charred body coming at her from below. She fought an urge to scramble onto the canoe's upturned hull.

Jack flung his arms around the other end of the canoe. 'Let's . . . flip her,' he gasped. 'Count of three.'

Vicki let the paddle float beside her. She slipped her hands beneath the submerged point of the prow.

'Ready?'

'Yes!'

'One, two, *three!*'

She hurled the canoe upward, turning it and sinking herself. Under water, she heard a metallic smacking sound. She bobbed up. Her shoulder bumped the canoe and she winced as pain exploded from the bite. She eased away and looked. The canoe was riding a little low, but upright. She swam to the paddle, made her way back to the canoe, and tossed it inside. It splashed.

'Get in,' Jack said. He held the other side. Just like before.

Vicki peered over the gunnel. The bottom of the canoe was awash with water, but Charlie wasn't there. She flung herself over the side, landing on her back with a splash. When she got to her knees, she saw Jack a distance away. The second paddle floated several yards ahead of him.

'Don't bother!' Vicki yelled. 'Get back here!'

He kept swimming toward it.

At least he's going in that direction, she thought. Toward the middle of the river. Away from the place where they'd left Charlie.

Vicki picked up her paddle. She swung her head around, first scanning the area near the canoe, then searching the river between her and the shore.

She almost wished she *would* spot Charlie.

Better to see him, even nearby and swimming closer, than not to know where he was.

215

Vicki hobbled astern on her knees. She leaned forward, slipping her paddle into the water, and drew it back.

Half expecting Charlie to grab it.

But he didn't.

The canoe moved sluggishly forward, turning.

Jack, she saw, already had the other paddle and was coming toward her. She stroked again. The prow swung farther and pointed at him.

'Hurry!' she shouted.

The distance closed.

Still no sign of Charlie.

Jack hurled the paddle into the canoe and flung himself in after it. He scurried to his knees. He jabbed the paddle down into the river and swept it back.

Vicki turned the canoe southward.

Soon, they were rushing over the river. The water inside the canoe slopped this way and that, splashing up Vicki's thighs, sweeping away, coming at her again like a small tide, rolling from side to side.

She paddled as hard as she could. She huffed for air. Every muscle from her neck to her calves felt stiff and heavy. The narrow slats of the floorboards punished her knees. The bite on her shoulder burned. But she dug the paddle deep and jerked it back and stretched forward and rammed it in again. Again. Again.

She didn't speak. She didn't look to see if Charlie was near. She stared at Jack's bent back and blinked sweat out of her eyes and kept on paddling.

At last, they rounded the end of the pier. Vicki steered toward the beach. The canoe sped alongside the pier. The instant it hit the beach, Jack leaped out. He dragged it a few feet up the sand. Vicki jumped over the side. She lifted her end. They ran the canoe to the place where they had found it. When they overturned it, the trapped water slopped out. They tossed the paddles under the canoe.

Vicki in the lead, they dashed across back yards. The water in her shoes made squeeshing sounds, and she was surprised to realise that she still had them on. All that swimming, and she'd been wearing sneakers. Could've gone so much faster without them. But she was glad to have them, now.

Finally, she rushed into the river and rounded the fence at the border of the public beach. She splashed her way ashore.

Safe on the beach, she hitched up her sagging wet shorts, then bent over and held her knees and tried to catch her breath.

Jack flopped onto his back.

'Get up,' she gasped. 'You'll tighten up. Gotta keep moving.'

With a moan, he pushed himself off the sand.

Heeding her own advice, Vicki straightened up. She walked in circles, back arched, head thrown back, hands on hips. Jack staggered backward, watching her. She was suddenly aware of her broken bra hanging loose from her shoulders. She felt one cup like a wadded hanky above her left breast. The other was crumpled beneath her armpit. The way her sodden T-shirt clung to her skin, she probably looked almost naked. She realised that she didn't care.

She only cared that she was away from Charlie. She was safe. Jack was safe.

'What's that on your shoulder?' Jack asked.

She glanced down at her shoulder. The T-shirt there was dark. 'He bit me,' she said.

'Jesus.'

'Are *you* all right?'

'My head hurts,' he said.

She went to Jack. She rested her hands on his sides. 'I was afraid you might drown.'

'I was never out cold,' he said. 'But the boat . . . it was pretty far off when I came up for air. I had a hard time catching up to it.' He moved closer to Vicki. His arms went around her and he eased her against him. She felt the rise and fall of his chest, the thumping of his heart.

'Thank God you're all right,' she whispered.

217

'Did he hurt you?'

'Not so much. Just the bite.' She squeezed Jack hard. 'It was so *horrible*. He tore my clothes. He . . . *pawed* me.'

'Was it Charlie?'

'Yes.'

'I don't get it. Why would Charlie . . . ?'

'He acted crazy. I don't know. Did you see him?'

'Not really. Just a glimpse.'

'He was . . . all burnt. Third degree burns.' A tremor passed through her. 'Jack, his skin was . . . incinerated. And he didn't have any eyes. And his head . . . one side was completely caved in. I mean, he should've been *dead*. Nobody could survive that kind of head injury.'

'Apparently, Charlie did.'

'What'll we do?'

'About what?' Jack asked.

'About him.'

Jack was silent for a while. His hands slowly rubbed her back. 'I'm in no mood to tell the search team, that's for sure. He could've killed us both. He *hurt* you. The hell with him. He's probably drowned by now, anyway. Or died of his injuries. Either way, good riddance. Let the bastard wash ashore. Or disappear forever. I don't care. I know he was supposed to be your friend, but . . .'

'That was Charlie, but it wasn't my friend. I *told* him who I was. He went ahead, anyway, and . . . he would've raped me, Jack. That's what he wanted to do. That burnt-up . . . he wanted to *rape* me.'

Shuddering, she pressed her face to the side of Jack's neck. He held her tight for a long time. Slowly, the tremors passed. Vicki's strength seemed to seep out of her. Only Jack's stout body kept her from slumping to the sand.

'Do you think you can walk as far as my house?' he asked.

'I'd rather go home. To Ace's. You'll come with me, won't you?'

'You bet.'

'Good,' she said. She kept her arms around him. 'In a while?'

CHAPTER TWENTY-FOUR

'Would you like a drink, or something?' Vicki asked as she turned on a lamp in the living room.

'That can wait until you've taken care of yourself,' Jack said.

'I'll hurry.'

'Do you have an old towel for me to sit on?' he asked, plucking at a leg of his damp shorts.

Nodding, she headed for the hallway. She thought how odd it was that Jack had ended up here in the house tonight, after all. She felt a small stir of excitement, but it was blunted by the weariness of her body and the leaden weight in her mind left by the encounter with Charlie.

When she reached the linen closet, she took down her beach towel. She carried it back into the living room, where Jack waited. She gave it to him. 'You might want to get out of your shorts,' she said. 'You can wear this, if you want. We haven't got a robe or anything large enough for you. I can put your stuff in the drier a little later.'

'I'm fine,' he told her. 'Go ahead and don't worry about it.'

'Back in a while,' she said.

In her bedroom, Vicki took her robe out of the closet. She found a nightgown in a drawer. Then, she shambled back down the hallway to the bathroom and shut herself inside.

Rump against the door, she bent down. She pulled off her shoes and socks. The shoes had sand in them. Sighing, she staggered to the waste basket and dumped the sand.

219

She remembered the car accident during her sophomore year at college. Tim was driving.

One of the guys I didn't marry, she thought.

They were on their way back to campus on a stormy night when a car ran a red light and broadsided them. They'd both walked away from the crash with nothing more than a few bruises. But this is how she'd felt afterward, waiting in the rain for the police to arrive. Her muscles like warm liquid. Her mind dim and out of focus. Exhausted, dazed, hardly able to stand on her feet.

Hands braced on the sink, she leaned forward and peered at herself in the medicine cabinet mirror. Her damp hair hung in ropes around her face. Her eyes looked vacant. Her skin seemed pallid in spite of the tan. She had a dark smudge on the right side of her face, and wondered vaguely where that had come from.

Stepping back, she glimpsed the way her T-shirt looked. Wet and dirty. Clinging. She had taken a moment, before leaving the park, to reach inside and arrange her bra. Otherwise, Jack would've had an eyeful. Which would've been all right, she supposed. She really didn't care much, one way or the other. Too messed up to care.

She only glanced at the shirt's torn, filthy, blood-spotted shoulder. Then she pulled it up over her head, wincing as the fabric came unstuck from her wounds, feeling the loose cups of the bra fall aside once the shirt was no longer there to hold them. She slipped the straps off her arm, and looked
'*Uh!*'

She flinched rigid. Her hands flew up and stopped, inches from her blackened breasts.

She understood, now, how she got the dirty face and shirt. She stared down at herself, moaning.

Her chest, both her breasts, her stomach and sides were smeared with dark soot. Hand prints. Smears. Streaks and swirls left by Charlie's burnt fingers. One broad, black smudge was low on her belly. She knew it didn't stop at the elastic of her shorts.

She lowered the shorts and stepped out of them.

The black stopped just above her pubic hair and swept sideways to her hip. At her hip were a few scratches, red trails in a field of char.

She drew a fingertip across the grimy top of her left breast. The filth was *greasy*.

That's why it hadn't come off in the river.

It's what you get on your fingers, she thought, if you picked up a grilled steak. One that's well-done. One that's been burnt to a crisp.

She suddenly gagged. And gagged again and again, her eyes watering as the spasms hunched her over. She didn't vomit, though. She supposed that her medical training, especially her time as a resident in the ER, had pretty much cured her of that. She'd seen such stomach-turning sights, day after day, that they had finally ceased to disgust her.

But *this* disgusted her.

This was *on* her.

When Vicki stopped gagging, she stood up straight, took deep breaths, and wiped her eyes. She felt a little better, now.

Just clean it off and forget about it.

Regular soap, she thought, might not do the job.

Crouching, she opened the cupboard beneath the sink and took out a can of scouring powder. Its label boasted 'grease-cutting action.'

With that in her hand, she stepped away from the sink and looked around. The mirror showed that her back, from just below her shoulder blades to her waist, was nearly as filthy as her front. From lying on Charlie in the canoe, she thought. Twisting herself, she saw that the backs of her legs also bore smudges.

Jack, she thought, may have a long wait.

When she finished drying, she checked her towel. It looked clean. The mirror was fogged. With a corner of the towel, she wiped an area clear. She inspected her shoulder.

221

Charlie's teeth had left a pair of discoloured crescents. Far apart. His mouth, she thought, must've been open very wide. The incisors had broken her skin. Four uppers and four lowers. The edges of the wounds looked ragged.

That's a pretty nasty bite he gave you.

Weird, she thought. I just treated Melvin for a bite, now I've got one.

Must be going round.

She smiled grimly at herself in the mirror.

We've got something in common. We can compare notes on our bites. Sure thing.

She gave no more thought to Melvin as she soaked her wounds with hydrogen peroxide and taped pads of gauze in place. Then she turned her attention to the scratches on her hip. They were minor. She dabbed them with the disinfectant and didn't bother to apply a bandage.

Takes care of that, she thought.

She put on her robe, carried her nightgown into her bedroom, then shut the door and slipped the robe off.

Turning slowly, she studied herself in the mirror. Her wet hair was a tangle. But her body bore no traces of the greasy ash. Her pallor seemed gone, replaced by a rosey hue.

The hot shower had not only brought colour to her skin. She felt as if it had also awakened her, washed the daze out of her mind and turned her exhaustion into a rather pleasant laziness.

She slipped the nightgown over her head. It drifted down her body like the caress of a cool breeze. Its pale blue fabric gleamed in the lamplight.

Quickly, she brushed her hair. She considered blowing it dry, but Jack had already been waiting too long. She put her robe on, and hurried from the room.

She found Jack sitting on the couch. He smiled when he saw her. 'You look fabulous,' he said.

'I sure feel better.' She knew she was blushing. Partly the compliment. Partly the fact that he was wearing the beach

222

towel like a skirt and she doubted that he had anything on beneath it. My idea, she reminded herself.

But her mind was fairly clear, now, and she found herself reluctant to join him on the couch.

'Sorry I took so long,' she said, stopping in front of the coffee table.

'I took the opportunity to clean myself up some. At the kitchen sink.'

He still had the dark smudge of a bruise on his forehead. It must've been coated with soot before he washed. He'd probably had some of the stuff on his hands, too, from when he pulled Charlie off her at the bottom of the river.

'How about that drink?' she asked.

'What are you having?'

She shrugged. 'Why don't we go out to the kitchen? We'll have a look around and see what looks good.'

He stood up, holding onto the towel. When he was on his feet, he tightened the towel's tuck at his hip. 'This is a . . . somewhat compromising attire,' he said, a sheepish look on his face.

Vicki smiled and found herself relieved by his embarrassment. 'What's it compromising?'

'My modesty?'

'I don't know, it covers more of you than your shorts did.'

'Doesn't feel that way,' he said, and followed her into the kitchen.

His blue shorts were spread flat on the counter by the sink. 'I'll go ahead and throw them in the drier,' Vicki suggested.

'Aah, don't bother.'

'You want to climb into damp pants when you're ready to go home? It's no trouble, really.' She pulled the moist leather belt out of the loops and picked up the shorts. Something jangled. 'You'd better empty your pockets,' she said. As she swung the shorts toward Jack, his briefs dropped out of a leg hole. He ducked and made a one-handed grab for them while he clutched the towel at his waist. Missed. Then snatched them off the floor and wadded them. But not fast enough to prevent Vicki from seeing that they were bikini-style and bright red.

Only slightly brighter red than his face.

Amused, Vicki almost said, 'Snazzy.' But that would probably just fluster him more. 'They're only drawers,' she said.

'Yeah,' he muttered, and took the shorts from her. He removed a key case, checked the other pockets, and looked around as if searching for the drier.

'It's out back,' Vicki explained.

'I'll go with you.' He rolled his shorts up, deftly planting the briefs inside so that Vicki didn't get another glimpse of them, and cradled the bundle against his belly.

He's awfully self-conscious about those things, she thought as she opened the back door and stepped outside. The concrete patio felt cool under her bare feet.

I'd sure be embarrassed if *mine* fell on the floor in front of *him*.

A hot sick feeling suddenly pulsed through Vicki as she was hit by the memory of Charlie ripping her panties off.

It's all right, she told herself. It's over.

She felt the grass, wet and soft on the bottoms of her feet, wisps of it sliding between her toes as she crossed the lawn.

We made it out of there. We're at Ace's, now. I'm safe. Jack's safe. Charlie's far away.

She pictured him under the water, a maimed shape blacker than the river's darkness, still searching the depths for her, still clinging to the flimsy torn rag.

Don't think about him, she told herself. It's over.

Over, sure.

You think you had nightmares *before*?

Nightmares, I can handle. It's the real-life shit that's getting hard to take.

She opened the laundry room door, felt the trapped heat wash over her, and flicked the light on. Jack followed her inside.

'Cosy,' he said.

'Hot as a huncher,' Vicki said, borrowing Ace's language

224

– and with it, some of Ace's bravado. She walked past the enclosure of the spare toilet, past the washing machine and tubs, and pressed a button to open the door of the front-loading drier. Even before she looked inside, she remembered that she had forgotten to take her laundry out. Laughing softly, she crouched down to remove her things. 'I saw yours, now you see mine.'

'Good. I'll feel a lot better.'

Into the laundry basket at her side she tossed washcloths, towels, socks, a sundress, shorts, blouses, her bikini, a skirt, panties and bras of every colour.

When the drum was empty, Jack handed his rolled shorts to her. She shook them open inside the drier, watched his briefs flop out, then shut the door, straightened up, and started the machine.

Jack picked up the basket.

'Oh, you can leave that here.'

'No problem. You just lead the way in case I lose my towel.'

In the kitchen, she took the basket from him and set it on the floor near the breakfast table. Then she opened the cupboard where the liquor was kept. 'What'll you have? The hard stuff's in here. There's beer and wine in the refrigerator, soft drinks . . . I'm having Scotch.'

'Scotch is fine,' Jack said.

As she filled the glasses, she asked, 'Ice?'

'Maybe one cube. Don't want it watered down too much.'

She dropped one ice cube into each drink, and gave a glass to Jack. They went into the living room. Vicki realised that she was no longer concerned by the fact that he wore nothing but a towel. She sat down beside him in the middle of the couch and turned sideways, sliding one knee onto the cushion. The robe fell away from her thigh. She glanced down. The blue satin of her nightgown was glossy in the lamplight. It was short enough to show a lot of leg. She thought, Looks okay to this kid, and didn't bother to adjust the robe.

'Here's mud in your eye,' Jack said.

Vicki leaned toward him and clinked her glass against his. Easing back, she took a drink. The Scotch went down, spreading heat, making her eyes water. 'Oh, that's good.'

'Hits the spot,' Jack said. '*Burns* the spot.'

'Ugh, don't mention burning.' She said it half-joking, and wished she hadn't.

'Are you going to be all right?'

'I'm feeling better all the time.' She took another drink. 'How about you? That's a mean lump on your forehead. Do you want some ice for it, or something?'

'No, it's fine.'

'Do you have a headache?'

'That's a leading question.' He smiled. 'How about you?'

'My head's about the only thing that doesn't ache. I probably won't be able to *move*, tomorrow.'

'Hate to tell you, it is tomorrow.'

'I'm gonna be wasted.' I'll have to take Charlie's appointments and mine, she realised. Maybe Thelma can cancel some of them. She looked at the digital clock on the VCR. Four-seventeen. 'Geez.'

'I'd better drink up and go, or you won't get any sleep at all.'

'Gonna go home in your towel?'

'My pants should be dry pretty soon.'

'There's no hurry,' Vicki said. 'I mean, I don't want to keep *you* up. Have you got court or something?'

He shook his head. 'Just a deposition at two. I can sleep in.'

'Lucky duck.'

'You must be exhausted, though.'

'I'm not really eager to be alone just now.'

'Neither am I,' Jack admitted. He set down his glass and held his hand out toward Vicki. His fingers were trembling. 'Look at that. I never shake like that.'

Vicki took hold of his hand and squeezed it gently. She brought it down and rested the back of her hand on her

226

thigh. She took another drink while he reached out with his other hand and picked up his glass. He moved closer to her. She felt the softness of the towel push against her knee.

'I'm sorry I got us into that,' she said. 'They *told* me to stay out of it. I should've listened.'

'There was nothing wrong with searching for him.'

'It nearly got us both killed.'

'Nobody could've foreseen that he'd attack anyone.'

'There's been so much weirdness lately. Pollock, now this. And I keep getting into it.'

'You mean the guy who was murdered by that nurse? How were you involved in that?'

'Ace and I were at the Riverfront on Saturday night. Pollock came to our table and caused some trouble. This guy we were with, Melvin, threatened to kill him. Later that night, Pollock *was* killed. We figured Melvin might've had something to do with it, so we talked to a policeman the next day. I guess he thought we should mind our own business, and he told Chief Raines about us, and that's how come I got such a lousy reception at the bridge tonight.' She took a sip of her Scotch, and sighed. 'I guess they don't appreciate civilian interference.'

'Raines likes to do things his own way,' Jack said. 'I've had some run-ins with him, myself. On behalf of my clients,' he added. 'It's been my experience that he's stubborn, narrow-minded and stupid.'

'But otherwise a wonderful guy,' Vicki said.

'From what I've heard, Dexter Pollock wasn't much better.'

'In addition to all the above, he was a tyrant and a lech.'

'Otherwise wonderful?'

'About the best thing that can be said for Pollock is that he's dead.' Vicki grimaced. 'I shouldn't have said that. I mean, I'm sorry he's dead.'

'But not very.'

'Hardly at all.' She changed position, swinging her bent leg down, turning forward, resting her feet on the coffee table and settling into the cushion behind her. Jack scooted closer. He lifted his arm. She eased forward to let him lower it across her shoulders. He didn't touch her wounded right shoulder. Instead, his hand slipped behind it and curled around her upper arm.

'At the Riverfront,' she continued. 'Pollock started sniffing me. Said I must have an odour that attracts crazy people. I dumped my beer in his lap.'

Jack shook his head. 'You *are* a tough broad.'

'You should've heard what *he* called me.'

Jack caressed her arm. 'That's the incident that led to the threat?'

'Oh, he retaliated and flung his beer at me. Right in my face.'

'Good thing he's already dead, the bastard.'

'I'm liking you more and more,' Vicki said. She patted his leg. Leaving her hand on the towel, she took another drink. Her cheeks, she realised, were beginning to feel a little numb.

'So who's this Melvin? Is he just a casual acquaintance, or is he someone I need to worry about?'

'Don't worry about him. That's my job.'

'What do you mean?'

'He's apparently smitten with me, and he's crazy as hell.' She fingered the nap of the towel. 'That's partly what Pollock meant about me attracting weirdos. Melvin's as weird as they come. He gave me a *car*.'

'That doesn't sound so weird.'

'Wouldn't be weird if we were engaged or something. We've never even gone out together.'

'Glad to hear it.'

'He just likes to *do* things for me. Maybe even things like killing Pollock to pay him back for what he did at the bar. Wouldn't surprise me. He doesn't have loose screws, he's *missing* screws.'

'He can't be all that crazy if he's smitten with you.'

'Oh no?' Vicki asked, looking at Jack.

228

He leaned forward, turning himself, setting his glass on the table as his arm eased Vicki away from the cushion. When she faced him, their eyes locked. She felt him take her glass. He bent away from her, putting it down. Then both his hands were on Vicki's back, guiding her closer. She held his sides, brushed her lips against his, then felt the soft pressure of his mouth. She closed her eyes as they kissed. Her mind seemed to spin slowly – the Scotch and the deep weariness – and she felt herself sinking into the dark, peaceful place where there was only the comfort of knowing Jack was with her, kissing her, and everything was right.

She was on the diving raft with Jack, standing in the darkness, holding him, the raft rocking gently under her feet as they kissed. He lifted her nightgown. She stepped back and raised her arms. As he drew the gown over her head, she closed her eyes. She stood there, trembling, the warm breeze sliding over her skin, and waited for his touch. He kissed her breast. The mouth on her nipple felt crusted and greasy.

NO!

She clutched the charred head and thrust it away from her and staggered backward as Charlie, black and eyeless and wearing a beach towel around his waist lurched toward her, reaching out. She teetered on the edge of the raft. Windmilled her arms. Then tumbled backwards.

Flinched as she fell, and jerked awake.

She was in bed. Daylight filled the room. Gasping for breath, she sat up. Her heart was thudding. Sweat trickled down her face. Beneath her robe, her nightgown felt glued to her skin. She pulled the robe open as she scooted off the bed. The movement awakened a hot ache in her shoulder, lesser aches in the stiff muscles all over her body. Standing, she shook the robe off. She peeled the damp, clinging nightgown over her head. With a shaky hand, she lifted a corner of the sheet and used it to dry her face.

The clock on the nightstand showed 7:58.

At least I didn't oversleep, she thought.

An hour before she had to be at the clinic.

229

Charlie.

A chill swept over her body as memories of last night's attack rushed through her mind. She rubbed the gooseflesh that pebbled her arms, and jumped as the alarm clock blared. She lurched to the nightstand and silenced it.

She didn't remember setting the alarm.

Maybe Jack did it.

The last thing she could remember was kissing him. Had she actually fallen asleep while they kissed? What did he do then, carry her into the bedroom and set the alarm so she wouldn't be late for work?

She heard the distant ringing of the telephone. It rang only twice. She went to the dresser. As she pulled a football jersey over her head, she heard footfalls in the hallway. A knock on her door, then the door opened. Ace looked in, grinning. 'Told you he'd call,' she said. 'Bet he's been up all night, kicking himself.'

'You're half right,' Vicki said. She brushed past Ace and hurried to get the phone.

CHAPTER TWENTY-FIVE

'Dr Chandler's with a patient right now,' Thelma said. Though she looked composed, her eyes were red as if she'd been crying recently. 'She's very busy this morning, Melvin. May I schedule an appointment for you?' She glanced down at something on her desk. 'There's an opening next Wednesday at . . .'

'I just want to talk to her for a minute,' Melvin said. 'About this.' he held up the bandaged hand.

'As I explained, she's very busy. Dr Gaines . . . we lost him last night.'

'Lost him?'

'There was a terrible accident up on River Road. He's still missing and . . . we don't hold out much hope for him.'

'I'm sorry. Gosh.'

'So I hope you can appreciate that this is a very difficult time, just now. I've been on the phone all morning, rescheduling appointments to ease the burden for Dr Chandler. So if you'll be patient and give us a few days to sort things out . . .'

Melvin turned around, scanning the deserted waiting room. 'I don't see anyone,' he said.

'I've just explained to you,' Thelma said, an edge to her voice. 'I'm *cancelling* today's appointments. As many as possible. If you'd like to come back next week . . .'

'I'll just sit and wait. Maybe she can find a minute for me.'

Thelma pressed her lips together and glared at him. But she said nothing. Melvin turned away. He stepped over to an easy chair, sat down, and settled into it gently. The cushion pressed against the furrows Charlie had scratched into his back. They hurt a little, but not much. Compared to all the bites put in him during the past week, the scratches seemed like nothing more than a minor irritation.

But they itched through the bandages Patricia had applied.

He'd found her asleep when he returned from dealing with Charlie. He woke her up. She yelped with alarm and threw her arms around him. 'What happened?' she blurted. 'What'd he *do* to you?'

'Not near as much as I did to him,' Melvin said.

He told her all about it while they went into the bathroom and he shed his damp, filthy clothes. The back of his shirt was split apart. Standing behind him, Patricia ran her fingertips lightly down his scratches, making him squirm. In the mirror, he saw that his face – especially around the mouth – and neck were smeared with the same kind of black grime that had darkened his shirt and pants.

He filled the tub with hot water. He climbed in, and Patricia got in with him. Kneeling behind him, she lathered

231

his back and rubbed it gently with a washcloth. Then, she rubbed harder. 'Ow! Stop that!'

'It doesn't want to come off very good,' she said. He told her to get the Goop from under the sink. It was a lotion that he often used after returning from work at the service station to clean car grease off his hands. She left the tub and came back with the jar. She spread the slimy lotion over his back. When she rinsed it off, she said, 'It's like magic! Let me do your front.'

She climbed out. Melvin scooted toward the rear of the tub to make room for her. She stepped in and knelt between his legs. Holding the jar in one hand, she peeled the sodden bandages off his shoulders and chest and tossed them onto the bathroom floor.

'You're just so covered with hurts,' she said, a sorrowful look in her eyes as she gazed at his wounds.

'Thanks mostly to you,' Melvin said.

She nibbled her lower lip. 'I'm sorry. I try to be good. I love you, Melvin. I don't *want* to hurt you.'

'I know,' he said. Something seemed to tighten inside his chest and throat. He looked at the trails of scratches remaining on Patricia's breasts and belly from the tantrum she'd thrown last night. Because she'd *missed* him. Most had faded to pinkish lines. Others were dark with thin crusts of scab. He saw that the Face of Ram-Chotep seemed to be healing well except for one corner of the Mouth, which she'd opened during her rage. The bite wound on her forearm was covered with a wet bandage. 'You shouldn't hurt yourself, either,' Melvin said.

'I know. I'm sorry.'

She scooped up a mound of the white Goop with her fingers and spread it over Melvin's face. As he watched her eyes, he wondered about the tenderness he'd lately been feeling toward her. She's dead, he thought. She's nothing but a goddamn zombie.

But *my* zombie. She loves me.

Nobody had ever loved him. Maybe his parents, but that

was doubtful, the way they used to treat him. Certainly no girls had ever looked at him with anything but contempt.

Except Vicki, and now Patricia.

Vicki was the only *live* one who was ever nice to him. But it was pretty clear she didn't love him.

She will, he told himself, and closed his eyes. I've just gotta be patient and keep being good to her.

His plans were already bringing rewards. Though Vicki made him take the car back, the gift must've pleased her – she'd asked him out for drinks at the Riverfront. Pretty soon, they'd be having dinners together, maybe going to the show. They would be kissing goodnight. Then, she would start asking him into the house and they'd hug and make out.

He felt Patricia bathing his face with warm water, then swirling the slippery lotion over his shoulders and chest. He imagined her hands were Vicki's hands. Someday soon, they would be. He opened his eyes just a crack, reached out to her breasts, and caressed them. They would be Vicki's breasts, cool and smooth and slick, the stiff nipples pushing against his palms. He felt a swelling rush of desire. If only this was Vicki. Here and now. He'd won her over, at last, and she was living with him, sharing his tub, sliding her hands over his chest, and down, wrapping her fingers around his erect penis.

'You missed me, didn't you?' Patricia's voice.

He opened his eyes. He had left dark hand-prints on her breasts. 'I sure did.'

Her hand moved up and down beneath the water, lightly stroking him.

'Do you love me?' she asked.

'Sure I do.'

'I'm glad you got rid of Charlie. I hated him.'

'I know.'

'You won't make any more, will you?'

'I don't know.'

'We don't need anyone else.'

'I don't want nobody else but you.'

233

'I love you so much, Melvin.'

She'll never stand for having Vicki around, he thought. She was jealous as hell about Charlie, and Charlie wasn't even a gal. She'll go apeshit when Vicki moves in.

I'll need to get rid of her before then.

Cut off her head? Maybe that'll work.

He felt a hollow ache inside that stole the pleasure from his groin.

Can I do that to her? he wondered. I'll have to.

She's dead anyway, so what does it matter?

It matters, he realised. She loves me and she's good to me and I like her more than I've ever liked anyone except Vicki. But I'll have to get rid of her.

Melvin heard footsteps. Then a voice. Vicki's voice. Though she spoke too softly for him to understand the words, he could see her through the sliding doors of the receptionist's window. She was standing beside a counter back there, talking to Thelma. Beside Vicki stood an obese woman with hair like a grey helmet.

Vicki looked wonderful. Her blonde hair was golden, her skin a mellow tan, her eyes clear and blue. Her doctor jacket hung open, showing the front of a blue silken blouse that was open at the throat.

Melvin's pulse quickened.

She glanced at him, then faced Thelma again, said a few more words, and walked away. The fat woman stayed by the counter for a while. Then, she opened the door, passed through the waiting room without glancing at Melvin, and left.

Thelma got up from the desk. She walked around the end of the counter. She turned toward the door.

All right!

She opened it. 'Dr Chandler will see you now.' She held the door for Melvin, then led the way down the corridor to the same room where Vicki had treated his hand last week.

'She'll be with you in a minute,' Thelma said, and left him alone.

Melvin sat on the paper-covered examination table. He took a deep, shakey breath and let it out slowly. His heart was pounding fast. He felt trickles of sweat dribble down his sides.

Then, he heard footsteps. Not the clack of heels like Thelma wore – the whisper and squeak of rubber soles.

Vicki entered the room. Her white coat was buttoned shut, and she had closed the button at her throat.

She's made herself nice and proper for me, Melvin thought. That'll change. One of these days, she'll be as eager as Patricia. I won't be able to *keep* the clothes on her.

He pictured her naked. But she had the Face of Ram-Chotep carved on her torso.

No, it won't be like that. I won't have to do that to Vicki. She'll be alive, and *still* want me.

'Good morning, Melvin,' she said. Though she didn't smile, she didn't look as if she'd been crying. 'Are you having more trouble with your hand?'

'It's still hurting.'

'Shall we have a look at it?'

'I think so,' he said. Last night, Patricia had applied a fresh bandage after the bath. The hand had looked good. But the hand was his excuse for being here, and he wanted Vicki to come over to him and unwrap it.

He held the hand out to her.

She approached, stopping when her thighs were almost close enough to touch his knees. With one hand, she held his hand steady. With the other, she began to peel the tape loose. She smelled clean and fresh, a little like lemons.

'I heard what happened to Dr Gaines,' he said. She stiffened slightly, and the grip on his hand tightened. 'Thelma, she says they haven't found his body.'

'No. They haven't.'

'I'm real sorry for you. I guess he was a good friend.'

Vicki nodded. She seemed distant, withdrawn.

235

'So, you're running the clinic all on your own, now?'

'For the time being,' she said.

'That's gonna be a lot of work. Maybe you better hire somebody to help out.'

'I imagine I'll have to.' She unwound the last of the tape and peeled off the gauze pad. She turned his hand over, inspecting the wounds on both sides. 'It's looking a lot better,' she said.

'Yeah. Still hurts, though.'

'That's to be expected,' she said, not looking up at him. 'I'll put a fresh dressing on it, and you can be on your way.'

'You're acting like you want to get rid of me.'

'I'm very busy.' She stepped over to a cabinet. There, she opened the shallow metal drawer. She took out a roll of gauze and a tape dispenser. On top of the cabinet, she found scissors. She came back to him and began to bandage his hand. She worked quickly -- and not very gently.

'Something wrong?' Melvin asked.

'Everything's just peachy.'

'You mad at me, or something?'

'Mad? I wouldn't say that.'

'What'd *I* do?'

She squeezed the last stip of tape into place, released his hand, and stepped back. She looked down at the scissors in her hand, then tossed them. They landed with a clatter on top of the cabinet. She stared at Melvin with narrowed eyes. 'What *did* you do, Melvin?'

He felt heat rush to his face. 'What're you talking about?'

'You killed him, didn't you?'

Melvin forced out a laugh. 'Hey, I'm supposed to be crazy, but I don't go around killing people. I'm into resurrection, not murder. *Was* into. Back when I tried to jump-start Darlene. Resurrection, not murder.' He shook his head. 'That's wild. Where'd you ever get an idea like that?'

Vicki didn't answer him. She gazed steadily into his eyes.

'He cracked up his fuckin' car! I didn't have nothing to do with it!'

236

'Not Charlie. Dexter Pollock.'

'What?'

'You heard me.'

Melvin huffed out another laugh. 'Boy, you've got some imagination on you.'

'Do I?'

'Some nurse nailed Pollock. Everybody knows that. The cops even know who she is. Patricia something. A nurse. Geez. *Me* murder Pollock? That's wild!'

'Is it?'

'Come onnn! You're pulling my leg, right?'

A corner of Vicki's mouth twitched.

'They say *I'm* crazy.'

'You can tell me, Melvin.'

'Are you nuts?'

'Maybe. Maybe I'm nuts to think you meant it, Saturday night, when you said you'd like to kill him. Maybe I'm nuts to think you hated him for what he said – what he *did* to me. Maybe I'm nuts to think you cared enough about me to make him pay for it.'

'*Jesus*,' Melvin muttered.

'Maybe I'm nuts to want to thank you.'

'Thank me?' The words came from him in a hoarse whisper.

This can't be happening, he told himself. It's a trick, or I'm dreaming, or . . .

'I suppose I *am* nuts,' Vicki said.

'I wanted to kill him,' Melvin told her. 'I wanted to tear him to pieces. I *do* care about you. I . . . But I didn't kill him. I shoulda, maybe, but I didn't.'

'Then get out of here,' she said in a tight, hard voice. 'And stay away from me.'

'But . . .'

'You either don't trust me enough to admit it, or you were too chicken to kill the bastard for me. Get out!'

Stunned, Melvin hopped down from the table. Vicki sidestepped out of his way. When he was in the corridor, the door slammed at his back.

'I guess maybe I *am* nuts,' Vicki said. She stared down at her lunch, and shook her head.

'Certifiable,' Ace agreed. 'Holy God in a basket, what were you thinking?'

'I don't know. Seemed like a good idea at the time.' She lifted to top of the sesame bun off her hamburger. The broiled patty reminded her of Charlie. Wrinkling her nose, she covered it and pushed the plate away.

'Better eat,' Ace told her. 'A busy gal like you, you've gotta keep your strength up.'

'My appetite's shot.'

'What on earth possessed you to run off at the mouth like that?'

Vicki shrugged. 'I was just feeling so tired. I figured, why not confront him with it?'

'If he did kill Pollock,' Ace said, 'it wasn't such a smart move. I do't care how adorable he thinks you are, if he's afraid you know too much, he might decide to . . .'

'Terminate me with extreme prejudice?'

'You read too many damn books, hon. If that means kill your ass, yeah. He might try something like that to save himself.' She bit into her chili dog. 'He really might,' she added, her words coming out muffled.

'I know. That occurred to me.'

'Then why . . . ?'

'By the time I thought of it, I'd already accused him. Since it was too late, then, I changed my tactics and acted as if I would've considered it a favour if he *had* killed Pollock. So he wouldn't think I'm a threat. And also, I thought maybe I might get him to admit it. I don't know whether he believed me or not.'

Ace swallowed her mouthful of food. She wiped chili off her lips with a napkin. 'That wasn't such a hot move, either, hon.'

238

'Probably not.'

'No probably. You as much as told him that he failed you by *not* killing the man who insulted you.'

'But he did it, Ace. I know he did. When I said I wanted to thank him for it, he got this odd look on his face.'

'He's always got an odd look on his face.'

'He said, "Thank me?" And I got the feeling he regretted denying it and was really close to confessing. He *wanted* my approval. He ached for it. But he just wasn't quite convinced that I really meant what I said, so he backed off.'

'My pal, Nancy Drew. What's next on the agenda?'

'It wasn't planned, Ace. It just happened.'

'Keep after him, maybe he'll break down and admit it. Maybe just a little more urging. Take him out to dinner tonight, woo him a little, show him you were serious . . .'

The suggestion made something flutter inside Vicki.

What if I tried it? she wondered. I can't! Christ, a date with Melvin? But what if I *could* get him to confess?

Then what? Tell Raines? That jerk wouldn't listen to me anyway.

He'd listen to Jack, though. Or we could go to the DA.

Ace, chewing and staring at her, suddenly looked alarmed. 'Hey, I was *kidding!*'

'Don't worry, I wouldn't have the guts.'

'Don't even think about it. Christ! Why did I open my trap?'

'But just suppose I did get him to admit it. They'd have to investigate. They might find real evidence . . .'

'What do you care? Pollock was a pain in the ass!'

'That was no excuse to murder him. He didn't deserve that.'

'Stop it, would you? You're scaring the shit outa me! If he killed Pollock, let the high-and-mighty cops nail him. That's their job, as they've pointed out in no uncertain terms. It's none of your business.'

'It is my business, Ace. He did it because of me – because of what happened at the bar.'

'Horse squat. He did it because he's a fruitcake. *If* he did it. Maybe he did, maybe he didn't. But you can't hold yourself responsible. Just forget about it. My God, why are we even discussing this? It's crazy. Forget Melvin. Forget he exists. You've gotta look out for number one.'

'From that angle,' Vicki said, 'it makes even more sense. He's never going to leave me alone. Never. He'll just keep . . . *at* me. But if they can get a conviction, he'll be sent away for years. He may *never* get out.'

Ace, with a look on her face as if she were in pain, muttered, 'You're really seriously gonna do it, aren't you?'

'I don't know.'

'You've got a date with Jack, remember? I was standing right there. Seven o'clock, his place. Remember?'

'It'd only take a couple of hours to . . .'

'Well, don't do it without me. He won't try anything if I'm along.'

'He won't confess, either.'

Back at the clinic, Vicki found two patients in the waiting room. 'I'll start seeing them in just a few minutes,' she told Thelma. She borrowed the telephone directory, and hurried into her office.

Melvin's phone rang three times before he picked up.

'Who's this?'

She squeezed her eyes shut.

'Who the hell is this?'

She pressed a hand to her pounding chest and said, 'Vicki.'

'*Vicki?* Hi!'

'Melvin, I called to apologise. I . . .' She sucked a shakey breath into her lungs. 'I'm sorry about the way I behaved this morning. I was tired and upset, but I shouldn't have . . .'

'No sweat. Honest.'

'Well, I'd feel better if you'd let me make it up to you. Would you like to have dinner with me tonight? My treat. I was thinking about the Fireside Chalet.'

'Yeah? Just you and me?'

'Just you and me.'

'Great. Uh . . . what time you want me to pick you up?'

She'd planned for that one, and had a story ready. 'I need to run over to Blayton Memorial this afternoon, so . . .'

'Want a lift?'

'No, that's fine. I've got Ace's car. It'd be a lot more convenient for me if I just meet you at the restaurant.'

'Yeah, I guess.'

'That way, I can just stop in on the way back from the hospital.'

'Yeah. I guess that makes sense.'

'So why don't we meet at the restaurant at about six o'clock? Is six all right for you?'

'Sure. Great. I'll get dressed up real nice for you.'

'Me, too. See you then, Melvin.'

'Yeah. See you then.'

She hung up. Her heart was racing. Tilting back her chair, she folded her hands behind her head and took slow, deep breaths. I did it, she thought. I actually did it. I'm committed now. I *should* be committed. To an asylum.

But if it works, I'll be rid of him. Maybe for good.

When her calm returned, she looked up Jack's name in the directory. She found two numbers, one for his rooms and one for his office. She dialled the office.

After the second ring, a woman answered the phone. 'Good afternoon, Law Offices of Jack Randolph.'

'Is Mr Randolph in?'

'Who may I say is calling?'

'Vicki Chandler.'

'Just a moment, please.'

Seconds later, Jack said, 'Hi. How's it going?'

The sound of his voice suddenly made her feel a lot better. 'Not as bad as I expected. Thelma cancelled most of the appointments, so it's nothing I can't handle. The thing is, I'll have to be a little late tonight. I should be able to make it over by about nine, if that's all right.'

241

'I guess I can live with that,' he said. 'We'll eat fashionably late.'

'I'll have to eat before I come over. I've got a dinner engagement.'

'Oh. Okay.'

'It's nothing. I just . . . have to do it. I'll explain when I see you.'

'You don't have to explain anything, Vicki.'

'Don't worry, I will. It should be interesting. If I survive.'

'Now I am worried.'

'It just won't be any fun, that's all. I'm not exactly looking forward to it. But we'll be in a public place, and I'm driving myself, so nothing's going to happen.'

'What *are* you doing?'

'I'll tell you all about it when I see you.'

'Vicki.'

'I really can't go into it right now. It's a long story, and I've got a couple of patients waiting. I'll see you at nine, okay? Earlier if possible.'

'Well . . . Fine. See you then.'

'Bye, Jack.'

CHAPTER TWENTY-SIX

Melvin's heart quickened when he spotted the red Mustang in the parking area alongside the Fireside Chalet.

Vicki had actually come.

All afternoon, he'd wondered about the invitation. Was it for real? Maybe it was just a dirty joke. In school, he'd been the butt of plenty. Darlene Morgan herself had asked him to be her date for the junior prom. But that was right after the movie *Carrie* played for two weeks at the Palace Theatre, so Melvin didn't fall for it. There on the phone, right in front of his mother, he told Darlene to eat shit. And always wondered, afterward, if the bitch really would've gone through with the date.

But Vicki was here. She really intended to have dinner with him.

It seemed so incredible.

I knew it would happen, he told himself as he swung into the parking lot.

But not this soon.

Or ever, really.

He realised this was like his experiments. He had *known* he would succeed, but deep inside he'd expected failure. Which made the success all the more sweet.

She knows I killed Pollock for her. That's why she's doing this. It's her way of thanking me.

Unless she wants to get me for it.

Either way, I better not tell her the truth.

He pulled into a space two cars away from Ace's Mustang, and climbed out. He'd been sweating, even in his air-conditioned car. Now, the heat seemed to bake him. His face dripped. Trickles of sweat slid down the nape of his neck and soaked his tight collar. Beneath his sport coat, his shirt was plastered to his back and sides. His underwear was stuck to his rump.

He wanted to look good for her, not like a sweaty pig.

When he opened the restaurant door, cool air rushed out against him. He entered the dimly lighted foyer. Ahead, a gal in old-fashioned clothes stood behind something that looked like a speaker's stand. She was busy talking on the telephone. Looking around, Melvin noticed a sign that read 'Restroom' over the entrance to a recessed area. He hurried that way, and pushed through the door marked 'Gentlemen.'

Instead of towels, it had blowers. He hated those things. Stepping into a stall, he used toilet paper to dry himself. Then, he went to a sink and checked himself in the mirror. He thought he was fine except for his necktie being crooked.

Until now, he hadn't been able to see how he looked in

243

his jacket and tie. To keep Patricia from being upset – she would've thrown a fit if she knew he was having dinner with Vicki – he'd told her that he needed to work at the station tonight. He'd carried his good clothes out to the car earlier, while she was watching television. When he kissed her good-night and left the house, he was wearing his greasy coveralls. Alone in the garage, he stripped and dressed himself for dinner.

Melvin straightened his tie. He ran a comb through his slicked-down hair, gave himself a wink, and left the restroom.

He walked up to the girl behind the lighted stand. She was a slender brunette, a few years younger than Melvin, and pretty in spite of the expression on her face. She looked at him the way she might look at a pubic hair floating in her soup. 'I'm supposed to be eating with Dr Vicki Chandler,' he said. 'She here?'

'This way.'

He followed her. She walked fast as if trying to get away from him.

The bitch.

He wondered how she'd enjoy having cellophane wrapped around her face.

Then, he saw Vicki. She was seated in a high-backed booth along the wall. She smiled up at him, blushing. He sat across the table from her.

To Melvin, she always looked beautiful. Tonight, however, she was more stunning that he had ever seen her. Her golden hair seemed to float around her face. Her eyes were as blue as the sky on a cloudless summer morning. She wore a single thin gold chain around her neck. Her pale blue blouse, gleaming like silk, was open wide at the throat, open all the way down to a button just lower than her breasts. Between the folds, he could see the shadowed slope of her left breast.

'You look very nice this evening, Melvin,' she said.

'You too. You look great. Gosh.'

'Thank you.' She lifted a half-empty glass and took a drink.

When she set it down, a few grains of salt speckled her lower lip. She curled her lip in over her teeth and licked the salt off. 'Would you like something from the bar?' she asked. 'I'm having a margarita.'

'Yeah, that'd be great.'

'I got here a little early,' she said.

'Figured you'd better get a drink in quick before I showed up?'

'Don't be silly.'

A waiter stepped up to the table. Melvin was glad it wasn't the bitch, but he didn't look at the man's face. Instead, he watched Vicki smile up at him and say, 'We'll have two margaritas.'

When the waiter was gone, he said, 'I bet he wonders what you're doing with a guy like me.'

'You shouldn't put yourself down all the time, Melvin.'

'Beauty and the beast.'

'I wouldn't be here if I thought you were a beast.'

'How come you *are* here?'

Her head tilted slightly to one side. 'Because I want to be. I think . . . I haven't been very nice to you.'

'You been okay. You been fine.'

One shoulder shrugged a fraction. Her blouse, Melvin noticed, didn't cling smoothly to it. As if she wore a pad of some kind between the shiny fabric and her skin. Some kind of a female underthing, he supposed. But the other shoulder didn't seem to have it.

'To be honest,' she said, 'I really was a little frightened of you, at first. The night I came into town, for instance. I mean, the last time I'd seen you was the Science Fair and that pretty much freaked me out.'

'Freaked everyone out,' he said.

'But I'm not frightened of you, anymore. Now that I've gotten to know you better, I've seen that you're sensitive and thoughtful.' Smiling, she shook her head. 'Nobody ever gave me a car before.'

'You made me take it back.'

245

'But the thought was very generous. And I can understand how . . . It seems like everybody's always dumped on you. So it makes sense if you might feel the only way to gain affection is by giving things to people.'

She *does* understand, Melvin thought. He felt a tightness in his throat.

'You don't have to give me gifts, though. I like you for who you are, not for what you give me.'

'That's . . . real nice.'

The waiter arrived with the drinks. He set them on the table, a small napkin under each glass. 'Would you like to enjoy your drinks for a few minutes,' he asked, 'before I bring the menus?'

'I think we'd like to see them now,' Vicki said. She smiled at Melvin. 'I'm starving, how about you?'

He nodded.

Maybe she's starving, he thought. Or maybe she just wants to hurry things up and get finished and get away from me.

If that's it, why's she here at all?

The waiter handed a menu to Vicki, then gave one to Melvin. 'Would you like a few minutes to look them over?' he asked.

'A couple of minutes,' Vicki said.

He went away.

Vicki didn't open her menu. She set it aside. So maybe she's not in a big hot rush, Melvin told himself as he set his own menu down.

She lifted her margarita toward him. Her hand wasn't steady. The surface of the drink trembled. 'To knights in shining armour and damsels in distress.'

Didn't Pollock say something about knights when we were at the Riverfront?

That's what she's getting at, Melvin thought. She's toasting me for nailing the bastard.

He clinked his glass against Vicki's, and took a sip through the grainy salt on its rim.

'Do you like it?' she asked. 'The drink?'

'It's a little like lemonade.'

'It's strong, though. It has tequila and Triple Sec.'

He nodded as if he knew that.

'Well,' she said, 'shall we see what they've got?'

They studied their menus. The prices stunned Melvin. He had never eaten at a restaurant this nice, and never imagined that the food could cost so much. The price of the top sirloin was almost ten times the amount he spent for one at the grocery.

She can afford it, he told himself. She owns the whole clinic now. Thanks to me.

Still, the prices made him feel uneasy.

Maybe I'll pay for us, he thought. That'd make it all right. She said this was her treat, though. It might be rude if I try to pay.

'Their steaks are very good here,' Vicki said.

'Is that what you're having?'

'I think I'll have the prawns.'

The prawns, he saw, were less expensive. 'Go on ahead and have a steak,' he said, keeping the menu in front of his face so she couldn't see him blush. 'It's on me.'

'Melvin, no. I'm paying. I insist.'

'Hey, I got money I don't know what to do with.'

Her fingertips suddenly curled over the top of his menu and eased it down. She looked him in the eyes. His embarrassment fled as he felt a soft warm glow spread through him. 'My treat,' she whispered.

'But if you want a steak . . .'

'I don't even want to look at one.' She drew her arm back slowly. In the dim light, it was dusky and sleek. 'I want prawns. You may have whatever you wish. Have steak and lobster, if you like. Don't think about the cost.'

'Okay. I just wanted to . . .'

She touched a finger to her lips. 'You've given me so much already.'

'You made me take the car back.'

'That's not what I mean,' she said, 'and you know it.'

247

The waiter stepped up to the table. 'Are you ready to order, now?'

'I think so,' Vicki said. She glanced at Melvin. 'Have you decided?'

He nodded. He hadn't decided. He raced his eyes down the menu while Vicki talked to the waiter, didn't know what half the dishes were, didn't know if he should go ahead and order steak.

'And you, sir?' the waiter asked.

'I'll have the same as her,' he said, and felt a wonderful sense of relief when the waiter took his menu.

'And bring us a bottle of the Buena Vista Sauvignon Blanc,' Vicki added.

'Very good.' The waiter left.

'We having wine?' Melvin asked.

'Don't you like it?'

'Sure.' Grinning, he rubbed a hand across his mouth and felt crumbs of salt fall off his lips. 'We ain't careful, we're gonna get snockered.'

'We're celebrating,' she said.

She trying to ge me drunk? he wondered. Or trying to get herself drunk?

She was already near the end of her second margarita, and her face had a rosy hue that wasn't there earlier.

She's just nervous, he thought. He remembered the way her hand had trembled when they clinked glasses. It's our first date, she has a right to be nervous. I'm pretty shaky, myself. But if she keeps putting down the booze . . .

She won't be in any shape to drive home.

I'll get her into my car.

Melvin's heart was suddenly pounding so hard he wondered if she might hear it.

'What're we celebrating?' he asked.

She finished her margarita, sighed, set down the glass, and licked the salt from her lips. 'What're we celebrating?' she asked, as if questioning herself. She leaned back. She stretched her arms across the top of the booth's cushion. The

248

movement made her blouse pull slightly against the undersides of her breasts. 'Us,' she said. Her voice was soft,
solemn. 'We're celebrating us.'

'That's . . . real nice.'

'A friend like you is very rare. I know you're too modest
to admit you took care of Pollock. But that's all right. The
thing is, I appreciate it. He was terrible to me, and you made
him pay for it. It isn't just that I'm grateful. I *am* grateful.
But it's more than that. It's that you cared so much. You
actually risked your life for me. He might've *killed* you, or
the cops might've got you . . .' She pressed her lips together.
She looked as if she might begin to weep. 'I've never known
anyone so gallant.'

Melvin swallowed, fighting the lump in his throat. 'I . . .
I'd do anything for you.'

Leaning forward, Vicki reached her hand across the table.
Melvin covered it with his hand, felt its gentle squeeze. He
saw her look away. She drew her hand back moments before
the waiter arrived with salads and a basket of bread.

Damn it! Why'd the bastard have to show up and ruin
things?

When he was gone, Vicki stared into Melvin's eyes for a
moment. Then, she began to eat.

Melvin picked at his salad. The white, lumpy dressing had
a sour taste. He didn't like it, but the way he felt, he doubted
that he could eat anything right now. His thumping heart
made him light-headed. He felt hollow inside, and aching.
Pushing the salad aside, he took a drink.

'You don't like the salad?' Vicki asked.

'The stuff that's on it.'

'Bleu cheese dressing. It's my favourite.'

He sipped his margarita and watched her eat. After a few
bites of salad, she took a roll from the basket and ate half
of it before returning to her salad. She barely spared him a
glance as she worked on the food. And she ate so slowly.

Melvin wanted her to rush and get done and talk to him.
She was almost finished when the waiter arrived again.

This time, he had the bottle of wine. He showed the label to Vicki, and she nodded. Then he uncorked the bottle. He poured a dab into her glass. She tasted it, said, 'Very nice,' and he filled both glasses. He set the bottle on the table.

Then, he was gone.

Vicki ate a big chunk of the bleu cheese. She set her fork down on her salad plate, wiped her mouth with a napkin, and lifted her gaze to Melvin. 'I'm sorry you didn't care for the salad.'

'That's okay.'

'You should try a roll.'

He shrugged.

'Are you all right?'

'Yeah. Sure.'

'I didn't upset you, did I? What I said about . . . my feelings for you.'

'No. Yeah. I guess. I don't know.'

'You're not angry, are you?'

'Gosh, no.'

She drank the last of her margarita. 'I hope you're not worried that I might tell. I mean, it's our secret. I wouldn't breathe a word about it to anyone, not even to Ace.' Smiling, she shook her head. 'No one would believe me, anyway. They're all certain the nurse did it. Patricia something?'

'Maybe she *did* do it. That's what the cops say.'

'You don't have to play games with me, Melvin.'

Maybe you're the one playing games, he thought. But he couldn't bring himself to say it. He didn't want to believe it. This was all too good to be real, but why *can't* it be real? Resurrecting Patricia had been too good to be real. It had happened, though. This could be happening, too. Vicki might honestly like him – even love him – for what he'd done to Pollock.

'I'm curious about something,' she said. 'You don't have to tell me, but . . . it was fascinating the other night when you explained about digging up Darlene and setting up your

250

science project. So how on earth did you manage to make it *look* like Patricia . . . took care of that creep?'

'Can't we talk about something else?'

'Sure. I'm sorry.' She took a sip of wine and looked around as if searching for the waiter.

'Somebody could hear us.'

'I shouldn't have asked. Forget it. I mean, I'm interested, that's all. But I can understand how you might be afraid of saying anything . . . too specific. It's okay. Don't worry about it. Ah, here comes the food.'

This time, Melvin felt grateful for the waiter's interruption. It saved him from getting in deeper. He didn't know what to do. Vicki was pushing to find out *everything*. Maybe she needed to be convinced that he really had done the job on Pollock. Maybe she was starting to doubt it. What if she should decide he *wasn't* involved, after all?

The waiter left, and Vicki began to eat.

Melvin looked down at his plate. Steam was rising off the asparagus and white rice. The prawns were smothered in a brownish sauce that smelled strongly of garlic. He forked one and tried it.

'Good?' Vicki asked.

'Yeah.' He supposed it was very good, but he had no appetite. He went ahead and ate, anyway. He ate, and drank wine, and watched Vicki. Though she sometimes glanced up at him, she didn't speak.

I should've told her, Melvin thought. I'm gonna lose her.

Then he reminded himself that she had eaten her salad with the same concentration. It's just the way she eats. Doesn't mean nothing.

What if I do tell her? he wondered.

That would mean explaining about Patricia. Would Vicki even believe him? She'd believe, all right, it he showed her Patricia.

Can't do that.

He could just imagine the scene. Patricia would fly into a jealous rage and Vicki, herself, might freak out when she realised what he'd been up to. Killing, resurrecting, *living* with a zombie. Even if she could accept all that, she was bound to figure out what he and Patricia had been doing together. That'd be bad enough, even if Patricia was just a regular person. But doing it with a zombie?

Can't ever let her find out, he decided.

She isn't gonna find out, long as I keep my mouth shut. I'll get rid of Patricia before Vicki ever steps foot in my house. She'll never know.

When she finished eating, she picked up the wine bottle and inspected it. Melvin saw that there wasn't much left. They had both been refilling their glasses during the meal. She poured more wine into Melvin's glass, then emptied the bottle into hers. 'Would you like some coffee or dessert?' she asked.

'I don't know.'

They'd have more time in the restaurant if they lingered over coffee and dessert. He wanted more time with her. But it would be even better if they were alone.

Maybe we can go someplace.

She has her own car. Ace's.

But she's had a lot to drink.

'You wanta have another margarita or something?' he asked.

Smiling, she shook her head. 'Oh, I don't think that'd be such a good idea. I know my limits. I wouldn't be in any condition to drive.'

'I'll drive you. You can leave the car here.'

The waiter showed up. 'Would you care for coffee?'

'No, I think we're all done.'

'Very good. Did you enjoy your meal?'

'Everything was delicious,' Vicki said.

He left.

Vicki lifted her purse off the seat beside her and set it on her lap. Melvin felt a pressure growing inside. As soon as she paid the bill, they would be leaving.

What'll happen then?

'I oughta drive you,' he said. 'You've had a lot to drink.'

'Don't be silly, Melvin.'

'We can take Ace's car. I can come back and get mine.'

'What would you do, walk all the way over here?'

'Sure. It ain't far.'

'I appreciate the offer,' she said. 'I really do. But that'd be so much trouble for you.'

The waiter returned. He had the bill on a small plastic tray. He set the tray on the table. Vicki quickly picked up the bill. She studied it for a few moments, then took cash from her purse. She placed three twenties on the tray, covered them with the bill, and smiled at Melvin. 'All ready?'

'Don't you gotta wait for your change?'

Shaking her head, she scooted to the end of the booth and stood up. Melvin saw that her blouse hung loose past her waist, draping the top of a white, pleated skirt. The skirt covered her almost to the knees.

She waited for Melvin to rise, then took hold of his hand. Her warmth seemed to flow up his arm. He felt as if his heart were swelling.

This is so great, he thought. This is so great – it *can't* end. We'll go somewhere, now.

It'll be *her* idea. Just wait and see. We'll get into the parking lot and she'll say, Why don't you follow me in your car? We can go to my place. Ace isn't home. We can sit around and have a drink and talk some more. I'd like that, wouldn't you?

It'll *happen*. That's just what she'll say. She just paid for my dinner, for Christ sake. And she still wants to know how I wiped out Pollock.

He opened the door for Vicki, and they stepped into the night.

'Will you walk me to my car?' she asked, still holding his hand.

'Sure.'

They started across the parking lot.

'Did you enjoy your dinner?' she asked.

253

'Being with you.'

She gave his hand a gentle squeeze. 'We'll do it again soon, all right?'

'Yeah.' Melvin felt himself sinking. She was getting ready to tell him goodnight. She wasn't going to say they should go somewhere now. Her suggestion that they soon have dinner again didn't help dispel his gloom. He wanted to be with her now – tonight. 'Next time, I'm gonna pay.'

'Next time,' Vicki said, 'maybe you'll trust me enough to be honest about things.'

Her words, though softly spoken, struck him like a punch. 'I *trust* you.' He sounded whiny to himself.

Vicki stopped beside Ace's Mustang, released his hand, and took the keys out of her purse. She faced him. 'I wish you did, Melvin. I don't know what kind of relationship we can have, if you feel you need to keep things from me. Frankly, I'm a little disappointed. If you can't be open with me . . .'

'I'll be open. It was just . . . we was in a restaurant.'

'We're not in the restaurant, now. Nobody's anywhere around.'

'Can't we go someplace? Can't we go someplace and talk? Like maybe your house?'

'Ace is there.'

'Well, how about we just drive? We can park someplace and . . .'

'I have to get home. I can't be away from a telephone. One of my patients is about due . . .'

'Huh?'

'I might have to deliver a baby tonight. In fact, we're lucky we made it through dinner. I can't go anywhere but home, Melvin. I'll give you a call in a few days.'

'A few days?'

'I need some time to think. I'm not at all sure about things anymore.'

'Just 'cause I didn't tell you about Patricia?'

'I don't care about that. I'm interested, but . . . it's the

254

fact that you're keeping me closed out. You're afraid to *reveal* yourself to me. That's what hurts.'

His mouth was dry, his heart slamming. 'What if I tell you I sent Patricia to waste him?'

'Did you?'

'Maybe.'

'See? You still won't open up. What do you think, I'm going to tell the police? Do you think I've got a tape recorder here, or something?' She suddenly pulled open her purse and thrust it toward his face. 'Look. You see a recorder in there?'

The lights of the parking lot were bright enough for him to see a billfold, a compact, a tube of lipstick, and a small pack of tissues inside the purse. Nothing that resembled a tape recorder.

'Satisfied?' Vicki asked. She snapped the purse shut, whirled around, fumbled with the keys, got one into the door lock and opened the door. She tossed her purse onto the car seat. Then, she turned and face Melvin. She shook her head. 'I . . . I don't know what's wrong with me. I'm sorry. Will you forgive me?'

'Well, yeah. Sure It's all right.'

Leaning forward, she brushed her lips lightly against his mouth. 'I'll call you,' she whispered.

He stood there speechless, amazed and thrilled, and watched her climb into the car. The door thumped shut. The engine stuttered to life. The headlights came on. The driver's window slid down.

Lurching forward, he reached through the window and clutched Vicki's shoulder. 'It was Patricia,' he blurted. 'She did it, but I made her do it. Hypnosis, that's how. Okay? Okay?'

She reached across her body and pressed Melvin's hand down on her shoulder. 'I'll see you tomorrow night,' she said. 'I'll call. Ace is going away, so we'll have the house to ourselves.'

She released his hand. She slowly backed up the car, and he felt her shoulder slide away.

CHAPTER TWENTY-SEVEN

She pressed herself against Jack. He embraced her. The muscles of his chest and arms were big and hard. Wrapped by him, Vicki felt small, protected, safe. She kissed him. She opened her mouth and tasted Jack's lips and tongue.

It was like standing in the first rays of sunlight after a night of awful darkness and numbing cold.

Too soon, he eased away from her and shut the door. 'That was well worth the wait,' he said. He reached out and lightly stroked her cheek. 'You look wonderful. And a little rattled.'

'It wasn't much fun.'

'Can I get you something to drink?'

'Coffee?'

He nodded. He took her hand, and led her across the foyer. They entered a living room that seemed huge and plush compared to Ace's. The thick carpet felt soft under her shoes. 'This is very nice,' she said.

'Did you have any trouble finding your way?'

'Not much,' she said. In fact, she had been so distracted and dazed by the encounter with Melvin that she'd driven past the street and didn't even notice her mistake until she found herself a block from Ace's house.

She bashed her forearm against a dining room chair.

'Ouch!' Jack said. 'You all right?'

Grimacing, she let go of his hand and rubbed her arm. 'Like you said, I'm rattled. And a little . . . tipsy. I had a drink before he got there. I don't think I could've faced him

256

sober. Then, I wanted to loosen him up so we both kept drinking.'

'And who was this mystery date?'

'Melvin Dobbs.'

'You're kidding.' He led her into the kitchen, past a break-fast table, and pulled out one of the stools at the serving counter. While he held her steady, she climbed onto the stool. She leaned over the counter and braced herself on her elbows. 'Crazy Melvin?' he asked. 'That's who you had dinner with? The guy who's smitten with you? The guy who's missing a screw?'

'That's him.'

Jack frowned at her from the other side of the counter. 'Why?'

'I wanted him to admit killing Pollock.'

'And did he?'

'He did.'

Jack's eyes widened.

'That missing nurse? Patricia? He said he hypnotised her and made her do it.'

'Good God.'

'Yeah.'

'Do you believe him?'

Vicki nodded.

'Well.' Jack rubbed his jaw. He turned away and walked over the the coffee maker at the far end of the kitchen. 'No wonder you wouldn't tell me what you were up to.'

'I just didn't want you to worry. Or try to talk me out of it.'

'I would've done both,' he said. He scooped ground coffee into the filter and looked around at her. 'I knew you had guts, lady, but . . .'

'But you didn't realise I'm crazy?'

'I wouldn't go so far as to say you're crazy. Hey, you might slug me again. But why did you do it?'

'He has to be put away.'

Jack slid the filter into place, poured water into the top of

257

the machine, flicked a switch that turned on a red light, and came back to her. He stood at the other side of the counter. 'Why do you suppose Dobbs made this confession to you?'

'He wants me to . . . approve of him. I let him believe he was doing me a big favour by killing Pollock. I mean, Pollock had insulted me in front of him. I as much as told him I thought it was great that he'd . . . stood up for my honour. By nailing the guy.'

'So he told you what he knew you wanted to hear. Whether or not he actually did the deed.'

She stared up at Jack. 'Hey, whose side are you on, here?'

'Who do you think?'

'You're making it sound like the whole things was a waste of time. God, I damn near *seduced* him.'

'Under which circumstances, any reasonable man – not to mention social outcast with questionable emotional stability who has been fantasizing about having you as his lover – would've admitted almost anything.'

'Come on, don't say that. It was awful. He . . . he *loves* me, Jack. And I encouraged it. I felt like the biggest liar of all time. I felt like such a shit, and you're telling me it means nothing that he confessed?'

'No, I'm not telling you that. His confession would be admissible in court.'

'So it's real evidence?'

'It is. But very weak. Any decent attorney would have no trouble at all convincing a jury that it was given under a form of coercion. You were dangling yourself in front of him like bait. Confess, and I'm all yours.'

Vicki felt herself blushing. 'I didn't say that.'

'From what you've told me, the implication must've been pretty clear to him.'

'So is it evidence, or isn't it?'

'It's enough to set an investigation into motion. It's probable cause for a search warrant.'

'Even to Raines?'

'He'd be a fool not to act on it.' Jack smiled. 'Of course, he *is* a fool. But Bob Dennison isn't.'

'Who's he?'

'The District Attorney. And also my fishing buddy.'

Vicki felt a grin stretch her face. 'Well, it sure pays to be well-connected.'

'That it does. One way or another, I'm sure we can arrange it so that Dobbs will be visited by the authorities first thing in the morning.'

'Then what?'

'We hope they find something tangible.'

She nodded. 'Like Patricia.'

'Or her body. In fact, with what they apparently have on that woman, any physical evidence of her presence in the house should be sufficient grounds for hauling Dobbs in. And you never know what they might find. Pollock's service revolver. His badge. Even some of his blood might've gotten into the house. If Dobbs was involved, there's a very good chance they'll find something to tie him in.'

'Suppose they don't?'

'Then you're in trouble. Dobbs will know you're the one who fingered him, and he might not love you anymore.'

'There's a mixed blessing.'

'You've gone this far. I don't suppose you'd let a little matter like that stop you.'

'I don't suppose I would.'

'We'll see to it that he doesn't get a chance to . . . visit his displeasure on you.'

'Thanks.'

Jack looked over his shoulder. 'Coffee's ready. Do you take cream or sugar?'

Melvin wished he could read the fucker's lips.

He had a very good view of Vicki's back. She had been sitting on the stool since he found the kitchen window. For a while, he hadn't seen anyone else. Then the man had come up to the other side of the counter and started talking to

259

her. The angle was good, so Melvin could see him beyond Vicki's shoulder.

A big guy. He looked like a goddamn football player. He wore a white knit shirt that showed off his muscles.

Melvin didn't know who he was. He for sure wasn't the pregnant lady, though.

Keeping a safe distance back, Melvin had followed Vicki when she left the restaurant's parking lot. He wished she would drive faster. He ached for her to reach Ace's house. Though he couldn't be *with* her, at least he could watch her – find a window and spy on her. That'd be something. He was sure she'd change clothes as soon as she got there. He might get to see her slip out of that shiny blouse, step out of that long white skirt, maybe even take off the rest.

If she didn't take off her clothes, it would still be great to watch her. He knew he could look at her for hours, and every moment would be exciting.

But Vicki didn't drive to Ace's house, the way she'd said she would.

She lied to me, Melvin thought.

Did she lie about *everything?*

His mind reeled with confusion and loss.

Then, her car stopped at a curb. Melvin slowed down. He drove by just in time to see her reach the front door of a big two-storey house.

I know! he told himself.

He felt like a fool for doubting her.

It was nothing. Instead of going straight to Ace's house, Vicki had decided to pay a visit to the pregnant gal. Just look in on her, check on her progress.

She'll be there for a few minutes, then she'll head on home.

It's all right, after all.

Melvin parked near the end of the block. He thought he might wait in his car, but he quickly grew restless.

What if I'm wrong? he wondered. What if she's in there with a guy?

260

No, not Vicki. She wouldn't. No.

But Melvin couldn't get the idea out of his head. He wanted to believe in her, to trust her. But he had to know.

He walked back to the house.

Most of the windows had curtains that were shut, but not the kitchen. The curtains there were wide open.

First, he saw only Vicki. Then the guy stepped up to the counter.

Melvin tried to convince himself that the guy was the *husband* of Vicki's patient. She could be asking about the wife's condition. Any contractions yet?

Bullshit.

Who *is* he? What're they talking about?

It was like watching a drive-in movie without any sound. He could see Vicki and the guy perfectly. But the window was shut and an air conditioning unit hummed loudly nearby, so he couldn't hear a damn thing.

If only he could read the fucker's lips.

Vicki turned sideways and slid off the stool. She stepped around the end of the counter. The guy was saying something. And watching her.

Melvin couldn't read his lips.

But he could read his eyes.

'How long have you lived here?' Vicki asked.

'What?' Jack called. 'You've got to speak up.'

'Wise guy.'

Jack smiled at her from the couch. It looked soft and comfortable, but Vicki had settled into an easy chair a short distance from the corner where he was sitting. 'What'd I do wrong, this time?' he asked.

'You bought a white couch and you gave me black coffee. I don't think the two would go well together.' She raised the cup to her lips. Steam drifted up, hot against her face. She took a sip of the coffee, and sighed.

'Take a chance,' Jack said.

'I'm fine here.'

261

'But out of reach.'

'We can admire each other from afar.'

'Should I confess to something?' he asked. 'Would that get you over here?'

The words made her stomach tighten. 'Don't rub it in, okay? I don't like what I did. It was a rotten trick.'

'Not nearly as rotten as committing murder. If your maneuvers end up getting Dobbs put away, you've done society a considerable service. You'll have taken a killer off the streets. That counts for a lot.'

'I suppose.'

'No supposing about it. It's certainly possible that Pollock wasn't his first victim. And might not be his last, if he isn't stopped.'

'Possible, I guess.'

'That nurse, for instance. He told you that he hypnotised her?'

Vicki nodded, and took another drink of coffee.

'Pretty far out. But we're going on the assumption that he was telling the truth, right? So, if he put her into some kind of trance instead of just asking her politely to knock the guy off, that means she wasn't acting on her own volition. She was compelled to kill Pollock. So what happens to her afterward? Is Dobbs going to let her go on her merry way?'

'He could get her to forget everything that happened while she was under hypnosis,' Vicki said. She frowned into her coffee. A thought, a new idea, a realization heavy with portent was stirring somewhere deep in her mind. She concentrated, trying to force it to the surface. But Jack spoke again, distracting her.

'The nurse might forget it, but the cops know she was involved and they're looking for her. If they got their hands on her, they might make her remember.'

'If they hypnotised her again,' Vicki said, 'they might be able to get the truth.' What *was* that thought? Where'd it go?

'And if Dobbs knows enough on the subject to persuade

someone to commit murder – I imagine that takes quite an expert – then he'd have to realize she's a threat to him. As long as she's alive.'

'Yeah.' Vicki searched her mind. It was like swimming under murky water, hunting a message hidden deep in the weeds along the bottom.

And having to come up for air when Jack spoke.

'It's my guess,' he said, 'that Dobbs has already killed the nurse. Eliminated the only person – except for you – who can tie him in.'

Vicki held up her hand.

'What?'

She shook her head and gazed into the coffee. She submerged herself again, thought of herself as taking a deep breath and plunging into the darkness. Going deeper. Her mind was a river and the lost thought was down there someplace. *Come on, where are you?*

Suddenly, Charlie Gaines was on her back, clinging to her, groping her, driving her down. The horrors of last night rushed in. She could feel him, feel the ache in her lungs . . .

'What's wrong?' Jack asked.

His words wrenched her to the surface. The coffee was shivering, the cup tinkling against the saucer. She rose carefully out of the chair, placed the cup and saucer on the table, then stepped around the table and sat down on the couch close to Jack.

He slipped an arm around her. She leaned against his side.

'I didn't mean to scare you, Vicki. But the fact remains that you've put yourself at considerable risk by . . .'

'It isn't that,' she said. 'I had . . . I flashed back to last night. Charlie. In the river.'

His hand gently covered her wounded shoulder. 'I'm sorry. You know, with all this Dobbs business, I'd almost forgotten about Charlie. That must've been so awful for you.'

Looking up at Jack, she managed a smile. 'Hey, it wasn't all bad. Afterward was pretty nice.'

'Till you conked out on me.'

'I hope you minded your manners.'

'It wasn't easy, but . . .'

The lost thought burst to the surface of her mind, full and clear. As if it had waited for her to stop searching, then popped up to surprise her. 'My God,' she muttered, stunned by what she suddenly knew. *Knew*.

'Honest, I was a perfect gentleman.'

'Hypnosis. That's how . . .' She squeezed Jack's leg. 'Melvin killed Charlie.'

'What?'

'Oh, Jesus. Melvin . . . he was doing me another favour, the scum. First, he gave me the car. Then, he "defended my honour" by making Patricia kill Pollock. And then . . . then he got hold of Charlie. He knew I owed money to Charlie. He knew I wasn't a partner at the clinic. So he got hold of Charlie and *helped* me.'

'That would explain a lot,' Jack said, staring at her, understanding. 'If Charlie was under Dobbs's influence when he called me in Monday morning . . .'

'I *knew* something was wrong.'

'I remember. You were concerned about his health, thought he might be dying.'

'Melvin made him do it. Hypnotised him, just like Patricia, and told him to make me a partner, make me *inherit* the whole clinic . . . Oh, damn it. The dirty . . . it wasn't any accident last night. Charlie's crash . . . Melvin must've staged it. He was *giving* me the clinic.'

'It makes sense,' Jack said. 'It's all supposition, but it sure fits neatly into the pattern. If he really did hypnotise Patricia and compel her to murder Pollock, which he's admitted, then the rest of it follows.'

She stared into Jack's eyes.

He believed her. He knew. She didn't have to convince him.

Something seemed to tear inside her.

She turned and hunched herself down against Jack's chest. He put his arms around her.

264

'I killed Charlie,' she whispered.

'No.'

'I did. I killed him.'

Jack held her gently. She could hear the quick beating of his heart.

My damn mouth, she thought. I murdered him when I told Melvin I wasn't a partner. When I told him about the loan.

'And Pollock,' she murmured. 'And Patricia, if she's dead. I killed them all.'

'Shhh.' Jack stroked her hair, carressed her back. 'You didn't do any of that.'

I stopped at Melvin's station. Bought gas from him. Thought the Arco might be closed. Couldn't wait for morning to fill the tank. That's how I started it.

No, I started it back in high school. Didn't tease him. Didn't torment him. I was nice to him.

I was nice to him, and two people are dead. Maybe three. Three lives.

Because of me.

Melvin, face pressed to the window screen, watched through a gap in the curtains. A tiny gap. No more than half an inch, but enough.

He saw Vicki when she twisted around on the couch, saw when she huddled against the big man's chest, saw when he put his arms around her.

The filthy, lying cunt!

CHAPTER TWENTY-EIGHT

'You might be wrong about all of this, you know.'

'I'm not wrong.' She rubbed her face against the soft knit fabric of Jack's shirt, feeling his sturdy chest beneath it, feeling his warmth. 'It was his way of . . . courting me. They'd all be alive.'

'You can't take the blame on yourself.'

'None of it would've happened.'

Jack's hands moved slowly up and down her back. In a gentle, soothing voice, he said, 'I was a prosecutor in Detroit for a short time. Before I moved here. I moved here because I couldn't stand it. The brutalities, the viciousness I saw every day. My last case, the one that finished me . . . two guys walked into a liquor store with shotguns. The owner, a fellow named John Baxter, didn't give them any trouble. He handed over all the money in the cash register. It was a lot of money. And the robbers had it in their hands. Then they proceeded to blast everyone in the store. They killed Baxter in front of his wife. She was bagging a six-pack of Pepsi for two teenaged girls who'd stopped by on their way home from the junior high down the road. They killed the wife and both girls. They killed a mother whose three kids were waiting in their car while she ran in for a carton of cigarettes. They killed a guy over at the paperback rack. And a stock boy who showed up when he heard the shots.'

'Horrible,' Vicki muttered.

'About as horrible as it can get,' Jack said. His caressing hands stopped in the middle of her back. In a low voice, he said, 'We got a murder-one conviction against the money in the cash register.'

Vicki raised her face and looked him in the eyes. 'Is that some kind of a bad joke?'

'A lesson,' he said. 'A lesson in blame. That pair of mutants went into the liquor store because they wanted the money in the cash register. In spite of that, you apparently think it's absurd to blame the money for the slaughter those seven people. Isn't that right?'

'Of course.'

'Then how can you blame yourself for what Dobbs may have done because he wanted you?'

'How can I not?' she asked.

266

When she said that, she saw tears come into his eyes. He turned his head away quickly. Vicki raised a hand to his cheek. She eased his face around, stretched upward and pressed her lips to his mouth.

She sank into a warm, quiet place where there was only the feel of him. The moist softness of his lips and tongue. The gentle pressure of his hands. The firm muscles of his chest. The smooth skin she caressed through the shoulder and side of his shirt.

But she was twisted so, to hold him this way.

'I'm breaking,' she finally whispered against his lips.

'Can't have that happen,' he said. 'You're too precious to break.'

She brushed her lips against his, then climbed off the couch. She looked down at him. He was slumped against the cushion, big arms hanging at his sides, knees spread. His white shirt was askew, his hair mussed. His mouth, open just a bit, had a reddish hue around the lips from pressure and rub of the kissing. He gazed up at her with eyes that seemed, somehow, both calm and eager. She watched them lower slowly down her body, and up again, and linger on her face.

Her heart pounded. Her mouth suddenly felt parched.

Jack raised an eyebrow. He glanced at the length of the couch. 'Shall we stretch out, or . . . ?'

'What's upstairs?' Vicki asked.

'The bedrooms.'

'Show me?'

He pursed his lips and blew softly, not making a sound. 'Just a thought.'

'And a fine one, at that.'

Vicki stepped out of the way, and Jack got to his feet. They crossed the living room, walking side by side, almost touching. At the bottom of the stairway, Vicki reached across his back and rested her hand on his hip. He moved in against her. She felt him caress her shoulder blade, sliding the slick fabric against her skin. Together, they climbed the stairs.

As they walked along the second floor hallway, she looked

at him. He faced her and smiled. She bumped him with her hip. His smiled widened.

They entered a room, and he flicked a light switch. A lamp came on beside the king-sized bed. The bed was made, the rest of the room tidy.

Vicki halted just inside the doorway.

Suddenly doubting.

He was a man who lived alone. His bedroom shouldn't necessarily be a mess, but . . .

He'd cleaned it up. Gathered the dirty clothes, hidden the clutter, put on fresh sheets.

Knowing I'd be here.

Knowing.

In the back seat of his car, Melvin stripped naked. He struggled into his greasy coveralls and pulled the zipper up. Then, he pushed his bare feet into the old leather shoes he liked to wear at the station.

Outside, he opened the trunk. He took out his tyre tool. It had a lug wrench at one end, a prying wedge at the other. It felt good and heavy in his hand. He lowered the trunk lid. Holding it down, he turned his back to it, hopped up, and drove it down with his rump. The latch made a quiet click.

He swung the bar, slapping it into his left hand as he walked toward the house.

I'll fix the bitch, he thought. The dirty, lying whore.

He couldn't stop *seeing* her. The way she turned on the couch and pressed herself against that bastard's chest. The way she kissed him. And how the guy's hands moved on her back as if he *owned* her.

The images sickened him. He felt as if cold hands were wringing his guts.

She'll be sorry. She'll be so sorry.

Melvin hurried alongside the house to its rear. The windows back here were dark. The patio, dim in the moonlight, was a concrete slab with a couple of lounge chairs and a barbeque.

The screen door wasn't latched. It squeaked as he eased it open. Holding it away with his back, he tried the knob of the inner, wooden door. Locked.

He rammed the wedge of the tyre tool into the crack between the door and the jamb just where he figured the lock tongue should be. He threw his weight against the bar. The wood made crunching sounds. It bulged out, cracking. He drove the bar in deeper, working it back and forth, thrusting it, feeling the give of the lock's steel tongue.

The door swung inward.

He stepped into the house, drawing the screen door slowly shut. The kitchen was dark except for a glow of light spilling in from the entryway.

He listened. He heard only the pounding rush of his own heartbeat.

When he took a step, the sole of his shoe made a scuffing sound. He squatted down and loosened his laces. He stepped out of the shoes. The linoleum floor felt cool and slick under his sweaty feet.

He took a deep breath. He felt so tight and cold and shaky inside. If only he could calm down.

Calm down and enjoy what he was about to do.

He wished he could feel some excitement.

The kind of thrill he got when he nailed all the others.

But he couldn't. He hurt too much.

She had hurt him too much.

Now you're gonna pay for it. You don't fuck with Melvin Dobbs.

Silently, he made his way toward the light.

'Something wrong?' Jack asked, stepping up behind her. She felt the light pressure of him against her back. He put his hands on her sides. His warm breath stirred her hair, made her scalp tingle.

'It's . . . going awfully fast.'

'It doesn't have to.'

'I know I'm the one who suggested . . .'

269

'In the heat of the moment.'

'Yeah. I was a little carried away.'

His hands slipped around to her front. They made small circles, sliding the blouse against her belly. Vicki felt as if warm oil was being spread on her skin. She caressed the backs of his hands, his wrists and forearms.

'Shall we go downstairs?' he asked.

'I don't know,' she whispered.

She remembered her regret that she hadn't made love with Paul that morning so long ago on the driving raft. It had been their last chance, and she had missed it. There had been other men . . . a few . . . but she'd loved none of them.

Do I love Jack? she wondered. It comes down to that, doesn't it?

She knew that she cared for him, that she desired him. But love?

The feelings that she'd had for Paul certainly weren't there – the intimacy, the mystery, the ache of longing when they were apart. But maybe you only get that once. Maybe that's all they hand out, and Paul was it.

She had refused to settle for anything less than what she'd known with him. She'd looked back on their times together as the way it *should* be. Nothing afterward had even come close.

Jack comes close, she told herself.

I can't go through the rest of my life crippled by the memories of how it was with Paul. It was a brief, wonderful time, but it's gone. Forever.

And Jack's here.

And who knows about tomorrow. This could be it, our one and only chance, and if I don't take it maybe years from now I'll look back and wish . . .

'You're trembling,' Jack said.

'I know.'

'Let's go on down to the living room.'

She guided his hands down the front of her blouse and up beneath it to her belly. As they drifted over her skin, she unfastened the buttons. She sank against him, reaching back and holding the sides of his legs. His hands moved slowly, lightly roaming as if he were a blind man who could only know her by touch, whose hands were his eyes and he wanted to see the texture of her skin and memorise every curve and hollow. Their slow exploration brushed her blouse open. Soon, they curled over her brassière. Her nipples, already hard, ached against the lacey cups. She didn't want the fabric in the way, shielding her from the feel of his skin.

She wanted to reach up and open the catch at the front of her bra. She didn't do it. She rubbed his legs, and let Jack go on in his own way.

Come on, she thought. The bra.

A corner of her mind was amused by her impatience. Wasn't she the one who'd thought they should wait, see each other many times, slowly growing more intimate, slowly moving closer to a distant night when they would finally complete their long journey?

Then, she felt him unhook the clasp. Lowering her head, she watched his hands slip beneath the black lace cups. She moaned at the feel of him. His mouth pressed the back of her head. He roamed her breasts, his touch so soft it was like a warm wind. His fingertips drew circles on her nipples. Too lightly. Tormenting her. Making her squirm.

She reached behind him and squeezed his buttocks. As if this were a signal, he squeezed her breasts, kneaded them. Breathless, she brought her hands up, pressed his hands hard against her, then peeled them away and turned around and embraced him and found his mouth.

Melvin stopped in the hallway near the open door and leaned against the wall. Moaning, gasping sounds came from inside the room. The creak and squawk of bedsprings.

He knew what they were doing.

They wouldn't be doing it for long.

He wiped his lips with the back of a hand.

271

They're making it easy for me, he thought. I'll be on top of them before they know I'm there.

'No. Wait.' She sounded winded. 'Not yet.'

'What's wrong?' A man's voice.

'It's rubber time.' Melvin could almost see her smiling as she said it. Smiling and panting, her breasts rising and falling as she gasped for air, her naked body shiny with sweat.

'A rubber? Are you kidding?'

'I just don't want to take any chances.'

'Aren't you on the pill or something?'

'I'm not worried about birth control.'

'You think I've got diseases?'

'Would you rather argue, or . . .'

He moaned. A moan of pleasure. Melvin wondered what she was doing to him. He could guess.

In a low voice, the guy said, 'Hang on, I'll get one.' The bed creaked. There were quiet footfalls on the carpet.

Melvin raised the tyre tool, though he didn't think the guy would leave the room.

'I hate these things.'

'I know. It's like wearing a glove.' She sounded amused. 'Come here and give it to me.'

'That's not how they work.'

She laughed.

There were more footsteps. The bed squeaked again. Melvin heard the tearing of the condom's foil wrapper. He lowered the tyre tool and rested it across his leg.

'Think it'll fit?' the guy asked.

'Braggart.'

Then the guy went 'Uhhhh. Yeahhh.'

Melvin could picture her unrolling the thing down him. He could almost feel the tightness of the cool moist tube, feel her fingers through its thin latex.

He'd gone to whores a few times over in Blayton. They'd made him wear one. But they'd made *him* put it on.

'There,' she said. 'All set.'

Melvin ran his tongue around inside his dry mouth. He

took a deep breath. His heart was drumming. He was hard, and saw that the front of his coveralls jutted out like a tent.

The bed groaned.

'Oh, yeahhhh.' Him.

'It . . . doesn't feel like a glove to me.' Her.

'What does it . . . feel like?'

'A telephone pole.'

'Yeahhhh.'

Time to party, Melvin thought.

He pictured blood flying, spraying his coveralls.

Can't have that.

He rubbed his mouth. Crouching, he set his tyre tool on the hallway runner. He stood and slowly lowered the zipper of his coveralls. He shrugged the garment off his shoulders. It dropped around his feet, and he stepped out of it. Then he picked up the steel bar.

Panting, he leaned against the wall. It was cool against his back and rump. He listened.

'Oh . . . oh.' She sounded as if she was being beaten to death.

Any minute, Melvin thought.

'Oh! . . . Yes . . . Oh yes.'

Melvin stepped into the doorway.

A lamp beside the bed cast bright light onto their thrashing bodies. The guy was stretched out on top of her, half kneeling, his white rump flexing as he ran himself into her. Her hands were clenching his buttocks, Her legs were spread wide, knees high, heels digging into the mattress, pushing herself up to meet his thrusts.

Melvin walked silently toward the end of the bed.

He couldn't see their faces, so they couldn't see him.

She kept bucking herself up against the guy, gasping and murmuring. 'Oh . . . Oh God . . . Yes . . . In, in.'

Melvin pictured himself ramming the iron right up lover-boy's ass. That'd be a kick, but it wouldn't do the job.

He leaped onto the bed and dropped his knees onto the guy's rump, onto her hands.

273

Driving him down. The guy grunted.

She squealed.

'How's that for *in*,' Melvin gasped. Felt his knees sliding away. Threw himself forward and clutched the wet nape of the guy's neck, stopping the slide, and swung the bar.

The impact made pain blast through his bitten hand and streak up his arm to the shoulder.

But it sure did a number on lover-boy. Knocked his head sideways. Sent a spray of blood slapping the wall.

'No!'

She had blood flecking her face. Her eyes looked ready to pop out of their sockets.

'Yes,' Melvin said, and smashed the lug wrench end of the tool once more against the man's crushed temple. This time, the blood flew up spattering Melvin's face and shoulders. The limp body suddenly rocked beneath him. His knees slipped down the backs of the legs. He flopped, and before he could scurry up something trapped under him – one of her hands – twisted and clawed his thigh and shoved between his legs. He flung himself backward just as it found his genitals. The hand clamped shut. The fingers bumped him. They didn't catch hold, though. Missed their chance to squeeze and crush, missed their chance to disable him. But the bump was enough to send a shock-wave of nauseating pain through his body.

He hunched over and grabbed the back of the dead man's leg to hold himself steady. He needed a second. Just a second to recover.

But the bitch didn't give it to him.

She lurched and twisted, throwing the body sideways, tumbling Melvin off the bed. His back slammed the floor. The guy landed on top of him. And she was on top of the body. Melvin could feel her up there, jostling the body, her weight shoving the bastard's butt against his face as if she were trying to smother him with it.

She wasn't up there long. Just long enough to untangle herself. Then she either rolled or fell off the pile. She hit the floor beside Melvin. He heard her hit, couldn't see her. Not until he flung himself over, toppling the body away.

She was scuttering toward the door on her hands and knees, whimpering, looking back over her shoulder. Melvin crawled over the body, got to his feet, and went after her. She pushed herself up. She stumbled into the hall. Melvin lurched through the doorway. She was already a few strides ahead of him. He cocked back his arm, ready to hurl the bar at her head. But what if he missed? Then he'd be without his only weapon and *she* might pick it up – use it on him. He kept the bar in his hands and raced after her.

But she was faster.

She's gonna get away!

He lost sight of her when she darted into the kitchen.

She's gonna get out the door and start screaming!

Melvin's shoulder hit the doorframe. He bounced off, grunting, and stumbled into the dark kitchen. And spotted her. She wasn't going for the door. Her pale figure was at the counter, reaching out, her back to Melvin.

He slapped the wall, raced his hand down it, and found the switch plate. He flipped the switch. As light filled the kitchen, she whirled around.

A butcher knife in her hand.

She stood there, gazing at him, blinking sweat out of her eyes, gulping air. Ropes of wet hair hung over her eyes. Her face was dripping, sweat mixing with the guy's blood and running down, dripping off her jaw. Her chest was heaving, her breasts shaking. Her wet skin gleamed as if slicked with oil.

She looked beautiful. Like some kind of warrior goddess.

Melvin stared. He *wanted* her. He'd only wanted to kill her, but now he ached for the feel of her savage body under him, writhing and slippery.

Beneath the desire, he felt a chilly stirring of fear.

'All right,' she gasped. 'End . . . of the line . . . fucker.' She took a step toward him.

Melvin fought an urge to back away. He bent over a little and raised the tyre iron. 'Come 'n get it.'

She suddenly rushed him, snarling, feet slapping the floor, knife slashing.

Melvin's heart seemed to freeze.

She's gonna kill me!

He swung at her face. The iron bar knocked her jaw crooked. He saw her eyes roll upward as her head was whipped aside. At the same instant, he felt a streak of warmth across his belly. Not pain. Just a long line of heat.

But the blow from the tool had done it's job.

He watched her spin away, head tipped back, arms flying out, knife sailing from her hand. She crashed against the floor, slide sideways on her belly, then lay motionless.

Melvin looked down at himself.

She got me!

He felt sick as he stared at the wound. It was five or six inches long, straight across the belly, just below his navel. A curtain of blood flowed down from it, sheathing his groin and thighs. His penis was shrinking, getting smaller and smaller as if it wanted to hide.

He fingered a raw edge of the cut. Peeled it back like a lip. Not very deep. But now it was beginning to hurt. To *really* hurt.

'You bitch!' he shrieked. 'Look what you done!'

She moved a little.

He hurled the bar. She flinched and gasped 'Uh!' as it gouged the skin of her shoulder blade. It didn't stick, though. It bounced off and skittered across the linoleum.

Melvin, forearm to his slashed belly, hurried to pick up the bar.

It had come to a stop beside the knife.

He picked up the knife, instead. When he straightened up, he saw that his legs were red all the way down to his feet.

He stepped over to the sink, being careful not to slip and fall on his own blood. There, he found a moist dishrag. Knife

276

clamped between his teeth, he folded the rag and pressed it against his cut.

'You hurt me bad, you bitch.'

She just lay sprawled there. She bled where the bar had torn her skin.

Melvin remembered that she'd flinched and made a sound. So she wasn't out cold. Dazed, maybe, but not unconscious. Still able to feel pain.

He straddled her and sat on her back. With the tip of the knife, he prodded her wound. She made a quick, high bleat and her muscles fluttered under him.

Melvin peeled the rag off his cut. He squeezed it into a tight ball, blood spilling out between his fingers. Then lay the knife between her shoulder blades, grabbed her hair, lifted her head off the floor, and stuffed the rag into her mouth.

If she was dazed, she came out of it when Melvin drew the blade across her brow. She gave a spastic jerk as if jolted by a charge of electricity. She shrieked into the rag. She rammed her hands and knees against the floor, started to push herself up. Melvin cut with one hand. With the other, he yanked her hair. With a wet, tearing sound, her scalp peeled back. He kept his grip on it and rode the crazed, screaming woman like a horse for a moment before she threw him.

He hit the floor, rolling. And got to his knees.

And held up the thatch of hair. It swayed, the flesh from the top of her head sprinkling a circle of blood.

'Scalped ya,' he said, grinning as he panted for air.

She wiped blood out of her eyes. Looked around. Scurried toward the tyre tool.

'No y'don't!'

Melvin sprang up. His feet flew out from under him. His rump pounded the floor.

Slipping and sliding on the blood, he crawled toward her.

She got a hand on the tyre tool.

He pounded the knife down into her back.

She flopped. She made a wet smacking sound when she hit the floor.

Melvin pulled the knife out, raised it high, and stabbed Ace again.

CHAPTER TWENTY-NINE

Vicki squeezed him as hard as she could, crushing him against her, then let her arms flop onto the bed. She slid her feet down the backs of his legs, and lay spread-eagled beneath his weight. He was still deep inside her. She was filled with him, peaceful and tired.

Jack pushed himself up enough so his face was above her. His chest no longer tight against hers, air came in, cool against her hot, damp skin. He stared into her eyes, searching them. He looked very solemn. After a long while, he said, 'I think I love you, Vicki Chandler.'

She felt as if her heart were swelling. She reached up and held his sides. 'I think maybe I love you, too.'

He eased down and gently kissed her mouth. When he pushed himself up again, he smiled. 'And it's not just your body.'

'Oh, sure thing.'

'I can take it or leave it.'

'Right.' She flexed muscles, tightening them around the hardness inside her, and watched Jack's eyes widen.

'On second thought. . .,' he whispered.

She reached up and pushed her fingers into his damp hair. She drew his head down. She kissed him. She felt him start to move a little, squirm a little, tentatively pressing this way and that as if exploring the soft walls that held him.

'And one for the road?' she asked.

The exploration stopped. Jack raised his head. 'You're not going to leave, are you?'

'Indeed I am.'

'Why?'

She didn't want to leave. More than that, she didn't want to cast a shadow over their time together by ending it with an argument. 'Deep, dark reasons,' she said, and tried to look mysterious.

'Stay. Please.'

'I didn't bring my toothbrush.'

'I have a spare.'

'Oh yeah?' She smiled. 'Whose is it? Anybody I know?'

'It's new.' He had such sadness in his eyes. 'It's . . .'

'It's not about a toothbrush, honey.'

'What *is* it about.'

'You and me.'

'But I thought . . .'

'I'd love to stay. And sleep with you. And wake up in the morning in bed with you beside me. And have breakfast together. It would be wonderful. But I won't. That's something . . . I'd rather save.'

Jack nodded. 'I guess I understand. Something special. To save for another time. Like, for the honeymoon.'

She felt heat rush to her face. Her throat went tight. 'Yeah, like for . . . that.'

She stared into his eyes.

'I can feel your heart,' he said.

'I should think so.'

'Don't worry, I'm not going to drop the big question on you. You're not the only one around here who can save things for later.'

She felt neither disappointment nor relief, only the sense of wonder and excitement at knowing that he wanted her. He'd said that he loved her, but some people spoke those words easily. Now, he had gone so much further. He had let her know that he needed her in the midst of his life, part of him.

279

'Oh, Jack,' she whispered. She wrapped her arms around his broad back and kissed him. Gently at first, feeling tender and comfortable and glad, but soon with urgency as he began to move on top of her, began sliding himself within her hugging depths. His tongue entered her mouth and she sucked its thickness as he thrust, pounding her into the bed.

After bandaging himself in the bathroom, Melvin returned to the kitchen. He pulled the knife out of Ace's back. Then he turned her over.

'Not so tough now, huh?' he asked.

She looked like a *wreck*. A bald wreck. She still had lots of hair on the sides, but the top was a raw, skinned dome. It made her look a little freakish, like Lon Chaney in *Phantom of the Opera*. And all that red on her face and shoulders reminded him of Sissy Spacek in *Carrie* after they dumped the bucket of blood on her head at the prom. Her crooked, hanging jaw made her look like . . . Melvin couldn't think of a movie character. That part of her just looked like Ace after a run-in with a tire tool.

The rest of her looked like that sexy babe in the second *Howling* movie. The one who kept howling and showing off her big knockers.

For a moment, staring down at her, Melvin regretted messing her up so badly. If he hadn't ruined her looks, he might've taken her home and brought her back to life.

But that had never been the plan, anyway.

The plan was just to kill her ass.

Vicki's best friend.

See how she likes it.

Lying cunt.

He dropped the knife onto Ace's belly. Then he picked her scalp off the floor and gave it a toss. It dropped with a soft splat onto one of her breasts. He laughed at the look of it there. Then he moved it down to where the knife was. He grabbed her wrists and began dragging her.

A heavy thing.

His sore muscles ached, and he remembered that he'd been bent over just the same way, towing a body, last night in the river.

Killed Pollock for her. Killed old Gaines for her. She owns the fucking clinic because of me, even if she doesn't know it.

Told me I'm special.

Got rid of me and went straight to that big fucking asshole and started making out with him.

Gonna be real sorry, though.

Winded, dripping sweat onto Ace's face, he wanted to just let go and leave her in the hallway.

But his idea was neat. It was worth some work.

So he kept on dragging her. She was leaving faint maroon ribbons on the hallway carpet.

Somebody's gonna have a real job, he thought, cleaning up all this.

He dragged Ace past his coveralls lying in a heap beside her doorway. And kept on dragging her. Finally, he got her into the bedroom at the end of the hall.

This had to be Vicki's room..

Leaving her on the floor, he sat on a corner of the bed to catch his breath. His bandage had come unstuck during the long haul. It hung by one end. Blood was all over his belly and groin and legs. He pressed the bandage into place again, but the tape wouldn't cling. So he just held the bandage there until he could breathe again.

Then he let it dangle. He dragged Ace to the bed, jammed his arms underneath her body, gritted his teeth, and lifted.

Like picking up a damn horse.

But he got her onto the bed. He tugged and shoved until she was lying in the middle. Then he jammed a pillow under her head to prop it up. He arranged her arms so they stretched straight out away from her sides. He spread her legs wide. He admired the display for a few moments, wondered what to do with the scalp, then draped it over the toes of her right foot.

Nice.

He could just see the look on Vicki's face when he showed her.

Melvin found the knife on the floor beside the bed, where it had fallen when he lifted Ace. He took it with him, and went down the hallway to Ace's room. The dead guy was face-down, the broken side of his head against the carpet. The carpet looked as if it had soaked up gallons of blood. Melvin bet that if he stepped on it, over there, the blood would squish up between his toes.

Clothes were scattered over the floor near the foot of the bed. Jockey shorts, shoes and socks, a blue shirt and slacks.

A uniform?

He picked up the shirt. It had a colourful sleeve patch that read, 'Ellsworth Police Department.' A badge swung on its chest. A plastic name plate over the other breast pocket identified its owner as 'Milbourne.'

'Holy shit,' Melvin muttered. ''Nother cop.'

Cops carry guns.

A bright yellow jersey of some kind lay in a heap, partially covering the guy's pants. Melvin picked it up. A nightshirt with Minnie Mouse on the front. Once the shirt was out of the way, he spotted Milbourne's gunbelt and revolver.

Grinning, he waved it at the corpse. 'Thanks, buddy. Left mine home.'

The gun would come in handy when Vicki showed up. Without it, he might've been forced to mess her up. Now, he wouldn't need to get rough.

Just stick it in her face, she'll do what I say.

Step this way, sweetheart. Got something to show you.

My Ace in the hole, he thought, and chuckled.

He took the revolver and knife into the bathroom. He set them on the edge of the sink. Then he tossed his bandage into the waste basket. The bandage on his right hand was loose so he shucked it off and tossed it. Most of his other bandages, he noticed, were hanging and about to fall off. A couple of them were gone, must've ended up on the floor someplace.

Well, none of the bites were all that fresh anymore. The only wound that really mattered was the slice across his belly.

He wondered if he had time to take a shower.

Nice to be all squeaky clean for Vicki.

Bad news, though, if she walked into the house while he was under the spray. He wouldn't even hear her.

Just make it quick, he decided.

He stepped into the tub, skidded the plastic curtain shut, and turned on the water. When it felt hot enough spilling over his hand, he turned the shower knob. Spray spattered down on his back. He straightened up so it hit his chest. Head down, he watched the blood run down his skin. It turned the water pink in front of his feet.

The knife wound kept bleeding. Not much, though.

It reminded him of the Mouth of Ram-Chotep.

No stitches, though. No teeth.

He wondered if it needed stitches. Patricia could do that. She'd done a nice job sewing up the Mouth on Charlie.

Take Vicki home with him, he wouldn't trust Patricia with a needle.

She'd stick it in my eye.

Just have to get rid of her, Melvin told himself.

He pressed a washcloth against his wound, and turned his back to the spray.

Should've got rid of Patricia before, he thought. But he'd had no idea that everything would happen so quickly. It made problems.

He felt worn out.

He'd gone through so much, tonight.

And there was so much more to do. If only he could wish Patricia away. If only he could take Vicki home and not have to worry about dealing with that one.

Maybe keep Vicki in the trunk of his car. Go in the house without her, that'd make it easier.

If Patricia's as hard to rekill as Charlie . . .

He didn't want to think about it.

So much to do.

Made his mind feel soggy.

With a sigh full of weariness, he turned around and shut the water off. He held the washcloth to his wound, slid the curtain aside, and climbed out of the tub. Dripping, he stepped to the bathroom door and opened it. Cool air came in from the hallway. He listened. The house was silent.

Satisfied that Vicki hadn't arrived yet, he left the doorway and dried himself. He clamped the towel against his belly to stop the bleeding while he removed the adhesive tape and gauze from the medicine cabinet.

He used the entire roll of gauze, running the netted fabric back and forth several times across the length of his wound. It soaked up the leaking blood. The tape didn't stick well because his skin was slick. He kept wiping himself dry and adding more tape. Finally, the bandage seemed fairly secure.

He picked up the revolver and stepped into the hallway.

Though he liked the idea of being naked when Vicki showed up, he realised he would have to go outside, lead her to his car, drive her to his house. If he did that and somebody saw him not wearing a stitch . . .

He walked toward his coveralls.

Maybe wait till after she's here, he thought.

Might be awkward, though, trying to keep the gun on her while he dressed.

He put the revolver down, and climbed into his coveralls. They felt hot, confining. The fabric stuck to his damp skin. He left the front open, picked up the gun, and wandered up the hallway to Vicki's room.

He stepped inside.

His heart slammed.

He stared at the bed, at the stained coverlet and pillow.

Ace was gone.

Vicki, curled on her side, head resting on Jack's outstretched arm, lay motionless and stared at him. Only moments ago,

284

she had been caressing his chest and he had mumbled a few words too low and slurred for her to understand.

His eyes were shut. His mouth hung open a bit. He was breathing slowly. She wondered if he was asleep.

She hoped so.

Asleep, he wouldn't give her any trouble about leaving.

She didn't want to leave. She felt lazy and comfortable and safe. She felt as if she were home. This was where she belonged, and Ace's house seemed like a long, empty distance from here.

If she didn't go, she knew she would regret it. She did want there to be something held back, something saved for another time. Not saved for him alone, but also for herself. A special gift hidden away, anticipated.

They had given their bodies and their hearts. All that remained to give was freedom from the ache of parting. It was what they both wanted. It was what she intended to save.

For the honeymoon?

She would *make* it wait for then, no matter how badly she wanted to stay.

Slowly, she lifted her hand off Jack's chest and rolled away from him. The bed made barely a sound as she stood up. Turning, she looked down at Jack. Except for the slow rise and fall of his chest, he didn't move.

Vicki felt the soft breath of the breeze against her skin. It was comfortable, now, but it wouldn't remain quite so warm as the night went on. The bed's top sheet lay rumpled on the floor. She crouched and picked it up, and floated it down over Jack's sleeping form.

He didn't wake up.

Vicki shook her head. Disappointed in herself. Knowing her only concern hadn't been for Jack's comfort. A corner of her mind had hoped the touch of the sheet would disturb his sleep and he would try to stop her from leaving.

She found herself wanting to kiss him goodnight.

Right. Why don't you just shake him awake and be done with it? Or climb back in bed and go to sleep?

Leave or don't. Stop playing games.

Resolved . . . resigned . . . Vicki gathered up her clothes. She carried them into the hallway.

She considered turning off the bedroom light and shutting the door. But the room going dark might awaken him. The door might squeak.

So she left the room as it was, moved silently through the hallway and down the stairs. At the bottom of the stairs, she put on her clothes. She carried her shoes into the living room. There, she spotted her purse on the easy chair.

I ought to leave him a note, she thought.

Right, and maybe he'll wake up while you're writing it . . .

This isn't just another ploy to postpone leaving, she told herself. He's going to wake up alone. He'll miss me, and he'll be hurt that I snuck away. I *have* to leave him a note.

Vicki sat on the chair, opened her purse, and took out a notepad and pen.

Melvin's mind reeled as he searched.

Ace was dead, damn it! The dead don't get up and run away!

No?

Where is she?

The bedroom window was open, but its screen was still in place.

He dropped to his knees and peered under the bed.

He rushed to the closet and yanked its door open.

He ran into the hallway.

He felt sick and dizzy. This *couldn't* be happening. It was like a rotten dream. Running down the hall, he wondered if maybe it *was* a dream. Maybe he'd fallen asleep in the shower and he would wake up in a minute choking on water – and Ace would still be lying in the bed where she belonged. Still dead.

I'm not dreaming, he told himself.

Ace isn't dead.

Or Vicki or *someone* showed up while he was in the shower and took her away.

He raced into the living room. The carpet looked clean. If she'd come this way, there had to be blood. Unless someone was carrying her. Then, maybe . . .

The front door had a guard chain on it. She must've put the chain on so Vicki couldn't come in and surprise her with the cop.

She hadn't gone out that way.

Melvin rushed into the kitchen. His hip bumped a chair, crashing the chair against the edge of the table. He flinched, more from the sudden noise than the slight pain. Sidestepping, he swivelled his head.

The floor was smeared and splashed with blood over where he'd nailed Ace. There were even foot tracks.

But no Ace.

The screen door was shut. The inner wooden door with its splintered edge stood open.

He had left it open, himself, so . . .

He suddenly felt as if he'd been kneed in the stomach. He bent over, gasping, and stared.

At red smudges on the linoleum leading to the doorway. His gaze followed them backward to the messy area.

He groaned.

He could *see* Ace. See her staggering in from the hallway entrance, slipping and sliding through the blood, coming out of it on this side, tracking it to the door.

To confirm what he already knew, he stepped up close to the screen door and touched its handle.

Sticky. His fingertip came away stained.

'NO! NO NO *NO*..!' He slapped a hand across his mouth to block the shouts.

Gotta calm down, he thought.

She's alive. She's outside. She got away. She's gonna fuck up everything.

No.

He pushed open the door and leaped onto the patio. He scanned the darkness of the back yard.

I'll find you. I'll find you, you bitch!

There was some kind of room at the rear of the lawn. A laundry room or something.

Melvin ran to it, flung open the door and turned on the light. No blood on the floor. But he checked a small enclosure beside the door. Nothing in there but a toilet. He hurried past a washing machine, a basin, a drier. He jerked open a pair of cupboard doors at the end of the room. Then he rushed back outside.

What if she got over to a neighbour's house?

Cops might be on their way.

I bet she can't talk. Not the way I fixed her jaw.

They'd still call the cops.

He ran. He ran for the corner of the house. The grass was wet and springy under his bare feet.

He'd left his shoes in the kitchen.

No time to worry about them.

He dashed alongside the house.

All that mattered was getting to his car. Getting to his car before the cops showed up. And driving. Driving to the other house. And blowing that fucker's brains out. And getting his hands on Vicki.

Take her home.

What about Patricia?

That's a good one. The whole fucking world was falling on his head. Patricia was just one little piece of it. The least of his worries.

Just worry about getting out of here and getting Vicki.

When he reached the front yard, he stopped running. He stuck the revolver inside his coveralls and clamped it against his side. He scanned the lawn, hoping to find Ace sprawled on the grass. But she wasn't there. On the sidewalk, he looked both ways. No sign of her there, either.

He wished he'd parked closer. His car was at the end of the block. He wanted to run, but forced himself to walk.

He watched the neighbour's house as he strode by. Lights shone from its windows. He saw no one peering out at him.

Ace might've gone to the house on the other side, he told himself.

Might've gone *anywhere*.

He kept looking back, half expecting to find someone rushing up behind him, yelling – maybe someone with a gun.

At last, he reached his car. He climbed inside. With a trembling hand, he fumbled the key into the ignition. His heart gave a sickening lurch as headlights appeared on the road ahead.

Cops?

He threw himself across the seat and lay there gasping, listening. The sound of the car came closer, closer. Passed him and faded.

Staying down, he twisted the key. The engine caught.

He pushed himself up, glimpsed the red tail-lights in the side mirror, then put the car into gear and turned the corner.

A car was parked in Ace's driveway.

She hadn't said anything about having company tonight. Maybe assumed I'd be staying at Jack's, Vicki thought, so she didn't bother to warn me.

She swung the Mustang to the curb across the street from the house.

Now what? she wondered. I don't want to blunder into something.

She wondered who the man was.

Maybe it's not a man.

Of course it is.

Ace had broken up with Jerry a couple of weeks ago, and hadn't mentioned seeing anyone else. She'd had no dates since Vicki moved in.

Maybe she made up with Jerry.

Could be just about anyone, though.

289

Vicki sighed. She'd been so reluctant to leave Jack. It had taken all her willpower to resist the urge to stay with him. Now this. If she'd known Ace had company, she probably wouldn't have left.

Maybe I should turn around, she thought, and go back. No. I made my decision. It was the right decision. And I'm here.

Vicki climbed out of the car. She crossed the street and went up the walkway to the front door. She rang the bell. Waited. Rang it again.

That's plenty of warning, she decided.

She unlocked the door and opened it – three inches before the guard chain snapped taut.

Great, she thought. Hope they're not asleep.

She pressed the doorbell a few more times and heard the chimes ring through the house.

'Come on, gang,' she muttered.

Leaning forward, she eased her face into the gap and called, 'Ace? Ace, it's me. You want to let me in?'

Nobody answered.

Okay. They must be in Ace's room with the door shut. Either asleep or at a bad place to stop, too busy to be interrupted.

Vicki pulled the door shut. She dropped the keys into her handbag, and walked around to the back of the house. Light spilled out through the screen door. The wooden door was open.

If the screen's locked . . .

She tried its handle. The door swung open and she stepped into the kitchen.

And went numb.

Blood. Bloody smudges of footprints. And over there . . . over near the centre of the kitchen . . . .

God what happened here!

Gazing at the blood, she took a step forward and kicked something. She looked down. A man's leather shoe. One of a pair just in front of the door. Crouching, she picked it up

290

and turned it over. The sole was stained with black as if
someone had walked through spots of grease in it.

Melvin? Melvin was here?

Maybe *still* here.

His car in the driveway?

God, Ace, no!

'ACE!'

A sudden noise like a chair scuffing the floor made Vicki
flinch and jerk her head to the right. She dropped the shoe.

Curled under the kitchen table, staring at Vicki through
the bars of chair legs, was a naked woman.

'Ace?' Vicki whispered.

Didn't look like Ace. Not with that bloody, distorted face.
Not with that raw dome of skull. But the body . . .

'What did he do *to you!'* Even as Vicki heard herself blurt
the question, she was lunging at the table. She looped the
straps of her handbag over her head so the bag hung against
her chest, then flung the nearest chair out of the way. She
hurled the table up, overturning it. The vase of flowers flew
off and hit the wall. The edge of the table crashed against
the floor. She dropped onto her knees in front of Ace.
Hunching over, she saw blood spilling from two gashes on
her back. It came out in slow trickles.

Knife wounds? How deep? How much damange had the
knife done, penetrating her?

No way to tell.

But if all the blood on the kitchen floor was from Ace,
she'd bled a lot. And she undoubtedly had internal
haemorrhaging.

She might be dying.

Vicki rolled her over.

Ace stared up at her, blinking.

'It's all right,' Vicki whispered.

Though her front was smeared with blood, there were no
more wounds that Vicki could see.

Ace raised an arm. Clutched in its hand was a mop of
hair. She reached up as if offering it to Vicki.

291

'Hang onto it, hon. I'm gonna get you to a hospital.'

She lifted Ace's other hand. The pulse was weak.

She looked across the kitchen at the wall phone.

What if Melvin's still in the house?

He's not. He'd be on me by now.

But calling for an ambulance . . . the volunteer ambulance. The alert would sound through town like last night. The ambulance drivers would leave their homes, drive to the fire station . . . It might take ten minutes to get here. Or longer.

We could be halfway to Blayton Memorial by then.

'Come on,' Vicki said.

She straddled Ace, grabbed her sticky arms and pulled. Ace came up into a sitting position. 'You've gotta help,' Vicki muttered. 'Can you help?'

Scurrying around behind Ace, she squatted and hugged her beneath the breasts and lifted. Ace shoved her feet at the floor. Vicki staggered backward a step as the weight moved up against her. Then, Ace was on her feet – balanced, at least for the moment. Vicki rushed in front of her. 'Grab on.'

She felt Ace fall against her. But she was braced. She stayed up. As Ace's arms went around her shoulders, Vicki bent slightly and reached back. She clutched Ace's rump, thrust it upward and bounced.

With Ace on her back, she hooked her hands under the big thighs and lurched to the screen door. She used Ace's knee to punch the handle, releasing the catch. She rammed the door open and lumbered outside.

And ran.

She didn't think she *could* run, but she did.

Ace like a giant child riding piggy-back. Her weight pounding down with every stride Vicki took.

But Vicki stayed up. She kept on running. Alongside the house, across the front yard, her lungs burning, her legs leaden.

If only it were *her* car in the driveway.

292

Whose was it?

Who cares?

She only cared about getting to the Mustang. Far ahead. On the other side of the street.

She blinked sweat out of her eyes. She wheezed for air. Ace started to slide down. She tugged her thighs and boosted her higher and kept running. Over the sidewalk and across the street.

At the Mustang, she whirled around. Ace bumped the side of the car. Vicki released her legs. Ace let go. Bracing her up with a hand against her chest, Vicki jerked open the door. She flung the driver's seatback forward. Ace, turning, bumped against her. Vicki caught her, guided her, shoved her into the car.

Ace fell across the back seat. Facedown, she squirmed over the cushion.

Vicki raced to the trunk. She slipped the handbag straps off her head, dug out the keys, and opened the trunk. In the faint glow of the streetlights, she spotted Ace's blanket.

Ever since Ace had started driving cars, she'd kept a blanket in the trunk. *Never know when you'll wanta flop in the woods*.

Vicki snatched out the blanket, slammed the trunk, and rushed to the open door. Ace was on her side, curled up. Vicki leaned into the car and spread the blanket over her.

'Don't want the ER doctors drooling over your naked body,' she said.

The blanket was for warmth, not modesty. Standard treatment for shock.

Vicki slapped her haunch through the soft cover, then scurried out, threw the seatback forward and got behind the wheel. She started the engine, pulled the door shut, shifted and shot the car forward.

'Too bad you're in no condition to appreciate this, hon,' she called out. 'This is gonna be the quickest trip to Blayton in the history of man.'

293

As a professional courtesy, she supposed, Vicki was led to the deserted office of the chief of surgery instead of a waiting room. She was told to make herself comfortable. Then, she was left alone.

With tissues from a box on the desk, she wiped as much blood as she could from her hands and clothes. She wanted to sit down, but she knew that the back of her blouse must be bloody and she didn't want to make a mess on leather upholstery. Her skirt was clean in front. She twisted it around, then sat on the soft chair and leaned forward, elbows on her legs.

She flinched at the sound of the door opening.

I'm sorry, Dr Chandler, but we weren't able to . . .

The nurse who came in had a cup of coffee on a serving tray with a packet of sugar and a small plastic container of cream. 'Can I get you anything else? The kitchen is closed, but we have a vending machine in the lounge.'

Vicki shook her head. 'Thanks, I don't . . .'

The nurse set the tray on the desk in front of her. 'We've notified the police, Dr Chandler. They should be here shortly. They'll want to speak with you.'

She nodded.

'I'm sure your friend will be fine.'

'Thank you,' she muttered.

The nurse could be sure of no such thing, but Vicki appreciated the kind words.

When she was alone, she picked up the cup. She brought it toward her mouth. Coffee slopped out, splashing hot on her thigh.

She remembered joking with Jack about spilling coffee. Black coffee, white couch. That seemed like days ago. She wondered, vaguely, if he'd awakened yet and found out she was gone.

It took both hands to hold the cup steady. She drank, and set the cup down.

Jack. Thank God I didn't stay. Ace would've died for sure.

She might die, anyway.

Vicki wished she were with Ace in the operating room. She'd asked to join the surgical team, but the doctor had taken a quick look at her and shaken his head. 'I'm sorry,' he'd said. 'No way. You're in shock, yourself.' Then he'd instructed the nurse to show Vicki to the office and 'look after her.'

Vicki supposed the doctor was right about keeping her out of the OR. In her condition, she certainly couldn't have done Ace any good and her presence might've been a distraction for the others.

But she hated just sitting here, not knowing.

Ace could be dead right now.

She'd been unconscious by the time they reached the hospital.

She'll be all right, Vicki told herself. She'll be fine.

We'll pop open a bottle of Champagne for her homecoming, and get royally soused, and laugh about dumb things . . .

Vicki lowered her face into her hands and wept.

The nurse came in, followed by two men in slacks and sports shirts. Vicki stood up and faced them. Both men had thick moustaches. The older one, grey at his temples, wore a leather rig that held an enormous handgun upside down beneath his armpit. The other, with black curly hair, had a small revolver in a holster clipped to his belt.

Vicki tried to read the nurse's face. It looked solemn. 'Have you heard anything about Ace?'

'She's still in surgery. These men are detectives Gorman and Randisi from the police.'

Vicki wiped her eyes. She looked at the two men.

Randisi, the curly-haired one, said, 'We'd like to ask you a few questions about . . .'

'It was Melvin Dobbs. He did it.'

'Dobbs?' Gorman asked 'The Melvin Dobbs? The psycho? The guy they put away after he pulled the jumper-cable stunt on that dead cheerleader? What was it, ten-fifteen years ago?'

'That's him,' Vicki said.

Randisi glanced at the nurse. With a nod, she turned away and left the room.

'You were there at the time of the assault?' he asked.

'No. Melvin was gone when I got there. I *think* he was gone. I didn't look around. I just got Ace – Alice – out of there as fast as I could.'

'What makes you think it was this Dobbs psycho?' Gorman asked.

'It couldn't have been anyone else. He went to the house . . . because of me. I don't know why, maybe just to see me and talk, and maybe Ace tried to keep him out. See, he thought I was there. He was with me earlier, and I told him I was going home. Maybe he wanted to kill me or . . . abduct me or something. I don't know.'

'Had you quarrelled with him?' Randisi asked.

'I'd taken him out to dinner. I . . . baited him. I got him to admit he killed Dexter Pollock.'

The two policemen glanced at each other.

'I know,' Vicki said. 'Everyone thinks the nurse did it. Patricia Gordon. But Melvin *got* her to do it.'

'How did he manage that?'

Vicki almost told about the hypnosis. And how she suspected he'd also used hypnosis to persuade Charlie Gaines to make her a partner, then staged Charlie's crash. But she stopped herself. It would sound too much like hocus-pocus. These men might not buy it. Her credibility might start falling apart. 'I don't know how he did it,' she answered. 'He wouldn't tell me. But he *did* confess to making her kill Pollock. That was just before I left him. He must've got nervous, afraid I'd report him, so he went over to the house, thinking I'd be there.'

'Where were you?' Randisi asked.

'With a friend. Jack Randolph. At his house.'

'So,' Randisi said, 'you went to dinner with Dobbs, got him to confess killing Pollock, then you told him goodnight and went straight over to this Randolph fellow's place. Why Randolph? Why didn't you take your information to the police?'

'That's a good one,' she muttered.

'In what way?'

'I'd already told the Ellsworth police my suspicions about Dobbs killing Pollock. They acted like I was some kind of a flake.' She looked Randisi in the eyes. 'Which I'm not.'

'You don't seem much like a flake to me,' Gorman said.

'Who'd you tell in Ellsworth?' Randisi asked.

'Joey Milbourne. And he passed the word to Raines. I guess they had themselves quite a laugh.'

Gorman mumbled something. It sounded like 'dickheads,' but Vicki couldn't be sure.

'So you figured,' Randisi said, 'there was no point in taking your information to Raines. He wouldn't act on it, anyway.'

'That's right. The man I went to, Jack, is an attorney. We discussed the situation. He was going to wait for morning, then go to Raines himself. If Raines wouldn't listen to him, he planned to see a friend of his in the District Attorney's office. One way or another, we figured we'd get someone to pay attention.'

'They'll pay attention now,' Gorman said. 'Where does this Dobbs fellow live?'

'In Ellsworth. His house in on . . . Elm Street, I think.'

Gorman got a sour look on his face. 'That's in the city limits,' he said to Randisi.

'Where did the attack take place?'

'Ace's house is on Third.'

'Damn.' Gorman shook his head.

'What's wrong?' Vicki asked him.

'We're Blayton PD. We've got no jurisdiction in Ellsworth.'

'So it's Raines's ballgame,' Randisi said.

'We'll contact him right now. If he gives us any . . . trouble, we'll . . .'

'There's something else,' Vicki said. 'If he needs convincing. Dobbs left his shoes on the kitchen floor. I know they're his. I've seen him wear the same kind at the gas station he owns. And they have grease stains on the soles.'

'We'll see that Raines picks him up,' Randisi said.

'He gives us any crap, we'll do it ourselves.'

Vicki looked at the two men. 'I'm really . . . Thanks. You're terrific. I was starting to think *all* cops were dickheads.'

Gorman blushed. Just a little.

Melvin was down in his basement laboratory when Patricia called from the top of the stairs. 'They're coming. They just got out of their car.'

'How many?' he asked.

'Two of them.'

Melvin climbed the stairs, looking up at Patricia. She wore one of his bright blue Hawaiian shirts, and nothing else. The tails draping her thighs were parted slightly, letting him see a hint of her blonde curls. Above the single button fastened at her belly, the shirt gaped wide enough to show the sides of her breasts.

She looked just right.

Melvin had dressed her for the occasion.

As he reached the top of the stairs, the doorbell rang.

'You ready?' he asked.

Patricia nodded. She had fear in her eyes.

He kissed her gently on the mouth. 'Hey, don't worry.'

'I don't want to lose you, Melvin.'

'Ain't gonna happen. Just do like I said.'

The bell sounded again. Patricia turned around. Melvin followed her, watching the loose, glossy shirt shimmer on the moving mounds of her rump.

'Sure hope these cops ain't a couple of fairies,' he said.

298

Patricia glanced back at him and smiled.

The bell rang again.

Melvin stationed himself against the wall beside the front door. The door would conceal him when it swung open. Patricia slipped the guard chain free and looked at him.

Melvin nodded.

She pulled the door open just a few inches. She peered out through the gap. 'Yes?' she asked.

'I'm sorry to disturb you at this hour, but . . . This *is* the home of Melvin Dobbs?'

'Yes?'

'I'm Chief Raines of the Ellsworth Police Department. This is Sergeant Woodman.'

The chief himself, Melvin thought. And sounding pretty nervous. Probably hadn't seen this much of a pretty young babe in a long time. Probably trying for a look inside the shirt.

Did the chief realise he was in the presence of Patricia Gordon, RN, who'd nailed Pollock?

'Is Mr Dobbs home?' Raines asked.

'Yes, he's upstairs. Won't you come in?' Patricia gave the knob a pull and backed away. The door swung closer to Melvin. It blocked his view of the men, but he saw Patricia beyond its edge.

She kept walking backward toward the stairs. The shirt trembled over her breasts. The gap below the single button seemed wider than before. Her hair gleamed in the lamplight. Her thighs flashed white.

Melvin grinned.

He heard the men step forward. A shoulder and left arm came into view.

'I'll just call him,' Patricia said, stopping at the foot of the stairs.

' 'Thank you.'

She spun around. The shirt tail swished, giving a glimpse of her buttocks.

Melvin heard a soft breathy sound, almost a whistle.

'Melvin!' she called up the stairway. 'There are gentlemen here to see you.' She waited a moment. 'Melvin?' she called again. Facing the men, she shook her head and rolled her eyes upward. 'He must be asleep. Should I go up and wake him?'

'I'll go with you,' Raines said. 'Woodman, you wait . . .'

Patricia whirled and raced up the stairs, taking them two at a time, her shirt tail flapping.

Both cops bolted after her.

'Melvin!' she shouted toward the top. 'Cops! Run!'

Melvin stepped away from the door.

'Hold it!' Raines snapped, drawing his revolver, aiming it at her.

Patricia stopped. She turned around. She had popped open the button on her way upstairs. The front of the shirt was wide open. She raised her arms.

Both cops, guns drawn, stood at the foot of the stairway and gazed up at her.

Melvin aimed at their backs. He fired both his revolvers at once. He kept firing, pulling the triggers as fast as he could. Through the roaring blasts, he heard one of the men yell, 'OW! OUCH!' as the bullets knocked him down. The other was silent.

When both guns were empty, one cop lay face-down on the stairs and looked as if he'd been trying to hug them. The other, who'd succeeded in turning around after the first shot caught him in the shoulder, was sitting on the floor, leaning back against the stairs, his legs stretched out. That one stared at the ceiling and twitched as blood foamed out of his mouth.

Grinning up at Patricia, Melvin twirled the guns and jammed them into his pockets.

'Reckon its Boot Hill for *them* hombres,' he drawled.

Patricia rushed down the stairs. She leaped over the bodies and threw her arms around Melvin. She was shaking. She squeezed herself hard against him.

Vicki sat, leaning forward, elbows on her knees, waiting.

300

The two policemen, Gorman and Randisi, had gone away a long time ago to phone Chief Raines. Later, Gorman had returned alone to tell her how it went.

'Raines said he'd look into it,' he had told her.

'Look into it? Is that all?'

'He's not a great fan of yours.'

'I've noticed.'

'But he couldn't just ignore the attack on Miss Mason. Ace? Even a narrow-minded, stubborn cop like Raines has to do something about it if one of his citizens gets carved up like that. But he didn't want to believe that Dobbs was the perpetrator. Not on the basis of your suspicions. He said you've got a "burr up your ass" about Dobbs.' Gorman's face reddened when he said that. 'Sorry, but those were his words. He said you've been trying to get Dobbs put away so he'll stop . . . putting moves on you.'

'I guess we gave Milbourne that idea Sunday morning,' Vicki said. 'Joey Milbourne, one of his men. Dobbs had threatened Pollock's life right in front of us, and we told Milbourne that. But he wanted to know why we were out with Dobbs, and Ace had to go and tell him the creep has the hots for me. So Milbourne went and convinced Raines we were trouble-makers. So they didn't do anything about that bastard.'

Gorman shook his head. 'No accounting for fools,' he said. 'Any cop worth a damn would've pulled in Dobbs for questioning at that point.'

'So now Raines is willing to look into it? On the word of a flake with a . . . grudge?'

'I made it pretty clear he'd better.'

Vicki almost smiled. 'I bet you did.'

'I'm glad you told us about the shoes, though. That's what did the trick, finally made him decide there was sufficient reason to drop by the house and have a "chat" with Dobbs.'

'Tonight?'

Gorman nodded. 'He said he'd get right on it.'

Now, sitting alone in the office, Vicki looked at her wristwatch. Almost three a.m. Gorman had left her just after two.

Which meant that Raines had probably already had his 'chat' with Melvin.

Right now, Melvin might be in custody.

Or maybe he talked his way out of it, convinced Raines of his innocence.

That won't last long, she told herself. The minute Ace regains consciousness and names Melvin . . . she won't be naming anyone with her jaw in that shape.

Give her a pen and paper.

If she regains consciousness.

She will, Vicki told herself. She'll be all right.

She *can't* die.

My fault. It's all my fault.

Jesus, Ace, please.

Vicki lurched to her feet as the office door swung open. The nurse came in.

'How is she?'

'I haven't been told anything about her condition.'

Vicki nodded. 'Well, at least no news is good news.'

'I didn't say I had no news. Something came up. I thought you should know about it. We just got word to call in Dr Goldstein. He's our staff cosmetic surgeon.'

Vicki stared at the nurse.

A cosmetic surgeon!

For Ace's scalp?

They wouldn't bother, if . . .

'Oh, thank God,' she murmured.

'He's on his way right now.'

Vicki slumped into the chair.

'I don't know how long they'll be in there, but its safe to assume that your friend's in stable condition. Wouldn't you like to go home and clean up and get some rest? You've been through such an ordeal. You must be done in. And it'll be hours before you're able to visit with her. Why don't you call in around nine or ten, we can let you know when you'll be able to see her. Really. Waiting around here all that time . . . You'd feel so much better if you went home and slept for a few hours.'

Vicki nodded. 'Yeah,' she murmured.

Ace . . . she's going to live.

The awful tightness inside Vicki seemed to be melting, ice going soft, warmth flowing through her body, soothing, making her weak.

Ace.

You made it, Ace. You made it.

Vicki drove. She drove through the warm night toward Ellsworth, though she wasn't quite sure where she would go when she arrived.

She knew where she wanted to go.

Jack's house.

But she didn't like the idea of walking in this way, all covered with dried blood. Maybe she should go to Ace's house first, clean up, put on fresh clothes.

I can't, she realised. I can't walk through that kitchen.

Besides, it would be stupid to enter Ace's house alone. For all she knew, Melvin hadn't been caught. He was probably in jail right now, but what if he wasn't? What if she walked into the house and there he was, waiting for her . . . with a knife?

She considered turning the car around and driving to her parents' house. They had kept her room ready for overnight visits, and some of her clothes were there. She could shower, catch some sleep, then return to the hospital, which wasn't much more than five minutes from their house.

But she would have to do a lot of talking – explain everything. She didn't feel up to that. And why upset them with all that had been going on? They'll be sick when they find out. Might as well spare them the agony for as long as possible. Once it's all over . . . really over, Ace recovering for sure, Melvin behind bars for sure . . . that would be the time to let them in on it.

Pay them a visit tomorrow . . . today, she reminded herself. It's been Wednesday for hours. See them this afternoon or tonight. That's soon enough. Spare them till then.

She parked in front of Jack's house. Leaning away from the seat back to climb out, she felt her blouse peel away from the upholstery.

You're in for a shock, Jack old pal.

When she stood up, her legs trembled. She held onto the open door to steady herself. The lack of sleep, the tension, carrying Ace on her back, the relief she'd felt during the past half hour or so – they had taken their toll. The nurse had been right. She was 'done in.' Not only sore in the arms and back and rump and legs, but deep-down weary.

She took a full breath. Even her *lungs* felt heavy and tired.

It's almost over, she told herself.

She swung the door shut, shuffled around the front of the car, moaned when she stepped onto the curb, and pointed herself toward Jack's lighted porch.

It would feel so good to hold him, sink against his strong warm body.

First a shower.

She wondered if she would be able to stay on her feet long enough for a shower.

Maybe Jack'll go into the tub with me, hold me up.

The thought of that sent a stir through Vicki that pushed away some of the weariness.

She tried the door. It was locked. Of course. She'd made sure it was locked when she left. She pressed the doorbell and waited, hoping the sound was loud enough to wake him.

Before she could press it again, the door swung open.

304

CHAPTER THIRTY-ONE

Staring at her, Jack stepped away from the door and let Vicki enter. She pushed the door shut.

'What happened to you?' he asked.

He was frowning. He looked pale, and Vicki wondered if he had been up for a long time, worrying.

'I came from the hospital,' she said. 'I took Ace there. Melvin attacked her tonight.'

'My God,' he muttered. He reached out and pulled Vicki against him.

'I'm a mess,' she warned.

'Who cares.' He stroked her back.

She put her arms around him. His terry robe was soft under her hands.

'Was Ace hurt badly?' he asked.

'He . . . really wrecked her. But she's going to make it. I'm sure she's going to make it. The cops went to pick up Melvin. I'm such a mess. I'm so tired.'

'It's all right.' He gently stroked her back.

'I'm getting blood all over you.'

'Doesn't matter.'

'Can I use your shower? I . . . I'd like to get clean. And sleep. Is it okay if I sleep here?'

'Of course.'

Easing away from his embrace, she shook her head when she saw the hint of rust-colour her blouse and skirt had left on the front of his light blue robe. 'Sorry,' she muttered.

'It'll wash.'

'We can throw it in the laundry like your shorts.'

'Not wearing any,' he said.

'I didn't suppose you were.' Her heart quickened and she felt a warm spreading glow.

She smiled up at Jack as she remembered his embarrassment when his skimpy briefs had fluttered to the floor of Ace's kitchen. That seemed like weeks ago. It was only last night. Tonight, the place on the floor where they'd dropped was smeared with Ace's blood.

Vicki's smile died.

'Come on,' Jack said. He took her hand and led her to the stairway.

She saw her note taped to the top of the newel post. Brushing it with a fingertip, she said, 'Didn't you read it?'

His face looked blank. 'I was asleep till you rang the doorbell. I hurried right down.'

'Don't you want to read it now?'

'It can wait. You're here. That's all that matters.'

Vicki felt a small pull of disappointment. Didn't he *care* what she'd written to him? Though the note was brief, it told of her love for him, her regret for sneaking out while he slept, her hopes that soon there would be no need for her to leave. She glanced back at it as she climbed the stairs. The note looked abandoned.

He's right, she told herself. What's the big deal? I'm here. We're together. That's what counts.

At the top of the stairs, he released her hand. 'You go ahead and take your shower. I'll phone the police and make sure they've arrested Melvin.'

'All right.' She didn't want to be left alone. But it would be good to know, for sure, that Melvin was in custody. 'When you're done, why don't you come in . . . and wash my back?'

Jack grinned in a way that made something go tight inside her. There was nothing of tenderness or love in that grin. It looked wolfish, leering. She supposed it was meant to be amusing, but it seemed awfully inappropriate.

'Very funny,' she muttered.

Walking through the hallway, she glanced back at him. He hadn't moved. He was watching her, hands thrust into the pockets of his robe. For a moment, she was reminded of the way Pollock used to look on those mornings when he waited for her in the apartment corridor to lecture her, to ogle her.

She entered the master bedroom. Staring at the bed, she was filled with a rush of memories: the feel of him inside her, his gentleness, their soft words, his hinting of marriage, the way she had ached with love when she covered his sleeping body with a sheet before leaving.

None of that fit in with the harsh, lusting way he'd looked at her in the hall.

What had changed?

Maybe nothing.

He's tired, she told herself. I'm tired. It was nothing. He was trying to be funny and I'm just not in the mood for it. Too much has happened.

She stepped into the adjoining bathroom, snapped the light on, and shut the door. Her hand curled around the knob. Her thumb jabbed its lock button down.

That's ridiculous, she thought. What's the matter with me? *What's the matter with him?*

You invited him in, and now you're locking the door?

He gave me that look.

Big deal. Forget it.

Shaking her head, she turned the knob. The lock button popped out with a quiet ping.

She moved in front of the mirror, and curled her lip when she saw herself. So much like last night. But instead of black, greasy smudges from Charlie's body, it was stains of blood from Ace. Even her chin, though she'd wiped it with a tissue at the hospital, had a reddish smear.

Quickly, she turned her back to the mirror. She slipped her blouse off, reached back and draped it over the edge of the sink. Then, she removed her bra.

The blood had soaked through to her skin. Her chest, her breasts, her belly – all were marred by faint spots and blotches as if she'd been sunburned through a torn garment gaping with holes.

She turned toward the sound of the door swinging open.

Jack stood there in his robe.

The nasty leer was gone, but his eyes lingered on her. She

had an urge to cover her breasts . . . but that'd be absurd.

'Did you make the call?' she asked.

He nodded. 'They arrested Melvin. They've got him in jail.'

'That's great,' she said. But she felt no relief, only uneasiness about the change in Jack. 'Is something wrong?' she asked.

'No. Everything's fine. And you look . . . terrific.'

'I wish you wouldn't stare at me like that.'

He came toward her. Vicki took a step backward, then stopped herself.

This is Jack, for godsake. Jack.

He took her by the shoulders, drew her forward, and kissed her. His mouth felt quick and eager. More urgent than before, but so familiar. It opened. It sucked her lips, slid down and licked her chin. Where the blood stain was.

'Don't,' she murmured.

Then moaned as a hand moved to her breast. His other hand tore the bandage from her shoulder. She flinched as the tape pulled her skin.

'Jack.'

He said nothing. He squeezed her breast. He squeezed her bitten shoulder. The surging pleasure and pain and made squirm.

'You're . . . hurting.'

His mouth went away from her chin. He sucked the side of her neck. Her mouth fell open and she writhed, gasping. She dug her fingers into his buttocks through the thickness of the robe, and pressed him hard against her.

He no longer squeezed her shoulder. The hand roamed down her side, rucked up her skirt, hooked her panties down around her thighs.

His wet mouth slipped over her skin. He kissed her shoulder. Licked the wounds left by Charlie's teeth last night.

'Don't do that,' she murmured. 'Hey, come on.'

He bit.

Fire bolted through her body. She jerked rigid and cried

308

out. His teeth sank deeper. She shuddered in spasms of pain as she felt them grinding her.

When she tried to twist away, he clutched her buttocks with both hands, lifted her, turned her, slammed her against the bathroom wall. The impact snapped her head back. It struck the wall. Her vision exploded with brilliant lights, then dimmed.

She told herself to move, to struggle. But her body wouldn't respond to the commands of her dulled mind.

She was aware of Jack sucking blood from her shoulder. She heard wet smacking sounds, slurping sounds. She felt no pain. Just pulling sensations.

Then she felt herself being impaled.

He sucked and thrust, pounding her limp body against the bathroom wall.

It went on and on. Vicki tried to lift her arms, wanting to make it stop. But they flopped uselessly at her sides, bumping the wall each time he rammed.

Later, she realised the wall was no longer against her back. Instead, there was the cool tile of the bathroom floor. She gazed at the ceiling. It took her a moment to become aware that Jack wasn't on top of her. She tried to lift her head, couldn't.

She heard thumping, splattering sounds. Familiar sounds. Water bashing down, filling the bathtub beside her.

The noise shut off.

Jack loomed over her. He straddled her hips, staring down. His robe hung open. Across his belly, just above the navel, was a white strip of bandage. It looked like a mouth, the mouth of a strange design carved on his abdomen, drawn in lines that were threads of dried blood, leaking in places, droplets trickling down his skin . . . an upside-down pyramid inside a circle . . . ovals like eyes at the corners . . . the bandage its mouth.

A face. An evil face.

Something from . . . black magic? That changed Jack, made him evil.

309

And her mind pulled a memory out of its dense fog – Charlie sitting behind his desk at the clinic, specks of blood appearing on his shirt.

She gazed up at Jack's face. His mouth and chin glimmered with blood. Her blood. She searched his eyes. They looked down at her, wide, frantic, somehow both gleeful and frightened. She saw no hint of the Jack she had known, had loved.

'Melvin,' she muttered. 'Wha . . . wha'd he do . . . to you?'

The wild glee vanished from his eyes. His face twisted with fear and rage. 'You filthy rotten slut!' he squealed. 'You made me do it.' He swept down, bending at the waist, and his open hand smacked her cheek, rocked her head sideways. 'I wasn't supposed to touch you, damn it! You *made* me! He won't like it. He won't like it one bit! It's all your fault!'

Squatting beside her, Jack rammed his arms under her back and legs. He picked her up, lurched forward, and dropped her.

Into the bathtub. The cold water clenched her, covered her. but cushioned her fall. Softly, she bumped the bottom of the tub. She curled upward and caught a breath before Jack's hand clutched her face and pushed it down. The hand went away. She thrust herself up, gasping, and saw Jack climb into the tub.

He reached down for her feet. She jerked her legs back, knees rising out of the water, but he crouched and grabbed her ankles and pulled them toward him. Her back slid. Her face went under.

Forcing her eyes to stay open, Vicki watched him through inches of water that swirled pink from the blood of her shoulder. He stood, holding her legs up, yelling words that sounded faint and mushy.

Her heart felt like a bludgeoning club. Her lungs burned. *What did Melvin do to him?*

He's gonna drown me.

She squirmed and kicked, but he didn't loose his hold. She shoved her hands against the sides and bottom of the tub, trying to push herself up. And she *did* get closer to the surface, but Jack raised her legs higher. Her head pressed the bottom. Through the blurry pink, she saw her legs nearly straight up, saw her pubic hair and belly out of the water, felt her rump against Jack's legs, felt ripples on the undersides of her breasts. He almost had her standing on her head.

I'm gonna die, she thought. Jesus, this is it.

Then he shoved downward. She felt her back slide, her body unbend and enter the cold water, her head rise as it ran up the slope at the rear of the tub. Her face broke the surface and she gulped air.

Jack, crouching, still held her ankles. He glared at her. 'You won't tell him a thing!'

Vicki jerked her head from side to side.

'I didn't bite you, I didn't fuck you! Right?'

'*Right,*' she choked out.

'You came back and you were bloody so I let you take a shower. I wanted you clean for him.'

'Yes! Yes!'

'You're not going to tell on me.'

'No!'

'Promise?'

'Yes!' With a palsied hand, she splashed water as she drew an X on her submerged chest. 'Cross my heart. I promise. Please.'

Jack released her ankles. He stood and climbed out of the tub. Vicki sat up. 'Get out of there and dry off. You can wear this,' he said, and pulled the robe off. He tossed it to the floor, turned away from her, and reached for a towel.

He kept his back to Vicki and rubbed himself with the towel while she clambered over the wall of the tub. She flopped onto the floor, panting.

'Don't just lay there.'

The ceiling seemed to be spinning slowly, tipping.

'Move it!'

'My shoulder,' she muttered.

A dry washcloth fluttered above her, dropped onto her

311

right breast. Still on her back, she folded the cloth and pressed it gently against the torn flesh of her shoulder.

Moaning, she sat up.

Jack opened the bathroom door. 'I'll be right back,' he said. 'Don't try anything.' He stepped into the master bedroom.

Throwing herself forward, Vicki scurried on hands and knees toward the door. She was almost there when Jack spun around. He lunged for the door. She smashed it shut with a swing of her fist. The door slammed. She rose on her knees. Reached for the knob. For the lock button.

The door flew at her, knocked her hand aside, crashed into her forehead.

She came awake in darkness, her head throbbing and spinning. She didn't know where she was, but her wet hair forced the memory of looking up at Jack through the bathtub water. She remembered what he'd done before throwing her into the tub. She tried to think forward, to getting out of the tub, but the memories stopped with her still under water and thinking she would drown.

She knew she was no longer in the tub. She was on a cushion. She was wearing something dry and warm on top, sodden and chilly lower where it clung to her rump and legs. Jack's robe? She remembered him wearing it when he squatted in the tub and grabbed her ankles.

Was she on the bed in Jack's master bedroom?

She tried to push herself up. The dizziness flipped her stomach. She grabbed the edge of the cushion and dragged herself sideways and vomited onto the floor.

When she finished, she rolled away from the edge. Lying curled on her side, she saw a seatback in front of her. There was dim light above it. And a head. A head that turned. A face that was a pale oval, dark smudges for its eyes and mouth. Jack.

The face turned away, and Jack kept on driving.

She knew where he was taking her.

312

To Melvin.

She tried to make herself as small as she felt, snuggling her back against the rise of the seat cushion, drawing up her knees, hugging her breasts through the heavy softness of the terri cloth robe.

Taking me to Melvin, she thought.

Following orders.

'Jack?' Her voice sounded small and far away. 'What did he do to you, Jack?'

'Remember what I said about telling,' he warned.

'I remember. I won't say anything. What did he do to you? How did he make you . . . we *loved* each other.'

'That so?'

'Oh, God,' she moaned.

'You're Melvin's,' he said. 'That's all I know. I wasn't supposed to touch you, just pretend I was your boyfriend and bring you back to him. That's all. But you had to flaunt yourself and tempt me, you damn whore, and I lost my cool.'

'It's that . . . *thing* . . . on your stomach. That face or whatever it is.'

'I wouldn't know.'

'Do you know who I am?'

'Vicki.'

Her heart seemed to jump, pumping blood into her head, making it throb. Squinting against the pain, she sat up. She scooted across the seat, away from the vomit, and swung her feet to the floor.

Jack twisted the rearview mirror so he could keep an eye on her. 'Don't even think about trying something. Last time, I almost broke your head open.'

She settled down against the cushion and stared at the back of his head. 'What's my last name?' she asked.

'I wouldn't know.'

'What do you know?'

'He drove me to the house and told me to wait for Vicki and take her to him. And not to mess with her. Remember that.'

'Jack. You didn't. You didn't mess with her. I'm not Vicki.'

'Bullshit.' He turned the car onto Elm Street. With a glance out of the window, she saw that they were only a block from Melvin's house.

'You'll find out when we get there,' she said. 'Melvin's really going to be mad.'

She felt the car slow.

'I know Vicki,' she said. 'She was supposed to show up at your house? Why? I don't get it.'

'Melvin knew you'd come back.'

'Not me. Vicki. Was she there tonight? After I left? I don't . . . Has she been . . . has she been *going* with you? Behind my back?'

Jack stopped the car. He twisted around and stared at her. 'What're you trying to pull?'

'That rotten bitch! Melvin wants her? He can have her! I'll take you to her. I know right where she is. Turn the car around.'

Jack shook his head. 'He said the gal who comes to the house would be Vicki. You're the one who came to the house.'

'But I'm not Vicki. I'm Jennifer Morley.'

'Wait. No. That's crazy.'

'I can prove it. My purse.' She paused. Her head felt as if it were splitting down the middle. 'You can see my ID. Where's my purse?'

'Back at the house.'

'Well, didn't you look in it? Why didn't you *make sure* before you . . . God, you're stupid. Melvin's gonna cream you when you walk in there with me. Jesus!'

'You're Vicki.' He didn't sound sure. 'You're just trying to trick me.'

'That note I left on the banister. If you'd read it, you'd know who I am. I signed it. I signed, "Love, Jennifer". Take me back to the house and I'll prove it. You've got the wrong person!'

'Melvin'll know.' He faced forward. The car began to move.

'I can be *yours*,' Vicki blurted. 'If you take me to Melvin, I'll be *his*. He didn't send you out to get me. He sent you for Vicki. So you won't be disobeying if you keep me for yourself. I can be yours, and I'll help you get Vicki. You can take her to Melvin, and keep me. I love you, Jack. I want to be with you, not with Melvin. Please.'

'I don't know,' he muttered.

'Jack. You want me, don't you?' Leaning forward, she reached over the seatback and placed her hands gently on Jack's shoulders. They hunched for a moment as if he expected an attack. She caressed him through his knit shirt.

He stopped the car. In front of Melvin's house.

'Keep going,' Vicki whispered, brushing her lips against his ear.

'No,' he said. 'You're going in.'

Her hands tightened on his shoulders. She saw herself grabbing his face, going for his eyes, gouging into them with her fingernails. The pain should incapacitate him, giving her a chance to flee. Blinded, he wouldn't have a chance of overtaking her. She'd get away.

But this was Jack, *her* Jack. As brutal as he'd been to her, it wasn't his fault. Melvin had him controlled. Somehow. And maybe it wasn't permanent. But if she blinded him . . .

As he pulled the key from the ignition, Vicki rammed him forward. He slammed against the steering wheel. The car horn blared.

She threw herself against the door, levered its handle and stumbled out. She had a stranger's legs, weak and trembling. But she kept them under her, staggering toward the rear of the car, looking back when she heard the driver's door squeak. Jack lurched into the street. She ran.

She sprinted, chin tucked down, arms pumping, legs flying out, bare feet pounding the blacktop. Though pain crashed through her head with every heartbeat, her legs began to feel right. Her own legs, her own body, running – just as she had run every morning, but this time with an urgency she'd never known before.

She heard Jack behind her. His slapping shoes. His huffing breath.

He'll never catch me!

She dashed up the centre of the road. She felt the breeze in her wet hair, on her face, on her chest and belly and legs. The robe, hanging loose, flapped behind her like a cape.

I can run like this all night, she thought. I can run right into the police station.

(Lot of good *that* would do.)

An intersection. Glaring brightness from the left.

She snapped her head that way.

A car rushed toward her, bore down roaring, then shrieking. Shrieking, though she thought she was safe from it, strides beyond its path.

She twisted around in time to see it hit Jack.

Even over the noise of the brakes, she heard the thuds of the impact. The bumper struck the side of his leg. It kicked both his legs high. His body shot over the hood. His head crashed through the windshield.

The car came to a stop just beyond the intersection.

The driver's door swung open. As a man climbed out, Vicki pulled her robe shut and tightened its cloth belt.

She wondered whether to run or stay.

There's no more reason to run, she realised. Melvin's house, far back from the road and alone on the block, was more than a hundred yards from the intersection. She could keep an eye on it. She could get away in the man's car at the first sign of Melvin's approach.

And Jack was no longer a threat.

'He ran right in front of me!' the man called to her. He sounded scared. 'You saw it, didn't you? Was he chasing you or something? What's going on?'

She walked toward him. 'He was after me,' she said.

'Wow. Oh, wow.' He stood beside his car, turning, looking

at Vicki, then at the body sprawled motionless across his hood, then at Vicki again.

In the glow of the streetlights, he looked vaguely familiar. A short man, black hair in a crew-cut, eyes small and too close to his broad nose. 'Hey,' he said. 'You're someone. Vicki?'

She nodded.

'Wes,' he said. 'Wes Wallace. You remember me?'

'Sure.' From school. He used to pal around with Manny Stubbins. 'How're you doing?'

'Jesus. Not bad till a minute ago. Jesus H. Christ on a rubber crutch.' He walked closer to the body. Vicki stayed beside him. 'Who was it?'

'Jack Randolph,' she said, and felt a sudden aching tightness in her chest.

'You say this guy was chasing you?'

'He . . . he'd attacked me. I got away. He was trying to get me again.'

'Hey, so I'm some kind of hero, huh?' He leaned over the side of the car, and stared. 'Sure busted my windshield. Maybe I better try 'n get him out, you know?' He clutched the back of Jack's belt and pulled. The body didn't move. 'Shit. Hung up.' Reaching through the hole in the windshield, he grabbed Jack by the hair and lifted. Then, he dragged the body backward and let the head down on the hood. He gave it a close look, and groaned. 'God, last time I saw something this bad was when Kraft and Darlene . . .' He turned away, holding his mouth and gagging.

Vicki saw Jack's head. Its crown was caved in. One eye had popped out, and dangled by the optic nerve against the side of his nose.

'Oh, Jack,' she whispered. He was no longer a monster, he was Jack again, the man she had held in her arms only hours ago, who had been in her and part of her. Bending over, she lay her arms across his back, pressed her cheek against him.

And felt a slow rise and fall as he breathed.

317

Vicki whirled around. 'Wes! He's alive.'

Wes was hunched over, vomiting.

'Hurry! Come here and help.' Not waiting for him, Vicki turned again to Jack. She pulled his limp arms down against his sides and shoved his spraddled legs together. She clutched him by the shoulder and hip, pulled, tried to roll him over.

Then Wes was beside her. 'Alive? Can't be.'

'Help me turn him over.'

Together, they tumbled Jack onto his back.

'Oh, wow,' Wes muttered. 'Look at that.'

Vicki looked.

A triangular shard of windshield glass was embedded in Jack's throat. Its point had entered his esophagus, but the jugular and carotid hadn't been severed. Wes peered at it, his face inches above the glass.

A hand grasped Vicki's wrist.

She looked down.

Not Wes's hand. Jack's.

It seized her like a manacle. Gooseflesh like a swarm of spiders scurried up her back.

She looked at Jack. His one eye opened slightly, slid toward Wes.

'I'll be damned,' Wes said. 'I guess . . .'

'Look out!' Vicki cried when Jack's other hand darted up. Wes started to rise away. Vicki flung herself against the side of the car and leaned and reached for Jack's hand as it tugged the glass shard from his throat. But he was too quick. For either of them. Vicki reached and missed and Wes was unbending and Jack slashed.

Blood spouted from Wes's neck. It splashed Jack's face. Wes lurched upright, grabbed his throat and walked backward stiffly, blood shooting between his fingers.

'No!' Vicki shrieked. She twisted away from the car, trying to tug her wrist from Jack's grip, and saw Wes fall. His legs just gave out and his rump hit the blacktop and he sat there, spraying the front of his jeans.

She threw herself sideways, all her weight against the hand

squeezing her wrist. Her muscles strained. She felt as if her arm might pop from its socket. But Jack didn't loose his grip. As he slid off the hood, she reached with her other hand and snatched his thumb. She struggled to pry it away from her wrist. Jack dropped to the street, landing on his knees, staggering to his feet. She stumbled away as he came at her.

With a gristly ripping sound and a pop, his thumb broke. Vicki jerked her hand free.

Before she could spin away, his other hand grabbed a lapel of the robe. He yanked her up against him. She faced his wide frantic eye, his empty socket, his hanging, swaying eye.

The blow came fast. His knee? It blasted Vicki's breath out and lifted her off her feet.

CHAPTER THIRTY-TWO

Patricia, bent over the body of Chief Raines, prodded the green ooze back inside the gash with the fingers of one hand while she stitched the wound with the other. She was tugging her needle gently, pulling the thread, when the doorbell rang. She flinched. The needle jerked. The stitch pulled out with a silent tearing of skin.

She looked at Melvin, her eyes wide.

'I'll take care of it,' Melvin said.

'More cops?' Patricia asked.

'Maybe, maybe not.'

'Shouldn't I go up just in case? I can do my thing again.

'Stay here and finish up with Raines.' Melvin backed away from the lab table. He crouched over the heap of clothing they'd removed from the cops. He had dropped the handguns on top of the pile. All four of them. Three were cop guns –

.38 caliber Smith & Wessons, blue steel with four-inch barrels. One was his own Colt .44.

He'd emptied his .44 and Milbourne's .38 into Raines and Woodman.

The doorbell rang again.

'Melvin!'

'I'll take care of it.' He grabbed two .38s and charged up the stairs.

By the time he reached the top, he was labouring for breath.

These fucking better not be more cops, he thought.

As he hurried through the hallway, he pointed both guns at his eyes. The blunt tips of bullets showed in the cylinder holes of just one.

'Shit,' he muttered.

He dropped the empty revolver to the floor.

At the front door, he flicked on the porch light and squinted through the peephole.

Felt a tight squeeze of shock and joy.

He released the locks, swung the door open, and stepped backwards as Jack entered the foyer.

He gaped at them.

At Vicki, at Jack.

Vicki hung limp in Jack's arms, her arms and legs dangling, her head drooping, her eyes gazing into space. Her hair looked damp and stringy, but otherwise . . . ah, so beautiful. She wore a powder blue robe that had fallen open. Melvin stared at her pale breast, its dark nipple, the sleek curves of her ribcage and belly and hip, the smooth side of her buttock, her long tapering leg.

Her beauty seemed all the more perfect compared to the ruin that was Jack.

The top of Jack's head was broken flat. His face was sheathed with dripping blood. And that *eye*. It dangled against his cheek like a bloody, peeled egg.

'What'd, you have some trouble?' Melvin asked.

Jack shrugged and grunted. Melvin saw the raw slot in his throat, and realised why he wasn't talking.

'Anyone after you?'

Jack turned, swinging Vicki, and rocked her back and forth as if gesturing out the doorway with her knees.

Melvin stepped past him. From the stoop, he saw his car parked at the curb and another car far down at the end of the block standing crooked just the other side of the intersection. Its headlights were on.

He wanted to ask what it was doing there, but Jack was in no shape explain anything.

'Take her down to the basement,' he ordered. Then he shut the door and hurried towards the distant car. The grass in front of the house was wet and slick under his feet. Already, he could feel sweat making his silk robe cling to his back. He didn't *want* to be all hot and sweaty for Vicki.

Pain in the ass, he thought. The last thing he needed was to go running around like this. Now, when he finally had Vicki, he had to go chasing off. He should be inside with her.

Always some kind of fuck-up.

He felt cheated. As if the party had started without him. He wanted to *be* there. Instead, he was missing out. And getting himself breathless and sweaty.

His frustration changed to worry when he realised he wouldn't be there when Patricia saw Vicki.

Shouldn't have told Jack to take her down.

Shit!

He'd planned to get rid of Patricia before Vicki came along.

Should've taken care of her soon as the cops was dead, he told himself.

But he hadn't even thought of it. Too busy.

As soon as the cops were killed, he'd left Patricia alone and driven Jack home. When he returned, he found her trying to drag one of the bodies down the basement stairs. And *still* didn't think of wiping her out, even though Jack

321

was all set and waiting and might show up pretty soon with Vicki.

After helping to move the bodies into the basement, Melvin had allowed her to do most of the work involved in resurrecting them. And never gave it a thought that time was getting short.

Stupid!

Now, she was down there and so was Vicki.

Shit!

She better not try nothing!

Huffing, Melvin rushed past the rear of the car. And saw a body lying in the street.

What the hell happened here?

Jack must've run into trouble, all right. But it looked as if he'd taken care of it.

Good fella, Jack.

Melvin approached the body. Standing above it, he recognised the bloody face. Wes.

Manny's gonna be pissed, he thought. The two guys were best buddies, and Wes was always hanging around the station when Manny was on the job.

Wes was a jerk.

The jerk's throat had been slashed open.

Melvin was suddenly quite pleased with himself. It had been a smart move, using Jack to bring Vicki in.

Good thing he didn't blow the fucker's head off and leave him dead in the house, the way he'd planned while he drove there from Ace's place. He'd almost done it the minute Jack opened the door. And came even *closer* when he found out Vicki was gone. It had suddenly occurred to him, though, that Jack might be useful. So he'd forced the man, at gunpoint, to drive him home. Got him inside and down to the basement, then whacked him with the barrel. It had been a cinch, wrapping his head in cellophane while he was out cold. Dead, and not a mark to show for it. With Patricia's help, they lifted him onto the table and got to work. They were down there, still at him, when the cops showed up.

Once those two bastards were cancelled, Melvin had returned Jack to his own house. To wait for Vicki.

'Did a great job, old pal,' he muttered. 'Got Vicki for me *and* you wasted shit-for-brains.'

Bending down, Melvin set his revolver on the pavement. He grabbed Wes by the ankles and dragged him to the car. The socks, at least, weren't bloody. With keys from the ignition, he opened the trunk. He frowned at the body, wondering how to get it in without messing his good silk robe.

He looked around. The streets were deserted. The few nearby houses were dark at the windows.

Nobody's watching, he told himself.

They'd be out here by now, rubber-necking, if they'd seen the car or body.

So he took off his robe. He rolled it carefully and set it on the roof of the car. Strange, being naked in the street. He felt the breeze on his hot, sweaty skin. He was getting hard. He thought about the way Vicki had looked, her robe hanging open.

Vicki. Patricia!

Shit.

As fast as he could, he rolled Wes over, grabbed him under the armpits, hoisted him up, and dumped him head first into the trunk. He moved the legs out of the way. Then he lowered the lid, turned around, and bounced his rump on it until he heard the latch click.

He opened the driver's door. The overhead light came on. Glass from the windshield littered the seat, but most of it was towards the middle. So was most of the blood. From Jack's head? Had his head smashed the windshield? Was that how it got flattened?

Melvin brushed off the seat, climbed into the car, and drove it to the curb. He shut off the engine, killed the headlights, and opened the door. The ceiling light came on again. he looked down at himself. A small smear of blood on his chest. But both hands were red, and he'd used a hand

323

to brush glass off the seat, so he probably had blood on his rump, too.

He didn't want blood on his beautiful robe.

Maybe Wes kept a towel for wiping the windshield.

Again, Melvin thought of Patricia in the basement with Vicki. She won't try nothing, he told himself. Wouldn't dare.

But he leaped from the car, threw its door shut, snatched his robe off the roof, and rushed to pick up his revolver.

'*Damn* him,' Vicki heard. It was a woman's voice. It seemed to come from a great distance. 'I'm not good enough for him? He prom . . . Put her down.'

Vaguely, she was aware of her legs being lowered. She felt a cool cement floor under her feet. Her knees buckled, but she didn't fall. Someone behind her (Jack?) had an arm tight across her chest, pinning her against his body.

She saw the arm below her breasts, saw her bent legs and the grey floor. The floor was spotted and smeared with bright, fresh blood.

She tried to lift her head, but it seemed like too much trouble.

Bare feet and legs came into her view. Then a shirt. A glossy blue Hawaiian shirt, hanging open. The person in the shirt was a woman. She stopped in front of Vicki, less than an arm's length away.

Vicki raised her head enough to see the slash across the woman's belly, just above the navel. It was cross-hatched with stitches. From the look of the healing, the wound was a few days old. This is what Jack must have under his bandage, Vicki thought. Though the shirt covered the sides of the design, she could see parts of the circle and pyramid and eye-like ovals, the same as Jack had, but faint. Faded, pink lines on the woman's white skin. Almost gone.

A hand, slick with green fluid, reached out and grabbed Vicki's chin and lifted her head.

The woman had blue eyes, short blonde hair hanging in

324

bangs across her forehead, a sprinkling of freckles over her nose and cheeks.

The nurse? Vicki wondered. The one who killed Pollock? 'Patricia?' she asked. Her voice came out weak, little more than a whisper.

'Yeah. And you must be Vicki.' She let go of Vicki's chin. 'You're not so hot. What's he want you for? Huh? He's got me, why's he want you?' She looked upwards. 'Where's Melvin?'

Jack grunted.

'MELVIN!' she yelled. No answer came. She called his name again. A grin spread across her face. 'He's gone? Well, now, Jack, go upstairs and keep him out. Don't let him down here.'

He made another grunt, this one rising like a question.

'Do it! *I* brought you back, I can make you dead again.'

Jack's arm went away. Vicki sank to her knees and slumped forward. Her face pushed against Patricia, eyes against the stitched wound. She heard the quick footsteps of Jack climbing the stairs.

Her hair was yanked, her head jerked backwards. Patricia gazed down at her.

'By the time *we're* done, Melvin won't want you anymore. He'll toss his lunch just looking at you.' A hand flashed down at her, fingers hooked to rake her cheek.

She twisted her head and felt a quick scrape of fingernails as the hand swept by, nearly missing. The hand swung back at her. Pounded her nose. Then she was falling. Her back hit the floor. Blood was spilling from her nostrils. She licked at it as she pushed at the floor, trying to rise. Then she was sitting up, braced with straight arms.

Patricia sneered down at her. Legs spread. Hands on hips.

'You know Raines and Woodman?' she asked.

For the first time, Vicki noticed the men.

Two of them. Standing on either side of Patricia and slightly behind her.

325

Dead men. Dead like Jack. *I brought you back, I can make you dead again.* Dead like Patricia.

Dead, but not down.

Vicki's mind seemed to freeze.

The two cops (one was the chief, all right) both stared at her with frenzied eagerness in their eyes. Their faces were doughy white. Their bodies, from the neck down, were sheeted with blood.

The taller cop had dime-size entry wounds in the chest and belly, a bigger wound to the shoulder. He was leering at Vicki, rubbing his hands together.

Raines must've been shot in the back. His torso was pocked with big pulpy exit wounds, red globs and strings hanging out here and there.

Along with the rest of the wounds, each man had a horizontal slash above the naval, green fluid oozing from the stitched lips.

She saw Patricia's mouth move, heard a voice that sounded as if it came from far down a tunnel. 'Let's go to it, fellas. Have at her.'

Patricia sat on Vicki's legs.

The cops rushed forward. They dropped to their knees, Raines on her left, Woodman on her right. She swung at their reaching hands, trying to knock them away as she lurched and writhed under Patricia. Then, her wrists were pinned to the floor.

She felt hands – sliding, rubbing, squeezing, digging, twisting and pinching her.

She saw Patricia, beyond the moving arms, lean down and bite the back of a hand that was tight on her breast. The fingers trembled open. The hand let go. Patricia dropped lower, mouth wide. She felt the woman's tongue on her breast, felt the edges of her teeth.

Then Raines's face blocked her view. His mouth covered hers. His tongue thrust in.

She screamed into his mouth and heard a gunshot.

When Melvin saw Jack blocking the closed door to the basement, he groaned.

He wasn't sure what he'd expected. Patricia throwing a fit, maybe.

Not posting a guard.

'What's going on down there!' he blurted.

Jack stood motionless.

'Get outa my way!'

Jack didn't move.

'Damn it! I'm your master! Move!'

Jack shook his head, his loose eye swinging.

Melvin raised his arm, aimed the revolver at Jack's good eye, and pulled the trigger. The gun blasted. The eye vanished. Jack's head crashed backwards against the door. It bounced off the wood, and Jack raised his arms. Melvin lurched away from the reaching hands.

The fucker's blind.

Just like Charlie, he remembered. And Charlie damn near killed me.

'Stop!' he yelled.

Jack grabbed Melvin's neck and started squeezing.

Melvin jammed the muzzle into the gash in the centre of Jack's throat. Half the barrel vanished inside the wound. He fired. The blast flung Jack against the door. The way his head drooped and rocked, Melvin guessed that the bullet had severed the spinal column, Just as he'd hoped. He watched Jack slump to his knees and topple forward.

He dragged the body out of the way.

He flung the door open.

Saw Patricia and Woodman and Raines on their knees on the basement floor. All three huddled over a sprawled body, their hands on it. All three looking up the stairway at Melvin.

'GET AWAY FROM HER!' he shouted.

As he rushed down the stairs, the two cops looked at Patricia. She nodded. They started getting up. Patricia stayed where she was, sitting on Vicki's thighs.

Melvin stopped at the foot of the stairs.

Vicki lay motionless except for the rise and fall of her chest as she gulped air. Her arms were still inside the sleeves of the robe, but the robe was wide open. Her skin was slick with blood. As the cops backed away, Melvin crouched and looked closely at her body. She had awful-looking bite marks on one shoulder. Except for that, her skin seemed to be unbroken.

'Get off her,' he told Patricia.

'It's not fair.' Her voice trembled. Tears filled her eyes. 'I love you. *She* doesn't love you.'

'She will. Same as you. Get off her. Now.'

Patricia sniffed. She wiped her tears away with the backs of her hands. And stared down at Vicki and peeled back her lips, baring her teeth. For a moment, Melvin thought she might lurch forward and try to bite Vicki's face, ruin her looks. But he had given her an order, and she seemed to know it was her duty to obey. Her chin shook. She rubbed her eyes again, then stood up and backed away.

Vicki hung limp in his arms as he lifted her and carried her to the table. He stretched her out on top of it. She lay there, gasping for breath, her gaze fixed on the ceiling.

Stepping back, Melvin glanced at Patricia. She stood beside the pile of clothes from the cops, head down, sobbing quietly. The cops had retreated to a corner of the basement. They stood side by side, staring at Vicki.

'Forget it,' Melvin warned. 'She's mine.'

He went to the basin, turned a faucet on, and dampened a towel. Then, he returned to Vicki's side and began to mop the blood off her face and body.

She squeezed her eyes tight as if trying to shut out what was happening.

She looked beautiful and helpless. The rage Melvin had felt against her, earlier that night, was gone. He felt only tenderness and loss.

It wasn't supposed to turn out this way. He'd been so good to her. He'd given her the car, he'd killed Pollock for

328

bothering her, he'd made Charlie give her the clinic. She was supposed to like him and be his girl.

But it was too late for that.

It had all fallen apart.

There would be more cops, soon. They'd come for him. The only way to have Vicki was to go away with her in the car. They'd live like fugitives.

But they'd be together.

Melvin tossed the towel aside. She was as clean as he could get her, for now. Except for the raw wound on her shoulder, she looked fine. Wonderful. He would bandage the shoulder later, and maybe there would be time for a shower before fleeing.

The thought of showering with Vicki brought a warm stir to his groin. He caressed her. Her skin felt damp and chilly from the moist towel. It had goosebumps. He felt her muscles quivering below the surface.

He looked over his shoulder at Patricia. She was staring at him, crying. 'Bring me the cellophane,' he said.

She nodded.

He bent down and kissed Vicki's mouth. Her lips were trembling. 'It's gonna be okay,' he whispered. 'It won't hurt much.'

He heard a metallic click behind him.

Whirled around.

Saw Patricia aiming a revolver at him.

Heard a roar and felt the bullet slam his chest.

Vicki, rigid and shaking, waiting for her moment to strike out at Melvin, bolted upright at the crash of the gunshot. Melvin hit the table. The back of his robe was embroidered.

THE AMAZING MELVIN.

Above the Z of AMAZING was a ragged hole.

He dropped out of sight.

Vicki flung herself off the table. She sidestepped, eyes on Patricia.

The woman was staring at Melvin's body.

329

But the cops were watching Vicki.

She dashed for the stairway.

They raced for her, silent except for their feet slapping the concrete.

She leaped, kicking high, her foot catching the third stair.

A tug at the shoulders stopped her.

The robe. One of the cops had grabbed the flapping end of the robe, had pulled.

She tried to shrug out of the garment.

But already she was hurtling backward down the stairs.

They were all over her. Tearing her flesh with their teeth.

She screamed and heard her scream and flinched and opened her eyes.

She was in the basement. Sitting on the cement floor, her back against the stairs, her arms high, wrists bound with rope and tied to the banister.

Though her head throbbed and all of her body felt sore, the robe was open and she could see that she hadn't been devoured. Nor had a design been carved on her abdomen – no pyramid inside a circle, no eyes, no stitched slot of a mouth. Her skin was red in places, scuffed and scratched, but uncut and unchewed except for the burning shoulder hidden beneath the robe.

She scanned the basement.

She was alone.

Even Melvin's body seemed to be gone.

She listened. There was the sound of her heartbeat, and nothing else.

Groaning as hot pain surged through her body, she pushed herself up to the next stair. With her teeth, she reached the clothesline connecting her bound wrists to the banister. She began to chew it.

She listened. Still nothing.

Had they actually left her?

It seemed too good to be true.

When the rope finally parted, she used her teeth on the knots at her wrists. They loosened. She slipped her hands free, grabbed the banister, and struggled to her feet. She turned around. The door at the top was open.

Slowly, she climbed the stairs.

Her heart jumped when she spotted the body beyond the doorway. Jack. But he was down.

She stepped around his body, watching it, careful not to get close. His head was turned away so she couldn't see his face. The back of his head was blown out. So was the nape of his neck. But she didn't trust him to be dead.

Standing near him, though out of reach, she stared at his back. Finally, she knelt and pressed a hand against his knit shirt. There was no warmth. She lifted one of his hands, and felt the stiffness of rigor.

At first, she was relieved.

Then she wept.

She knew she should hurry and get out of the house. The others might be nearby, just in another room, or upstairs, or maybe they had left the house and would be returning soon. But she stayed there on her knees, face buried in her hands, crying for Jack and for herself and wishing for a way to go back in time and do something different and make all of it not happen.

Finally, she forced herself to stand.

She limped to the front door and pulled it open. Brilliant sunlight stabbed her eyes.

CHAPTER THIRTY-THREE

The scream that woke Vicki from a nightmare of being stalked by corpses wasn't her own. Pulse hammering, she climbed from bed and raced through the dark house to Ace's room. She flipped the light on.

Ace was sitting upright in bed, panting, her yellow Minnie Mouse nightshirt clinging to her body with sweat.

Vicki sat on the edge of the mattress and took hold of her hand.

'Melvin?'

'Who else? Shit. You'd think I'd be over it by now.'

'It may take a while,' Vicki said. 'Like years.'

'Here we are, our bods good as new – almost, and . . .'

'Better than new, in your case.'

'Yeah, right.' Smiling Ace patted her belly. She hadn't been noticeably overweight before the attack. Now, she was slim. By cutting back on her meals, she had managed to keep off most of the fifteen pounds she'd lost while her broken jaw was wired.

The only remaining mark of her encounter with Melvin was the thin faint line of a scar just below her hairline. The hair had started growing in white where her scalp had been reconnected, but she had used that as an excuse to visit Albert's New You Beauty Emporium in Blayton from which she emerged with her hair short, swept-up, spiky and purple. What are you going to do, Vicki had asked, 'Join a rock band?' To which Ace replied, 'It's *me*, don't you think?'

'Better in some ways,' Ace said. 'But the damn nightmares. And half the time I feel like hiding in the nearest closet.'

'Me, too.'

'And crying for no reason. Really sucks, you know? How come our minds won't heal like our bodies?'

'Not as tough, I guess.'

'We're a couple of tough old broads.'

'You said it.'

'In the springtime of our spinsterhood.'

'Yeah, sure. This is the first night you've spent alone in a week.'

'Obviously, a bad mistake. Didn't have any crap-sucking nightmares when there was a guy in here with me. A mistake I've got no intention of repeating in the near future.'

'How long does Gorman have the night shift?'

'Jesus, I don't want to know. Maybe I'll have to change my schedule, stay up till he gets off.' Ace looked at the clock beside her bed. She groaned. 'Get out of here and let me get my beauty sleep.'

'Sure you're all right? I'll stay with you.'

'Get. I'm fine.' She waved a hand at Vicki.

Vicki squeezed her hand, then stood up. 'Guess I'll go out for some fesh air.'

She saw concern come into Ace's eyes. 'Do you have to?' 'I'll lock the door.'

'I'm not worried about me, hon.'

'Well, don't worry about me. I'm fleet of foot and tough as nails.'

'It's nothing to joke about.'

'I know. But I need to get out and run. I can't keep putting it off. I need to.'

'Shit. Be careful, huh?'

'Yeah. Sleep tight.' Vicki flicked the light off as she left the room.

She walked down the corridor. In her dark bedroom, she slipped her nightgown over her head. As she dressed for running, she thought about Ace's concern. Jack's body had been found where she left it in the house, but Melvin's body was missing. Patricia, Raines and Woodman had also vanished. Along with two cars.

Maybe Melvin had survived the gunshot. Maybe Patricia had taken him away and nursed him back to health.

But Vicki didn't believe it.

The bullet had killed him. And while Vicki was left bound at the foot of the basement stairs, unconscious, Patricia had cut on Melvin. Cut one of those weird designs and made him come back. Then, they'd driven off together. Two cars gone, so Raines and Woodman had probably taken off on their own.

Four of them out there. Zombies. Somewhere. Doing God knows what.

Thinking about it, Vicki felt a chill squirm up her back.

But for weeks she'd given up her morning runs, and she could feel the need for the calming exertion, the touch of the morning breeze on her quick body.

She looped the chain with its key and whistle around her neck, and walked to the front of the house. Before opening the door, she told herself it was perfectly safe.

They're gone.

The cops were still looking for them.

Some of those were very nervous cops – those who'd listened to Vicki and shaken their heads as if they thought she had slipped a gear or two, but who'd later looked at Melvin's collection of video tapes. They had pretended to think the tapes were faked. But she could see the change in their eyes.

Those cops believed.

She was sure they'd kept it to themselves.

Raines and Woodman were described in the press as missing persons, possible victims of Melvin Dobbs and Patricia Gordon. Dobbs and Gordon were wanted for the abduction of Vicki Chandler and for multiple homicides. They were considered armed and extremely dangerous.

But not zombies.

Vicki had told herself, countless times, that they would've been caught by now if they weren't far away.

She told herself that, again, as she stood at the door, wanting to go out and run, but afraid.

There's no need to worry.

She left the house. On the sidewalk, she looked up and down the block. She studied shadows cast by the streetlights. Satisfied that nobody lurked nearby, she stretched, twisted, touched her toes. Then she sat on the cool concrete, spread her legs and swivelled, reached to her toes, straining, finally limber enough to grab the soles of her shoes.

She got up and began to run. Twice, she circled the block, unwilling to venture farther from the house. But she felt a longing to break away. Ignoring the small pull of fear in her stomach, she headed for downtown.

Except for a few delivery trucks, the main street was deserted. She dashed past the Riverfront, past Ace Sportswear and the lighted doughnut shop with its delicious aromas, felt her legs begin to weaken as she sprinted past Handiboy, and slowed down in front of the clinic. By the time she reached the park at the north end of town, she was huffing and her legs felt like warm lead.

She slowed to an easy jog. And stopped at the top of the hill. Staring down, she saw the pale strip of beach. The dim shapes of the playground equipment. The slide and swing set.

Empty.

No Jack.

Her eyes grew warm. Her throat tightened.

She walked down the slick dewy grass of the slope, remembering how she'd fallen on her butt the morning she first met him. He had been a stranger, then, watching her from atop the slide.

For just a while, he had filled the empty place in her heart.

Now, he was gone.

Vicki walked on the sand. She climbed the metal rungs of the ladder and sat on top of the slide. The platform was damp. The wetness soaked through the seat of her shorts, but she didn't mind. She was sitting where Jack had sat, and she felt close to him.

From here, she could see the dark slope. She wondered if he'd been amused by her klutzy fall. After the fall, she had gone down to the shore. He must've watched her. She'd been itchy from lying on the grass. She'd stepped into the river and picked up a stick and used it to scratch her back. She'd been thinking about Paul, aching with the memory of the early morning she'd been with him on the diving raft.

The raft, now, was out of sight, hidden beneath a thick fog.

There had been fog that last morning when she was with Paul. A heavy mat of it that covered them as they embraced. Nobody could have seen if they'd made love. But they hadn't, and she remembered standing in the water, full of longing and regret, wishing she could go back to that time.

All the while, Jack had been watching. From here.

She'd been daydreaming about the only man she had ever loved, and the man she was about to love had been sitting here on the slide, watching and wondering about her.

She closed her eyes and imagined the feel of Jack's big body against her, his mouth . . .

Sucking her shoulder, biting as he thrust, ramming her against the bathroom wall.

Her stomach clenched and she whimpered. Snapping her eyes open, she flung herself forward and shot down the wet ramp of the slide. She flew off its end, stumbled through the sand.

Ran, the memory pursuing her.

Paused only long enough to pull off her shoes and socks, then splashed into the river and dove. The chill of the water shocked her mind clear.

She thought, this is crazy. What am I doing?

I have a right to be crazy.

She arched to the surface and swam, swam towards the diving raft. She couldn't see it through the fog, but she knew right where it was.

It was home, that diving raft. It was where she had been happy and innocent and in love before the bad times came, before the loneliness, before the horror.

Treading water for a moment, Vicki heard it. Soft, familiar slurping sounds of the river's surface lapping the oil drums that buoyed it up. She swam towards the sound, and the weathered old wood appeared through the gauze of fog.

She climbed the ladder. She stepped onto the platform. It tipped and rolled gently beneath her.

Turning around, she looked towards shore.

There was no shore, only fog, pale in the moonlight.

She was surrounded by fog, alone on her raft, safe.

But shivering. The air, which had seemed so still and warm before she plunged into the river, now felt like an icy breath

336

blowing through her sopping clothes, against her dripping skin.

She sat in the centre of the platform. She drew her legs up tight to her body and hugged them.

She sat there, shaking.

The sun will come up in an hour or so, she thought. It'll burn off the fog. It'll dry me and warm me.

She could swim ashore now and return to the house and take a long hot bath.

But it was good here.

She didn't want to leave. She wanted to wait for the sun.

After a while, the chill seemed to fade and her shivering stopped. She lay flat on the raft, her face on her folded arms. The planks grew warm beneath her.

Her eyes drifted shut, but she opened them quickly. With sleep, dreams would come.

The platform moved gently beneath her. The water lapped at the drums. Sometimes, birds cawed and squealed. Far away, a motor sputtered to life and Vicki imagined a man setting out in his boat to begin fishing.

Her eyes slid shut.

She was alone in a canoe. It seemed that Jack should be with her, but she didn't know where he was. Had he gone in for a swim? The night was clear, moonlight casting a silver path on the water. She turned the boat slowly, scanning the river for him.

And saw, off in the distance, the faint shape of a swimmer.

She called, but no answer came.

The swimmer came closer.

What if it's not Jack?

Fear made a cold, hard place in her stomach.

Splashing sounds came from the other side. She jerked her head in that direction, spotted another swimmer.

More splashing from behind. She twisted around. Still another pale shape was moving towards her through the water.

A fourth appeared beyond the prow of the canoe.

337

Another off the starboard side.

Oh Jesus! I've gotta get out of here!

She dug her paddle into the water. It lurched and was jerked from her grip. It flew high and hit the water far away.

Hands clutched the gunnel. The canoe tipped. A head bobbed up.

She stared at the broad face, the slicked down hair, the bulging eyes and thick, grinning lips.

'Did you save yourself for us?' Melvin asked.

'No!' she gasped. 'Get away!'

The canoe tilted the other way as black hands grabbed the gunnels. The head that burst from the surface was charred and eyeless.

'He wants you, too,' Melvin said. 'Charlie's always wanted you.'

They both began climbing into the canoe. Patricia, naked except for a nurse's cap, was suddenly perched on the prow.

Vicki backed away. Hands clamped her knees, halting her. The hands of Raines and Woodman, both in the water, leering up at her from the sides of the canoe.

And someone was still swimming towards her. A vague, pale shaped in the water's blackness.

Jack?

It must be Jack. He'll save me.

'Jack!' she shouted. 'Help! Quick! They've got me!'

And Jack's voice came from the swimmer. 'Save some for me, folks.'

Melvin laughed.

All of them came at her. They threw her down. They piled on top of her, clawing, biting, ripping. She twisted beneath them. She writhed. She felt her belly split open. Someone bit her thigh. Her left breast was torn off and she saw it bulging from Patricia's mouth. Then Jack's face loomed above her. It came down, loose eye swinging. She felt the slimy eye slide against her cheek, felt his mouth cover hers, his tongue thrust in. She twisted and bucked, trying to push him off. The canoe capsized.

338

Cold water clutched Vicki, filled her mouth and throat.

Wide awake, she struggled to the surface. She grabbed the ladder of the diving raft, coughing and gasping, shaking from the terror of her nightmare.

When she could breathe again, she climbed the ladder. She staggered onto the platform and rested there on her hands and knees. Something was hanging from her. She lowered her head more. Her T-shirt was ripped down the front. Its dripping edges swayed. Her left breast was bare, the shoulder strap of her bra dangling from the cup bunched beneath it.

Vicki pushed herself up. resting on her haunches, she studied herself in the faint light seeping through the fog. And pressed her lips tight as she gazed at the tangle of scratch marks on the pale skin of her breast and chest and belly.

She could hardly believe that she had done this to herself.

But she remembered tearing her nightgown once, soon after her arrival in Ellsworth. So she must've done this.

She had not only torn her clothes and skin, she had put up such a struggle against the demons of her nightmare that she had pitched herself into the river.

The body heals, why not the mind?

Could the mind get worse instead of better? She'd had horrid nightmares before, but nothing that caused her to do anything like this.

With trembling fingertips, she explored the scratches. Only those on her belly were deep. The skin there had been plowed up in furrows.

She pulled at the rumpled fabric of her bra and lifted it over her breast. She tucked the strap down inside.

And heard distant splashing sounds.

Her back jerked rigid. She listened.

The sounds, which seemed to come from behind her, were those of someone swimming.

She felt as if her wind had been punched out.

This can't be happening. I'm awake.

Am I?

339

Vicki sprang to her feet and whirled around. The platform dipped. She grabbed the ladder's uprights and held herself steady and gazed into the fog.

The swimming sounds came closer.

She saw a yard or two of black water beyond the raft before the whiteness closed off her view.

She heard only one swimmer.

Who is it? Melvin? Charlie? Jack? One of the others?

Maybe all of them were coming for her, the rest of them approaching from below the surface. They don't need air, she thought. They're dead.

How do they know I'm here?

My shoes, she thought. I left my shoes and socks on the beach.

Oh, Jesus!

'LEAVE ME ALONE!' she cried out.

The sounds of the splashing stopped.

'VICKI?'

A man's voice. Almost familiar.

'I'm sorry,' it called through the fog. 'I didn't mean to scare you.'

'Who are you?'

'Paul. Paul Harrison. We used to . . .'

'PAUL?'

He swam out of the fog and reached out with both hands and took hold of the ladder and looked up at Vicki. She stared down at him.

'Permission to board?' he asked.

Vicki nodded and backed away. Her heart slammed. She struggled to breathe.

He climbed the ladder and stood in front of her, slim and dusky in the vague light, bare except for clinging white undershorts.

A body she had seen countless times in cut-offs and swimsuits, a body she had held tight and caressed. So long ago.

So damn long ago.

Vicki shook her head. 'This . . . is impossible.'

'I heard about your problems,' he said. His voice was almost the same as she remembered it. A little deeper, more confident. 'I was in Guam until yesterday. I got into San Diego and ran into an old buddy. He told me about it. He didn't know it was you, but he remembered I used to talk about a girl in Ellsworth, and . . .' His voice went husky. 'Oh God, are you all right?'

Vicki didn't answer. She rushed to him and threw her arms around him.

He held her. He stroked her hair, her back.

His skin was wet and cold, then warm where it pressed her. There was muscle where he used to feel bony. But his body fit against her the way it used to, as no other body ever had, as if it had been made especially to join with Vicki's body and complete her.

'You're really back?' she murmured against his neck.

Paul nodded.

'I can't believe it.'

'Believe it,' he whispered.

'How did you find me?'

'It wasn't easy. I figured Ace would know. I called her about half an hour ago. She said you'd gone for a run. I remembered you and the river, so I tried the beach.'

'Saw my shoes and socks.'

'I *hoped* they were yours.'

'You could've called out, you know.'

'I wanted to surprise you.'

'You scared the hell out of me. I thought *they* were coming for me.'

'You don't have to worry about them anymore. I'm here. Nobody's ever going to hurt you again.' His hands tightened on Vicki's back, pressing her hard against him. 'God, I've missed you.'

'I've missed you, too,' she murmured. 'God, so much. I thought I'd never see you again.'

'I always wanted to come back and look you up. I just didn't have the guts. I'm a leatherneck with one enormous yellow streak. I figured you'd met someone else, probably got married, had kids. I didn't want to know. I figured I'd missed out.'

'You didn't miss out.'

'Ace told me you're . . . single.'

'I been saving myself for you, hon.'

He laughed softly, and Vicki tipped back her head and watched his face come slowly down and waited for the feel of his mouth.

One Year Later

CHAPTER THIRTY-FOUR

'Nobody move or yer dead meat!'

Meg Daniels jerked with alarm at the rough shout, and dropped her loaf of bread on the floor. She stared at the two men standing in the 7–Eleven's doorway. A tall man with a revolver in one hand, a nylon satchel in the other. A shorter, stocky man with a sawed-off shotgun. Though the Bakersfield night was balmy, both men wore long coats. And ski masks.

Side by side, they strode towards the counter.

Meg wanted to back way, but she didn't dare.

The tall man dropped his satchel onto the counter. 'Fill it up,' he told the clerk.

The stocky man turned to Meg. He studied her through the holes of his mask. She trembled as she watched his bloodshot eyes roam down her body.

With the muzzle of the shotgun, he nudged her left breast through the thin fabric of her tank top. 'Nice,' he muttered. 'Real nice.'

'Don't . . . hurt me. Please.'

'Aw, I wouldn't *hurt* . . .'

The blast of a gunshot roared in Meg's ears. Whipping her head sideways, she saw the back of the tall man's coat puff out. Blood sprayed from a hole below his shoulders. But he didn't fall. Instead, he shoved his revolver towards the clerk and fired. His bullet slammed into the clerk's chest. The clerk staggered backwards, dropping his gun. He was still on his feet when the stocky man swung the shotgun and fired. The clerk's face from the mouth up flew apart in an explosion of red. Then he flopped out of sight behind the counter.

The tall man leaned forward, reached into the open drawer of the cash register, and started taking out money. He scooped up bills, tossed them into his satchel, and reached for more.

Meg, dazed, stared at the back of his coat.

The hole there was the size of a half-dollar. Blood was spilling out of it.

But he kept stuffing the bag with money.

'Yer coming with us, honey.'

The words seemed to come from a great distance. Meg thought, Is he talking to me? Must be. Nobody else in the store.

'Hey, you!'

She turned her head. The stocky man was looking into her eyes.

'You got a problem with that?'

She shook her head.

The tall one closed his satchel and lifted it off the counter. He turned towards Meg. He had a leaking hole in the middle of his chest.

Why isn't he dead? she wondered.

'We're taking this one with us,' said the stocky man.

'Fine by me, chief. She's a knockout.'

Grabbing the front of her tank top, the stocky man yanked Meg forward.

And out of the store.

Towards a waiting black van.

'Would you like another drink?' Graham asked, seeing that she had nothing left in her glass but ice and a red swizzle stick.

She shook her head. Her hair swayed, shimmering golden in the soft lights of the cocktail lounge. 'Not here,' she said. 'But if you'd like to come up to my room..?'

'You're staying here at the hotel?'

Instead of answering, she opened her clutch purse and took out a room key.

'Well, now,' Graham said.

'This is your lucky night.'

'I'll say.'

He could hardly believe his luck. He'd been striking out so many times since JoLynn left him and he moved to Tucson. Even when he did score, it was with women who were as desperate as he was: they were older, or plain, or fat, and all had personalities that were either bland or grating on the nerves. On a scale of one to ten, they ranged from about three to five.

This gal, Patricia, was at least an eight.

Lovely, golden hair. Warm blue eyes. A sprinkle of freckles across her nose. A quick, sly wit that tended towards the sarcastic but stayed short of mean. And a slim, lithe body that her dress did little to conceal.

More like a negligé than a dress. Low cut and glossy white, with spaghetti straps and a slit that showed her left leg all the way to her hip. The smooth way it flowed down her body, Graham *knew* she wore nothing underneath.

She had only two minor flaws, or she would've been a ten for sure.

A face that was slightly too long. Not long enough to make her seem horsey, just enough so she couldn't be considered gorgeous.

And she was pregnant. Not grossly pregnant, but enough so her belly pushed out the front of her gown.

Graham was keenly aware of what was pushing out the front of his slacks as he climbed off the barstool. He buttoned his sport coat, hoping to cover it.

Patricia took hold of his hand.

'Burrr,' Graham said, smiling.

She smiled. 'Cold hands, warm heart.'

As they walked through the cocktail lounge, he thought about how her chilly hand would feel on his hot flesh.

They walked through the hotel lobby and entered one of the elevators. It was empty. Patricia pressed a button for the

347

second floor. She looked at him and licked her lips. 'I'm going to devour you,' she said.

He said, 'Jesus.'

The elevator doors slid open. She led him through the corridor, and unlocked the door of 218. Graham entered first. No lights were on. When she shut the door, the room was dark except for a pale glow coming in through the glass doors on the far side.

She moved into his arms. He felt the firm mounds of her breasts and belly pressing against him. He kissed the side of her long, cool neck. He caressed her bare back. He ran a hand down to the slitted side of her gown, stroked the skin of her thigh and hip, inserted his hand beneath the fabric and found the silken smoothness of her rump.

She eased away from him, and for a moment he wondered if something was wrong. But only for a moment. Then she was undressing him: taking his coat off, opening his shirt and casting it aside, tugging at his belt, unbuttoning his waistband, skidding his zipper down, crouching as she drew his slacks and underwear down to his ankles.

He squirmed at the touch of her lips, her tongue.

'Delicious,' she whispered.

Then she stood up.

'Go in the bathroom,' she said.

'Sure. What for?'

'I like to do it in the shower.' She nodded towards the darkness of an open doorway. 'I'll be along in a minute. I'll make us drinks and bring them in.'

Incredible, he thought.

He took off his shoes and socks, kicked his feet free of the pants, and went into the bathroom.

He turned on the light. The brightness made him squint for a moment. Then, he saw himself in the mirror.

One nervous-looking guy.

Ain't nerves, buddy.

Jesus!

Shaking his head, he grinned at himself. His mouth was

348

parched, so he stepped to the sink and turned on the faucet. He used a hand to cup cold water to his mouth.

He straightened up and turned off the water. He wiped his wet hand on his belly. He looked at himself again in the mirror, and again shook his head.

This can't be happening.

But it sure is.

Trembling, he stepped to the tub. He ran the water until it felt good and hot, then turned a handle and watched the spray shoot out of the shower nozzle. It felt cold for a moment, then hot. He climbed into the tub. He slid the frosted door shut, and waited beneath the beating spray.

She likes to do it in the shower.

Oh man oh man.

First, we'll wash each other.

He could *feel* it, feel her soapy hands sliding all over him, feel her breasts slick under his latered touch.

Graham moaned as he saw her vague form through the shower door. He couldn't see much, just the pink tint of her skin.

The door slid open.

He saw the hammer in her upraised hand.

Saw the face behind her shoulder, bulgy eyes gazing at him, thick lips grinning.

The hammer crashed against his forehead. He fell. The back of his head slammed the bottom of the tub.

A shadow of consciousness clung to him.

'Turn off the water,' he heard through the ringing in his ears. Patricia's voice.

The spray stopped.

The two seemed rimmed with electric blue light as they climbed into the tub. They were naked.

'Shut the drain, honey,' Patricia said. 'We don't want to lose his blood.'

She crawled over him.

They both crawled over him.

He felt their teeth.

*

349

'Okay,' Vicki said. 'We're here.' She rested her paddle across the gunnels. Paul did the same. The canoe glided silently over the moon-sprinkled surface of the river.

Paul looked over his shoulder at her. 'We're where?' he asked.

'The special place.'

'We're in the middle of the river.'

'So we are.'

She crawled towards him, the canoe rocking gently as she moved. Paul turned around.

On her knees, she spread the blanket. She lay down on it, feet towards Paul. Lifting her head, she watched him come to her.

'What's the idea?' he asked.

'Gee, I don't know.'

Vicki turned onto her side. Paul stretched out next to her.

'Hope we don't get run over by a powerboat,' he whispered.

They moved closer together until their bodies touched.

'I've always wanted to do this,' Vicki said.

'The Huckleberry Finn in you.'

'Finn never had it so good.'

She hooked an arm over Paul's back, slid her other arm beneath his head, drew herself more firmly against him. She could feel his heartbeat and the soft warm touch of his breath on her face. The river gently lifted the canoe, turned it, lowered it, rocked it.

Something thumped the hull.

Vicki flinched.

'Just a piece of driftwood, or something,' Paul said.

Rigid against him, she listened.

'Hey, what's wrong?'

'What was it?' she whispered.

'I'll check.' He stirred, but Vicki clenched him hard against her body. 'I can't check if you're going to hang onto me like that.'

'Stay down.'

'Vicki.'

'Please.'

'Okay. God, you're shaking.'

'Just hold me. Hold me tight.'

'I'll do better than that.' He rolled, climbed onto her, covered her with his body.

'No! Get down here!'

'Oh,' he muttered. 'Aw, Vicki.'

She fought to hold onto him, but he pushed himself up and leaned out over the river. She heard a swish of water. Then he brought up a club of tree branch. He held it above her for a moment. Chilly water streamed off it, splashing her face and running down her cheeks. Then Paul flung the branch away. It plopped into the river.

Straddling her, he took off his shirt. He gently dried her face with it. 'Just driftwood,' he said in a low voice. 'It wasn't Charlie Gaines coming up to get you.'

'I'm sorry.'

'Don't be.'

'I've been looking forward so much . . . I thought it'd be so *neat*.'

He rolled his shirt and tucked it beneath Vicki's head. 'You just lie there, I'll take us back to shore. The bed may not be as romantic, but it'll be a lot more comfortable.'

Reaching up, she caressed his chest. 'I don't want to go.'

'Maybe next year.'

'Next year, I'll still wonder if he's down there. And the year after that. He's never going to be found.' She slipped her hands around Paul's sides and drew him down onto her. 'If Charlie's after me, let him come.'

'Maybe we'd better go home.'

'I don't think so.' Vicki pressed her open hands against Paul's ears and shouted into the night, 'HEY, CHARLIE! CHARLIE GAINES! IT'S ME, VICKI! NOW OR NEVER, OLD FRIEND! COME AND GET ME, OR FOREVER HOLD YOUR PEACE!'

For a long time afterwards, they lay motionless in the bottom of the canoe – listening.

352